THE ARTEMIS ADVENTURE

To Jim
Enjoy!
Thanks for the
support.
Alice
(AKA Dorothy Rice Bennett)

March
2018

Dorothy Rice Bennett

outskirts
press

Also by Dorothy Rice Bennett

NORTH COAST: A Contemporary Love Story

GIRLS ON THE RUN

What Amazon readers are saying about

NORTH COAST: A Contemporary Love Story
by
Dorothy Rice Bennett

★ ★ ★ ★ ★

"Dorothy Rice Bennett describes her characters with rigorous emotional honesty, which allows the reader to easily relate to the characters' strengths and flaws. This book is a wonderful tribute to the importance of genuine relationships and the hope we hold that even after life-shattering events, the gift of friendship can bring a new light and warmth to our lives...."

"This is a wonderful and truly gentle love story, and a story of kindred souls giving to one another. For all who have ever felt the growth of emotions as you have fallen in love will have those beautiful memories rekindled with this story...."

"I loved this sweet tender love story. It's not just a love story between two women but also a love story of a group of friends as well as a love story of self. Set in the beautiful Northern California coast, the author takes us into the place and the heart of the women about who she's writing...."

"Finally, a great love story that evolves. Not just a roll in the hay, but a learning experience for both partners. The writing was excellent. I enjoyed this book immensely. I couldn't put it down....."

"I really enjoyed this book…Finished it in less than a day. It's not the typical "lesbian romance"—It's even better! I'll look forward to more good reads from this author…."

"I appreciated a lesbian romance novel that was set on the North Coast, that dealt with older women in community, and that addressed some of the long-term effects of internalized homophobia…."

"Undeniably, the book is a good love story. The reader is engaged in women who experience processes of loving others and the intricacies of developing an intimate lasting relationship. A wonderful read for those who have relationships come and go, yet still desire fulfillment…."

"This is one of those books you cannot put down! It is quite well written with engaging, distinct characters and a strong story. Great job on your first novel, Dorothy…."

"This book is a well written love story that is understandable to all audiences. Every relationship is unique and real. North Coast is a breath of fresh air!"

What Amazon readers are saying about

GIRLS ON THE RUN
by
Dorothy Rice Bennett

★ ★ ★ ★ ★

"Dorothy Rice Bennett has published another lesbian romance novel that appeals not just to lesbians, but to anybody who has ever struggled with the question of who they are or who they are supposed to be. Girls on the Run follows two protagonists through a natural and sweet progression of new love...."

"Interesting, kept my attention all the way through. Sweet love story that brought me to tears several times...."

"Girls on the Run was a captivating novel of friendship, love and the evolution of family dynamics. I enjoyed the book and have passed it on to my daughter to read!..."

"This is my first time reading a novel from Dorothy Rice Bennett and I can say that it will not be my last. Dorothy did a wonderful job of crafting a complex story of two young ladies and detailing their development from being on the run across the United States to the life that they eventually setup for themselves in San Francisco..."

"Great book keep my interest all the way though. The characters were wonderful, I really felt I knew them. I think all kinds of people would enjoy this book...."

"Great read. Like the setting. Love the characters and interaction with neighbors and family…"

"There is something in it for everyone to relate to and not once did I think the characters were too young for me (76) to relate to. A few scenes brought tears, more brought smiles. A great, easy read and not one to be missed…."

What CURVE Magazine says about

GIRLS ON THE RUN

"…Jennifer and Stacy couldn't be more different when they first meet, and it seems highly unlikely they'd even be friends, never mind more. But the journey they undertake, and the decisions they have to make together once they get to San Francisco, brings them very naturally together into a wonderful friendship. ….this underlying story is very well paced, completely believable and delicately done."

For aspiring young women everywhere

1

Kiki's Star

As Kiki lay on the warm rooftop and gazed skyward at the stars, she made up her mind. She was definitely leaving.

Her mama and papa were screaming at each other in the apartment two floors below. This ongoing marital battle erupted in semiweekly yelling bouts, and Kiki needed to escape the uproar. She had learned that the best way to keep her own sense of balance was to come up the stairway to the roof, spread an old blanket, and lie down on her back. If she was lucky—and it was a clear night with minimal smog—she could see the moon and stars overhead.

Kiki was not an expert on astronomy. Although she didn't know the official names for the star constellations, she loved looking up at the night sky. At first her favorite star had been the really big, bright one that she could always spot even when she found it in a slightly different place. After she had spent months just lying still and focusing on its bright light—while lost in her own teenage fantasy world—she noticed a smaller star just down and to the right of the big one. This one seemed to blink at times. The star would disappear and then come back. Kiki decided, with a touch of amusement, that maybe this star was communicating with her.

Someone from Kiki's high school had read a book about mythology and told her of a Greek goddess named Artemis. An archer who wandered through the forest in search of adventures, accompanied by her faithful dog, Artemis was strong and independent—kind of an outsider who acted on her own. Although Kiki had never seen a real bow and arrow in the South Bronx, and a dog would be a luxury in her family, she liked the idea of Artemis's free spirit and named her blinking star after the goddess.

Kiki had slipped away to the rooftop during the past several months, weather permitting, to have some privacy to think about her life. The Rodriguez apartment was crowded and cluttered, with six people sharing it—her three brothers as well as Kiki and their parents. At the moment there were only five, because her oldest brother Raul was serving time in prison. Besides that, Javier was seldom home, since he hung out with his gang, and Kiki feared that he would eventually end up dead or in prison as well.

A product of the American melting pot, Kiki bore the name Patricia Loretta Cristina Rodriguez. She felt like a Heinz-57 mutt, with her mostly Polish mother and her Puerto Rican-Filipino father. She was third among the family's four children. Only Gusto was younger. With difficult and often-absent older brothers and an alcoholic father, Kiki had been forced to take care of herself at an early age. Her gut feeling was that lack of money and a chaotic upbringing—not to mention being a female—would make adult life very challenging.

Just turned eighteen, Kiki was five feet, two inches tall with an athletic build. She had large brown eyes that sparkled, wavy dark hair that fell to her shoulders—when not pulled into a ponytail—and an olive complexion. She was pretty, with full lips and two dimples that showed when she smiled. Kiki felt self-conscious about her nose, which seemed, to her, a bit too pug for her face, and she had a slight scar over one eye—a scar she had acquired when she hadn't ducked soon enough as two brothers sparred with each other during a family fight.

Kiki had just finished her junior year in high school. *One more year,* she thought to herself, *and you can start college and get out of this depressing world.*

Kiki heaved a deep sigh. *Yeah, what a dream. What chance did she have to go to college, really?* She had worked for an elderly Jewish baker until he had a stroke and his store was closed. Now she couldn't find another job, and the little savings fund she had spirited away for school kept shrinking instead of growing. No matter how creative she was in hiding her stash, Javier was smarter. When he needed drug money, he turned her room upside down until he found cash or something else he could sell. Kiki would scream at him and pound his shoulders with her fists, but he would just shrug her off, take her money, and nothing would change.

It seemed to Kiki that Mama and Papa's fights were becoming worse, and with the sweltering days of summer upon them, they would be at it almost every night. Kiki was sure there was nowhere in the world more hot and humid than a South Bronx apartment in August.

She lay on the steamy roof and watched Artemis blinking at her and knew that it was time to do something. Scary as the thought was, it was time for her to leave. Out in the world, under those stars, there had to be someplace better than this. If she didn't go now, she might never escape her family's cycle of poverty and crime.

A door closed quietly nearby, and a familiar form dropped down beside her.

"I thought I'd find you here," whispered Manuela. "I didn't bother knocking on your door when I heard them yelling."

The two teenage girls lay quietly for a moment, each watching the night sky. They had been best friends since grade school. They knew each other so well that they hardly needed words to read each other's thoughts.

"Artemis is bright tonight," Kiki finally commented, pointing her finger at the twinkling star low on the horizon.

"Yeah," Manuela nodded, her chocolate brown eyes studying Kiki.

Kiki sighed. "I'm doin' it," she said. "I'm leaving."

A look of pain crossed Manuela's round face. "Really?"

Neither spoke for a long moment. "You wanna come?" Kiki finally offered.

"Oh, Kiki, I wish. But I got school and Ramon. I couldn't run out on Ramon. I mean, he's beginnin' to talk marriage, an' I—"

Kiki reached for Manuela's bronze-skinned hand. "I know, Manuela. I just had to ask. You're my best and dearest friend."

The two girls continued to hold hands as they lay and looked upward, each one lost in thought. Kiki felt the soft warmth of Manuela's larger paw. She would miss the reassurance of that hand.

Aware that it was really late, Kiki stood up and pulled Manuela to her feet. The other girl towered over Kiki. They embraced for a long moment.

"I'll miss you, Kiki," Manuela whispered, as a tear slid down her cheek.

"Me, too. I'll write when I can, okay?"

"Okay."

Kiki opened the heavy metal door that led to the roof, and they walked carefully and quietly together down the dark, graffiti-scarred stairway to apartment 3A. They held each other once again briefly, and then—when Manuela had disappeared after waving a final goodbye—Kiki entered the dark and now blissfully silent apartment. Her papa had passed out drunk on the couch, and her mama had gone to bed. Kiki sighed with relief. Tonight might be easier than some.

Stepping inside her tiny bedroom, Kiki shut the door. Closing it made her personal space—which barely held a twin bed, dresser, and a small desk—even more sweltering than usual, but she needed privacy. She stretched out on her bed as the hint of a breeze puffed at the yellowed curtains hanging at her open window. Staring in nighttime dimness at the peeling paint on the ceiling, she attempted to make a plan. She would sleep, as much as she could, and then split in the morning. She'd take her money and her duffle bag and leave everything else, what there was of it. Thinking about Manuela—and being glad that her friend had stopped by so that one person knew she was about to leave yet wouldn't tell—Kiki finally drifted off to sleep.

She awoke suddenly when the first hint of morning light crept through the cracked windowpanes. Rolling out of bed, Kiki hurriedly showered, and dressed. Then she began to pack. Pulling her PE duffle bag out of the closet, she tossed in her personal bathroom supplies. She added two changes of underwear, a couple of T-shirts, socks, a pair of shorts and some long pants, and a fleece hoodie. She laid a jacket on the bed. It was worn but made of soft black leather—something Javier had won in a gang squabble and then given to her because it was too small for him. Her heavy hiking boots sat on the floor; she would exchange her slippers for them when she was ready to leave.

Kiki threw the bag back into her closet and strolled out to the kitchen, acting as normally as she could manage. Mama was silent, nursing a black eye, and there was an air of tension about her from last night's battle. She was fixing her usual breakfast of hash browns, which Mama made fresh and called "rosti," along with beans, rice and tortillas for Papa.

Clearly hung over, Papa was smoking a cigarette and trying to absorb the morning paper. Javier apparently hadn't come home again last night, because at the table there was just Gusto, who was barely fifteen.

Kiki pushed down anxiety as she seated herself and quietly studied everyone. She wanted to press their images into her memory, because she had no idea when she would see any of them again. There were things that maybe she should say, but words might create an alarm, and she didn't want that, so she swallowed hard and kept silent.

Mama put the food on the table and commanded as usual, "Here, eat."

Papa grunted and awkwardly juggled his newspaper, cigarette and fork. His eyes were fogged and watery.

Kiki sighed. Maybe slender, handsome Gusto, who dug into his beans and rice with a vengeance, still had possibilities. She hoped so, because he was a nice kid, yet she really wondered. She looked down at her plate of food but her stomach was tied in knots. Although she would need a good meal in her for the road, her mouth felt like cotton.

Mama turned from the stove, stared at Kiki and grunted. "Patricia Loretta Cristina Rodriquez, you eat! I'm not wastin' good food." She waved a finger menacingly in Kiki's direction.

"Yes, ma'am." Kiki struggled to swallow a bite of hash browns.

Mama pointed at Javier's empty chair. "Where's Javier?"

Gusto looked up. "He ain't home."

Mama swore under her breath. "He'll end up like his brother, rottin' in a jail somewhere, if he don't get knifed or shot first."

There was silence, as they all tried to clean their plates. No one wanted to anger Mama and start another fight.

Finally, Kiki pushed away her chair. "Well, I'm gonna look for a job again today. So I better get going."

Mama looked at her directly. Her eyes softened and a little smile crossed her face. "Good luck, baby."

Kiki melted and rushed to be embraced in her mother's fleshy arms. "I love you, Mama," she said with tears in the corners of her eyes. Silently to herself, she admitted, "*I'll miss you, Mama.*"

Papa grunted. "You better find somethin' soon, bambina. Now you eighteen, you gonna hafta start payin' rent around here. You got a whole bedroom, while the boys gotta share."

Mama flared. "Shut it, Pablo. She's knows what she's gotta do."

Kiki backed away from the tension and fled to her room, where she waited breathlessly. A few moments later, she heard her papa stand up and, with a heavy step, bang out the front door headed for work. Soon after that, Gusto followed on his way to summer school, and her mama soon left for her job in the meat market down the street. After the door shut for the last time, the apartment was quiet.

Huddled for a moment on her bed, feeling overwhelmed, Kiki struggled to pull herself together and remember her goal for the day. She had to get far enough away that they couldn't come after her. She was of age, and she had the right to leave, but that wouldn't stop her papa, or Javier, from coming to find her and forcing her to return home.

"You'd think they would be glad to see the last of me, since I'm just another mouth to feed," she muttered aloud. "But, no, I'm part of the glue that holds this family together, so they want me here." She sighed. *It was time to live for herself, if she was ever going to have a life.*

Kiki looked around the room at her favorite dolls, movie posters, and high school souvenirs that she might never see again. As she surveyed her life history, she thought of two other things she must take: her beat-up camera and a book of souvenir matches from the Waldorf Astoria Hotel. She might need matches for something, and the matchbook recalled one memory of something beautiful in New York.

Kiki wrote a vague note to her family—which they would find later in the day—saying she loved them and would be in touch. Then she emptied all her secret hiding places of her remaining savings, along with a Greyhound ticket from Newark to Pittsburgh that she had purchased in advance. She had figured out that non-express, slower buses were cheaper, so she had paid for the first leg of her trip. She sighed as she looked at her small roll of money and the ticket. This wasn't much to get her to California.

Kiki left the building, shouldering her duffle bag and jacket. Her pockets and boots were lined with cash. A slim wallet holding her only identification was stuffed in a jeans pocket.

With her entire body a bundle of nerves, Kiki walked hesitantly to the nearest subway station. Going underground, she paid her fare to Penn Station. From there she would switch to a New Jersey line that would take her to Newark within an hour. She figured it was the quickest way out of New York. Once in Jersey, she could board the Greyhound headed west.

At a Penn Station kiosk, Kiki bought a bottle of water and a U.S. map. She felt dumb not to have thought of this before and picked up a map for nothing or next to nothing somewhere in the neighborhood, but it was too late now. Although Kiki trusted that the Greyhound would eventually get her to San Francisco, she was used to being in charge and wanted to have some idea where she was headed. Logically, she knew enough to keep the morning sun at her back when going west. Yet once the New York skyline was out of view, she would need more than Artemis to guide her—after all, her star was only visible at night, and then only on clear nights at that.

Kiki studied the map while she rode the subway, her stomach aching as each mile took her farther and farther away from the South Bronx, her family, and the only world she had ever known. Looking at the map kept her from staring too much at the strangers around her, but she soon noticed they, too, were focused on books, newspapers, cell phones, and not each other.

At one stop, two women got on the subway together, giggling. Then they threw their arms around each other and kissed. Noticing them out of the corner of her eye, Kiki blushed and buried herself more deeply in her map. Then she found herself—she didn't know why—glancing at them as they stood arm in arm talking and laughing as the train hurled itself with jerking motions through the underground tunnel.

When she reached her New Jersey stop and left the subway station, Kiki surveyed the buildings around her and recognized how different everything looked and that she was standing on totally strange turf. Her heart began to pound in her ears. *Calm down*, she told herself. It was too late to be sorry that she had started this big adventure, but she was now feeling very unsettled. She had heard people were nicer and more helpful out West. Yet before she would reach California, she had days and nights to endure on a bus. Feeling waves of fear pass through her body, Kiki suddenly realized that despite her macho tomboy exterior, inside she was really a kitten. *And right now a scared one at that.*

Nervously taking deep breaths, Kiki strode toward the Greyhound Station.

2

Grace

Kiki sat in the crowded passenger area waiting for the Pittsburgh bus. There was little to do but study her map and check out the people around her. Everyone, regardless of age, seemed to be looking at, or punching words or numbers into some kind of phone or tablet. She wished she had one of them, but there had never been the money to buy such things. Even if she had been able to get one—or if a brother had dumped a pilfered one in her lap—she would not have been able to afford the service to use it. And there would have been no sense in asking her parents to help. Javier had a smart phone, but he supported it with his thievery and used it for his gang activity. She wasn't ever going down that route, no way. Any money that came to her, for the short time she'd had a job, had helped her mama or been tucked into her own "escape fund."

Kiki perched on the edge of the waiting room seat and felt isolated by her poverty. The people sitting around her, she assumed, probably weren't rich if they were riding the bus. Yet they obviously had more than she did, which was almost nothing. Kiki took in a deep breath and let it out slowly. She should have brought an old paperback to read. But she hadn't, so she had little to do to fill the time. Kiki sighed and resigned herself to watching people come and go and listening to the loudspeaker announcing bus departures.

Eventually, Kiki's stomach began growling and just as she wondered what to do about it, her bus was announced. Buoyed on a wave of excitement, Kiki grabbed an energy bar at a station kiosk, quickly paid for it, and moved along with a crowd of travelers through a doorway to the parked buses.

After finding the right bus and showing her ticket to the driver, Kiki looked wide eyed at the metal steps before her. After inhaling a few deep breaths, she managed to climb on board the big Greyhound marked for Pittsburgh.

The bus was nearly full. Kiki walked up the aisle searching for an empty spot and finally located a seat next to an elderly gray-haired woman, who glanced up at her with apparent relief when Kiki asked if she could sit there. Kiki figured the woman was glad it was a girl wanting to sit by her, instead of a man. Since Kiki felt safer that way, too, she gave the older woman a tentative smile. Watching others put their belongings in the overhead storage compartments, she stuffed her duffle bag and jacket up there, as well.

Kiki settled into the seat, took a sip from her water bottle, and then started looking around. Everyone nearby was already taking out phones and tablets. As the bus pulled out of its parking space and onto the roadway, Kiki noticed a sign that announced free WiFi onboard. Even the little woman next to her had a smart phone and was checking it for something. Kiki shrugged and mused that the only modern device she had with her was a credit card. Fortunately, she had applied for that when she worked at the bakery and her mama had cosigned for it. Kiki had rarely touched the card but it came in handy when she bought her bus ticket online at the local library. Thankfully the bill had already come and she had paid it. Now she didn't dare touch the card until she had a new address. Otherwise the bill would go to her parents' apartment, and they could start to track her by her purchases. Maybe they'd just be glad she was gone. However, she wouldn't know that for sure and she couldn't take a chance on giving herself away.

Kiki was aroused from her personal ruminations by the lady next to her. "Are you from Newark?" the woman asked. Kiki took a closer look at her and noticed that she was very slender with deeply veined hands. She had rounded shoulders and wore thick glasses.

A bit startled but amused by her courtesy, Kiki hesitated. "No, New York," she finally replied. She had to speak strongly to be heard over the noise of the bus engine.

"I'm from Jersey City," the little woman said engagingly, with a smile that exposed crooked teeth. "I'm going to Pittsburgh to see my sister."

"Oh." Kiki had already noticed the difference between her own Bronx accent and the woman's New Jersey speech. She was amused at the sound of "Joisey," or something very similar.

"You going to Pittsburgh?" Behind the glasses, the woman's eyes twinkled.

Kiki hesitated. *How much should she admit?* "Well, to begin with, anyway. But I have an aunt in California, and I'm going out there to visit." *Surely this woman wouldn't know anyone important or be able to reveal where Kiki was going.*

"You look kinda young, if you don't mind me saying so, to be crossing the country all alone."

Kiki smiled. "I'm eighteen. I'm kinda short, so that makes me look younger. Maybe I'll always look young, because I don't think I'm gonna grow any taller."

The woman slipped her phone back into her purse. "My sister isn't well. She's in a nursing home. I try to go to see her whenever I can, because I'm afraid one of these days, she'll slip away." Her expression turned sad.

"Hmmm," Kiki replied gently. "It's nice you take time to see her. How do you get to the nursing home from the bus?"

"I have a niece, my sister's daughter. She'll pick me up at the bus station, and I'll stay with her. Then she'll take me to the nursing home tomorrow."

"You are lucky." Kiki sighed and was quiet for a moment.

The woman's glasses had frames the color of gold with little rhinestones at the temples. She seemed to be studying Kiki.

"You ever been on a bus like this before?"

"No, first time." Kiki felt her stomach begin rumbling, so she pulled the energy bar out of her pocket. It wouldn't last long, but it was better than nothing.

While Kiki bit into her snack, the older woman pulled an apple out of her purse, along with a napkin, and carefully started to eat. "You reminded me that it's past lunchtime." She smiled, pointing to Kiki's quickly disappearing bar.

They ate in silence, after which the woman wrapped the apple core in her napkin and stuck it out of the way. Then she leaned back into her seat, pushing a button to recline a bit. In moments she had drifted off to sleep.

Kiki watched her for a little while but was glad for the relative quiet. She wanted to look at the scenery, because what she saw out the window was a whole new world for her. First Newark and its suburbs that looked a little familiar. Then expansive fields, with lots of brilliant green trees, and gradually rolling land. Kiki vaguely remembered from geography class that a big part of the country she would cross today was called the Appalachian Mountains. That would explain the hills and all the greenery.

According to Kiki's map, they would pass through the rest of New Jersey, which wasn't too far, then part of Maryland, and almost the whole state of Pennsylvania. There were a few stops and one transfer in Baltimore. They wouldn't arrive in Pittsburgh until late that evening. Almost midnight, if she remembered correctly. *What would she do then?* Kiki sighed and told herself not to worry—she'd figure something out. Meanwhile, she was safe and, since she had no amusing gadgets, she'd just have to figure out how to entertain herself and practice the art of being patient.

An hour later, the older woman stirred again. "Are we in Pennsylvania yet?"

Kiki shook her head. "I'm not sure." Then she remembered. "Oh, we transfer buses in Baltimore, and that's still in Maryland, I think. So, we're, like, not in Pennsylvania yet."

"I've been remiss." The woman suppressed a yawn. "My name is Grace. Grace Grazinsky." She delicately extended her thin, boney hand.

Kiki smiled warmly as they shook hands. "I'm Kiki. There's a whole string of names after that, so I won't bother you with them." She thought that Kiki was enough to share under the circumstances.

"I always forget about Maryland. I guess I'm getting old."

When the bus arrived in Baltimore, the Pittsburgh passengers faced a nearly two-hour layover before their next bus left at 6:20 p.m. Being familiar with the station, Grace guided Kiki to the restrooms. The women's rest area wasn't terribly clean, and along with bus passengers, it was obvious that homeless people made use of the station's facilities. Kiki felt very uncomfortable. *Could she be called homeless now?*

Watching Kiki looking around with wide eyes, Grace suggested, "I've been here several times, and I found a Subway not too far away. It's a hike, but it's better than living on energy bars and sitting here. And we have plenty of time to go there and back."

Kiki nodded, feeling relieved, and she walked with Grace outdoors and away from the terminal. Thankfully, the sky was partly cloudy and it was not as hot as Kiki expected. A touch humid, but she was used to that. She threw her duffle over her shoulder and draped her jacket across the top of it. She thought about Grace pulling her suitcase and offered to help. With obvious gratitude, Grace accepted.

Grace reached for Kiki's remaining free hand, and Kiki responded willingly. It felt good and provided protection for both of them. They walked carefully through an industrial zone and past a large casino and then had to negotiate their way across a major thoroughfare. Kiki moved carefully and looked out for Grace; they eventually reached the Subway with safety. Grace suggested that Kiki order a foot long sandwich, eat half of it, and save the other half for later. "Get some chips and a drink, because there is a special, and it will be cheaper." Grace ordered ham and American cheese on flat bread, with lots of vegetables. Kiki picked out her sandwich hesitantly. She didn't do *this* everyday. Finally, she settled on beef and Pepper Jack on an Italian roll and followed Grace's lead with lots of fresh vegetables. When they got to the checkout, Grace paid for both of them.

Kiki objected, but Grace shook her head. "I wanted to come here, and I wouldn't have felt comfortable by myself. You were kind enough to join me—and you're hauling my suitcase—so please let me treat you."

Kiki accepted, uncomfortable about it yet relieved at the same time. She had so little cash to spend. She thanked Grace.

After Grace pointed out an empty table, Kiki stowed the luggage by her chair where it couldn't disappear, and they sat down. Kiki devoured her sub. She hadn't realized just how hungry she was. Grace ate hers rather daintily and yet she put her sandwich away with real dispatch. They each saved half, wrapped up the remains, and then walked briskly back to the bus depot.

Kiki studied the big gambling emporium as they passed it for the second time.

"I've been tempted to go gambling," Grace admitted to her with a chuckle, "but I haven't done it yet."

Kiki shook her head, looking away from the casino. *Not even tempting, at least not at this moment.*

Finally, Grace and Kiki boarded their next bus, which made steady progress into Pennsylvania. Nearly four hours later, there was a twenty-minute rest stop, and then at 11:15 p.m., the big Greyhound arrived in Pittsburgh.

Kiki felt very tired after so many hours sitting on the bus, and she was sure that her traveling companion must be exhausted. She hoped that Grace's family would actually be there to meet her.

True to her promise, Grace's niece, Linda, met the bus. Linda appeared to be in her mid forties; she was attractive and well groomed. Grace introduced Linda to Kiki. "Kiki's from New York and is headed to California. She'll get another bus out of here tomorrow morning."

Linda smiled and shook Kiki's hand. She tilted her head slightly, frowning in thought. "Where are you spending the night? Surely not here in this bus station?"

Kiki started to say something, but she didn't really have an answer. She had nowhere to go. Blushing, she looked at the floor, feeling suddenly ashamed.

Linda put a hand on Kiki's arm. "Look, Kiki. Why don't you come home with us. I can drop you off back here in the morning when I take Grace to see her sister."

Kiki was astonished. "Really? I—I don't know what to say."

"Don't say anything. Just come. You've passed the Grace test, and you are welcome to stay with us overnight."

At first, Kiki didn't understand what Linda meant, but she later figured out that Grace had a long-standing habit of picking up people in need of a little help, especially if they were kind to her. Linda admitted to Kiki the next morning that these folks were always nice, so she and her husband, Rob, didn't mind having them briefly in their home.

After the three women piled into Linda's Volvo, Kiki could hardly keep her eyes open as Linda drove quickly through quiet streets to a

Pittsburgh suburb, stopped at a modern two-story house, and parked the late model SUV in the two-car garage. Linda introduced Kiki to her husband Rob, and there were greetings all around.

Grace had first dibs on the guest room, so Linda made up a bed for Kiki on the living room sofa. Whatever they had offered, Kiki thought to herself, was surely more comfortable than trying to sleep at the bus station sitting up in a chair, while attempting to guard her belongings, and worrying about being attacked or kidnapped—or whatever else might possibly happen in such a public place.

Since it was very late, the others disappeared quickly into bedrooms. Feeling the luxury of air conditioning in the house, Kiki pulled a blanket up under her chin and fell into a deep, exhausted sleep.

The next morning, she awakened to the sounds and smells of food cooking. Rob was seated at the kitchen table reading a newspaper, while Linda made breakfast. Grace came out of the guest bathroom and motioned Kiki to go next.

After Kiki had dressed and put her belongings back in her duffle bag, they all sat around the table and talked for a little while—the social conversation they had missed the previous evening. Rob seemed very interested in Kiki's goal of reaching California via Greyhound. "You must be a very determined young lady to cross the whole country that way," he observed with a friendly smile.

Kiki felt a bit uncomfortable but she tried to take his comments in stride. "Well, I'd like to see family I've never met, and if all works out, I'm gonna stay in California and go to college."

"Wow," Rob replied, "Very impressive goal. I wish you all the luck."

An hour later, after saying goodbye to Grace and Linda, Kiki stood in front of the bus depot. For a moment she felt emotionally torn about boarding the next bus. These were such nice people. Rested and with a belly full of home cooking, she already sensed an attachment to them. She would miss Grace and her kindness. *But,* she said to herself, *you are on an adventure, your adventure. You have to keep going.*

Swallowing hard, Kiki watched the SUV pull away and then went inside the building, where she stood in line to buy a ticket to her next destination. The counter agent informed her that the fare to St. Louis was much more than she had expected and, surprised, she asked the clerk why.

"If you got here on a ticket purchased in advance on the Internet, it was cheaper. At the depot, it costs more."

Kiki sighed. "So I guess I should pay my way to San Francisco, if that's where I'm going?"

The clerk nodded. "That would be the cheapest."

Kiki frowned. This would get her closer to her aunt and uncle in Sunnyvale, but it would take most of her cash. When she reached into her jeans for her slim wallet to pay for the ticket, she felt something else there. Kiki pulled out her hand and found three twenty-dollar bills.

Amazed, Kiki wondered if it had been Grace, Linda, or Rob who had put them there. Now she had no way to say thanks. But she heaved a sigh of relief and whispered to herself, "Thank you, too, Artemis."

When she left the counter, Kiki possessed a ticket all the way to California, which was a good thing. The down side was that she again had a long wait for her bus. *Another day of sitting and waiting with nothing much to do,* she sighed. Walking around the station, she found a kiosk with paperback books and selected one. Reading a detective thriller kept her occupied for most of the morning, although intermittently she had brief attacks of nerves, worrying about her family. She looked around for Papa and Javier. When she didn't see either of them anywhere in the bus station looking for her, she relaxed again and returned to her book.

About noon, Kiki ate her soggy sandwich from the evening before and thought about Grace and hoped she was seeing her sister and that they were having a good visit.

After a slow afternoon that seemed to last forever, and a can of Coke along with an energy bar that didn't make a very satisfying dinner, Kiki finally heard her bus announced and she boarded. Luckily, she found a seat alone and was relieved because she wanted to rest. She felt dull and exhausted.

It was nearly 7 p.m. before the bus left Pittsburgh. That evening, that night, and into the next day, Kiki dozed, woke up periodically, and dozed again. As she looked out the window, in her sleepy haze, she remembered a few big cities, some smaller towns, and between them endless farmlands.

Later that next afternoon—Kiki's third day on the road—at nearly dinnertime, the bus stopped in Salinas, Kansas. It was only a thirty-minute stop, but she went to the restroom and found a little something to eat. She told herself she had to have food, and the next day they would make great strides in getting across the country. She had a bit of a headache, but a soda and a ham and cheese sandwich helped. Other travelers were now talking about Denver and the Rockies, and she knew she had come far from home.

Shortly after they left Salinas, there was a loud bang, and the bus suddenly rocked back and forth. The driver slowed and gradually pulled off onto the shoulder of the freeway. Once stopped, he climbed down from the bus to identify the problem. Inside, everyone chattered. "Not again," someone muttered with annoyance.

The driver, an older man with a noticeable paunch, climbed back up the bus steps. "Sorry folks, there's going to be a delay. We've blown a tire, and I'm calling for help from the nearest repair facility. We'll be here for a while, and then we'll go on to our next stop in Goodland."

An agonizing forty-five minutes later, a big tow truck appeared. A large bus tire was rolled into place, and there were thumps and bumps heard from below. Then the passengers piled off the bus, to lighten the load, while the tire was changed. A couple of men stared at the remains of the old tire, which was pretty much shredded.

Finally, they were given the okay to re-board, and the bus moved back onto the highway, headed for the next official stop.

In Goodland, Kansas, the Greyhound rolled up in front of a local McDonalds for a planned meal break of thirty minutes. Since they were way behind schedule, the driver ordered, "Hurry it up," as several passengers climbed off the bus. Kiki, wanting to use the restroom, took her jacket and duffle bag with her for safekeeping. She felt dirty and decided to clean up a little. When she got inside the fast-food restaurant, it seemed that others had the same idea, and there was a long line.

Kiki tried to be calm while waiting for her turn, and then she hurried. She quickly used the toilet, cleaned up, put everything back in her bag, and scurried to the counter to pick up a dollar ice cream sundae, because she didn't feel filled up from dinner. Then Kiki rushed outside to get on the bus.

Only the bus wasn't there.

Kiki stopped dead still in front of the McDonalds and grasped her ice cream sundae for dear life. She felt shocked and devastated. *The bus had left her behind!* Now she was standing in front of the one business that was still open in an agricultural community that probably rolled up its carpet by dusk. There were a few buildings along the street where the McDonalds was located, all looking dark and closed, and then nothing except flat land. *She was absolutely nowhere and with no bus.*

Her heart pounded in her throat. *How could they have left without her?* She tried to think. *She hadn't been talking much with anyone and maybe someone saw her take her duffle bag with her, and thought? But her ticket was for San Francisco, so why wouldn't the driver have known she was missing? Now what was she to do?*

She walked back inside the McDonalds, where the counter clerk told her there wouldn't be another bus until the next evening. Between now and then she was stuck.

With sagging shoulders, Kiki went outside again. She looked up into the dusky sky. *Where was Artemis?* The evening was clear, and Goodland had few streetlights—she ought to be able to find her special star. She downed her ice cream and studied the heavens. Maybe it was still too early. And it looked different to her than from her rooftop in the South Bronx. After a few anxious moments, she located the familiar group of stars of which Artemis was a part. She relaxed. She saw her star. Artemis was there, small and pale in the fading daylight. With a sigh, Kiki accepted that somehow she would be all right.

Down the street, she noticed a blinking neon sign. Kiki suspected it was for a motel. After dumping her empty ice cream cup in the trash and with her heart still pounding a bit erratically, she walked toward the sign.

Kiki had been correct. She entered a dingy and plain motel office and approached the evening clerk. "My bus just accidently left me behind. I don't know what to do. I'm sure I can't find a solution until tomorrow, but I need a place to spend the night. Do you have anything that isn't too expensive?"

The clerk was a red-headed kid not much older than Kiki. He

started to give her a smirk and a smart reply, then seemed to think better of it.

"Well, we've been remodeling here," he explained, just a bit officiously. "Our rooms that have been fixed up are $49 a night. However, we have a couple that are sort of stripped down ready to be worked on, and I could let you stay in one of those for $35. It's clean but no TV or anything."

Kiki sighed. It was more money than she had to spare, but what could she do? "Okay," she agreed with a sigh, "I'll take it."

When she got to her room—key and towels in hand—the place was even less appealing than the clerk's description. But it was somewhere to sleep. Worn out from the long day on the bus and the lack of rest the night before, Kiki collapsed onto the sagging double bed. After a few moments of fitful tossing, she slipped into a deep sleep.

When footsteps along the outside corridor woke Kiki the next morning, she saw light around the edge of the blinds and knew she had to get moving. Although the bathroom was dismal, with trails of mold here and there, she needed a shower, so Kiki swallowed, grabbed the paper-thin towel and washcloth, and bathed in a tepid stream of water.

Once dressed in her only clean clothes, Kiki checked out of the room, hungry for something to eat. Since a complimentary breakfast was definitely not part of her room deal, she returned to the McDonalds, where an Egg McMuffin offered a cheap way to fill her stomach. She talked with an assistant manager who confirmed what she had been told the previous night—the bus that she had been on was part of a route that came through only once a day. The man had no idea if they would accept her ticket from the day before. There was only one other Greyhound that used the Goodland stop, and it was headed back east.

Wandering outside after she finished eating, Kiki hauled her duffle and jacket over her shoulder. What to do? Should she hang around until evening hoping to catch the Greyhound? Or should she try for a ride west? Maybe hitchhike? Look for a car or a truck? Thumbing her way was a scary idea, but waiting here was not getting her anywhere at all. It was using up her money, what little she had left, without moving her one foot closer to her goal.

Kiki wished she knew her aunt's phone number in California. She had an address but not a phone number. She had avoided writing ahead to her mother's sister because there was a chance word would get back to her parents. Kiki didn't trust anyone not to tell. Once in Sunnyvale and able to talk with her aunt about her home situation, she'd think about calling her family. She had all kinds of hope that her aunt and uncle might help her, but it was too soon to even think about that.

Kiki again glanced up and down the street. *Hadn't they passed some kind of gas station or truck stop on the way into town?* She looked up the road toward the freeway. Yes, there was a sign. She should explore what was there. She walked quickly up the street in that direction.

Kiki came to a small service area designed for truckers as well as autos and vans. The awnings over the gas pumps were quite high, and the spaces between the pumps were wider than usual. At the moment there weren't any vehicles around, but it seemed to Kiki that she had seen some the evening before when the bus came into town. At one side was a little convenience store, with a restroom door outside the building.

There was a wooden bench by the front door of the market, and Kiki sat down on it to think. Her trip, although scary, had begun according to plan, and Grace had helped her out in Pittsburgh. She had gotten this far, but now she was stranded, with no leads, stuck in hot, humid sunshine in the middle of Kansas. *A long way from home but still a long way from California.*

The morning became hotter and the bench harder and nothing happened. Eventually, Kiki stood up and went into the store to get a Coke. She asked the elderly clerk if truckers came by, and he nodded. "Yeah, sometimes. They see the McDonalds sign on the highway and come in to eat. Then they decide to gas up. But it's not predictable." He gave her a long look as if trying to decide what she really wanted to know.

When Kiki realized the man was studying her, she beat a hasty retreat outside and sat back down on the bench to drink her Coke.

The morning dragged on and flies pestered her. Nobody arrived who could help her. She realized as she sat there, getting more and more worried, that she was thinking about truckers because her papa used to talk about riding with truckers and how much fun it was. He had said he thought that professional truck drivers were safer than just getting in a car with a stranger.

Some vehicles eventually came into the service area, but no one seemed to have any potential for her. Kiki's mind drifted off to her friend, Manuela. She missed her. It would have been so much fun, and more protected perhaps, to share all of this, especially with someone as close as Manuela.

Kiki kicked rocks with her boots and studied the face of a young attendant, who was cleaning around the pumps. He looked pleasant and asked her once if she needed anything. She told him she was waiting for a Greyhound that was coming later in the day. He raised an eyebrow but left her alone. She began to get a feeling that her time on the bench was limited.

A station wagon rolled in, loaded down with a family of four and a dog. A girl, maybe ten years old, and a boy about seven. The mother made over the kids, and the father guided them all into the store for treats. For a moment, she considered approaching these people for a ride, but then she thought better of it. That wagon was already loaded.

Kiki settled back on the bench, sipped the last of her soda, and waited for the right person to rescue her. If someone didn't come before 7:30 p.m., she'd have to try to talk the Greyhound driver into taking her to San Francisco. What if he demanded more money? She didn't know what she would do.

3

Sal and Aisha

Sally Anne Turner needed to relieve herself. She didn't really want to move her eighteen-wheeler off the freeway for at least another fifty miles, but her bladder was sending clear signals that it was time to find a restroom. She had made a mistake in drinking that last can of iced tea. Although Sal loved iced tea on the road, it always went right through her. Time to take a break.

Then there was that noise coming from the underbelly of the trailer. Probably nothing; however, she needed to check. She couldn't afford a breakdown.

Sal calculated the possible places to stop. She had been along this route so many times that she knew every clean restroom and every spot with diesel. With a silent nod of her head, she decided to pull into the next town. It meant leaving the highway, but she felt that she had little choice.

Sal's bright pink cab—with "My Gal Sal" painted on the doors—was a familiar sight to truckers on east–west runs. More than fifteen years of driving had given her strong arm and shoulder muscles, which rippled as she gripped the wheel firmly and slowed for the exit ramp. Flipping on a turn signal and maneuvering the truck, she talked to a large German shepherd curled up in the passenger seat.

"Hey, Aisha, girl," Sal asked affectionately, "how would you like a chance to sniff some new territory and relieve yourself? I've got to go, so it seems only fair that you should get to pee, too."

Aisha sat up and offered a one-bark reply.

When Sal reached the familiar service station with its high awning and slowed the rig to a stop, she hopped down from the cab. Sal was a little on the short side, especially for a trucker; she had a strong, stocky build and a reddish-blonde ponytail that stuck out from under her pink ball cap that she always shoved on her head backwards. She pulled off her driving gloves and pushed them into the hip pocket of her jeans, checked all her tires, and then leaned down to inspect the underside of the trailer. For this she had to take off her dark sunglasses, exposing intense blue-green eyes.

Despite the funny noise she had heard, Sal found nothing unusual when she poked around. The trailer looked sound. Nothing loose. Relieved, she remembered her bladder and headed for the restroom. "I guess the noise will remain a mystery," she muttered to herself.

Her heart beating anxiously, Kiki stood up and hurriedly approached the trucker crossing the pavement.

"Excuse me, ma'am," Kiki said hesitantly.

"Not now, kid," Sal replied a bit gruffly, "Nature calls."

With a worried frown, Kiki watched the woman go toward the restroom.

When Sal emerged a few minutes later, lighter in bladder and in attitude, she remembered the girl, who was now standing beside the cab of her truck. A duffle bag hung from her shoulder.

Sal reached her in a few long strides and whipped off her sunglasses to gaze directly into Kiki's eyes. "Now, what did you want, young lady?" Sal was all business, yet her tone was gentle.

"Well, uh—" Kiki tried to find the right words. "I'm going to California, and Greyhound left me behind here last night. I just wondered where you are headed and if you ever take riders. I've been waiting here all morning and you're the first trucker that's come along."

Sal studied her for a moment, thoughtfully. "I'm on my way to

Salt Lake City," she spit out a bit impatiently while shoving her glasses back on, "but if you don't mind sharing space with that big German shepherd you see panting up there in the window, you're welcome to ride along, at least as far as Denver. How's that sound?"

The girl sighed with relief. "That sounds great. I don't know much about German shepherds, but you're the first woman trucker I've *ever* seen, and I'd be real grateful to go along with you."

Sal smiled and stuck out a hand. "Sally Anne Turner. Everybody just calls me Sal."

The girl returned the shake firmly. "Kiki—Jones, from New York."

Behind the dark glasses, Sal's eyes twinkled with amusement. "Kiki Jones, huh? Okay. I guess I can live with that. Stow your gear behind the seat and climb on up."

Sal walked away toward the convenience store and looked back, thinking. She wasn't sure she actually bought the "Jones" part, but she guessed the girl needed some privacy. She chuckled to herself and entered the market.

The counter attendant's nametag read "Harold." Sal passed him a credit card. "I wasn't planning to gas up yet, but since I'm here, I'll go ahead and fill up. That way I can have one less stop before Denver."

Harold swiped her card through his register. "Looks like you gonna pick up a rider," he observed, pushing the card back her way.

Sal nodded. "Looks like it."

Harold shrugged. "That kid's been sittin' here since the crack of dawn waitin' for someone to come along to give her a ride. I think she was about to give up when you drove in." Then he added, "We don't encourage people to hang around here lookin' for rides. I thought about calling the sheriff, but the girl wasn't botherin' anyone and she's just a kid. I didn't want to cause her trouble. I am glad that it's you maybe givin' her a ride. She worries me."

"Yeah, I get it," Sal observed with a nod. "The kid's got a little scar over one eye, but that doesn't mean anything. She doesn't look like a druggie, so I may let her go with me for a while. First, if it's okay to leave the truck, I'm going to get some real lunch."

Harold shrugged. "Sure. Nobody's gonna touch it."

Outside, Sal found her potential rider still holding her duffle bag and standing on the ground staring through the truck's window at Aisha. The shepherd was staring back. Sal sighed. "I hope you two will get along," she mused as she pulled down the big diesel hose and set it up. She smiled at Kiki once or twice as she worked.

When the meter showed the tank filling, Sal walked up to Kiki, still eyeing the dog. "You scared of Aisha? Come on." Sal opened the cab door and spoke to her pet. "This is Kiki Jones from New York. She's gonna ride with us for a ways. Now you be good."

Aisha whined.

Sal looked at Kiki. "That means okay."

Sal grabbed Kiki's bag, stepped up onto the cab's foot rail, and tossed the duffle and jacket over the front seat into the storage area. Then she jumped down again and looked at the gasoline pump numbers running.

"It's noon," she commented, looking at her watch. "You had lunch yet?"

Kiki shook her head. "I was too worried about getting a ride to think about eating."

Sal laughed generously. "Well, I guess it's a good thing I happened along. You might have died of starvation right here on that bench."

Kiki pulled herself up, a touch defensively. "I had breakfast at McDonalds."

Sal laughed. "Well, we'll go down the street to a place I know that is a little more original than McDonalds."

"You come through here often?" Kiki asked as she followed behind Sal toward the street.

"Sometimes," Sal called over her shoulder. "I do a lot of

cross-country hauls, and I hear from other truckers where the good places are to gas up, eat, or find whatever else I might need."

They hiked a couple of blocks, turned a corner, and there sat a little unpretentious café. Sal pulled open a screen door and motioned Kiki to enter. "Let's eat," she suggested with a lopsided grin.

The trucker led Kiki to a booth in the rear of the café and tossed a menu in her direction. "I've stopped here three or four times. The stuff is a bit on the greasy side, but the club sandwich is okay. The potato salad is pretty good, skip the soup, and desserts are *really* great. Fill yourself up—milk shake, whatever you want. I'd be willing to bet that among other things, you don't have much money, so this meal's on me. We've got a lot of miles to cover this afternoon, so eat hearty, and if you see something you want for the road, get it. We'll worry later about how you can earn your way."

Sal stood. "I'll be back in a minute. Order me a club, potato salad, Doritos, a chocolate shake, and a piece of that strawberry pie I see over there. Okay?"

Before Kiki could open her mouth to protest, Sal was already gone. The waitress appeared, and Kiki just shrugged and ordered two of everything Sal had suggested.

A few moments later, Sal returned. "I had to let Aisha out to relieve herself. I got so busy with my own problems that I almost forgot her. She's such a patient animal. I don't know what I'd do without her to protect me and the truck."

Their food arrived, and Sal tucked into her sandwich. With the first bite, she sprayed herself with mayonnaise. She laughed good-naturedly and grabbed a napkin to wipe her shirt. As she did so, Kiki gave her a long look, because Sal's sleeveless denim top was unbuttoned a little, revealing a bit of her well-endowed bosom. Sal glanced up and smiled at Kiki. "You can dress 'em up but you can't take 'em anywhere," she chuckled.

Realizing that Sal must have seen her staring, Kiki flushed.

"That's a nice necklace you're wearing," she commented to cover her discomfort.

"Oh, the amethyst? Thanks. That was a gift from a friend—sort of a New Age thing, I guess. But I like it. I think it's pretty."

Sal changed the subject. "So you came all the way from New York City?"

"Well, actually, from the South Bronx, and I caught the Greyhound in New Jersey," Kiki admitted.

"And they let a Jones into the Bronx?" Sal asked, lifting an eyebrow.

"Well, that's what I've been telling everyone, just to protect myself. My name's really Rodriguez. Kiki Rodriquez."

Sal nodded. "Now that I'll buy. You look more like a Rodriquez than a Jones, with those chocolate eyes and that dark wavy hair, not to mention your beautiful olive complexion. I'm so Anglo-Saxon pale—I just love skin that has more warmth and color."

Kiki blushed and looked away.

Sal smiled kindly. "Well, Kiki Rodriguez, I didn't mean to embarrass you. I think we'll get along just fine. Now tell me, why the sudden yen for California? You look a little young to be hittin' the road—and which part of California is your destination?"

Kiki sipped the chocolate shake. "We—my family—don't have much money, and I have this dream of going to college. There's just no work in the South Bronx. My papa says I have to pay rent, now I'm eighteen, and I can't do that, let alone save for college. I got tired of being poor and not seeing a way out. I just decided to split and start over somewhere else. Maybe I can have a better life."

Sal's eyes softened. "Life can be hard sometimes. Well, I wish you good luck. And are you headed for Berkeley or UCLA?" She asked, offering a little wink.

"I don't know," Kiki admitted. "I got family south of San Francisco, but I won't know if I can stay with them until I can tell them what I want to do. Whatever happens, I have to get a job and a place to live and save some money, before I can even think about college." She stirred her shake with the straw and suddenly looked a little subdued.

"You just get out of high school this year?"

Kiki sighed. "No, I was a junior. I'll have to finish later or get a GED."

"Oh." Sal's forehead creased with a frown. "You've got a lot of work ahead of you."

Kiki nodded as she finished her milk shake. Then she looked up. "Have you ever been to California?"

"Sure. I drive in and out of there all the time. My home base is Salt Lake City. Got a house there, and a roommate, kind of a real good friend, and my family is there. They're Mormon. I had to give that up because it didn't," she chuckled, "suit my lifestyle." She paused with a sideward glance at Kiki and then continued, "but that's a topic for another time. Yes, I've been all over California. I like the Bay Area the best. California's a big state. You'll figure out where you feel comfortable."

Sal ate quickly, and Kiki followed her example. The trucker looked at her wristwatch a couple of times as she polished off her pie. Meanwhile, Kiki excused herself to go to the restroom. When she returned, Sal had paid the bill and was heading out the door. Kiki hurried to catch up with her.

At the truck stop, Aisha was pawing at the window and wagging her tail. "Now that I told her you're my friend," Sal explained, "she'll be quite at ease. However, if someone tried to harm me, she'd go after them to kill."

Sal opened the passenger door, called Aisha down to the ground, and officially introduced her to Kiki. The dog smelled and licked her, and Kiki laughed as she felt a tickly sensation all over her body from the dog's inquisitive nose. She pushed Aisha away when she prodded between her legs. The dog looked up at her but accepted the limitation without resistance. Then, when Sal motioned to her, Kiki carefully stepped on the rail and climbed up onto the big bucket seat. Aisha jumped first to a spot near Kiki's feet, then over her shoulder and onto the long bench that crossed the back of the cab. The truck was not as big inside as Kiki had expected although the interior did have some personal décor. Sal had pictures on the visor and a colorful stone hanging from the rearview mirror. The cab felt homey, and Kiki began to relax. She felt she was really going to like riding with Sal.

"Well, fasten that seat belt, and let's get going," Sal instructed, and Kiki quickly did as told.

"We'll make Denver before dinnertime," Sal explained as she started the big engine and put it into gear. "It's only a couple of hundred miles via I-70. We'll have something to eat, and I'll get a cheap motel room for the night—probably won't cost much more for a second bed. Tomorrow I'll head over the Rockies and on to Salt Lake City. Since I drive alone, I can't make as many miles as some of the teams do. I hurt my back a few months ago, and sooner or later my spine begins to yell at me."

Kiki listened as Sal pulled the rig carefully out onto the street and turned in the direction of the freeway entrance. She watched Sal working the gears and pedals and became curious. "Is this a good job?" she questioned.

Sal looked at her and smiled. "Thinking about your career choices?" she asked with a grin. Then she added, a bit more seriously, "Driving can pay well, if you're skilled and find the right company. It's lonely unless you drive with a partner—a partner you enjoy—and it's hard on the body. Like any physical task, it becomes mentally boring and takes a toll on your health. You do control your hours, up to a point, you don't have many supervisors breathing down your neck, and nobody cares what you wear while you work or what kind of lifestyle you have."

Kiki nodded as if she understood completely. She didn't, especially about the "lifestyle," but it was Kiki's nature to think a bit about things that confused her. Then she'd ask questions when she had some sense of exactly what it was that she wanted to know. Kiki had always been a quiet observer.

"Have you always been a truck driver?"

"Well, I was in the Army for a few years. I applied to mechanic's school, because I didn't want to get stuck behind a desk, and along with working on trucks, I did some driving. When I got out of the service, I went to college for a little while, until I realized I didn't like studying all the time. I dropped out eventually and tried waitressing and a few other jobs. I missed being around the big trucks. Then I started driving for a company in Salt Lake and did that until I could put money down to buy a rig. I've been on my own for a little over three years now."

Sal gave Kiki a friendly smile. "That's about it."

Kiki watched the passing landscape for a few miles. "I don't know what I want to do, but I do know I want to go to college. There's just something inside, calling me."

Sal nodded. "Trust your senses. If you want an education, there's a reason. Go for it, and don't let anyone talk you out of it. Along the way, you'll figure out what you want to do with that education."

Kiki slid down in the seat and listened to Aisha's occasional panting from behind her shoulder. She couldn't believe her good luck. It seemed already that being with Sal was like having a big sister. Kiki had always wished she had a sister to talk to. She seldom talked to her mama because she was always so stressed and busy. Kiki was expected to help around the house, yet no one had much time to listen to her about anything, especially her feelings.

As she watched the landscape roll by, Kiki experienced a delicious feeling of comfort and power. She felt so good that she lifted her feet and stuck them, boots and all, up on the dashboard and stretched.

Sal looked her way with a slight frown and started to say something. Instead, she shook her head silently and returned her focus to her driving.

After a brief silence, Sal asked, "You left your family behind, what two or three days ago?"

Kiki nodded.

"That's a mighty gutsy thing to do."

"Yeah, I guess so. I'm scared but I felt I had to go." Kiki shrugged.

"Did you also leave a boyfriend pining away for you?" Sal inquired lightly.

Sitting up straighter, Kiki pulled her feet back off the dash. "No boyfriends," she offered with a little sigh. "I've never dated much. Like, there wasn't much free time. Mama worked, and I had to help out at home. Then there was homework for school, because Papa insisted on decent grades. Thankfully I could do that. And I had a job for a little while. I didn't have too much spare time, but frankly, I never cared about dating much. With three brothers, I saw just about as much of guys as I wanted in a lifetime." She wrinkled her nose to emphasize the point, and Sal laughed.

Kiki was briefly quiet and then added, "When I listened to the girls at school talk about boys—and how silly they became over them—I just couldn't find the same feelings inside myself. I guess I was kind of different, more independent, maybe a loner. Like, I don't seem to need boys around me."

"I see," Sal noted and let the subject drop.

There was a lengthy silence between them. Kiki was thinking about her family. Growing up she had too much of some things—anger in the house, drinking by her dad, trouble with her brothers—and not enough of other things, like warmth and affection. Or even like seeing movies, watching television shows, TV news, or learning what all that Internet stuff was all about. In some ways she was too smart, and in other ways she was really naive for eighteen. She understood that, without anybody telling her.

Sal remained quiet while observing Kiki's thoughtful frown from the corner of her eye, until Aisha's panting led her to suggest, "Kiki, there's a water bottle and a bowl behind the seat. They're for Aisha. Do you think you could pour her some water and see if she'll drink from the bowl?"

"Okay." Kiki was not sure how to handle this big dog but was willing to try. She unhooked her seat belt, scooted around, located the water bottle, and poured some water into the bowl—being careful not to spill it. She held it out to Aisha, and the dog lapped without hesitation. Kiki began giggling as she watched Aisha's big tongue slipping in and out of the water.

A short time later, they pulled into a rest stop. After everyone, including the dog, had gotten physical relief, Sal did a few moments of stretching to help her back. Then she climbed into the driver's seat beside Kiki and Aisha, who were busy becoming pals.

As Sal had predicted, it was time to eat when they reached Denver. She already had a cheap motel picked out, near a truck stop with a safe place for her to park the rig. Along the way into the city she pulled off the road long enough to pick up a pizza and some pop. In their motel room, Sal and Kiki shared a big pepperoni pan pizza and watched TV for a while. Aisha, having devoured her kibble, nibbled on the droppings in the pizza box and then curled up beside Sal's bed. Before long, Sal turned out the lamp.

"Sorry," she said to Kiki, "but my back's had it for the day. I need to get a long night's sleep."

"That's okay," Kiki replied. "Thank you for everything, Sal."

Kiki remained awake for a few minutes, thinking of the remarkable day and how fascinating Sal was to her. She was curious to know more about the trucker. It was so much fun to have a grownup to talk with, especially a woman. It seemed so different. Kiki thought about Artemis blinking somewhere up there in the sky and silently thanked her star for bringing Sal to her.

Early the next morning, they showered, ate breakfast, and then Sal gassed up. Kiki stood beside her and watched her handle the hose.

Sal looked at her. "We haven't really talked about this. I need to know whether you want to go on with me to Salt Lake City, or whether I should try to find you another ride over the mountains straight into California."

Kiki swallowed. *That was a bridge she didn't want to cross.* After a pause, she replied, "If it's okay, I'll go with you." Her eyes were wide, almost wild and threatening to fill with tears.

Noticing, Sal just nodded and didn't say anything else.

When Sal finished with the fill-up, she went to the office to sign off on the bill. Then they both climbed into the cab and Sal headed for the freeway. Salt Lake City. Some five hundred miles away.

"I go up to Ft. Collins and pick up I-80 and go across that way," Sal explained as they moved away from the service station. That meant nothing to Kiki; however, she was thankful that Sal was willing to share the information. Later Kiki would pull out her map and look up the routes, so she could understand what they were doing. There were a lot of ways to go over the Rockies, she soon realized.

Kiki's second day with Sal felt even more rewarding than the first. During the morning, they shared stories about their childhoods and compared the differences between growing up in Salt Lake City in a Mormon family and growing up in the South Bronx as part of a Polish-Puerto Rican-Filipino family. Now that New York had slipped farther and farther behind, Kiki discovered that she could laugh about things that had seemed so painful when she was in the midst of them. She admitted that many of the family issues revolved around her papa's drinking. "He can get jobs, but then he drinks and gets laid off or fired. He straightens up enough to talk himself into another job, and then the whole thing repeats itself. I know Papa's upset about my brothers being in gangs. Of course, his drinking doesn't help anything, and it makes Mama very sad and angry, so they fight."

Sal apparently thought she should lighten things, because she soon changed the subject to favorite sports and movies. Kiki didn't care what they discussed. She just enjoyed hearing Sal talk.

"What was your favorite class in—oh, let's say, seventh grade?" Sal asked.

"PE. I loved playing softball and basketball. My older brothers would never let me do anything, and seventh grade was the first chance I had to prove I could hold my own in sports."

Sal nodded. "I loved PE, too. I must confess that I had a terrible crush on my teacher, Miss Hodges." She laughed, perhaps remembering being thirteen.

Kiki blushed. "You, too?" Her eyes opened wide. "I thought that I was the only one who did that! Mine was Miss Castaneda, and she was really pretty. I was so impressed with my only Hispanic teacher that year, that I couldn't wait to get to PE class." Kiki suddenly laughed. Then she added, "I was always on this high, and I couldn't understand why everyone else didn't feel the same way I did."

Sal chuckled and then suggested kindly, "Well, I suspect several of them felt the same way. They just weren't as open about it as you seem to have been. And some of them may have been frightened to admit what they felt, for fear of what it might mean, or what others might think it could mean."

Kiki nodded, then scooted down in the seat and became quiet. There was something in what Sal had shared that was important, but Kiki didn't quite understand, and she didn't feel ready to explore it, at least not right now.

Sal, looking her way, seemed to realize that she had hit on a touchy subject for Kiki and kept quiet.

As the moments sped by, Kiki felt more keenly aware of what a good time she was having. This was so much better than her trip had been in the beginning, on the Greyhound. Aside from meeting Grace, long hours on a bus were a bit grim. Now, riding in the big cab, up high where she could see so much, and listening to Sal on her CB were really fun. Maybe it was Sal, too. She certainly enjoyed talking with her and felt safe with this very independent woman.

Salt Lake City, the end of their road together, loomed ahead at the end of the day. "Our fun is soon going to be over," Kiki commented with a touch of regret.

Sal nodded. "Well, we have a few hours to go yet. It's a long day." She gave Kiki a friendly cuff on the shoulder and then explained what would happen. "This evening, when we get to Salt Lake City, I'll be home for a while before I start out on another haul. You can stay there with my roommate and me, for a few days if you want, and we can look around for a ride for you to San Francisco. That's another long day's trip from Salt Lake, maybe ten hours."

Kiki nodded and grew quiet. She looked forward to arriving in Salt Lake City and checking out Sal's place. Although she wanted to go to San Francisco, she was enjoying herself so very much right now. It was going to be difficult to leave Sal behind. While Kiki wanted to reach California, she wished somehow that Sal were going there too.

4

Sal and Meg

Despite the fun she was having, Kiki grew tired by the afternoon and leaned against the window for a nap. She moved in and out of consciousness, and her mind intermittently replayed the mysteries and wonders of this second day with Sal.

That morning as Sal had pushed the big truck upward into the Rocky Mountains, Kiki had been awe struck by the scenery, which was so different from anything she had ever known. This part of the country was not like the rolling hills of Pennsylvania or Missouri, or the farmlands of Kansas and eastern Colorado. These mountains were beautiful but sheer, stark, bold, dramatic, and clearly dangerous.

After their early conversations, Kiki had been quiet for long periods of time. She could see that Sal was concentrating on shifting gears and keeping the heavily loaded truck under firm control as they rounded numerous curves and gradually worked their way in traffic toward the highest mountain elevations.

At one point, Sal had pulled off at a lookout to rest her back for a few minutes. This allowed Kiki a chance to just stare at the majesty of the Rockies. She had gotten film in Denver so she took a few pictures with her little camera. Sal and Aisha posed for her in front of a tall mountain peak, and Sal took a couple of pictures of Kiki with the Rockies behind her. Aisha sniffed around the guard railings and left her mark as she squatted to relieve herself.

The routine became comfortable, and as the day wore on, there was little either of them needed to say. Even Aisha, despite her occasional panting, was very quiet.

When they began a gradual descent on the western slope of the Rockies, Kiki started thinking again about herself and her life. And about Sal. She suddenly felt a sense of urgency. *She had to make the most of their brief time together.*

Breaking her long silence, Kiki suddenly asked Sal, "Are you intelligent?"

Sal laughed. "What makes you ask that question?"

"First answer my question, and then I'll explain," Kiki insisted.

Sal shook her head. "Well, I don't know what you mean by intelligent. By my own standards, I suppose I'm fairly smart. I always did well in school, if that's any measure. I can usually make decisions and solve problems, and I generally think of that as intelligent. I guess I'm not sure what you're looking for."

"Well, you talk different. I'm ignorant, I know that, but you talk so plain, so clear. I listened to people on the Greyhound, and they didn't talk like me. I recognized the Jersey accent, it sounds like 'Joisey' but after that I heard different sounds. You know what I mean? Mine's Bronx slang, and then there's Southern slang, and then there's other slang. You're different, more proper. More like in a book. I just wondered if that's a sign that you're real intelligent."

"Yeah, I'm probably intelligent," Sal mused. "However, the way I speak is more a result of where I grew up and the values that were important to my family. My father's a lawyer, and my mom taught school. They both placed a premium on proper speech, and I was corrected whenever I used a double negative, like 'I don't have nothing.' I did well in English grammar because it was expected of me. I've been a rebel in lots of other ways in my life, but clear, correct speech has been a habit for so long that I don't see any reason to stop." She smiled to herself, "I do have to admit, after years on the road, that my spoken English is a little more casual than it used to be." She laughed. "Those 'gonnas' slip in now and then."

Kiki was silent, and Sal studied her. "Do you think you are not smart because you speak like people in your neighborhood in the South Bronx?"

"Well, not exactly. But jeez, all I heard at home was dialects of Polish and Puerto Rican and Filipino and Yiddish and all spoken with this Bronx accent. A word like 'thought' comes out 'thawght.' And Bronx speech was different from Brooklyn, or Long Island. I know that much, but, like, it sounds kind of funny to me now that I'm not there. I hear you, and you don't talk that way."

Sal nodded. "You're talking about regional speech patterns. If I'd grown up in the South Bronx, I'd have been exposed to the same speech that you have been. Since Salt Lake City has a different local accent, I talk differently."

She paused a second and then added, "Now you can decide to change the way you talk, over time. You have to develop a good ear, which can be done. With practice, you can learn to speak any way you want. Personally I don't see your speech as a problem. I enjoy the way you talk," Sal commented. "It's actually kind of cute."

"Really? Jeez, that's strange."

"Kiki, I see you as intelligent. You've come from a tough background, and look at you. You're open-minded and adventurous and brave. You want something for yourself and you're willing to go after it. And you're eighteen and from what you tell me, you've avoided a lot of traps that your circumstances could have lured you into——drugs and alcohol, pregnancy, or a relationship with a tough and abusive male. To be eighteen, intact and still filled with dreams and enthusiasm, is no small miracle, and *you* created that. You must be bright and very determined to have done it."

"Wow," Kiki commented with a sigh. "I never thought of it like that."

"Well, hang onto that idea. It's important to see your strengths when you go out into the world. There's enough out there to scare and humble you without putting yourself down on top of it."

Kiki's olive complexion turned pinkish. She giggled. "You're embarrassing me. I'm not used to compliments."

Sal smiled and reached over and mussed Kiki's hair. Kiki smiled back but kept silent. As they wound their way gradually down through the mountains, she looked thoughtful. She turned over and over in her mind what Sal had said and savored it. She knew it was somehow significant.

At the same time, Kiki's curiosity had not been satisfied. She had other nagging thoughts and questions on her mind, and they were moving closer and closer to Salt Lake City. Kiki thought about Sal's offer to spend time with her there and what she should do about that. Most of all, she was curious about the photograph that was stuck in Sal's visor.

Kiki studied the picture, which was of a woman, who must be about Sal's age, somewhere in her thirties, who was standing in a blue scrub uniform and smiling warmly. She had short dark hair and hazel eyes and a relaxed manner. One hand was on Aisha's shoulder. The dog was sitting beside her and leaning into her body in a loving, protective way. Kiki assumed that she was the roommate that Sal had mentioned, and yet Kiki instinctively felt that a roommate—although admittedly she had never had one—wasn't important enough to put on your visor and take with you all over the country. That seemed more like a husband, or a wife, or a lover. And with Aisha in the picture, it all seemed like family.

Kiki chewed on this thought for a little while. And she studied Sal, with her muscular arms and pink baseball cap worn backwards on her head. She then observed the tension in Sal's jaw as she maneuvered the powerful semi and thought about how it must feel to be competing with men in a job that used to belong solely to males. Women in Kiki's world raised kids and held minor jobs in the neighborhood. Other than teachers at school and a few local bus drivers, she had had little contact with women who were making a life for themselves independently.

These observations brought up another subject Kiki had avoided earlier in the day. After a moment's consideration, she asked directly, "Are you a dyke?"

Sal smiled. "Why do you ask?"

"Just curious, I guess."

"Will it make a difference how I answer the question?"

"Probably not, but I'd just like to know."

"Well, I'm not sure what your frame of reference is, but I *am* a lesbian. If that means a dyke to you, then probably I am a dyke, although I don't usually think of myself in that way. Why do you ask?"

"I just never knew a dyke—or a lesbian—before. They don't exactly walk around my 'hood wearing nametags. In my school, they'd risk getting beat up by a mob. There were some tough, kind of masculine girls in school, but all I saw in that was that they could stand up for themselves."

Sal glanced at her thoughtfully for a moment. "I bet some of those tough girls were lesbians, yet to protect themselves they had to pretend to be straight, even to the point of beating up on lesbians so it wouldn't look as if they were lesbians too, or had sympathy with lesbians."

Kiki sighed. "Yeah, I can get that. I just don't understand all of it. Just like the women I saw kissing on the subway the other day. I was kind of embarrassed. I didn't know what to make of them."

Sal smiled at her gently. "You're not alone there. Most people don't understand. Sometimes *I* don't understand. However, it's why I'm not on speaking terms with my parents and why I don't go to the Mormon church anymore and a lot of other things—maybe even including why I drive a truck instead of doing a job that could pay better and be less tough on my body.

"Being a lesbian has shaped my life in many, many ways. Yet I still feel like a woman—not a man—and I do little womanly things at home like plant flowers. I don't ride a Harley. I don't do drugs or drink or hang out in bars or any of those stereotypes. I've been with Meg for six years, and that's a long time in anyone's world, straight or gay. Meg is a physician's assistant and she works long hours at a hospital. We feel very fortunate when we can be together for a brief time, before I go on the road again or she goes to work for a long shift."

Sal paused and returned her focus to her driving.

Kiki thought and thought. Then she asked, "Did you always know that you were a lesbian?"

Sal seemed to consider that question for a long time. "Well, not always. I dated boys in high school, but I found I was so much closer to my girlfriends. Boys didn't have the impact that I expected them to have, and I didn't dream of getting married and having a big family, like Mormon girls are programmed to do. I didn't understand my indifference, or rebellion, or whatever it was, for a long time. When I joined the service and was surrounded by women in the barracks, things happened. A woman approached me for a sexual encounter. I was curious and, after we experimented with each other, thoughts and feelings started to fall into place for me. However, being gay in the military is hard. It's why I finally left the Army."

"Where did you meet Meg?"

"When I was going to college. Meg was in nursing school at the time. We ran into each other at a campus event, and we really hit it off. We had a lot in common in terms of our backgrounds and our values, and I was mature enough to want a stable relationship. So was she. And it's worked."

Kiki was silent. Sal glanced her way questioningly. Finally, she asked, "Does this mean something to you?"

Kiki looked out the window. "I don't know."

Sal pursued the question. "Does it worry you? Do you think this part of me rubs off, like a disease, like you might catch it or something?"

Kiki shook her head. "No, it's not that. I just don't know what to do with all this new stuff I'm experiencing. Like, it's a lot."

Sal nodded. "You're right, it is. The minute you walked out of your apartment in the South Bronx, you opened up a whole world of new ideas and experiences, and you're going to grow and change in a multitude of ways you could never have dreamed of before. Don't worry about understanding it all. You'll sort it out eventually in your own way."

Kiki sighed. "Maybe I should have stayed home."

"Do you really mean that?"

Kiki shook her head. "No, I just feel scared of everything and real tired, like I need to sleep for a long, long time."

"I understand. Why don't you try to take another a nap? You might feel better after you rest."

Kiki wadded up her jacket for a pillow, put it by the window, and leaned against it. Within minutes she was asleep. Sal watched her and smiled to herself.

When Kiki started moving around and came back to the world, they had reached a town where Sal could pull off for a snack and a rest stop. Sal kept the conversation light. They kidded and laughed about the food and the place and Sal told some stories about silly things that Aisha had done over the years.

As they climbed back into the truck, Sal gave Kiki a warm smile. "I've been wondering," she asked, "How did you come by the handle 'Kiki'?"

Kiki laughed. "Well, I got a long string of names at birth. My mama preferred 'Cristina.' So that's what I was called. Then it gradually became 'Christy.' Gusto, my baby brother, had trouble with the sounds, and 'Christy' came out of his mouth as 'Kiki.' At first we all laughed, yet it stuck. I didn't always like it, but I'm so used to it now that I wouldn't recognize anything else."

Soon they were back on the highway, and Kiki watched the road signs roll by. They were getting close to Salt Lake City. It would be upon them before she was ready.

Early that evening, almost at dusk, they hit the suburbs of Salt Lake and in another hour, after winding through various neighborhoods, and beyond the city limits, Sal turned off the main road and carefully guided the truck into a wide drive which ran alongside a house, a bungalow surrounded by trees and gardens. She gave one honk on the truck's horn and then opened the cab door to allow Aisha, who was barking excitedly, to jump down to the ground and run free. They were home. And Meg was at the front door, running out to greet Sal and meet Kiki, who stood shyly by watching the two women hug each other warmly.

Kiki was invited in, and Meg brought out a dinner she had created for Sal's homecoming. There was plenty of savory meat, steamed vegetables and tossed salad to share, and Kiki devoured her portion. After days of road restaurants, sandwiches, pizza, and energy bars, a home cooked meal tasted wonderful to her.

By the time they had finished ice cream for dessert, Kiki began to fade. Meg noticed and signaled to Sal, who quickly left the table to prepare a bed for Kiki in the spare room. Then Sal showed Kiki how to find everything that she might need. Half asleep already, Kiki wandered off to bed, having barely the energy to wish them good night. In moments she was sound asleep.

Sal and Meg sat at the dining room table and talked for a long time, sharing the events of their individual lives over the past few days. Sal told Meg about Kiki and her incredible journey and how responsible Sal felt toward the eighteen-year old. Meg nodded in understanding. "I do trust that you know what you are doing," she observed gently.

Sal paused for a moment. "I know that Kiki is very young and vulnerable and that, as a consequence, I'm walking a fine line with her," she finally commented.

Meg patted her arm. "Glad you're aware."

Giving Sal a warm smile, Meg stood and headed for their bedroom.

Kiki was up early the next morning. After they all downed a quick breakfast, Meg rushed off to the hospital, and Sal took Kiki with her to unload the truck. They drove to a warehouse in a downtown industrial district, where Sal unhitched the cab from the trailer, so the warehouse crew could empty it. "The trailer will sit here empty for a while," Sal explained, "and then it will be loaded for my next trip back east."

Once they had dumped the trailer, Sal planned to take Kiki on a brief tour of Salt Lake City. Before they went very far from the warehouse, however, Sal pulled into a car wash big enough to hold her rig. "Now," she laughed, "this is where you're going to earn your keep. You're going to help me wash the truck!"

Kiki was only too glad to help, and she and Sal climbed around the cab and soaped it down and hosed it off. Sal kept feeding the machine quarters. Kiki did a good share of the physical labor, and they kidded each other while they worked. When they finished, the pink truck shone; Sal and Kiki had to towel off because they had sprayed nearly as much soap and water on themselves as the semi.

"Now we'll drop the cab off at home and get my pick-up," Sal explained, as she pulled out of the car wash.

With Aisha between them on the bench seat of a blue Ford F-150, Sal drove Kiki by the Utah State Capitol, Mormon Tabernacle and Salt Lake Temple, one of the big malls, and a couple of neighborhoods where Sal had grown up. Kiki was fascinated with everything, so different from her own home. She was especially impressed with the many-spired Mormon Temple and studied the complex for a long time. "Was it hard for you to give up your religion because you are a lesbian?" she asked.

Sal sighed. "Well, it was very important in my family. We all went to church regularly. I really believed in it; however, when I realized I was a lesbian and would be shunned—or else they'd try to 'cure' me through some torturous counseling process—I decided that I could no longer remain loyal to that belief system. My own sanity and happiness in this life came first."

Kiki nodded, deep in thought. "I got a dose of Catholicism from my mama. My papa was Catholic in name but he didn't go to church. It was one of the things they argued about. I stopped attending mass after I got big enough to say no. Maybe someday I'll find the right religion for me. Until then, I just talk to Artemis."

"So far your personal star seems to have done right by you, huh?"

Kiki smiled. "Yeah, I think so."

After finishing their local tour, they stopped at a grocery to pick up items from a list Meg had handed Sal that morning. By the store entrance there was a bulletin board with several local announcements pinned to it. Sal spotted a notice of three college students headed to Berkeley and looking for a fourth person to ride along with them to share the cost of gasoline. She showed the message to Kiki and encouraged her to call the phone number listed.

"It may be a faster way for you to get to San Francisco than riding on a big truck," Sal suggested, "because there is the Sierra Nevada mountain range to cross upon entering California.

"It's a long trip yet doable in one day when you can zip along at the speed limit, rather than being held back by a heavy truck load. There will probably be more than one driver, and that will help too—both on time and expenses."

When the two returned to the house, Kiki swallowed her anxiety and made the telephone call. The girl who answered, Tina, seemed really happy to find another rider. She told Kiki that she and her boyfriend and another male friend were going to be leaving in a couple of days and would really be glad to have Kiki join them. The two made plans for their departure, with Sal providing instructions for finding the house.

During her last two days in Salt Lake City, Kiki did more sight-seeing and took a couple of long naps. She could feel her body letting go of tension. As she released the stress, she sensed just how tightly wound she had been after leaving home. Now she played with Aisha, enjoyed the wonders of TV, and sat one evening outside looking at the stars, trying to find Artemis. After reorienting herself to Utah's night sky, she finally located her twinkling star and smiled. "I can't believe it," she said aloud to her nighttime friend, "I think I know now what it is to feel happy."

On the last night before Kiki's departure, she and Sal took Aisha for a long walk. As they ambled through the neighborhood, which had houses spread widely apart and with large yards between—and while Aisha sniffed and did her business—Kiki confessed her conflicts. "Part of me wants to go to California, and part of me wants to stay here," she admitted.

Sal put her arm around Kiki's shoulders. "I can understand that. Yet you left your home with a dream, and I believe in honoring dreams. You need to follow your rainbow until you find the end of it. I don't know what lies there for you, any more than you do. However, it's important that you finish what you started."

Kiki frowned. "But I have all these feelings, and I don't know what to do with them," she said plaintively as a few tears began sliding down her cheeks.

"Kiki," Sal told her firmly, "you're a delightful young woman just coming into your own. You're strong, courageous and direct—and people are going to take to you. Oh, some will not understand you and others will be turned off by your bluntness, but you will make many significant relationships in your life. I can see that, because I have just a little more life experience than you do right now. You're hungry for life, and I'm the first person you've met who has given you a little time and attention. However, I'm not the only one who can be nurturing to you, and I don't want you to get stuck here. I don't think Salt Lake is your destination or that my way of being has, necessarily, anything to do with your own future. Do you understand?"

Kiki's shoulders trembled. "I think so."

"I like you, I care about you, I can be your friend—I want to be your friend. I also want you to find your *own* life, that unique life that's waiting out there for you."

Kiki turned and threw her arms around Sal. "Thank you. I'm sorry. I shouldn't be making demands on you."

Sal patted her gently. "It's okay, Kiki. You trusted yourself enough to leave home. Hang onto that trust. I think that life sort of takes care of us in its own way. And I rather suspect that it wasn't a coincidence that I happened along when you needed a ride out of that little town in Kansas."

Kiki laughed.

"There is some meaning in our paths crossing," Sal continued, "I believe that. I also feel sure that you must continue your trip to California. You have to connect with your aunt and see what's there for you."

Very early the next morning, a little white Subaru sedan pulled up in front of the house, and Tina, Rick, and Frank climbed out. Kiki had been watching for them and rushed outside to meet them. When she got a good look at the car, Kiki decided it was a good thing she didn't have many belongings, because a rack on top was already loaded, and the rear hatch was tied closed with a rope.

Sal emerged from the house with Aisha on her heels and talked with the students for a few moments, apparently trying to be sure that they knew the route and had a realistic plan to make it to the Bay Area by the end of the day. Kiki was relieved that Sal was helping assess the situation, because she hadn't a clue how to figure out if they were safe to travel with. All she could feel was her own apprehension. When Sal turned to Kiki and prepared to say goodbye, Kiki decided it must be okay. Sal was sending her off with a bag of sandwiches for the road and a bedroll that she kept in the truck, "So, no matter what happens, you'll always have a place to sleep."

Kiki told Aisha goodbye, while the shepherd thumped her tail and gave Kiki a wet kiss. Then Kiki moved into Sal's arms and held her close. After a moment, Sal directed her, "Now I want you to keep in touch. Call me collect when you get to the Bay Area, okay? Here's the address and phone number." She handed Kiki a piece of paper. "Write me, and someday, when you're settled, come back to visit, okay?"

Kiki looked at her with eyes that were pools of fear and sadness. She nodded, released Sal and climbed into the back seat of the sedan.

Rick backed the car out of the driveway and started to turn around. Then Sal waved him to stop. She came to the side of the car, opened the passenger door and reached in to give Kiki her pink baseball cap. "Take this as a souvenir of your trucking days. It's always brought me good luck, so maybe it will do the same for you."

"Oh, thank you, Sal," Kiki said, holding the cap as if it were made of gold.

Rick shouted something about needing to get on to California, so the car moved away as Kiki looked out the back window at Sal standing by the roadway and waving.

Frank looked around from the front seat. "Is that woman a relative of yours?" he asked. Before she could answer, he snickered at Rick, "She looks like some kind of dyke to me."

Kiki flared in embarrassed rage. "So what's it to you, anyway?" she demanded.

"Nothing," Frank grumbled, backing off.

Rick glared at him. "Come on, let's not ruin this before we even get started. We've just got to get through a day together."

So they sped across Utah, by the flat and shimmering desert of the Great Salt Lake, then on into Nevada and hours later into downtown Reno, where they stopped briefly. Frank and Rick both wanted to play the slots and round up a beer or two. Tina tailed along with them, but Kiki stayed beside the car. She looked at all the glittery signs for the hotels and casinos. It wasn't her world, and she shook her head. For this she had no ambition.

Just as Kiki was getting antsy, Frank, Rick and Tina came dashing across the street, mission accomplished. The guys had won a few dollars on the slot machines and had also scored some beers. They were happy.

Next they crossed the Sierra Nevada range on I-80. Along the way, they saw signs for the state of California, and Kiki felt very excited. At first the land reminded her of the Rocky Mountains, but gradually they came down into the vast farmlands around Sacramento, and then onto the ribbon of freeway that flowed into the Bay Area. Kiki was all eyes, especially when they passed rice fields after Sacramento, crossed a bridge at Vallejo, and went through Richmond, where the waters of the San Francisco Bay became visible through the car windows.

About this time, Frank pulled out a marijuana joint, lit it, and passed it around. Rick took a whiff and Tina gladly accepted it. Kiki shook her head. She had tried pot only once. After seeing her brothers move into a life of crime to support their drug habits, she had steered clear of all substances. To her, it just wasn't worth it. And Kiki didn't like it now, even the odor, when she was confined in the car with them. How safe were they on the highway, smoking pot? And of course, who knew how much of it they had with them and just what legal issues might be involved. *She didn't want to start her new life in jail.*

The three college students got rather giddy and silly; however, Rick controlled the car pretty well, until he took a wrong turn on the freeway and ended up on the I-580 headed toward East Oakland. As soon as Kiki felt herself turning away from San Francisco, she wanted out of the car. The gas gauge read almost empty, and before long they would be stopping for gas and she'd be asked for another contribution. She had put in her fair share when they had last filled the tank, and now things were getting out of hand. Kiki was ready to end this encounter. She didn't like any of them, anyway.

Rick and Frank started arguing about which exit to take to get turned around and go back toward San Francisco. Finally, Kiki asked, "When you get off the freeway to turn around, would you just let me out? I can take a bus or the subway or something."

Rick suddenly veered off on the next exit, did a U-turn in the middle of a block, and stopped. "You got it, lady," he yelled. The others giggled.

Kiki climbed out of the car, making sure she had her pink cap, which she shoved onto her head in the way Sal would wear it, her duffle bag and bed roll. She almost forgot her jacket, but Tina threw it out at her. "Thanks," Kiki called, as the three waved and Rick gunned the motor, leaving rubber behind.

In the gathering shadows of a summer evening, Kiki looked around this street corner in East Oakland, in a rather run-down neighborhood which she instantly realized was ethnic, and judging from the people out on the street, largely African-American. She sighed. *Now what?*

About a half block from where she stood, she saw a bus stop with a small shelter. To her right was a stucco wall and behind it a lot of tall evergreen trees. She walked toward the bus stop, yet her curiosity led her to examine the walled area to her right and to wonder what it was. It didn't match the neighborhood. There was an opening in the wall, and as she came to it, she saw a driveway with a gate and over the gate a wrought iron sign: "Montrose College."

Kiki looked around. No bus was coming at the moment. It was about an hour before dark, and she was hungry and had no place to spend the night. She was not sorry to be out of that car, but she realized immediately that this was certainly not the best place for a girl to be alone, especially after dark. The grounds to her right, with all the green trees, looked very inviting. Maybe she could find a place to spread her bedroll and spend the night and tackle San Francisco the next morning. *A college campus*, she thought. *Wow! That was almost too good to be true.*

Carefully, Kiki inched her way onto the grounds. There was a gatehouse with a guard a few yards up the road, and he was stopping each car entering the campus. He just waved at the ones going out. There was also a sidewalk on each side of the roadway. What would his reaction be to a young woman walking through the gate with a bedroll and a duffle bag?

She closed her eyes, took a deep breath, and walked ahead, trying to look both inconspicuous and as if she belonged there. Her heart pounded wildly. Whether she pulled it off, she never found out. The security guard received a telephone call just as she passed his booth, and he was so caught up in the conversation that he didn't even look her way as she walked behind him.

After Kiki was safely out of sight, she picked up her pace. There was a chapel on her right, a very unusual round building, and then a stucco structure with a sign "Music Department," and then a counseling center, and then a field with some buildings on her left that looked like dormitories and the library, and then the student union. When she reached the student union, the teashop was just about to close. She rushed inside, where a young clerk helped her with the purchase of a banana, a sandwich, and a bottle of apple juice and then, as Kiki left, locked the door behind her.

By the time Kiki came out of the student union, the campus was cloaked in deep shadows. It wouldn't be long until total darkness.

She had noticed a rather steep gravel footpath that led upward by the side of the music building, so she followed it. There were stone steps, many of them, and Kiki was winded by the time she got to the top.

Then she reached a wall, which opened outward onto a large stone structure, which she recognized from a high school history class as a Greek theater. Awestruck, Kiki tiptoed down the steps until she was at stage level. She dropped her gear, which felt heavier by the moment, sat down on the edge of the stage, and looked out at the sea of curved stone steps going upward into the hillside. Although completely mesmerized by the feeling of history in this building, Kiki still managed to eat her banana and the sandwich and wash them down with apple juice.

Shortly dusk turned to darkness. Then Kiki looked up at the stars and found Artemis, her ancient goddess in the sky. "Oh, Artemis," she whispered, "is *this* where you meant to bring me?"

Not knowing her way, Kiki could go no further in the fading light. Using the flashlight from her duffle bag to find a spot, she spread out Sal's bedroll in the back corner of the stage area, where two walls came together, and lay down to rest. She could smell something of Sal and Aisha in the fabric, and it made her feel sad yet also in some way safe. She lay there watching her star for a long time, musing about how her Greek goddess was up in the sky and how she was lying down here in a Greek theater.

Gradually Kiki's eyelids closed, and she fell asleep.

5

Jim

Kiki was startled into momentary wakefulness by the sound of chimes coming from somewhere nearby. It was barely dawn. Her mind registered the musical tones and then she drifted back to sleep. A few minutes later, the chimes sounded again. Eventually, she realized there was a pattern, like every fifteen minutes, with gongs on the hour. *This would take some getting used to*, she considered, when around 6 a.m. she finally woke up for good. Funny, she hadn't noticed the chimes the night before. Oh, well, she had been so tired that she might not have heard anything other than the sound of her own heavy breathing.

The sun was making shadows between the evergreen trees as its rays hit the concrete floor of the amphitheater. Kiki sat up abruptly. Her heart skipped a beat as, fully awakened, she recognized that she was still here in Oakland, California, on the grounds of a place called Montrose College.

Shaking the sleep out of her head, Kiki felt her stomach growling and realized that she really had to go to the bathroom. Climbing out of her bedding, she rolled it up, grabbed her duffle bag and jacket, and quickly but carefully headed in the direction of the teashop where she had found food the evening before. As she walked along an asphalt path, Kiki looked nervously around the college grounds. Except one person jogging, she saw no one. No security patrol, not a single car on the main street.

When she reached the tearoom, Kiki found a closed sign on the door and a notice that the shop would open again on Monday morning. Meals would be served over the weekend in the Mathews Dining Commons beginning at 7:30 a.m. Not having any idea where this dining hall was, Kiki momentarily felt overwhelmed. Aside from needing to eat, she was really afraid she would soon wet her pants.

While she stewed, Kiki studied a nearby bulletin board looking for a campus map. Unexpectedly, she heard footsteps as a young woman passed her with keys in one hand, a clipboard and whistle in the other, and walked to a door that opened onto an outdoor swimming pool facing the teashop. Clad in navy blue sweats, the woman unlocked the door and entered the pool area, where she pushed a button to roll back the pool cover and grabbed a broom to sweep the decking.

Kiki had a decision to make. She instinctively knew that anyone she talked with could decide she didn't belong here and call security. Then promptly have her removed. With her duffle bag and bedroll, she looked like a homeless person. Kiki would have called herself "an adventuress," but she felt sure that others might not view her the same way.

However, at this moment Kiki badly needed a bathroom, and ever since she had left home, help had somehow appeared when she needed it. Perhaps her good luck would hold. She approached the young woman, a tall blonde, who looked up with hazel eyes from her stooped position at the edge of the pool. Her blue jacket had "Julie" embroidered in gold letters on the chest.

"Excuse me," Kiki asked, "but I'm new here, and I wondered if you could tell me where to find the dining hall?"

Julie did not seem particularly surprised by the request. "No problem. It's just up the hill there," she explained, pointing. "You go down the street behind the teashop, toward the east and after about a half a block, you'll see a winding path to the left. Take it upward. It's a steep climb, but you'll find the dining commons at the top."

"Thanks!" Kiki said with relief. Then she risked another question: "Is there someplace where I can stow my things for a couple of hours?"

"Sure," Julie replied with a nod. "We have lockers in the dressing room. I can open it, and you can put your stuff there. The pool will only be open for swimming classes until 1 p.m., so just be sure to get back by then, okay?"

Julie showed Kiki the lockers and, leaving her alone, returned to the pool. While Kiki was shoving her things into the tight confines of a locker, she noticed that the room had toilets and a shower. She quickly relieved her bladder and then came out to the pool and thanked Julie, whom she realized didn't have a particularly suspicious nature.

Kiki's watch read 6:30 a.m., meaning that she had to tolerate her hunger for another sixty minutes. She filled the time by strolling around the campus. Relieved of her belongings, Kiki felt less conspicuous; therefore, she followed roads and pathways and examined every building, statue, bridge, and bulletin board that she passed. Within the hour she had decided that the campus was small, perhaps two to three city blocks wide and about the same long. Kiki could walk from one side to the other in a little more than ten minutes. It couldn't be very big. The roads were winding, and there was a stream cutting through the middle of the campus, which had a tall stucco fence around it and only one open gate—the one she had entered the evening before. A second wrought iron gate was carefully closed and chain locked. Kiki skirted that area carefully, deciding not to become a presence at that end of the campus.

Most of the buildings seemed old to her, especially the ones with the word "hall," which Kiki decided must be dormitories. They were all built of California stucco, just like she had seen in movies. She saw trees and plants everywhere, all kinds of them. Although she had taken high school biology, Kiki didn't know the names for very many of these trees, bushes, or plants. She did think they all were pretty. The tall trees that had pealing bark gave off a fragrance that caused her nostrils to open wide when she took a deep breath.

As she heard the chimes sound the half hour and started up the hill to the dining commons, she mused to herself that the campus was kind of like turf. Back home, in the South Bronx, everybody had turf. It was the territory immediately around your home, which you knew, felt safe in, and could in some way protect. Turf was usually limited to just a few blocks to the grocery one way, and the drug store another, and perhaps school, if you were lucky enough to live close to your school and didn't have to ride a bus. This campus was just about the size of her turf back home. And it was so beautiful that she wished she could make it *her* turf.

You're just visiting, she reminded herself, *getting a look at California, and seeing what a real college is like. That's okay, for an adventuress, isn't it? Just to look? Artemis was known for exploring the forest, accompanied by her hunting dog or a deer, because she protected nature and the animals. Wouldn't Artemis approve of her exploring this beautiful place?*

At the main door to the dining commons—where from seemingly out of nowhere people were assembling—a young and tiny Asian woman, Kiki thought perhaps Chinese, stood in a white uniform. She held a clipboard and a clicker in one hand and a punch in the other.

People ahead of Kiki held out cards and this staff person punched the cards and signaled them through. Kiki's heart pounded in her throat as she moved gradually up to the door, knowing fully well she did not have this magic card.

When Kiki reached the head of the line, the woman looked at her expectantly. "Do you have a meal ticket?" she asked, in heavily accented English, when Kiki didn't produce a card and just stared at her.

"No," Kiki confessed. "Is there any way I can eat here?"

"Yes, if you pay $3.50."

Kiki sighed with relief and smiled. "I can do that." She pulled money out of her jeans pocket and offered a $5 bill.

"Over there," the woman pointed. "See the register? Pay there, and then you can eat."

Once the transaction had been completed, and Kiki had succeeded in securing entrance to this enticing place filled with marvelous breakfast smells, she nearly ran up the steps to the main dining area located on the floor above. It had big glass windows all around, and people were moving with their trays along a cafeteria line, making selections. Kiki followed them, picking up a tray and looking wide-eyed at all the food choices. Watching the person ahead of her, she realized that the $3.50 allowed her to eat as much as she wanted. Kiki loaded her tray with toast and jelly, a ham slice, scrambled eggs, a banana, a glass of milk and another of orange juice. She found a small table in a far corner, sat down and started eating. Initially, her hunger led her to bolt the food, but she shortly realized she needed to take it easy. She inhaled a couple of deep breaths and tried not to gulp everything down.

It was not like Mama's home cooking, yet hungry as Kiki was, the food tasted wonderful to her. She cleaned her plate and almost went back for pancakes before deciding she had eaten as much as she could for one sitting. After watching someone else leave the dining area with fresh fruit, Kiki risked picking up an extra banana for later.

On her way back down the path from the dining hall, Kiki saw a man talking on a pay phone, and it suddenly dawned on her that she hadn't called Sal. Remembering that Sal had instructed her to phone, collect, as soon as she arrived safely in California, Kiki hung around until the man had completed his call and then pulled Sal's crumpled slip of paper from her pocket. Fishing out a couple of coins, she dialed the operator and got assistance for a collect call to Salt Lake City.

The phone on the other end rang for a long time and finally was answered by a woman. It sounded like Meg, a very sleepy Meg. The operator asked about accepting a collect call from California, and Meg agreed.

"It's Kiki," she practically shouted into the phone. And then, "Did I wake you? I'm sorry. Is Sal there?" The words just tumbled out.

"It's okay, Kiki. I worked late last night at the hospital, and Sal left early this morning for the East Coast. She won't be back for about ten days. She kept hoping you'd call last night, but finally she had to get some sleep before her trip. Where are you, and are you okay?"

"I'm in California, in Oakland, at a college called Montrose. Have you heard of it?"

"Montrose College for Women? Are you kidding?"

"It's a women's college?" Kiki asked. "I didn't know that."

"Yeah, a famous one. What are you doing there?"

"Well, just sort of hangin' out. It's great. Well, say hi to Sal, when you talk to her, and tell her I'll write her a long letter as soon as I have an address. Okay?"

"Well, thanks for calling. She'll be glad to know. Now, Kiki, I've got to go back to sleep."

"Okay, thanks, 'bye."

Kiki was sorry to have missed Sal; however, Meg's statement that Montrose was a famous women's college made her heart throb rapidly with excitement. That meant it was like Smith or Wellesley or those other colleges in the East—names bandied about sarcastically in her high school as places that "rich girls" got an education.

So, with her spirits even higher than before, Kiki bounced down the sidewalk toward the swimming pool. She had an idea, and she wanted to check it out. When she arrived at the pool, Julie was busy coaching a group of young girls swimming laps, so Kiki just slid by with a wave of her hand and went into the locker room. No one was there, so she took out her duffle bag, which didn't seem to have been disturbed, and got out a change of clothing and her towel, washcloth and soap. She went into the shower, stripped, and cleaned up, giving her hair a wash, too. The warm water felt really good, and she shivered delightedly at the idea that she was showering in the swimming pool locker room at Montrose College for Women.

After toweling dry, Kiki repacked her things, left the pool area and did more exploring. She had until just 1 p.m. to come up with a survival plan.

There was a bookstore in the complex, and it was open until noon. Kiki walked into the store and quietly browsed, at first seeing tall piles of text books for the new semester, and then finding a book about Montrose College history and another covering the 5,000 plants and trees growing on the campus—including the tall Eucalyptus trees, for which she now had a name. Kiki wished she could read these books yet knew she did not have the money to buy them. She had to save every penny until she could find a permanent place to stay and a job. Maybe someday, Kiki told herself, she'd come back here and get those books.

Leaving the bookstore somewhat regretfully, Kiki noted a post office next door with rows of mail boxes along the wall inside a covered entryway. A sign indicated the post office wasn't open until Monday. This must be Saturday, she reminded herself. Maybe that's why there weren't very many people around the campus. And it was summer. Maybe school wasn't in session now.

During her earlier tour around the campus, Kiki had passed the library twice. It was now 9:30 a.m., and the library was open. She risked entering, just to see what was inside. Maybe she'd find some information she could use. Once within the building, Kiki decided the library was beautiful, with all sorts of workstations, computer stalls, and comfortable chairs for reading—and stacks and stacks of books and magazines. Nothing like her outmoded high school library at home. She felt sure she couldn't take anything out, yet perhaps she could come in sometime to sit down and read. *Maybe she'd find a book about Artemis! She would remember that, for later.*

Kiki continued to stroll around the campus, feeling both anxious and excited at the same time. *She didn't belong here, but until someone forced her to leave, she could enjoy exploring it, right?* It was a world so beyond anything she had ever known, and as she walked and looked she became aware of how emotionally hungry she was. She didn't just need food to fill her stomach, she needed information and ideas to hope and dream about. And this campus seemed filled with much to feed her and her curiosity. She actually started skipping along the sidewalk for a moment. *This must be what Disneyland would feel like to a little child.*

While exploring Montrose, she discovered two construction projects. One of the dormitories was being remodeled and, even on a Saturday, there were a few workmen scurrying around that building. Maybe, she thought, they were trying to finish before school started for the next semester. She wondered to herself what the dorms were like inside and what it would feel like to live there.

The second project was some kind of renovation of an old building, a big white wooden structure that was located on an oval, across from the tower that held those chimes. Kiki walked around the fence that circled this old building. She thought it very interesting to look at, although she admitted that it wasn't her personal taste in architecture. However, it had a feel of history about it and looked to be the oldest building on the campus.

Just as she finished her tour around the fence—and was glancing at the upper floors and the ornate windows—Kiki nearly bumped into a security guard. Kiki instinctively backed up in shock, although she began to relax when she realized that this guard was a gray-haired woman, and she didn't look particularly formidable. Her uniform was different from the one worn by the guard at the entrance gate, and it had the name of a security service on it, not the college security.

"Sorry," Kiki apologized. "I'm just visiting here today, and I got curious about this building. I didn't mean to run you down."

The woman smiled, and her gray-blue eyes twinkled. "No problem."

"Do you know anything about it?"

The guard, whose named tag read "Shirley Franklin," nodded at Kiki and looked with obvious pride at the building. "A little. This was where the college began. Students and faculty lived here and all classes were taught in this building. Unlike most of the campus now, much of which is Spanish stucco, this building is a true Victorian. More recently it was a dorm until, because of its age, the structural integrity was questioned. They used it for administrative offices until the last earthquake, when it was badly damaged. Not that you could see—its foundation and such. It's an important historic building, so they raised funds to restore it."

"Is it fun guarding it?" Kiki asked.

A grin crossed Shirley's face. "Yes, and talking to people like you. When I'm here alone in the evening, as I often am, I like to imagine the old days when girls in their long skirts used to scurry up and down the staircases inside. It's a very lovely building. I'll miss it when this job is done." She winked at Kiki.

Kiki sighed. "I wish I could go to a school like this," she admitted in confidence.

Shirley nodded. "Me, too. It was beyond me, even when I was a girl. My friend went to Smith, back East. She was very lucky. I had to settle for a small community college. Yet here I am, having the time of my life watching over this old gal."

"Well, thank-you." Kiki waved and moved on. Shirley, she had noticed, had short, straight hair, wore no makeup, and her face was weather beaten. Kiki wondered what Shirley meant by "friend." *Maybe something like Sal's friend, Meg?*

Kiki dreaded the idea of taking a single step away from Montrose College. However, as the chimes—a "campanile" according to a sign—rang out the half hour, she noted that it was 10:30 and her time was running out. She had to stop looking around and focus on a plan.

She desperately needed a place to stay and a job. The food was good at the commons, but if she ate two or three meals there, she would be perilously close to broke. And nothing else would be open on the campus until Monday.

She looked around and sighed. She had a million questions and no one to ask.

Kiki sat down on a wooden bench for a moment, trying to figure out what to do. She couldn't camp out here forever. She should be on a bus to San Francisco and then that CalTrain to Sunnyvale. However, she almost choked at the thought. The City, which had looked so beautiful in the distance when they drove in yesterday, was huge, like Manhattan Island, and where would she start? The mere thought overwhelmed her.

The campus was much smaller, a turf Kiki could grasp—even if in her heart of hearts, she knew she was an eighteen-year old without money, job, home, or a high school diploma. Staying here was *so* beyond possibility.

"Well," Kiki said aloud, "this kind of thinking isn't going to get you anywhere." *A plan, she had to have a plan.*

Kiki decided to skip lunch, because in all honesty she couldn't afford it. She sat on the lawn, ate her banana and then got up and tossed the banana skin into a trash barrel. Then she returned to the pool area and retrieved her duffle and bedroll. Kiki noticed a sign that indicated the pool was open on Sunday afternoons. Since she didn't have a swimsuit or money for fees, the information was appealing, but hardly pertinent. She thanked Julie, who gave her a friendly smile and called, "Have a nice day."

At l p.m., Kiki was back on the sidewalk feeling conspicuous with her bedroll and duffle bag. Any minute, she was sure, a patrol car would come along and ask her who she was and where she was headed.

She was so new at this game, that no matter what she told them, they would know she was lying. Even the pink ballcap that Sal had given her, and which Kiki wore turned backwards the way Sal did, made her look different. Perhaps she shouldn't have it on, at least not right now. She removed the cap and stuck it in the top of her duffle bag.

While she stood trying to decide where to go next, Kiki noticed a maintenance man emptying a trash barrel. The man drove a small pick-up, and he pulled out the liner, put a tie on it, and tossed the bag into the back of his Montrose College truck. Next he put a new liner in the trash barrel, returned the cover, and drove off. Since this was Saturday, Kiki had an abrupt thought—*he probably would not return to pick up trash before the first of the week, especially since the campus was nearly deserted.*

Watching the workman gave Kiki an idea. She walked along looking for other trash barrels and found one near the music building, in front of the Greek theater where she had spent the night. She peeped into the trash barrel and saw that it was empty. The workman must have just changed the liner a few moments earlier. Glancing around to see if anyone was coming, she removed the top, lifted the liner out, put her duffle bag, bedroll, and jacket in the bottom of the can, replaced the liner, and slid the top back on. It was a bit smelly and undoubtedly not the cleanest place in the world, yet her things might be safely hidden there for a few hours. She told herself she would worry about other details later.

Again freed of her encumbrances, Kiki continued exploring the campus, hoping for some miracle to reveal itself so she wouldn't have to leave Montrose.

She saw a couple of cars arriving at the music building. Two young women climbed out of the cars, carried musical instrument cases up to front door, and went inside. Kiki waited a few minutes and then followed the path they had taken. The door was unlocked, and she walked into the building. There was a foyer and steps up to a big auditorium, which smelled of old wood and was dimly lit. As she checked further, she could see there were ornate paintings on the walls and a decorated wood-beamed ceiling. This looked like an assembly hall, or maybe it was the campus concert hall. The big room was very still. She moved silently back down the stairs—so as not to disturb the spirits of geniuses that must have trod there. The experience made her shiver with excitement.

Kiki heard sounds coming from one wing of the building, and she searched for the source. Several young women, she found, were in small rooms practicing their instruments. She could see them through little windows, as she moved quietly down the hallway. One room was empty, and she entered it. The room had a window looking out on a garden—the same garden that led to the Greek theater. *Aha!* Kiki felt the window latch, and it gave quite easily. *So, not only was the building old, it was relatively unprotected.* She opened the window a crack and left the room. She would check later to see if the window was still open.

Satisfied with what she had learned, and feeling she might be able to extend her visit for one more night, Kiki left the music building and walked back toward the campus entry gate. The security guard was busy waving to the driver of a car going out and stopping to talk to someone coming in. He scarcely even looked in Kiki's direction as she passed him on the opposite sidewalk—sucking in deep breaths and forcing herself to step casually without hurrying.

After passing through the gate, Kiki stood by the bus stop and tried to decide what to do. Cars whizzed by on this busy street, called logically Montrose Boulevard, and appeared to be headed for the freeway entrance a couple of blocks away. Well, Kiki decided, she could catch a bus and go into downtown Oakland or to San Francisco, or she could scour the neighborhood on foot. Wanting to stay near the campus and her precious belongings, she decided to check out the nearby possibilities first.

Although Kiki noted again that there was a declining neighborhood around the school—not all that different from home, although architecturally different, with lots of houses, many in need of paint—Kiki knew that people must eat and get gas and do other necessary things. Surely there were some businesses around, so she set out to find them.

The outline of a few buildings beyond the freeway underpass drew Kiki's attention, so she walked carefully under the massive and noisy concrete interchange, dodging a couple of fast moving cars. She found a little strip of businesses on the other side, including a plumbing company, a printing office, and an electronics repair shop, all looking rather closed up for the weekend. Kiki sighed and started to turn another direction when she spotted a pizza shop in the distance. It looked like a family type business, not part of a chain, so Kiki headed for it.

A bell jingled when Kiki entered the shop. The inside was dimly lit, with tables covered in red-checkered cloths and a long counter. A heavy-set, graying African-American man was rolling out dough on a table in the back. Behind him was a large, hot oven. At the moment there were no customers at the tables, although just as Kiki entered, the man stopped working to answer the phone to write down an order. His hands were covered with flour. He looked frustrated as the pen slipped out of his fingers and he stooped with an audible grunt to retrieve it. He completed the order, hung up the phone, and returned to his task. At the same time, he glanced at Kiki out of the corner of his eye, yet went on molding his pizza crust.

"Yeah," he finally called out, as the dough conformed to his demands, "can I hep ya?"

Kiki cleared her throat. "I, I was wondering if you need any help. I'm new in town and looking for work, anything so I can eat."

The man laid his crust in a pizza pan and began pounding a new ball of dough. "Ya *must* be new in town if yore hangin' out in dis neighborhood. Yore too pale to fit in, kid, unless ya be one o' dose Montrose girls—but they's all summerin' in Europe now, and none o' them would set foot in this place to work, or to eat pizza. So ya can't be one o' dem. So where *do* ya come from?"

Kiki ignored his attitude. She had heard attitude all her life. Attitude didn't cut very deep. "New York," she answered. "The South Bronx. Polish-Puerto Rican-Filipino. Good melting pot stock. However, you're right, not African-American, if that's the term out here."

The man laughed and regarded her more kindly. He gave her a closer look, and his dark brown eyes twinkled. "Yore okay, kid. Ya got any work experience that's in any way useful?" He looked amused yet still a bit dubious.

Kiki hesitated only a second. "I worked for a Jewish baker for about six months. I know how to make dough, if that's what you mean. I've been around ovens. I know when something's done."

He looked thoughtful as he pounded. "Well, I'd like to hep ya out, but I'm barely makin' ends meet right now, and I got a fam'ly to support. I can't be takin' on extra hep." He shook his head. "Mebbe later, if this damn recession ever gits over, jis' not now."

The phone rang as he was tossing his flattened dough into a pizza pan. On a sudden impulse, Kiki reached across the counter, picked up the phone before he could get to it, and with her other hand grabbed a faded menu and an order form. "Good afternoon," she greeted politely, "Thank you for calling—uh, Big Jim's Pizza. How may I help you?"

She listened as the voice made requests and she wrote down an order. "So, you would like a large pizza with ham and sausage, lots of cheese. That sounds great! Are you by any chance a mushroom lover? Because for just fifty cents more, we can top that pizza with our special giant mushrooms. Okay, great, add the mushrooms. And did you want something to drink with that? Okay, two large Cokes. And you'll be here in thirty minutes to pick it up? Your phone number please, so we can validate the order. 495-6677. Okay, we'll have your pizza ready. Thanks again for calling Big Jim's Pizza."

The pizza maker, obviously Big Jim, plopped down on a stool and laughed. He shook his head and his belly rolled. He looked at Kiki and tears came in his eyes. "Okay, kid, ya got yoresef a job—provided ya got papers. I don't want no illegal aliens around here, no trouble with the government, if ya get my meanin.'"

Her throat instantly tight, Kiki pulled out her wallet. "I've got my Social Security card and my high school ID card. Will that do?"

He looked at the cards she offered. "No driver's license?" He frowned.

"We didn't need cars much in the South Bronx. I'm just eighteen, and I don't drive yet," Kiki admitted.

The shop owner shook his head, sighed, and looked at her seriously. "Look, kid, uh, Kiki, ya got to git papers, proper papers. I got forms to fill out for Uncle Sam, and I don't want the IRS or ICE on my back. Kids come an' go, and often they ain't on the up and up, know what I mean? Ya seem sharp, for a little Polish, Filipino, whatever ya are, yet I gotta protect myself. I work long hours here, and I could use some good hep, but it's gotta be legal."

Kiki nodded. She swallowed nervously.

"I don't care if yore sleepin' in the street. Ya got to come up with some kind of address. Ya gotta go down ta the driver's license bureau and git a California ID card. It's a card that shows yore birthday and has yore picture, and it's used for people who don't have no driver's license. Ya'd best send for yore birth certificate back in the—where did ya say—the Bronx?"

Kiki's shoulders were beginning to cave in. *How long would all this take? And how would she survive in the meantime?*

"Look, I'm not tryin' to be mean," Jim explained, apparently sensing her disappointment. "I'm just protectin' myself—an' ya, too. 'Cause no matter where ya try to work, they gonna ask ya for the same things. I'm just bein' honest and tellin' ya what yore up against."

Kiki considered this. "I know I can find an address," she said, "to send for the papers. But while I'm doin' it, I still gotta eat."

"Well, I'll meet ya half way. Do yore part, and meanwhile I'll give ya $7 an hour cash and all the pizza ya can eat, twenty hours a week guaranteed. Now listen, ya gotta be here when I need ya and don' be late, 'cause I'm sure ya ain't gonna give me no phone number to call ya up. Ya don' show up, ya ain't got no job, clear?"

"Clear," Kiki agreed.

"Okay," Jim confirmed, "right now ya's on the clock. Ya start sweepin' an' cleanin' up here, the way it ought to be, only I don' have time to do it all, while I make up this fancy pizza ya just sol' on the phone. After I git done, I'll start teachin' ya how to make the bes' pizza you ever et. And 'fore ya go home, wherever yore hidin' out, ya'll have yore tummy full of Big Jim's Pizza an' salad with a big Coke an' rocky road ice cream for dessert."

Kiki smiled to herself and grabbed a broom. Glory Halleluiah! She had her first job in the state of California! *And only a block off the campus of Montrose College for Women.*

6

Kiki

Kiki worked with Jim until closing. Then, on his way home, he dropped her off at the front gate to Montrose. Kiki was stuffed with pizza and had a couple of extra slices in a napkin that might not spoil before morning. She also had several dollars in her pocket from the night's earnings, including a few tips she had made by waiting on tables. She was supposed to report to work again the next day at 4 p.m.

As he stopped to let Kiki out of the car, the big man made a request. "I know it says Big Jim's Pizza on the door, but just call me Jim, okay?"

"Okay." She nodded. "See you tomorrow. Jim. And thanks!"

Kiki was so exhilarated by earning her first money and by being fed by Jim's humor and his tasty pizza that she sailed by the security guard's station with hardly a thought. And the guard seemed uninterested in her, as if Kiki were a regular.

After she passed the music building, Kiki ducked behind the stucco structure, found her path, and crossed her fingers that the window she had left cracked open would still be that way. In the dark she became quickly confused and tried several windows before she came to the right one, which was still slightly open. After a bit of a struggle, Kiki was able to push the frame open far enough that she could climb into the room. First, however, she had to go get her things—if they were still there.

Despite scattered street lamps, the campus was eerily dark. There was only a sliver of a moon, its little glow dimmed by several low-lying clouds. Kiki still felt she had to be careful as she quietly moved back to the trash barrel where she had left her things. The barrel was beneath a street lamp, and she waited a few moments to make sure no traffic was coming before she pulled off the lid, removed the liner, and retrieved her clothing. After putting the lid back in place, Kiki quickly hurried breathlessly up the gravel path to the backside of the music-building annex, where she finally heaved a sigh and began breathing normally again.

At her special window, she tossed her things inside and then climbed into the room. Although it was very dark and smelled of old, musty wood, it still felt safer and in some ways cozier than sleeping out in the open as she had the night before. Also, just down the hallway, she knew there were restrooms. She sighed with relief.

Kiki propped open the practice room door, so it couldn't slam shut and tiptoed down to the restroom, taking with her a toothbrush and toothpaste. The night before she'd had to forego that luxury, and she didn't want to do it again. Moments later, with a relieved bladder and clean teeth, Kiki headed for her bedroll and her second night on the Montrose campus.

Hours of physical work in a new job and a full belly allowed Kiki to fall into a deep sleep.

After Jim had dropped her off at the college gate, he drove on toward his home a couple of miles away. When he arrived, the house—a small weathered bungalow—was silent. The girls were asleep, and his wife, Cora, was reading in bed.

Jim smiled because Cora was still awake. He had a story to tell her about his day's amazing experience.

Jim stripped out of his work clothes and ran a cool shower. Sweaty from working with the pizza ovens all day, he relaxed in the stream of water running on his skin. Then he slipped into some clean boxer shorts and crawled into bed beside Cora. Even after twenty years of marriage, three daughters, and a lot of financial struggles, Cora responded to Jim with affection and caring.

"How did it go tonight, sweetie?" she asked, nuzzling against him. "You smell so good from the shower."

Jim chuckled. "I was hopin' ya'd be awake. I had the strangest experience this afternoon."

Cora sat up. "What happened?"

"Well, this kid come in an' ast for a job. I tol' her I couldn' afford no more hep. She grabbed the phone the next call and sol' those folks more dan they ast for. So, I let her work the res' of the evenin' and even after payin' her off, I made more money. She's real good wit' the customers."

"She from the 'hood?"

"Well, I don' know. She ast to be let off at the gate to the college, an' it looked like she went in there—"

"You hired some rich kid from that school!" Cora sounded indignant.

"Now, Cora, listen to me. It's summer, an' school's out right now. I'm more afraid she's a runaway from somewhere. Says she's eighteen, but I don' think she's got a home. It's just a feelin' I got."

"Is she black?"

"Well, no," Jim admitted.

"You mean you hired some white kid!" Cora's voice rose and an eyebrow lifted.

"Cora Lee, now don' get all political wit' me. She ain't black and she ain't white, neither. She's some kinda mix, Puerto Rican, Filipino, Polish, or somethin' like that. Cora, she's a good kid, and she's good wit' our customers. They really took to her, 'cause she went out o' her way to serve 'em. She made 'em feel real important, and they ordered more an' they tipped more."

"Well, if it's good for business, I guess I can't say anything. However, you got three daughters and it seems like if you're hirin', you could use one of them."

"Cora, we been over this before. I don't want my girls to end up spendin' their lives behind a hot pizza oven. Ya clean hotel rooms, and I slave in dat pizza parlor. I want better for *dem* dan what we got."

Cora fumed. "Well, you know we aren't ever sendin' 'em to Montrose. That place must cost $40,000 a year. Maybe more. Our girls will be lucky just getting' into a community college."

"Well, this kid I hired ain't no rich kid, I can tell ya that. For all I know, she's jus' campin' at dat school, but as long as she shows up, gits the right papers, and heps me make more money, I'm gonna keep her on."

Cora let the subject drop and curled up next to Jim. He turned out the light and put his arms around her. "Even with dem gray streaks in yore black hair, ya is still the most beautiful woman in da world to me," he whispered to her lovingly. "I treasure every moment I can have with ya—even if ya git a might touchy at times and always full of opinions."

When Kiki awoke the next morning, a little stiff from another night in a bedroll on a hard surface, she experienced a new wave of curiosity about the college campus and wanted to continue exploring. She also had made a list in her head of things she would need, like a pen, a tablet of paper, and a small alarm clock. Then she had to come up with a mailing address, stamps, maybe a post office box. Kiki was planning on writing Sal a letter—she had so much to tell her—but Sal couldn't write back if she didn't have an address. Then there was the birth certificate she had to get from New York.

Today was Sunday, so there was little that Kiki could do about resolving these problems. She hid her things in the trash barrel again, because there was always a possibility that she wouldn't be able to get back into the music building that night. She had to keep her options open.

Kiki downed the leftover slices of pizza for breakfast and then hung out in the library until the dining hall opened for lunch. After eating what would be her main meal for the day, she strolled a little while waiting for the college's art gallery to open. Kiki had once visited the New York Metropolitan Museum of Art on a school trip and had been fascinated by the paintings and sculptures—however, there had been little opportunity to pursue an interest in art in her tenement neighborhood.

The gallery at Montrose was attractive although small. Kiki picked up a brochure at the entrance and walked around studying every image of the current exhibit of paintings and sculptures by Montrose graduate students. Kiki knew very little, technically, about art but she was quite curious. *How wonderful it must be for those fortunate enough to be able to study the arts*, she thought to herself.

At 3:30 p.m., Kiki tore herself away and walked along the main road to the campus gate, under the busy freeway, and to the pizza parlor. She was looking forward to seeing Jim. Even though she couldn't confess to him the full details of her current situation, he had befriended her and was really the only person she knew in California. Even though Kiki was excited about her big adventure, she was already feeling a bit lonely.

When the campus post office opened at 8:30 on Monday morning, Kiki was standing at the counter. The postal worker, an older Asian man whose bent shoulders might have come from years of sorting mail, came slowly to the counter. He was neither awake nor ready to deal with customers.

"Can I rent a post office box?" Kiki asked.

He raised an eyebrow. "You're kinda early, aren't you? School doesn't start for two weeks yet." He frowned and cleared his throat.

"Oh, well, I, uh, just wanted to be ready," Kiki said, hoping she looked and sounded like a student.

"$45 for the semester," he told her with disinterest.

"Oh," she sighed. She hadn't planned on having to spend so much of her little cache of money.

"Yep, these boxes rent by the semester or the year. A school year is $85."

Kiki almost turned away and then decided that she had better rent the box. She pulled out her little stack of bills and counted out a twenty, two tens, and five ones. She pushed the money over to the clerk, and he shoved a form and a pen back toward her.

"Just fill this out." He shuffled off.

Kiki stared at the form. *Now it was beginning—her battle with forms and addresses and legal issues.* Everything would have consequences, and she knew that she couldn't outguess them all. She was standing on a thin high wire, with no net to break a fall.

One step at a time, Kiki told herself with a sigh. Name she could handle. Address. *What address could she give?* Should she put her aunt's address down? Shoot! She hadn't contacted her aunt yet, and it might be a while before she could get to Sunnyvale. Well, she'd just have to put down the address of Big Jim's Pizza, since that was the only place where she had any connection. She'd worry about the rest later. People did move and change their addresses. That was life. So, despite considerable apprehension, she filled out the rest of the form.

The clerk asked for identification, and she showed him her social security card and her high school ID. He looked at the picture and her face and seemed satisfied. "No California driver's license?" he asked with a frown.

"I don't drive, but I'm going down to get a California Identification Card right away," Kiki assured him.

He looked her over for a moment and then nodded. The clerk gave her a receipt and the combination to a mailbox and showed her how to find it along the row outside. He told her she could get her mail any time night or day. And it was usually put out by 10 a.m. "Don't come bothering me before that. Okay?"

Kiki left the building both excited and worried. She had succeeded in getting a mailing address in California, yet in order to obtain her birth certificate, she would have to call New York and post a letter before the day was out. To do that, she would probably have to buy a money order. Having purchased the mail box, her cash was now running really low. *Ouch!*

A pay phone at the student union connected Kiki to information and then to NYC Department of Records. Armed with the information, she next had to go to the Montrose library, ask a librarian to help her download a form from the Internet, fill it out, photo copy her identification, then go to the post office to buy a money order and a stamped envelope.

Finally, Kiki completed the task, and her letter was off to New York. She sighed when it was done. Fortunately, she had recently passed her eighteenth birthday; otherwise, she could not have gotten a birth certificate on her own.

When she went to work that evening, Kiki was able to report to Jim, whose full name she had learned was James Garfield Williams, Jr., that she had sent off for the papers that would make her legal to employ. He seemed pleased and then put Kiki to work. By the end of the evening, she was making her own pizzas. When he dropped her off at the campus gate, Kiki practically danced her way through, because she was so thrilled. The guard nodded at her, and she waved back.

7

Mrs. Trang

Kiki awoke in the music-building annex very early the next morning. A kind of panic hit her in the pit of her stomach. Her secret stay on campus was about to become more precarious. Although classes were not in session, music students who lived nearby came early on weekdays to use the practice rooms. Kiki had seen a reservation list posted at the end of the hallway, and now she had to be out of the building almost before dawn to keep from being discovered.

While stowing her things in the trash barrel, Kiki sensed that this approach was not going to last and that her belongings were really beginning to smell. Keeping an eye out for security vehicles, she disappeared behind the Greek theater to hide until she could grab breakfast in the dining hall. Taking a back road along the campus fence, she discovered apartment buildings that seemed to be part of the college. Maybe that was why she saw a few people around, going in and out at odd hours when Montrose was generally deserted.

Later, while eating a big bowl of cereal with a sliced banana on top, Kiki came to a conclusion. *It was time to explore Oakland.* She had a little cash in her pocket from working for Jim, so she could go shopping. Items that she needed either weren't available or were too expensive on the campus, and she had to find a more realistic source of supply. She would go on this jaunt after breakfast.

Forcing herself to relax as she slipped past the morning security guard, Kiki waited for a local bus at the nearby bus shelter. One came by shortly, and as Kiki rode to downtown Oakland, she watched the neighborhoods, keeping alert for businesses that potentially might offer up more or better work and possible places she might rent a room or an apartment. Although some of the neighborhoods were only a cut above what she had left behind in the South Bronx, at least there *were* possibilities out there. Of course, there was always her aunt in Sunnyvale, but she felt very excited by these few days of being on her own. Kiki alternated between moments of absolute terror and moments of exhilaration because she was managing to live a secret life totally by her wits. *Did Artemis feel this way when she was out in the forest with her hunting dog and her bow and arrow? Independent, challenged to find her way and provide food for herself and her companion animal?*

Downtown Oakland held a mixture of angled streets, international language signs—mostly in Asian symbols—tall buildings obviously being used for something other than their original design, and a general lack of affluence. The city center was a bit daunting and discouraging to Kiki. So, she decided, the South Bronx was not the only down-and-out place in America, although this was certainly better than home. It just didn't match Kiki's Hollywood-inspired image of wondrous California.

While exploring and realizing almost immediately that this was a dangerous place for a young woman alone, Kiki did accomplish her primary mission. There were several thrift stores, and she managed to pick up items she really needed: a small alarm clock, two serviceable shirts, another pair of jeans to augment her skimpy wardrobe, a padlock—which instinct told her to grab when she saw it—a note pad and envelopes, a cheap pen, some extra shampoo, and soap.

On the trip back to Montrose, she felt good at having found what she needed. She also experienced new flutters of anxiety. Kiki was beginning to realize consciously that what had started out as a desperate and immediate solution for a night's lodging had evolved into some sort of personal intrigue to remain on the college grounds. She now asked herself: *To what end?* She couldn't go to school there. There was no possible or realistic goal in hanging out on the campus, and the longer she stayed the less she would want to leave. Yet it was the most beautiful place she had ever been in her life, and she knew that she had only begun to explore its secrets. *But what would happen when they caught her, as inevitably they would, sooner or later? Jail?*

Well, if something bad happened when they found her, Kiki decided, she would have to give them her aunt's address. They'd surely contact her aunt, and she hoped her aunt would help her. She was trespassing, and Kiki was certain that was illegal. Yet she hadn't hurt anything, not used much except a little water for a shower, or stolen anything from the school. Surely she hadn't committed a major crime, or had she? *Breaking and entering?* She sighed. Maybe it wouldn't be so bad, and until then, whatever "then" would turn out to be, she was learning and growing every minute.

Kiki was still contemplating these complex questions when the bus stopped across from the Montrose gate. She climbed down from the bus and then thought to herself, as she walked along the college's main road, that she had neglected to check in with Artemis the last couple of nights. Maybe she had lost touch with her guardian angel in the sky.

Just as her favorite star crossed her mind, Kiki noticed that the construction scaffolding had been removed—certainly that morning—from around the Willard Olsen residence hall. Holding her shopping bag tightly, she crossed a field and headed toward the large stucco building.

A construction company truck was just pulling away. However, the front door was still standing wide open. Although Kiki saw no workmen anywhere, she assumed that someone was probably still around. However, her curiosity won out. She cautiously mounted the front steps of the hall and then silently slipped into the foyer.

There was a living room with a fireplace at one end, large glass doors opening onto a garden, long sofas and comfortable-looking chairs, and a big piano in the far corner. The beige carpeting had a "brand new" smell. A small elevator beside the main staircase appeared to be quite new. There were hallways stretching both ways from the living room. Kiki walked down one of the hallways and peered into a student room—very simple, with bed, dresser and bookcase, closet, sink, and a window. Almost like the cells she always imagined that nuns lived in. Simple though it was, the room looked really inviting to Kiki, compared to her bedroll spread out on the hardwood floor of a music practice room.

Still not seeing a soul, Kiki explored the dorm completely, up one wing and down another, up the staircase to the second floor and then on to the third, where she found wonderful sleeping porches with adjoining study rooms. Now this would be where she would want to stay. Entering one of the porches, she felt it to be so peaceful, yet she thought it would be punctuated by the sun coming up in the morning, the breeze, the smell of all those flowers and plants, and the sounds of the creek and the campanile. *Paradise!*

When Kiki came back to the main floor, she noticed an open door leading to another set of steps, and she followed these steps down into a basement. There she found storage rooms, a recreation room with a big TV and a ping-pong table, several locked rooms off a corridor, and a laundry room with washers and dryers. Her eyes popped when she saw the washers and dryers. *She could sure use those!*

Throbbing with excitement, Kiki propped open a side door with a little stick, making sure it wasn't obvious, and ran to the bookstore before it closed for the day. There she purchased a small bottle of laundry soap. Then she retrieved her clothes from the trash barrel— none too soon, because she saw the maintenance worker down the street starting his rounds of trash pick-up—and ran back to the dorm, her heart pounding lest someone had returned and locked that door by the laundry.

No one had, so she slipped inside and threw everything she owned into the washing machine along with the soap and a pile of quarters. A light came on, and the washer began to work. Wow, Kiki realized, she was lucky the electricity was on, given that this building had been closed for renovations. Later she figured out from the aroma of something baking that there was a campus bakery located in the dorm basement only a few feet from where she stood, and perhaps because of it, the power and water had been left on.

Kiki didn't dare move from the room until her laundry was done, so she sat on the cold concrete floor until the wash cycle was complete and she had put her clothes, including her new shirts, into the dryer. Next she washed her bedroll and even threw in her duffle bag. As her clothes were being stripped of grime, Kiki's heart lightened. *Maybe Artemis was still watching out for her.*

While her clothes were drying, Kiki again propped open the exit door, ran to the tea shop and bought a sandwich, a container of orange juice and a banana, and returned on a full run. The door had remained propped open, and she was able to retrieve her things. She heaved a sigh of relief.

Kiki sat on the concrete floor and ate her light dinner hastily, then struggled with her new notepad to compose a letter to Sal. There was so much she wanted to tell her, and yet an inner voice warned her that since her situation was highly unusual, to say the least, Sal would be worried and maybe even take action. Kiki couldn't risk that, so she mentioned her job and the mail box, adding that she was staying *near* the college and exploring the campus. She didn't admit that she was still hiding out there.

But Kiki was lonely for Sal's company and she wanted—no, needed—to reach out to her, anyway she could. Her feelings about her family, when she stopped to think about them, were still mostly that of relief at being far away from there. Sal was different. She was so positive and kind. She spoke of dreams and the future, and she was making a life independently. She and Meg gave Kiki hope that somehow she could do it too.

As her laundry finally finished drying, Kiki sensed that the workday was over. The building had become very still. Maybe, if she were careful, she could get away with spending this night in the dorm. Gathering her things, she crept up the stairs again, avoiding areas where it looked as if the workmen might be putting on finishing touches, and crept up to the sleeping porches, where there was the most visibility. Kiki spread her bedroll on one of the mattresses and decided that if her cheap little alarm clock didn't go off the first thing in the morning, then the dawning light would alert her, so she could get out before being found.

That evening Kiki used her flashlight to go into the bathroom. She even risked taking a shower. There was no hot water on this floor of the building, and although she shivered as she washed her body and hair, Kiki felt ever so good afterward. In the study room adjoining the sleeping porch, there was a rack to hang out her damp towel and washcloth. She gave her teeth a good brushing and stretched out on top of her bedroll. With the tarp up, and the moon and stars visible over the trees in the summer night sky, Kiki was truly in heaven. She studied the sky between the tall Eucalyptus trees, until she found Artemis. "You're still there, and I'm still here," she whispered to her star.

The next morning, Kiki woke up happy and refreshed. Sleeping in a real bed was certainly wonderful. Seeing sunlight, listening to birds as well as the chimes, and smelling the Eucalyptus trees all helped her greet the new day with enthusiasm. Kiki rolled up everything, put it in the closet and closed the door. She set the hallway door handle so that it wouldn't lock behind her and slipped out of the building before the construction trucks pulled up for the day's work. She dropped her letter to Sal in a mailbox on her way to breakfast at the dining commons.

Everywhere Kiki strolled, she read posted signs and listened to conversations around her. She gradually figured out that although there were no summer classes currently in session, various groups used space for workshops and seminars, and so the campus was not truly deserted. Meals went on, if on an abbreviated schedule, buildings were open, administration and staff went to work. The comings and goings of all these people had been her protection, because otherwise, she would have been much more noticeable.

She didn't work for Jim again until Friday, so during the middle of the week Kiki was able to spend time at the library, where she hid herself in the stacks. Walking up and down, she saw a section on mythology and found a book on Greek goddesses. She flipped through the book, reading the sections that applied to Artemis. There were not a lot of facts, since this was all about myths, yet Kiki loved the idea that Artemis was on her own, kind of like someone who colored outside the lines. *Someone who did things her own way.* Kiki liked that and smiled when she read the words. *Was she being like the goddess right now?*

Leaving her fantasies behind, Kiki also managed to locate copies of a good map of the campus, a student guidebook, and a list of fall classes—all of which she could keep. Aside from the map, none of these things initially meant much, so Kiki studied the pages again and again, until from the jumble of words, a kind of order began to emerge.

During the week, Kiki also wandered into the Administration Annex, where she located the Admissions Office and asked for a guidebook for prospective students. The clerk pulled one from a drawer for her and then wanted a name and address for follow-up, so Kiki froze. She was saved by a phone call that distracted the clerk long enough for Kiki to grab the guidebook and flee the building.

Once she had read the manual, the student guidebook and list of classes, things began to make more sense. Kiki started to get a feel for classes, majors, and requirements. There were more similarities to high school than she had realized, like the way information built on itself. You take the first class in a series and then move on to the next level, like algebra one to algebra two. Since Kiki had wandered through high school exhausted, depressed, and emotionally spent half the time, she hadn't really thought much about the structure of things. She had only done what she had to do to pass.

Although Kiki enjoyed the luxury of her dorm penthouse for a few days, she knew that eventually students would return or she would be locked out, or both. She was right, of course, and very early on the following Saturday morning, she awoke to the sound of cars pulling up to the dorm. Young women parked and unloaded suitcases, taxis dropped off students, and parents arrived and ushered in their daughters.

The once silent dorm became a beehive of activity, and Kiki panicked.

Where could she go?

Then she remembered the rooms in the basement that she had first seen while she was doing her laundry. One or two of them were occupied by single Asian men who apparently worked in the bakery, but she had noticed one room that was empty and unlocked. So, grabbing her things from the sleeping porch, Kiki scurried down the back stairs, threw herself into the empty and dark basement room, and closed the door.

She hid there for the better part of the day, feeling overwhelmed by the feet that trampled overhead, the laughing and talking, the new students going by to check out the laundry room and other downstairs facilities. Her stomach growled because she hadn't eaten all day, and she needed to relieve herself; however, she was afraid to move. By 3 p.m., Kiki had to make some decisions, because she had to be at work by 4. The door to the room had hardware for a padlock, so she pulled from her duffle bag the combination lock that she had purchased in downtown Oakland, attached it to the door, and left the dorm by the laundry room exit.

At work, Kiki finally made it to the restroom. She also asked Jim if she could have a slice of pizza right away because she missed lunch. He nodded and watched with amusement as she downed the food in two bites. She was unusually nervous and dropped one pizza on the floor. Although Jim looked at her once or twice, he didn't say anything about her mistakes. He studied her as if he wanted to ask her if everything was okay, but she remained very self-protective and didn't open up, and Jim chose not to pry.

When Kiki returned to the dorm at nearly midnight, the front door was locked. So was the laundry room door. The second of her dreaded fears had come true. *Now what to do?*

Kiki walked around the building looking for another entrance and found nothing. She was sitting on the front steps contemplating her problem and the prospect of spending the night outside somewhere when a sports car drove up and parked. A young blonde-haired woman, accompanied by a companion who appeared to be a boyfriend, climbed out and the two started walking toward the dorm entrance. Although they were engaged in an obviously very personal conversation, the young woman noticed Kiki sitting on the steps and observed, "You look lost."

Kiki was startled yet managed to say, "I-uh, left my front door key in my room. Stupid me."

The blonde smiled. "No problem. I used to do that all the time. Here, let me open it for you."

She unlocked the door, and Kiki slipped through with an "Oh, thank you" and the young woman turned away to continue talking with her boyfriend.

With an audible sigh, Kiki tried to calm herself as she entered the living room, looked both ways down the corridors and then quickly dashed downstairs to the basement. *She had survived two of her dreaded fears—at least for now.*

Over the next few days, Kiki became an expert at dodging students, following others, and sliding inside doors. She had always been reasonably observant; now she became quite vigilant about looking at and remembering every possible detail around her.

She realized as she watched Montrose students come and go that she didn't really stand out, not nearly as much as she had feared. Most dressed casually, there was an international mix of various ethnic groups and cultural backgrounds, and many of the women were about her age. As long as she could hide her anxiety effectively and stroll around as if she belonged, Kiki would look like any other college student. Except for the backward ballcap, which she sometimes still wore.

Most of the time Kiki managed to get into the residence hall without difficulty, just by stepping inside when a group of girls were entering. They were almost always caught up in their own conversations and totally ignored her as she slipped through with them. Who wanted to bother to dig out a key from pocket or purse if it wasn't necessary? She would just smile and say, "Excuse me," and no one noticed her at all.

Kiki also learned to follow students to the dining hall and listen to the way they spoke, so she could improve upon her accent. She kept her ears open for survival clues—details about registration for classes, drop/add, and little bits of information like, "Dr. Simpson never takes roll in her class, so I can sleep in whenever I want to skip my 8 o'clock."

While eating a meal, Kiki would consult her catalog and class schedule to find out what Dr. Simpson taught. Little by little she pieced together her own fictional fall schedule, based on things that interested her and classes where her presence might not be noticed. It meant starting school a little late, she thought to herself, because she had to wait for all the record-keeping processes to finish. Suddenly, she realized she was *really thinking* of trying to sit in on Montrose classes. She sucked in several deep breaths to calm her nerves when she confronted herself with her own audacity. *You're actually going to do this*! Kiki thought to herself—and she didn't know whether to laugh or cry.

Kiki asked Jim to limit her hours to weekends—Friday evenings, most of Saturdays, and anytime on Sundays. These were times she could best get back into the hall after work without a problem. She figured out almost immediately that weeknights would be much harder, unless she returned to the dorm right after dinner. Kiki's earnings from this limited schedule would not provide sufficient funds to pay for food, laundry, and textbooks, even used ones. She had to buy her meals one at a time, because to get a meal card, she would have to have a student ID card. Of course, Kiki didn't have that—and had no way to get one. She decided to look for another or better job, maybe even on the Montrose campus.

When the drop-add period ended, Kiki began sitting in classrooms. She started with beginning psychology because almost all freshmen took it and the classroom was filled with two hundred faces. Freshmen didn't know everyone yet, another benefit. She quickly realized that the instructor might never notice her as long as she didn't do anything to stand out. By pretending she knew very little English, Kiki nodded her way into English as a second language, where her ethnic background helped her look the part. Although she soon realized she was head and shoulders over the other students, she picked up fine points of grammar that she had missed in high school, and the class wasn't really a waste. Kiki sat in on regular English literature and composition one day and it overwhelmed her. She scooted into art history, because the room was dark all the time while the professor showed slides. He never seemed to even notice his students, because he was so caught up in the beauty of the paintings that he was analyzing in intimate detail. Kiki also sat in on basic Spanish, again because her grammar was poor, even though the language had been spoken daily in her family.

Kiki's big challenge was economics. Survival in the world, she thought, meant understanding money, and Kiki knew she had too little of it. She read about the basic economics class and heard students talking about the instructor and saying that she was strict, yet very good. Her name was Helena Ramirez, and she had taught at Montrose for several years. Kiki tried to figure out how to get into her class but it was small, and Dr. Ramirez was reported to be very perceptive. Terrified to attempt sneaking into the classroom, Kiki tried sitting on the grass outside and listening to lectures through an open window. She couldn't catch every word—it was something about "guns and butter." She tried to read through the first chapter of the textbook in the library and felt terribly confused. Yet Kiki knew the economics class was important, so she kept going and sitting on the grass— scratching now and then when a bug gave her a bite—and leaving just before the students emerged from the old economics building. It was a white wooden structure that didn't have air conditioning and was located at the edge of campus. The lack of a noisy compressor helped Kiki catch some of what was being said in the class.

Despite her worries over money and her persistent anxiety about being caught, Kiki was having a great time. It was a surreal existence, yet more exciting and interesting than anything she could imagine. The only drawback was her loneliness. Although she saw Jim regularly, she couldn't be open with him. She envied the students who walked together around campus chattering, laughing, and enjoying each other's company. Kiki wondered: *Was Artemis ever lonely?* The book in the library had described her as a virgin goddess, which seemed to mean she never married or had children, and she went off alone in the forest—but she *did* have a companion animal, so maybe that helped.

After another week passed, Kiki's birth certificate arrived from New York, and she was able to go by bus to the driver's license bureau and fill out papers for a state identification card. When the form asked for an address and telephone number, she had no choice except to use Jim's business address, and she brought with her a pay stub to show that she was employed. She had to imply that she was living at the business address, and the clerk looked at her for a long time and heaved a sigh. "The form calls for two proofs of residence," she said, "and you don't really have even one." Kiki explained that she was living in a room behind the pizza parlor and wouldn't be getting any utility bills or anything, but she really needed some kind of local identification. Although the woman was clearly unnerved about it, she finally made a notation and stamped the form approved. Kiki's photograph was taken. Kiki was told that the card would be mailed to her within two weeks, and she asked that it be sent to her mailbox. The clerk nodded knowingly and let her go.

Soon afterward, Kiki received a letter from Sal. It was very pleasant, telling her a little about her latest trip to the East Coast and how she thought about Kiki. Sal mentioned Aisha briefly and noted that she was concerned about the precariousness of Kiki's life in California. The letter continued:

From your note, and what Meg told me of your phone call, I gather that you are hanging around Montrose College without being an official student. I applaud your daring, but please be very careful. Trespassing on private prop-erty could get you in a lot of trouble. Meg said you have good taste in selecting schools, ha, ha. Have you gotten in touch with your aunt yet? Let me know and keep in touch. Fondly, Sal.

Kiki sat on a bench, reading and rereading Sal's letter. She could tell that Sal was worried. She knew that she should take a day, find the way to Sunnyvale, and see her aunt and uncle. The minute she did that, however, she knew she'd never be returning to Montrose—her adventure would be over. Kiki was not yet ready to give it up.

The tearoom bulletin board sported many written treasures, and one day Kiki found a job posting for a dishwasher, Monday through Thursday afternoons, from 2 to 6 p.m., in the kitchen of the Mathews Dining Commons.

Since most of the classes Kiki was attending—however irregu-larly—were held in the morning, she could work that job in without losing anything other than valuable study time. Almost in financial desperation, she went up the hill to the dining hall and asked to see the person in charge.

Mrs. Trang, a middle-aged Asian woman who looked at Kiki through thick bifocals, came out to talk with her.

Nervously, Kiki introduced herself and asked about the job.

Mrs. Trang was pleasant but uncertain. "This is not good job," she said in somewhat halting English. "We Chinese family who have served this school for nearly hundred years. We do cooking and bak-ing and kitchen work for whole campus. Sometimes, there is delay in coming from China, and a job is not filled. So, then we post for students. There is very low pay plus meals, and job very hot, sweaty work."

"If it includes meals, that would be great," Kiki responded with enthusiasm.

"You are student, yes?" Mrs. Trang asked.

Kiki sighed. "Well, not officially. I, uh, live in the neighborhood and come here a lot. I saw a sign at the teashop."

Mrs. Trang nodded. "Tea shop, yes, teashop. But you not student?"

Kiki was starting to feel exasperated, yet she tried to remain calm. "Do I have to be? Are your regular workers students?"

Mrs. Trang seemed not to understand.

Kiki tried another approach. "Have any students asked about the job?"

Mrs. Trang shook her head. "No, no one ask. Is not good job."

"Well, can I take it temporarily? Until a student asks, or until one of your regular people shows up?"

Mrs. Trang raised an eyebrow. She considered that idea for a moment and seemed to see a way out.

"Okay, temporary. You take for little while, 'til student come or family arrive from China."

After this initial interview, Mrs. Trang showed Kiki around the kitchen and introduced her to various workers, most of whom smiled and nodded. Kiki could see that she would again be alone working here, because the machinery was loud and the workers spoke in Chinese. Yet it was a job and would provide meals.

So that afternoon, after filling out the paperwork and W-2 form, again relying on Jim's business address, Kiki became a temporary part-time employee on the campus of Montrose College.

8

Dr. Ramirez

Helena Fontana Ramirez, Ph.D., was known as a pacer. The veteran economics professor would cross to the blackboard and draw a chart, use her pointer to explain it, and then while giving examples, pace back and forth across the front of the room. Her students knew she loved teaching. From the roses always present on her desk, they guessed that she also loved the outdoors and the smell of flowers. Helena had admitted that she grew roses as a hobby, and it was widely known that she made sure the campus gardeners planted rosebushes outside her classroom. When the weather was warm, her pacing took her to open windows that allowed breezes to tempt her nostrils with beautiful fragrances.

This fall semester, as she paced back and forth, she kept noticing someone coming and going below the window. Then she would see the tips of boots sticking out as she glanced outside at the beautiful day and continued her lecture. These details might have been coincidental, yet when they repeated themselves, Helena began to explore. Never missing a beat of her talk, she moved ever closer to the window until finally she stared almost straight down onto Kiki's head. Apparently quite surprised, she paced back across the room, her forehead pulled into a frown.

On the next trip to the window, she suddenly called out rather loudly, "Would the young lady camped on the lawn outside my window please do me the courtesy of coming inside?"

Kiki bolted to her feet. Her first impulse was to run for her life. However, the professor's commanding voice resounded in her head, and she thought she had better do as told. *The jig was up.* Her heart pounded and she swallowed nervously. She had been anticipating this moment with dread. Her shoulders began to slump as Kiki climbed the creaky wooden stairs and entered the economics classroom, while all twenty-some student heads turned and stared at her. She blushed with embarrassment.

Helena motioned her to take a seat, and Kiki did so, as the class resumed and the professor continued her lecture without a pause.

When the class ended, the students trooped out, staring openly at the stranger.

Helena motioned Kiki to stay seated.

Kiki sighed. *Here it comes.*

Helena stood over her and looked down at Kiki, not unkindly. "I gather from your ongoing presence outside my classroom window that you have a burning interest in either me or economics, and I assume the latter," she said wryly, with a slight smile that took the edge off her obvious sarcasm. She paced again and Kiki stared at her, noting the short auburn hair streaked with white, the black-framed glasses, the professional look of her gray silk blouse and black skirt.

Kiki forced herself to nod. She was overwhelmed by this woman and didn't know what to say. She could not have prepared herself for this encounter.

"Why do you study economics from the grass outside, where you will be pestered by ants and other crawly creatures—and where you can only hear perhaps one third of what I am saying if the wind happens to be in the right direction—when there are empty seats inside the classroom?"

Kiki struggled to speak. "'Cause I'm not registered—for economics, I mean."

"Are you an auditor?"

Kiki squirmed. "Does it cost money, to be an auditor?"

"Yes, it's a registration like any other."

Kiki sighed. "Then I'm not an auditor. I couldn't pay the fee, whatever it is."

"So, you've been auditing, rather unofficially, then?" Helena raised an eyebrow.

"Yes, ma'am."

Helena paced, thoughtfully.

"You live in the neighborhood and just wander in to unofficially audit economics?"

Kiki swallowed and nodded. *What else could she say?*

Helena paced some more. "Interesting. Highly unusual, but very interesting. What is your name?"

"Kiki. Kiki Rodriguez."

"Well, Miss Rodriguez, I'm not quite sure what to do about your unique situation. I'll have to think about it. Meanwhile, I suggest that you do your unofficial auditing inside the room where you might at least learn something. I also suggest that you find a copy of the textbook in the library and take a stab at reading it. I also suggest that you find a copy of the morning newspaper and select a stock to follow. It is a classroom project to follow one stock throughout the year and track its progress in the stock market. Let me know when you've picked a stock, and I will give you more information about how to track it."

"You mean, like IBM?"

"Yes, like IBM. However, there are thousands of choices. Read the chapter in the text on how money grows and then select a stock. Have a good day, Miss Rodriguez. I'll see you next class."

Kiki ran from the room and up the street. She didn't know how to react. This was so unexpected and incredible! Dr. Ramirez was treating her like a student and was actually willing to teach her something! At this moment, she thought that Helena Ramirez was the most wonderful woman in the world. *Of course, later*—well, she'd have to worry about that then.

Attempting to calm down, Kiki stopped in the bookstore and looked at the price of a textbook for economics. Even used it was $25. She'd have to wait until she got her first check from the job in the dining commons, and then she would buy it. Meanwhile, she'd spend every available moment in the library.

When Kiki reached the dorm, she slipped in after another girl and failed to notice the three students following a few paces behind and watching her every move. She went down the stairs to her secret room in the basement and stretched out on the bed. What a day. She wished she could write to Sal and tell her all about it, but she didn't think Sal would understand, or approve of, the complexity of her life situation.

A few moments later, there was a knock at the door. Kiki jumped. This was another of her fears—the day someone would discover her room and report her presence to security. *How short lived was her success with Dr. Ramirez.* Kiki went to the door expecting to see a uniformed security guard.

Instead, she faced three Montrose students. One stared at her directly, and the other two watched the hallway. The first one asked, "May we come in?"

Kiki backed off and nodded. *What could she say?* She had no right to protect her space.

The three students moved inside and closed the door. Almost aggressively, they cornered her. The first—a stocky, dark-haired young woman wearing her locks short and spiky and sporting a bright red "I'm a dyke" T-shirt—was clearly the boss.

"I'm Karen Fullerton," she announced. "This is Sue Swanson, and this is Delia DeMarco." Kiki noted that Fullerton was Caucasian, Sue was African-American with milk chocolate skin and dreadlocks, and Delia was obviously of some kind of Italian extraction. Both Sue and Delia were casually clad and not as overtly political in appearance as Karen.

"Now you know who we are. Who are you?" Karen demanded.

"Kiki Rodriguez."

"Well, Kiki, we're all students in Economics 101, and we saw your little interaction with Dr. Ramirez this morning," Karen continued. "We were talking on the way back to the dorm and we realized that at different times each of us has seen you somewhere, coming or going. Always sort of slipping in or slipping out. And I've seen you in the dining hall."

Kiki nodded, her back ramrod stiff.

"So, looking at this room, with your sleeping bag spread out, and your rather modest collection of belongings, and knowing that you are shacked up in steerage with the Chinese cooks, I came to the conclusion that there is something rather different, shall we say, about your presence on this campus."

Kiki blanched.

"Com'on," pushed Sue Swanson. "Give us the scoop. Who are you and how did you get here?"

Kiki began sweating. She didn't want to tell them anything, but they had her. All they had to do was report her to security, and she was history. She might as well be honest. "I'm from New York. I got here by bus, a trucker, and some college students from Berkeley. I came to California to find a job so I can save up to go to college, and someone dropped me off here by the front gate. It was late at night, and I came in just to sleep somewhere, until I could go into San Francisco the next day and then find my aunt's house in Sunnyvale. It seemed like a safe place to rest. I didn't know it was a famous women's college until later, and it was so beautiful here that I just sort of stayed."

The three students looked startled. "Wow," Delia said.

"I found a job in a pizza parlor down the street," Kiki continued, "and slept anyplace I could find, until I managed to get into this dorm. I slept up on the top floor until the students arrived, and then I moved down here. I've been just sitting in on classes and working two jobs."

"Two jobs?" Sue inquired, her eyes wide.

"Yeah, I got a temporary job washing dishes in the dining hall."

Karen looked at her intently. "And nobody but us knows you're here?"

Kiki shook her head. "Not that I know of."

Karen plopped herself down on the floor and leaned against the wall. Sue and Delia followed her example. Kiki slumped down on her bed. "Wow, this is complicated," Karen mused. "You're living on this campus, going to classes, working here, without ever having applied for admission or being registered." She looked at Kiki sternly. "This is outrageous!"

Sue and Delia both glanced at Karen, waiting to see what she would do.

Karen paused a moment, as if thinking. "By the honor code, we should turn you in."

Delia spoke up. "But the honor code is for student behavior. If we know something about a student, say one who is, like, cheating or something, we have to tell and we can't cheat ourselves. If Kiki isn't registered, and she won't get transcripts or a degree, then she isn't bound by the honor code, and how are we bound by it?"

Karen thought. "Well, I'm sure in some way, if we see anything that's not right, we are supposed to report it. And this is definitely weird." Suddenly she slapped her knee. "But you know what, *I like it!*" She laughed.

Then Sue and Delia laughed, and then Kiki laughed.

Karen continued to think. Then she addressed her friends, "Okay, we'll have to vote on it, since it affects us all. My suggestion is that for the time being, we keep this under wraps. We could maybe make a deal of some kind."

Kiki sucked in her breath. "What kind of deal?" She knew about blackmail—it ran rampant in her neighborhood back home.

"Well, we could trade services. You could do some things for us, and we could do some things for you, and all of us could keep quiet."

"Like what?"

"Well, do you type?"

"Yeah, I passed typing in high school."

"Well, I'm a lousy typist. If you'd type a paper for me each week, on the computer at the library, I'd scout around and get you some things you need for your classes."

Kiki sighed. It would be hard, with two jobs and her classes and homework, but she supposed she could do it, or try anyway. *What other choice did she have?* "Okay, what else?"

Sue spoke up. "I hate doing laundry. You're camped next to the laundry room. I'll provide the money, if you could just see that my stuff gets through the washer and dryer once a week, and I'll help you out any way I can," she negotiated.

Delia nodded. "Me, too."

Kiki felt that all these tasks sounded like more than she could handle, yet she was really in trouble now and she couldn't see any other alternative but to accept the deal. Reluctantly, she agreed.

Late that afternoon, Helena Ramirez sat in her Volvo wagon stuck in a rush-hour logjam on the I-580 headed east to Stockton. Although freeway traffic had grown worse each year, braving it was the only way she could keep her farm. Shortly after Helena had started teaching at Montrose, she bought the place, near Livermore, with money inherited from her grandfather. She had hung onto this piece of personal sanity that was once in open country yet now increasingly the victim of suburban sprawl. The horses had long since been given up, yet there were still dogs and cats, a few chickens and a single milk cow.

Helena had managed to develop a teaching schedule that limited her stressful freeway drives to Montrose to three days each week. She had wisely bought a computer early in the game, and she could now do much of her work from home. When her eyes tired of focusing on the monitor, she could go outside and tend her roses. It wasn't a bad life, if a bit reclusive.

Of course, her campus acquaintances might have assumed she was more reclusive than she actually was, because Helena never entertained the faculty, staff or students at her farm. It was her secret hideaway. And that way no one knew a thing about PJ.

The traffic lightened a bit. Helena reached the edge of Livermore, took an exit ramp, moved away from the suburbs and gradually wound her way home. The trusty Volvo, definitely a relic, had made the journey thousands of times. The odometer had long since given up the ghost, and even her mechanic had no idea how many miles she had actually put on the car over the years.

When Helena turned into the front gate, which PJ always kept open for her, she surveyed the homestead, pleased with its white picket fence and traditional farmhouse having a wide front porch. Although the house dated back to the early 1920s, she and PJ had modernized it. Helena always sighed with relief when she arrived home.

She honked as she drove up to the house. PJ came out on the porch and waved, as she did every time Helena came back from her hectic jaunt to the college. PJ was a rotund woman with an equally round face and short gray hair. Her eyes had once been an intense blue but had faded a bit with age.

"Did you have a good day?" PJ chirped happily. She was still wearing her work clothes, stained with paint from various carpentry and repair projects.

"Very interesting. I'll give you the details at dinner."

"Oh! Should I prepare for a tale of economics or human relations?" PJ asked with a slightly suppressed chuckle.

"Human relations, I think," decided Helena, as she followed PJ into the house and stopped to pet Wiggles and Waggums, their two female rescue dogs of indiscriminate heritage. The dogs gave her a sniff and a lick and then returned to their favorite pillows.

PJ always had dinner ready when Helena arrived home, and the meal inevitably included a chilled glass of wine. Helena's contented look revealed just how much she appreciated this quiet time.

The two women sat together in the living room and sipped their wine and talked of the day.

"Dinner's still warmin' in the oven, so tell me, what happened today that's so special?"

Helena raised the wine glass to her lips for a sip and thought. "Well," she finally said, putting the glass back down on the coffee table, "two things. Both of them kind of threw me." She paused.

PJ grew impatient. "Come on, don't keep me hangin.'"

"Well," Helena began again. "You remember Karen Fullerton, that very outspoken young student of mine?"

"Yes, the self-styled leader of the lesbians. What has she done now?"

"Today she came to my class wearing a T-Shirt that announced 'I'm a dyke' in big letters across her chest. All during my lecture, I kept looking at it and felt distracted. At first I was almost offended. Then I realized why I was feeling that way, and I started seeing my whole life flashing before my eyes—you know what I mean?"

PJ shook her head. "I'm not sure where you're headed."

"When I began attending college, no one ever mentioned the word 'lesbian,' let alone 'dyke.' If a girl was suspected of any kind of unusual affection for another student, she was instantly expelled. I was just reflecting on how the world has changed so radically since then. Today this student can sit in my classroom proclaiming her sexual preferences for the whole world to see. I don't know whether to chuckle or scream. See what I mean?"

PJ looked at her tenderly. "Are you thinkin' about how much livin' you've missed?"

"Somewhat. I think now about how I had to lie to get through school myself and how I had to build up this mystique about myself to keep my personal life private. I was so lucky to find you, and we've had a good relationship all these years; however, it would have been nice to be able to acknowledge you. And to invite people here as our guests. You understand?"

PJ nodded. "I get it. And you see the kids today havin' it so much easier bein' open and not havin' to live with fear and shame about who they are."

"Yes, that, but you know, I even questioned myself this morning, about whether the lie is still necessary. We keep it up, year after year, and I wonder if we need to."

"Helena, my love," PJ said gently, putting her hand on her partner's shoulder, "are you wantin' to come out of the closet?"

"I don't know, PJ, I don't know," Helena admitted. And the two sat in silence for a long time.

Finally, PJ asked, "I thought there was something else that happened today?"

"Oh, yes!" Helena brightened. "I have a new student, the strangest student I've ever had."

"What do you mean?"

"Well, during the past few classes, I've had this feeling there was someone outside the building listening. I thought I must be dreaming. Today I verified that indeed there was a girl, about eighteen or so, sitting on the ground outside my window attempting to listen to my lecture and take notes. I thought it was ridiculous, so I had her come in and join the class."

"Is she a Montrose student?"

"I don't know. I didn't have time to pursue it today, but I get this sense about her. She's the right age, and she looks like a student, and she's very anxious to learn. You can see it in her face. She admitted that she's not registered for my class, and I wonder if she's registered at all. I suspect that she is walking onto the campus from somewhere in the neighborhood and just hanging out. As you know, our part of town is almost totally black—excuse me, African-American—and this girl is some exotic mixture, probably Hispanic or Filipino with something European mixed in. I just feel she hasn't a dime to her name, and for some strange reason, I want to teach her. I should mention it to the dean, or security or something, yet somehow, I don't want to. I just want to let her come and wait and see how she does. Don't ask me why, because it's not logical."

PJ looked at Helena thoughtfully. "Is she one of us?"

Helena shrugged. "I don't know. It's possible. She's very young, with big brown, hungry eyes and an intense yearning to learn. That could mean anything. So many of my students are privileged, and they're here for many reasons, not all having to do with a burning desire to get an education. This girl really *wants* to learn, and that is flattering to any teacher. So I'd like to share with her what I have to give, an appreciation for the value of economics."

PJ smiled. "And your friendship. You have that to offer. She may need a friend."

Helena sighed. "That's scary, even to hear you say that. I've kept my distance all these years."

PJ leaned over and kissed her on the cheek. "You'll know what to do when the time comes."

Kiki was more nervous than ever for the next few days. Karen and her friends, however, kept their word. No security patrolman knocked on Kiki's door, nor was she followed by security anywhere on the campus. Her job and the classes went on, and each day when she came back to the dorm, she found something under her door. A syllabus for a class she was attending unofficially, a used textbook for another class, a set of sheets for her bed with a note attached, "My mom sent me some new sheets for my birthday, so I thought you might be able to use these." Another day there was a note telling her that there was a bin in another dorm where clothes were kept for donation to charity, and that she should check it just in case there was something she could use. Kiki did not allow herself to feel angry or put down by these notes. Whatever was really meant, everything was useful for her survival. The sheets were nice, and she did need more clothing. She only had time to do her own laundry once a week, and she scarcely had enough clothes to keep going that long. One day there was a ticket to a concert, and she sat down and cried. She had been working so hard that she hadn't even stopped to think about all the cultural advantages of a college campus. This ticket seemed like a heavenly gift.

One day she found the biggest surprise of all: a key to the front door of the dorm. There was no note, so Kiki had no idea which of them had found a way to obtain the key. She almost didn't want to know, because whoever it was had taken a risk in getting it.

With that key Kiki could come and go at will, and one night she sat for a little while on the lawn behind the dorm and stared up at the stars. She found Artemis and told her star, "Geez, when I was in the South Bronx, sitting on the roof, I never knew there was a place like this, where I could see you and have such a wonderful life. Please, Artemis, help me find a way to make it last."

Tall, slender and very Italian, Annibella Carrera was the resident assistant for Willard Olsen Hall. She was an older student who was paid a small stipend to oversee the dorm. Back in the old days, there had been an official housemother, but in the wake of women's liberation, the dorms were now very open with few restrictions. So there was only one person with any authority in each hall, and she was a student, commonly known as the "RA."

It was Annibella's job to get to know the students, and since there were nearly a hundred thirty of them in Olsen, she couldn't accomplish this task immediately. She saw them coming and going, and there were a couple of general dorm meetings to give information on fire and earthquake preparation. Because she didn't yet know all the students, occasionally she would see a face that she did not recognize.

Early one afternoon, as she was returning from her senior English honors class, Annibella bumped into a student coming out of the dorm.

The student apologized and rushed on, but Annibella watched her go and felt some confusion. She had seen this dark-haired, olive-skinned girl several times yet could not get a handle on her identity. She decided to find out.

That afternoon when she passed Annibella, Kiki had been on her way to work in the dining hall. She was in the midst of doing three different projects for three classes and trying to oversee Delia's laundry at the same time. She was pushing herself hard because she had decided to tackle the work in her classes as if she were a real student. The courses were fascinating to her, and Kiki wanted to learn. When a professor announced the assignment for the next class, she would write it down and then proceed to do it. In psychology class, she had even taken one examination—without signing it. When the tests were returned, each student had to go up to the front of the room and pick up her exam. Kiki found hers in the pile, with a grade of 89, and a note that the unnamed student would not get credit for it. Kiki just left the exam sitting there and walked back to her seat. She dared not acknowledge it as hers. Thankfully, the professor was busy writing on the chalkboard and did not notice, or Kiki would have been caught right then.

She had resumed her seat, still looking at her exam lying on the professor's desk and knowing that she had learned enough to score a good grade. While it was exciting information, at the same time it just complicated things. Every step forward pushed Kiki deeper into the pit—wanting to stay and knowing that sooner or later she would be forced to leave. Much as she wanted to belong here, she had not graduated from high school nor had enrolled nor paid fees. Kiki was as out of bounds as she could possibly be. *Was this,* she wondered, *how illegal immigrants felt?*

Kiki's excitement over the psychology exam score had actually added to her anxiety and, rushing by Annibella, she dashed off to work confused by conflicting thoughts. When she reached the dining commons, she encountered a huge pile of dishes awaiting her—along with several cooks impatient for Kiki to load the dishwasher to provide them with supplies for the next meal and plate service for the dining room. An afternoon business meeting had put extra stress on the dining facility.

Kiki rushed here and there gathering dishes, rinsing them off and loading them into the big dishwashing machines, then unloading and stacking them. At one point, the spray attachment slipped out of her hand and left a big puddle on the floor. One of the cooks started yelling at Kiki to clean up her mess. At least that's what she thought he was saying, because he was shouting in Chinese and Kiki understood very few words. She ran to get a mop and bucket. On the way back she slipped on the wet floor and fell.

When she hit the concrete, Kiki nearly screamed in pain. Her ankle was badly twisted, and she had cut open her right arm. Mrs. Trang rushed to her aid and stopped the bleeding with a bandage; however,

Kiki's ankle was swelling quickly and might be broken. The kitchen supervisor did the logical thing. She called for an ambulance—despite Kiki's protests—to have Kiki transported to Highland Hospital, the nearest medical facility to the college and where students were sent for emergency care. The fact that Kiki was not a Montrose student was the last thing Mrs. Trang considered at that moment. Kiki was doing a student job and needed treatment.

Between gasps from the pain, and as she was loaded into the ambulance, Kiki tried to tell the EMTs that she couldn't go to an emergency room. The ambulance team, a man and a woman, just took her cries as a response to her injuries, shook their heads, and worked over her in the vehicle on the way to Highland's ER. What she wanted to say, and tried unsuccessfully to express, was that she wasn't a Montrose student and now everyone would know.

9

The Administrators

Melissa Johan, Montrose Dean of Students, shoved a pencil through her tightly curled black hair and scratched an itchy spot on her scalp. Whenever she became stressed about something, her scalp itched. And with her highly coiffed black hair, she couldn't get within three inches of her scalp if her life depended on it.

Melissa had creamy off-white skin and dark chocolate eyes. Of mixed race heritage, she was one of the first African-Americans to reach the higher academic realms at Montrose, and she was clearly very sensitive about her position and the importance of not making any mistakes—major mistakes, anyway. All eyes were on her, from the board of trustees to the freshman class, to potential students who had not yet applied to Montrose.

Her position brought with it a great deal of normal stress, and she was used to that. It came with the territory. Unfortunately, this report on her desk—following an urgent telephone call regarding a young woman hiding out on the campus and masquerading as a student—was more than she wanted to handle.

Melissa had lost not a single moment before contacting the head of campus security, and Harold Seitzman had remained closeted in her office for the better part of the afternoon.

Harold now sat across from her shaking his head in disbelief at her story. "I've been security chief here for nearly twenty years, and in all my days on this campus, I have never encountered such a dilemma," he observed with a touch of defensiveness.

Melissa held up a hand. "Harold, you have no reason to feel

attacked in this matter. You and your staff always do an excellent job of keeping our campus safe. You even came up with a workable plan for additional security after 9/11. You are good at your job. This situation is unusual to say the least, and what we most need from you is help in resolving it."

Melissa had been forced to take charge of the "Kiki Rodriguez problem" because the college's president, Dr. Anita Collins Ryerson, was on a speaking tour in Philadelphia and other cities along the East Coast and would not be back for a couple of weeks. Since this situation couldn't be ignored for that long, it fell to Melissa, as official backup to the president, to figure out what needed to be done.

After talking with Harold at length, Melissa quietly and privately spoke with the school's primary lawyer, the psychology department head, the campus chaplain, and Dr. Helena Ramirez, who seemed to be the member of the faculty who had been most aware of this Kiki Rodriguez—but who like many others, had not fully appreciated, or at least admitted to, the significance of this young woman's presence on campus.

Melissa also interviewed Mrs. Trang, who became quite upset and, with her limited English, not particularly helpful. The dean next called Annibella Carrera, who remembered seeing a young woman of this description in Willard Olsen Hall. After Annibella, Melissa interviewed a payroll clerk who had been processing paychecks for a Kiki Rodriguez for the past few weeks but didn't know there was a problem with her working in the kitchen. Melissa closed her eyes, shook her head, and dismissed the young woman.

Finally, she summoned Karen Fullerton, who had been seen speaking with the Rodriguez girl. Melissa always dreaded contact with Karen, not because she was a lesbian, although Melissa in her heart of hearts would have to admit she was not particularly comfortable around lesbian women. It was more Karen's overt political stance that bothered Melissa. Karen was at heart a rebel and her lesbianism gave her a platform from which to battle authority. Melissa and Karen had been adversaries a number of times during the past three years, and now that Karen was completing her final semester, Melissa was anxiously waiting for the day when she would graduate and take her aggressiveness somewhere else.

As soon as Melissa had finished questioning her, Karen Fullerton quickly whisked herself off to Kiki's room. With her well-defined rap on the door, she pushed her way into Kiki's pain-filled world and announced, "Well, you've been had. I just had a talk with Dr. Johan, and she's got to do something about you. What do you think?"

Kiki, nursing her sore ankle with the help of pain medication from Highland's ER, looked pale and exhausted. Her upper arm had required several stitches and was covered with a large bandage. "Well," she sighed philosophically, "it was a dream from the moment I walked onto the campus. I'm amazed it has lasted this long."

"Oh, come on, Kiki," Karen said sharply. "You came here for empowerment. Now is the time to grab it. Fight them, don't give in!"

Kiki groaned. "I don't feel up to fighting anyone, today. Maybe I'll feel better tomorrow."

Karen—perhaps noticing for the first time Kiki's pale face and just how depressed she was—backed off a bit. "Well, don't say anything you don't have to, don't agree to anything, and let me get you a lawyer. I can help you. Just don't let them bulldoze you, okay?"

Kiki nodded. Her eyelids drooped and Karen, after a moment's hesitation, left her alone to rest.

Two days later, Harold reported back to Melissa that Kiki Rodriguez came from the South Bronx, in New York, had finished the eleventh grade at a local high school with slightly above average grades, had no criminal record of any kind, came from a very disadvantaged family, and had left home quite suddenly. Her parents had attempted to file a missing persons report; however, since the girl had left a note, the police had not been inclined to pursue the case and had just filed the paperwork. The girl was technically old enough to be on her own and had apparently left home of her own volition.

Dennis McNally, principal legal counsel for Montrose College, came later that afternoon directly to Melissa's office from a court appearance. He too was quite concerned about the ramifications of the "Rodriguez situation."

Peering at Melissa through his thick horn-rimmed glasses, he announced, "You must realize that the school is quite compromised by this. No matter what decision you make, there are risks."

"Explain," Melissa encouraged him, after a deep sigh. Her shoulders were aching from stress over this matter. A masseuse's gentle touch would be really nice, but that was not possible at the moment.

"Well," Dennis began, "the young woman is trespassing on private property, plain and simple. You have every right to have her literally thrown out the front gate by campus security. You also have the right to have her arrested for trespassing, probably breaking and entering by staying in the music building with entry through a window and staying secretly in a dormitory. Even fraud for pretending to be a student. Some of it is a little shaky, yet you could pursue all sorts of legal grounds against her, if you so desire."

"Okay, what's the complication?"

Dennis paused thoughtfully. "More moral and political than legal. It's a fluke that she ever got in here. It's amazing that she's stayed undiscovered for what, a couple of months? She hasn't so far really harmed the college, but her presence here is a threat. If the press gets wind of this, she'll become some kind of heroine or martyr—and from what I've seen, this Karen Fullerton, with her sit-ins, marches, and speeches, is the perfect person to make use of Rodriguez for her own ends. And of course, our Ms. Fullerton has been smart enough to find this girl, when every responsible authority on campus has totally missed her existence. The front gate security guards are all red in the face with utter embarrassment."

Melissa stared at him with raised eyebrows that revealed she was clearly thunderstruck by the reality of his words. All Montrose needed was a public scandal.

"So," he continued, "you, all the administration, and the college reputation, are caught in the middle. The girl has made friends, she has attached herself to the campus, and she even has a job here. If you kick her out, you risk making the school into the villain, even though the girl is legally in the wrong. I can just see this story all over the Internet right now, going 'viral' as they say." McNally tapped his fingers on the arm of his chair nervously.

"If by a fluke," he added after a moment, "you should decide to turn the world upside down, and allow her to stay under some kind of agreement or let her continue studying here, and that story gets out, you will open the door for every down and out young woman in the country to show up at our gates and demand a free college education. It's a tough situation, because I'm not sure Montrose can come out of this totally unscathed, no matter what you do."

Melissa sucked in a deep breath. She looked out the window at the Eucalyptus trees, perhaps remembering her own student days. A Bostonian who could pass for white, she had lived then in a bi-racial world that had been simple by comparison. The political, social, and cultural roadmap of this country had become much more complicated post civil rights, women's rights, gay rights.

"Another thing," McNally went on, "is that this girl has cost us very little. She has used an empty room in the basement of a dorm and has consumed a few dollars in hot water and electricity. She has paid for her meals and whatever supplies she has used. She has sat in empty chairs in classrooms. Other than this ambulance ride, up to this point her visit has been a minor nuisance—not worth pursuing. However, it does raise issues with insurance coverage, student rights, the role of the college in the community, etc., etc., etc. The implications of her presence are endless."

"Well," Melissa sighed. "I guess it's time I meet this girl, face-to-face."

"Yes," McNally agreed. "But not alone. You need a committee to interview her."

"Isn't that a little heavy-handed?"

"I don't think so. She needs to feel the weight of what she's done. In an intimate situation, she might be very persuasive, win over your sympathy. You can't afford that. It's too touchy. You are going to need a consensus on this, because whatever the outcome, there will be consequences."

The dean nodded reluctantly. She clearly dreaded an encounter yet felt curious at the same time. With a sigh, Melissa made the phone calls and set up the inevitable meeting.

Annibella Carrera descended the stairs to the basement. This was the hardest situation she had faced since becoming an RA the previous year, and she had wondered as she lay awake the last two nights if she should have been smarter and figured out that this girl was hiding in the dorm. But then, no one else had figured it out either—at least no one who should have and had good reason to.

After walking down the dimly lit hallway, Annibella knocked on the door of Kiki's little room, and Kiki answered dully. She had known this moment was coming. She had limped to the laundry and washed her best pair of jeans and her nicest shirt and had found an iron to press them a bit. She still had only one boot on, with her other foot wrapped up, and she was still hobbling around on crutches. Her right arm was in bandages—the stitches had not yet been removed from her deep cut. Her pain was down, but she felt very little like taking on the world. She had spoken with a very worried Mrs. Trang, and she had called Jim to let him know that she couldn't work for a few days. Other than that, she had just waited. *Waited for this moment.*

The RA's automobile was parked just outside the laundry-room door, and Annibella helped Kiki get into the passenger seat of the Toyota Corolla and arrange herself. Kiki, who could count on the fingers of one hand the number of cars she had ridden in, was impressed that Annibella could afford something so nice. During the brief ride, she didn't have much to say, and neither did Annibella. When they reached the dean's office, Annibella touched her shoulder gently and wished her luck. That was all she said.

Kiki was led into a conference room and asked to take a seat. Across from her was Melissa Johan, the dean whose name had been running through Kiki's head for the past two days. Then she was introduced to Harold Seitzman, the head of campus security, and Dennis McNally, the lawyer, Dr. Rita Capehart, the head of the psychology department, and Dr. Nancy Raines, the college chaplain.

Kiki's heart pounded in her throat. *There were so many of them, and they all looked so serious.* She felt like she was on trial. *Which, of course, she was.*

Melissa Johan seemed pleasant enough to Kiki, and the others tried to look relaxed and unhurried. However, she felt them all staring at her. She remembered what Karen had said about not letting them pressure her.

Melissa began. "Miss Rodriguez, or Kiki, I'm not sure how you wish to be called—"

"Kiki will be fine." She flushed bright red.

Melissa smiled. "Kiki, then, we are all aware that you have been sort of an uninvited guest on our campus for several weeks. Since this situation is a bit unorthodox, to say the least, we need to ask you some questions about yourself and your reasons for being here."

Kiki looked around the room, felt the intensity of all those eyes and panicked. "Do I need a lawyer?" Her voice sounded tense and harsh even to her own ears.

Dennis McNally reacted quickly. "Ms. Rodriquez, or Kiki, this is not a legal proceeding. This is merely an informal interview."

"But it could lead to some kind of legal action, couldn't it?" Kiki's voice was beginning to rise from stress.

McNally quickly spoke up. "That is not our purpose—"

Rita Capehart suddenly interrupted. "Dennis, excuse me. This is rather an imposing group. We all know that. It must be totally overwhelming to this young woman. If you and Melissa and the others don't mind, I'd like to have a moment alone with her."

Melissa looked surprised, paused briefly and then nodded. "Okay, let's all relax for a minute. Rita, you can take Kiki into my private office."

Rita kindly offered to help Kiki up from her chair and put an arm around her as she led her into the next room and closed the door.

Once there, she showed Kiki to a comfortable chair and then sat nearby. "You look scared," she said very gently.

Kiki, who had never felt more alone and isolated in her life, let her head drop. *Oh, Artemis, she thought, what a mess I'm in.* "Yeah," she finally admitted aloud. "I don't know what they're going to do to me."

Rita nodded. "Are you afraid they're going to hurt you?"

Kiki sighed, barely able to hold back tears. "I'm afraid of being sent away. Or going to jail."

Rita paused and then asked, "Kiki, do you know how much power you have?"

"What do you mean?" Kiki looked up, surprised. She was feeling *anything* but powerful.

"Look at all these important people who have stopped their lives just to come and talk with you. Just by being here, you have turned this campus upside down. That's power. Right now you have an opportunity to choose *how* to use that power. To hurt or to help." The psychologist paused to let Kiki consider her words.

After a moment, Rita continued, "I honestly don't believe that anyone in that room, I or anyone else, is out to hurt you. And I doubt that you came here intentionally to hurt the school in any way. Right now, you have choices. If you give in to your fear and become defensive, you will start fighting, and then these administrators may find it necessary to fight back. On the other hand, if you are honest and open enough to speak your mind, your truth, you can use your power to turn them into your friends and supporters."

Kiki sat still and considered the professor's words. She remembered what Karen had told her about protecting herself, not giving in. "But what if——"

Rita interrupted her. "Kiki, try to understand this, despite your fear. If you fight them, they may have to fight you. If you can allow yourself to cooperate, then you empower them to cooperate with you. The choice is yours at this moment—a moment that may never come again."

Kiki stared at the floor. No one had advised her like this, except Sal. *Oh, how she wished she could talk to Sal. It was so lonely not having her close.* With her swollen ankle, Kiki hadn't even been able to get out at night to look at the stars and talk to Artemis. *Well, she'd have to decide on her own.*

She looked up at the professor, sighed, and then nodded. "Okay, I'll try my best."

When Rita and Kiki returned to the conference room, Rita nodded to Melissa, who visibly relaxed. The others, all taking their cue from her, sat back in their chairs and appeared ready to listen.

"Kiki," Melissa began, again, "what we would all like to understand is how you came to be on our campus, under these unusual circumstances. Could you just tell us, in your own words, what happened to you to bring you here?"

Kiki looked at her and then at each of the others, all expectantly waiting. She swallowed. "Well," she began, her South Bronx accent breaking into her speech as she began telling her story, "I've always wanted to go to college. Like, what do you want to do when you grow up? Go to college."

She told them about having a job and losing it, her parents fighting and her brother being in jail, her papa demanding rent from her, and how she began to fear that she would never have a chance for any future unless she got away. And about the bus that left her behind in Kansas and Sal the woman trucker who picked her up and how Sal spoke excellent English and valued education, and about the college kids who brought her to the Bay Area.

"When they started smoking pot and acting weird and getting lost," she recalled, "I knew I had to get away from them. I asked to get out of the car, and they just dropped me off, right at your gate. I didn't know where I was or that it was a college, at first. It was late, almost dark outside, and I was tired and lost and the trees looked beautiful, and since I had a bedroll I thought I could maybe sleep safely inside the fence until morning. I just came in to rest for the night." Tears started to spill down her cheeks, and she wiped her face with the back of her hand.

Rita got up and brought her a box of Kleenex.

"Where did you sleep that night?" asked Harold Seitzman.

"In that outdoor theater in back of the music building. I just put my bedroll down by the corner of the building."

Kiki began feeling a little better, because they all were now leaning forward and seemed interested in her story. "So, the next morning, when I woke up, I just started to do what I needed to do to survive, like get something to eat, go to the bathroom, you know. And whenever I needed something, it just showed up. It was like a miracle to me, and I kept getting more excited about being here, and after a while I couldn't imagine being anywhere else. So, I just kept staying and staying.'"

Dennis broke in. "Did you sleep in the Greek theater again?"

Kiki shook her head. "No, I went into the music building and found a window that would open in a, like, small room with a piano in it. I crawled in that window with my things and slept on the floor for a couple of nights."

"Where did you keep your things during the day?" asked the head of security. "We would have seen you for sure, if you had walked around all day lugging a bedroll."

"I hid my things in the bottom of a trash barrel I found by the music building, until I got into Olsen Hall when the fence was taken down. Once I saw the inside of the dorm, I really wanted to stay there. I don't know how to explain it. It's like if you're a kid, and you think you'll never see Disneyland, and then one day, you're standing right in the middle of Disneyland—well, you wouldn't want to go home until you'd been on every ride, would you?" She stopped for a moment and cried silently.

The administrators all looked at her thoughtfully and with great patience.

Kiki dried her eyes, looked up, and then continued. "I knew I couldn't afford to go to school here. Since I only completed the eleventh grade, I have another year of high school before I can even think of college, and then I'd have to save money and find a school and get admission. That's the real thing. And then there's this dream, and I'm living this dream and I'm here and I just didn't know how to let it go." She sniffed a couple of times.

Melissa interrupted. "But while you're in this dream, you managed to figure out how to get into a complete schedule of freshmen classes, to get syllabuses, study, even take exams, from what I gather. Dr. Ramirez says you've turned in work in her class, and I understand there was an anonymous test score of 89 in psychology which might belong to you."

"Yes," Kiki admitted, flushing. "That was my test. I didn't put my name on it, because I wasn't registered, and I knew that it might lead to me. It was enough to know I could pass the test."

Before anyone was able react to her amazing story, Kiki continued, "I did have help. Some students from the economics class brought me books and papers that I needed and sheets for my bed. I think the key to the dorm came from one of them. I don't know for sure, because it was just shoved under my door. We had a deal that they'd keep quiet about me if I typed papers for them on a library computer and did their laundry. I didn't mind because I learned a lot about grammar by typing their papers. They all had a much better education than me—my school in the South Bronx wasn't the greatest."

Seitzman looked thoughtful for a moment. "So these girls were kind of blackmailing you," he suggested.

Kiki looked at him, taken aback. "Well—"

McNally chose to cut off this line of questioning and quickly put in, "And you held two jobs while doing all this."

"Yes, sir," Kiki admitted. "I left home with a little more than $300, but after a bus ticket and some meals, I had almost no cash when I arrived in California. The campus mail box was $45, and I had to send for my birth certificate to get a job, so I didn't have much left. If Jim Williams hadn't hired me right away at his pizza parlor, I don't know what would have happened to me."

The Rev. Nancy Raines, who had been watching quietly until now, spoke up. "Kiki, what do you want most?"

Kiki sighed. "To stop running. It's been exciting but it's hard. I hope you don't send me to jail, because I didn't mean any harm, and I tried not to use anything I didn't have to. Although I know having the key was wrong, I had to sit outside sometimes for an hour at night before someone would come by who was going into the dorm, and I was really tired and sometimes cold after working at the pizza shop. So I was glad to have the key. It was like a miracle when I found it."

Nancy Raines persisted. "After this is all settled, what do you want?"

"To find a place to live, official like, and get a job and finish high school and then apply to college, the right way."

"How long do you think it will take you to be ready for college?"

Kiki looked down at the floor. "A long time, I'm afraid."

Nancy asked, "Would you consider going back to New York?"

Kiki shook her head. "No, there's nothing there for me. My mama and papa have too many troubles. Jobs are hard to find. I have one brother in jail and another one on his way there. There's no way for me to get ahead in the South Bronx. I have to make it on my own."

McNally pushed back his chair. "Well, Kiki, I think that's all we need to hear from you right now." He glanced at the others. "The dean and I and the rest of this committee have some thinking to do, and meanwhile, I believe the dean will agree with me that it's best for you to go on with what you are doing right now, healing from your accident in the dining hall, sitting in on classes if you feel able, and being patient. For the moment, you don't have to do anything. We'll be talking with you again soon, and hopefully we can work out something to resolve this uncomfortable situation."

He paused for a moment to let this sink in. Then he added, "One thing, though, you have some very vocal friends. For right now, it would be best for you to keep a low profile about this meeting and any others that we might have. Do you think you can do that?"

Kiki looked around the room. No one looked angry or spiteful. She glanced at Rita Capehart, who smiled at her kindly. "Okay," she agreed, "I'll just go on and wait."

The group of administrators stood up and watched quietly as Rita Capehart gave Kiki a hand in getting to her feet and then led her to the door, which Rita opened for her.

Annibella was waiting in the hallway. She drove Kiki back to Olsen Hall and commented to her along the way, "Kiki, I gather you handled yourself very well in a difficult situation. I've always believed in honesty myself, even though it isn't easy in a complicated world.

I suspect you were open and frank, and I hope that your candor will work for you. Have a good evening."

Back in the conference room, Melissa and her panel of experts looked at each other in a long, long silence. Each was clearly mulling over Kiki's story. All of them came from backgrounds of privilege, at least in comparison to this teenager. In their careers they had undoubtedly seen poor students, they had all known some moments of financial duress, yet none of them had likely experienced the kind of abject poverty from which Kiki had emerged.

Nancy Raines finally broke the silence. "I think we all have a lot to consider—and maybe a lot to be personally thankful for."

Melissa shoved a pencil back and forth across the pad in front of her. "I know I don't know the answer right now. All I have are a lot of questions. For example, what are the absolute limits on residency in California to be eligible for grants in aid and scholarships, when is the next SAT exam to be given, and is there someone who has the time to coach Kiki Rodriguez and take her to the exam—who knows, it might be given in Sacramento, for all we know—and Dennis, whatever happened to that early admissions program we had back in the '50s and '60s? I know we don't use it anymore, but was it taken off the books?"

Nancy stood up, crossed the room and turned in the doorway with a slight smile on her face. "I'm free and willing to coach, and my car has plenty of gas. Just let me know."

Rita grabbed her purse. "You sound open-minded, Melissa, and I'm glad. A score of 89 percent on a freshman psych test by a high school student is promising, to say the least—I'm glad you noticed the potential as well as the problems."

Dennis rose to his feet. "Well, Melissa, although you've always had the reputation of being the toughest Dean of Students this school's ever had, I think you're a softy at heart."

"Be quiet, Dennis," Melissa chuckled.

Harold Seitzman shook his head. "Well now that I know who she is, you can be sure we'll be keepin' an eye on her."

"But subtly, Harold, very subtly," Melissa commanded.

10

Nancy

Rita Capehart and Melissa Johan met for a hasty luncheon in the privacy of Melissa's office. The dean's secretary had ordered salads from the tea shop and personally delivered them with large paper cups filled with iced tea. These two busy women enjoyed each other's company and treasured an occasional lunch amidst their ongoing campus responsibilities.

Rita tucked into her salad. Between bites, she asked, "So how is the investigation coming?"

Melissa nodded as she pushed a forkful of salad into her mouth and held up a hand to ask Rita to wait a minute. After swallowing her food, she commented. "It's coming. Dennis found there is nothing in the charter to prevent us from admitting a potential student without benefit of a high school diploma—provided that student meets all the normal standards and requirements. In this case, without a SAT score or anything, we're on totally unknown ground."

Rita paused, fork in mid air. "I take it that you are actually trying to find a way to admit this girl to the college," she observed.

"Well, I don't know. I can't make any decision myself, anyway, until Anita gets back from the East Coast. She'll have to be consulted and may have strong feelings about what we do. I have no idea what her thinking would be, and it's not something to drop at her feet long distance. Of course, it would be my luck that Sonia Yakimari is in Southern California on a recruiting trip this week, and as Director of Admissions, this is really her baby to deal with. But at least, I can do research so that Anita and Sonia can have data with which to make a decision."

"It's sticky, either way," Rita noted.

"Yes," Melissa agreed.

"How's John?" Rita asked, changing the subject in the direction of Melissa's marriage partner.

"He's fine. Up to his ears in legal briefs, as usual, but he's very aware that I'm preoccupied with something at the college. I'm not sure that I want to bring him into this, so there's a little wall right now."

Rita toyed with her salad. "You know, I've lost a lot of sleep over this girl, since we had that meeting," she commented. "She seems so terribly young, if you know what I mean. She's eighteen, yet she's *very* young and quite naive. All feelings, emotions and hungers. It was quite remarkable for her to make it all the way here from New York and even more remarkable for her to hide out for such a long time. I wonder about her staying power over the long haul, if by the wildest stretch of the imagination you decide to admit her formally as a student."

"What do you mean?"

"Well, she took off from home rather suddenly, on a fantasy trip, and if it gets tough here, which it will eventually, she might wake up one morning and decide the pressure is too much—and we could be left holding the bag. She has a real story to tell, if she wanted to tell it."

"I see," observed Melissa with a thoughtful nod.

"Honestly, my own intuition tells me that she is a good kid. I don't sense any maliciousness in her. In fact, she appears amazingly free of bitterness to be coming from the kind of background she has suggested. That's good. I also sense that she is very vulnerable. She's open to being manipulated—by Karen Fullerton, for example—and the politics of a campus are different from what she's known on the streets in the South Bronx," Rita explained.

"So what are you suggesting?"

"Well, if you are going to put her through a SAT exam to determine her college potential, I think you should also give her some personality tests, at least the MMPI-2, so we can get a handle on her level of personality integration. She's probably had inadequate parental nurturing, her siblings appear to be a negative influence, she has had little on the material level, and who knows about her emotional stability."

Rita looked at Melissa to see if she was getting the point and then added, "The majority of our students come from comparatively privileged backgrounds where they have been empowered to believe in their worth before they apply to this school. Few of our students, even those on scholarships, are as disadvantaged as this girl. Hiding out alone is one thing. Fitting in with a group of students is another. And fitting in with whom? Karen Fullerton has a hidden agenda for Kiki's rebellious actions here at Montrose, and Karen will use it for her own greater good. We both know how persuasive Karen can be."

Melissa thought for a moment. "Okay, so we test her. And if she comes up okay?"

Rita dropped her fork into her salad and pushed the bowl aside. "Then I would feel a bit safer in recommending her admission, if that is in fact what you all decide. I would also suggest that she be connected with an advisor who could do some personal counseling with her, as much as she wants or needs. I would gladly volunteer for that—I don't mind finding the time for her, and I wouldn't want to trust her to an intern who'll get all emotionally gooey over this wondrous kid and not be able to keep a clear perspective."

"So, it sounds like you think we're going to admit her."

"I don't know. I can tell that it might be a real possibility."

Melissa chuckled. "Then you are quite the mind reader, because I haven't the foggiest idea what will happen. I'm just collecting data."

Rita smiled. "Right, Melissa."

Kiki was invited to take the Minnesota Multiphasic Personality

Inventory. Just the name was a bit daunting; however, she agreed to take the four-hour test as much out of curiosity as to any real understanding of its purpose. Colleges, she considered, seemed to be places where lots of exams were taken. She certainly could handle this one.

When Kiki had completed the examination, Rita Capehart personally scored it and then wrote a confidential report to Melissa Johan. It summarized: "Basically normal range on scores except one area and an indication that she was honest in her answers. The area of concern is sexuality. While most eighteen-year olds are interested in sex and sexual subjects, her score indicates either sexual repression or possible homosexuality."

Melissa looked over the report. "This was my concern as well," she admitted to Rita when they spoke again. "Karen Fullerton has already befriended her, and perhaps we will find that this girl is coming out as a lesbian. If so, so be it. At the same time, she is very young and seemingly inexperienced, and I would like her to figure this out on her own, not out of peer pressure. More reason for some good counseling, if she stays on campus." She looked at Rita. "I'm glad you are willing to take her on for a few sessions, if we get to that point."

Each evening that week, Kiki met with Nancy Raines. They used her office in the college chapel to prepare for the SAT, which Nancy explained was an achievement test that helped determine college aptitude. She pulled up a chair for Kiki, who maneuvered herself into the seat and stowed her crutches. The two then sat next to each other looking at sample questions for the exam.

Nancy was small and quiet, a gentle young woman with blonde hair and deep blue eyes—the first woman minister the college had ever hired and one who was *very* sensitive about her visibility and her position. Like Melissa, Nancy was being watched, and it was apparent that she had to do well for other women to follow in her path. And it wasn't easy. At this moment in time, organized religion had a very low approval rating among many college-age students—especially as diverse and international as this liberal-arts campus was. Based on her own experiences, Nancy knew that students were often in the process of re-evaluating and breaking away from parental values and edicts. Additionally, those from Asian backgrounds often came armed with practices of prayer or meditation that differed from those of major Western religions. Ultimately, Nancy found that she had a real challenge in reaching out to the more mature staff and faculty members who would occasionally come to services and the few students who did attend. Her flock was definitely *small* on Sunday mornings. To justify her position at the college, she also did personal counseling and taught religion classes.

When she sat down with Kiki the first evening, Nancy knew immediately that coaching her was going to be fun. Kiki clearly was hungry to learn. She was open-minded and absorbed every thought, idea, and concept that came her way.

The downside was that Kiki's educational background was relatively poor, and Nancy had to call upon her own vast store of patience—learned during several summers of tending sheep on a Wyoming ranch—to stay in tune with Kiki as she tackled grammar, literature, and math concepts for which she was poorly prepared. And they had only a week to get ready for a SAT exam being offered in Berkeley the following Saturday.

Nancy realized it was a daunting task for both of them. She started off simply. "Ok, let's pretend you are a farmer with a dozen sheep. And three of them run off. How many sheep to you have left?"

"Nine, of course," Kiki responded with a giggle.

"Good." Nancy smiled. "You will have questions that are harder than this one, but this gives you the idea. You read the question carefully, and don't jump to conclusions until you feel sure, or until it's the best guess you can possibly make."

Kiki nodded.

"For example," Nancy continued, "you have a dozen sheep. Two females give birth to two lambs and one female gives birth to one lamb. How many females with their lambs do you then have?"

"Should be eight, I think," Kiki said, after a moment's thought.

"You are right. The point is that you have to be careful to be sure of exactly what is being asked. Not just lambs, not just females, and not all the sheep together. The answers will offer you all those choices—seventeen, five, and eight. All those could be correct depending on *exactly* what the question is." She told Kiki to take her time, count on her fingers, makes notes with a pencil, whatever she needed to do, and just not to jump to a conclusion.

Kiki smiled. "Okay, I think I have the idea."

Nancy went through a series of basic math questions. Each one was more difficult. Kiki eventually stalled and looked frustrated, and Nancy stopped at that point. She moved on to English grammar and literature, beginning again with fairly easy questions that would give Kiki an idea about how to tackle the exam.

When both became tired, they quit and planned to meet again the next day.

Melissa called Nancy for an update, and the chaplain was honest with the dean. "Kiki can learn it, but if you want her to take the exam right away, her scores will reflect her lack of preparation. Only you know how low a score you can allow in justifying her admission as a college student—unless you are trying to prove that she *can't* do it."

"Well," Melissa replied a bit uneasily. "Do your best. She has to take the test on Saturday. Just tell *her* it's practice. And it is! If she can't do it this time, it's practice for the next time, whenever she's ready."

Yeah, Nancy thought, as she hung up the phone. If they didn't allow Kiki to stay now, when would she ever find the money and the courage to try again? *Get real, folks!*

When the two finished their next evening of studying, and before Kiki returned to Olsen Hall, they sat together on the steps in front of the chapel and watched the stars. Nancy also was a stargazer, except unlike Kiki, she knew the proper names for many constellations and individual stars.

"I have my own star," Kiki confessed. "See up there where that big one is shining? Then look to the right, just down a bit, and see that one that blinks? That's mine. Although I don't know the real name, I call it Artemis, after the Greek goddess. She's my guide, and I talk to her. I used to go up on the rooftop in the South Bronx and just lie there for hours watching her and thinking."

Nancy smiled. "That's very special. Artemis was very strong and independent. I think you've made a good choice. So, keep your star, and don't change anything just because someone tells you that the name is wrong. Okay? If she's Artemis to you, then she's your star, just that way."

Kiki looked at her in the pale light cast from a street lamp. "Karen Fullerton told me that you're a lesbian," she said, somewhat shyly.

"Yes," Nancy answered, "I am. I don't hide it, and didn't hide it when they hired me. However, I also keep a low profile. My being a lesbian makes my job harder in some ways, because there is still so much homophobia in the world, although at times I find I can be a friend to someone who needs one."

"How did you know that you were a lesbian?" Kiki asked.

Nancy, whose blonde hair framed an oval face, grinned warmly. "It's a long story, Kiki, and one I don't mind sharing under the right circumstances. At the moment, however, I have two questions for you—are you trying to resolve something about your own sexuality, *and* are you discussing this subject now to avoid dealing with your feelings about the SAT?"

Kiki burst into laughter. "The answer is yes to both questions, I guess," she admitted.

"Well, what *are* you feeling about the SAT?"

"Terrified."

Nancy smiled gently. "With good reason. It's a scary test." She touched Kiki's arm. "There is so much riding on it, for you and for everyone else who takes it. Colleges everywhere use this test in ways that don't always make sense. It isn't going to be easy for you, because the test measures so many intangible things and is subtly biased culturally."

She let Kiki think about that for a moment.

Kiki glanced at her and asked, "You mean there are things I won't know because of where I grew up?"

Nancy nodded. "It's not fair; it's just the way it's done. So don't fault yourself for not being able to answer every question."

Kiki shrugged.

Nancy patted her shoulder and then continued, "Because the questions have multiple choice answers, you'll do best if you trust yourself. Rule out answers that are obviously wrong, and then pay attention to your gut level instinct in choosing between the ones that sound most correct. Your first guess is usually your best. I think you'll do fine on some chunks of the test; there will be other areas which will overwhelm you with large words and sophisticated concepts."

Kiki heaved a big sigh.

Nancy paused and then added, "If a question makes no sense to you, skip it and go on to others that feel more familiar. I expect your literature scores will be much higher than your math scores, but Montrose College really doesn't concern itself seriously, as a liberal arts campus, with math unless you have professed an interest in a math- or science-oriented major. What they want to know is how well you stand up in a stressful, testing situation and to know if you can handle the English language and literature well enough to compete effectively with other Montrose students. Since the current enrollment is very international in scope, with many students having learned English as a second language, I think you stand a chance to score well enough to be admitted."

Kiki looked at Nancy with surprise. "Really?"

Nancy nodded. "Well, in terms of the test itself. There are so many factors involved in college admissions that I have absolutely no idea what President Ryerson will say when she returns, or Sonia Yakimari, Director of Admissions, who is due back on campus tomorrow. You may just be practicing for admission to this or another college somewhere down the road; however, since you've been given this opportunity, it's worth it to try, isn't it?"

Kiki thought a moment. "Yes, but I am really frightened. I can't sleep at night. I keep thinking about all these things, and I still have to focus on the classes I'm attending right now. It's hard."

Nancy agreed. "You're right, it is. You didn't carve out an easy path for yourself when you left home and set yourself down in the middle of a prestigious women's college in California. Since you're here, just do the best that you can."

Kiki struggled to her feet. "Well, I need to get back to Olsen Hall. Thanks for all the help."

Nancy smiled. "I'll see you tomorrow evening."

Kiki had mastered the crutches she would be using for the next couple of weeks and rather than asking Nancy for a ride, she took off on foot and crutches across the meadow toward Olsen. Even with her SAT manual tucked under one arm, she was able to navigate just fine.

Watching her go, Nancy grinned and shook her head. *That girl had guts.*

Sonia Yakimari peeped into Melissa's office. Sonia was petite, with sparkling brown eyes, shining black hair, and a warm, open smile. She was the perfect college recruiter, because everyone loved her instantly.

"Hi, Melissa," she greeted.

Melissa looked up from a pile of papers. "Oh, hi, Sonia. You're just the person I wanted to see. How was your trip?"

"Great, really great. I found several prospective students in the LA area and a few in San Diego. Really quality girls who are quite enthusiastic about our program."

Melissa smiled. "That's good, really good."

Sonia raised an eyebrow. "I found a note that you needed to see me right away. What's up?"

"Well," Melissa acknowledged, standing up and going to close her office door. "You're never going to believe what happened while you were gone." She launched into an hour's detailed account of Kiki Rodriguez, an improbable story that held Sonia spellbound.

"You're right," Sonia admitted when Melissa had finished the tale. "I don't believe it. However, I guess I'm going to have to. So we have these choices—kick her out, have her arrested, or consider admitting her as a student? No diploma, no money, no SAT scores, nothing? Right now, not even an application for admission? That's quite a lot to swallow in one sitting," Sonia commented.

"Yes, it's been a lot for all of us. Imagine Harold's reaction when he found that this girl has been on campus for several weeks and his security patrols never noticed anything out of place. She's been going in and out of every building and attending classes, and no one has said a word."

Sonia shrugged. "Well, obviously President Ryerson will hit the ceiling when she gets back. As far as arresting this kid, I know I'm not any legal expert, yet wouldn't we have had to do that immediately, for it to stick?"

"I suspect so. However, I don't think having her jailed is very desirable to anyone. Too much chance of the story getting out to the press, for one thing. I think the real question here is whether she is suitable for admission, formally, to Montrose. That's what we're going to have to decide."

Sonia nodded. "Yes, I agree. As for my office, I want two things right off—to interview her personally, and to get some SAT scores on her. I might as well have her fill out an application for admission, just in case."

Melissa looked at her questioningly. "I take it that you are not totally opposed to her being admitted?"

"I don't know enough to take a position on Kiki Rodriguez one way or the other. It's certainly a strange way to get into college, but I can assure you that if this girl hadn't found us, we would never have found her. Maybe there's a reason she's here, so I'm not going to rule out any possibility, without exploring everything first. "

Late the next afternoon, Kiki met Sonia Yakimari, Director of Admissions for Montrose College for Women. Kiki was suitably in awe, partly because Sonia obviously had a complex family tree, like Kiki's, and because Sonia was young, energetic, and attractive—all things in a woman that would undoubtedly impress someone like Kiki.

From her side of the desk, Sonia saw a nervous teenager who was still struggling with crutches from her accident in the dining hall kitchen. Sonia chose to overlook her appearance and was soon impressed by Kiki's openness, desire, and positive attitude. Her story left the administrator emotionally affected. Sonia did feel that Kiki was very young to be carrying such a load of responsibility. At the same time, the administrator felt that life *also* would have been hard for Kiki back home, and that here she was making sacrifices on her own behalf, rather than because of family issues. Perhaps it was worth it.

After listening and considering, Sonia decided to offer Kiki an application for admission to Montrose. She asked Kiki to fill out all the pages and submit the form as quickly as possible.

"If you need help, come back to this office, and we'll sort it out," Sonia offered before Kiki left.

Kiki sat on her bed in the dark basement room and looked over the application. She was totally overwhelmed. The form was lengthy and demanded all kinds of things, from letters of recommendation, to information on high school interests and activities, to a lengthy essay on why she wanted to attend this school. After she read the entire application, she curled up on the bed and cried. It was just too much.

As luck would have it, Karen Fullerton stopped by that afternoon. She was excited to see the application in Kiki's possession. Karen immediately termed it a good omen. When Kiki, obviously upset, told her that she couldn't fill it out, Karen took over. "Look, it's no big deal," she explained. "I'll help you with it. We'll put together something that will impress the hell out of them."

Kiki studied her. "I need your help, I can see that. But whatever we put in this application has to be honest, okay?"

"Okay," Karen agreed, with one raised eyebrow. It obviously would not have been her personal style.

Karen sat down on the bed beside Kiki, and the two of them went over the application very carefully. With prodding, Kiki thought of a couple of high school teachers who had liked her and might write something on her behalf. She also thought of Sal, who expressed herself very well, and was a recent, if brief, acquaintance who knew how much Kiki wanted an education. Karen thought that Sal, if available, was acceptable, as long as the high school teachers wrote good letters. Then Kiki would be all set.

"Now," Karen laughed. "See how easy it is. You write a note to those two teachers, telling them of this wonderful opportunity you have and asking them to support you with good letters of recommendation. They'll be impressed to know you're possibly going to school at Montrose College, and they'll bend over backwards to help you."

Kiki looked at her doubtfully.

"Believe me, I know teachers' egos," Karen affirmed, giving Kiki a little tap on the arm. "We'll FAX your requests, so they can get their letters back here quickly. Stress that you need these *now*, this week if possible, for this semester, not next semester, nor next year. Call your friend Sal in Salt Lake City. Hopefully, she'll be in town and not on the East Coast or somewhere else. Now, why do you want to go to school here?"

Kiki thought for a moment, "Well, because I see all these women doing wonderful things, and I've never seen that before. And I want to do something with my life, and I feel that if I can see and learn from these women, I can become like them. Does that make sense?"

"Sure, you need role models. Your family couldn't provide them for you, and this school could—better than a co-ed college, where men might dominate in the classroom. So, you're saying you don't just want to go to any college, you specifically want to go to a women's college. Right?"

"Well, I hadn't thought of it that way, yet I was really excited when I found out that Montrose was a college for women. The idea made it seem special somehow."

"Just say that, in your own words. Put all your excitement and enthusiasm into a letter about why you want to be in this very place, right now, and what an education here would mean to you. After you write it in your own way, I'll help you dress it up a little."

Kiki was ecstatic, her tears having dried. "Oh, thank you, Karen. This is wonderful!"

Late that evening, Kiki called Sal in Salt Lake City. This time Sal was home and was very happy to hear from Kiki. It had been weeks since they had talked.

"Are you okay?" Sal asked with concern.

"Oh, yeah. I've had two different jobs, one in a pizza place—I think I wrote you about that—and one washing dishes in the college dining hall. I fell and sprained an ankle; otherwise, I'm just fine."

Sal was surprised. "You mean you're still at Montrose?"

"Yes," Kiki admitted enthusiastically, "and I'm in the process of applying for admission."

"Don't you have to graduate from high school first?"

"Well, they have some program here, where they can admit you after your junior year in high school. And while it's not for sure yet, they're letting me apply."

"I take it you're not hiding out anymore, thank God."

"No, they caught me, when I fell in the dining hall. It's a long story, and they're not sure whether they're going to kick me out or admit me. It's the craziest thing. I'm taking some test for admission they call the 'SAT' next week and I'm filling out paperwork. Which is why I called. Do you feel you know me well enough to write a letter recommending me?" Kiki asked the question a bit hesitantly.

Sal was quiet for a moment. "Kiki, I'm really flattered. However, do you think I'm what you need, a truck driver?"

"I have two letters coming from high school teachers. You saw me in a totally different way, on the road, and very recently. Could you just write about your impressions of me as a person and my goals?" Kiki was scared Sal would say no.

Sal laughed. "Sure, Kiki, I'll whip something up tonight. Where do I send it?" Kiki gave her the proper name and FAX number for submitting her letter and thanked her.

Sal then added, "Well, just promise me one thing—when you finish, invite me to your graduation. I'd get a big kick out of that."

Kiki laughed. This whole thing made her feel giddy. "Of course, Sal, I want you to be there. If you hadn't let me ride with you, I might still be stuck in Kansas."

So the letters were promised, and Kiki wrote her essay. When Karen saw it she was impressed. Then she showed Kiki ways to make her sentences stronger and more persuasive.

"Isn't that lying?" Kiki asked, "if I get help beyond my own ability?"

Karen grinned with amusement. "Kiki, nobody in the world ever did absolutely everything perfectly without some help along the way. Everyone gets help with college applications. And don't kid yourself. If they let you in, by the time you graduate, you'll be writing so well that this will look like kindergarten to you. No sweat."

That night Kiki sat outside on the dorm steps looking up at Artemis blinking back at her. "I don't know what to think or feel, but my life right now is really incredible," she told her star.

11

President Ryerson

In misty fog, on Saturday morning, Nancy Raines drove Kiki to Berkeley, to a small educational complex near the University of California campus, where the SAT was being given. Kiki struggled to get out of the car and to organize herself and her belongings around the crutches.

"Are you going to be okay?" Nancy asked, leaning over from the driver's seat.

"Yes, I think so," Kiki acknowledged with a sigh. "It isn't the crutches so much as being scared about the test."

"You've done everything you could to get ready. Try to relax and just do what you can. I'll be back at noon to pick you up."

"I'll be here," Kiki assured her.

"Good luck! Remember, just trust your gut feelings."

Nancy waved and pulled away from the curb. Kiki watched her go and then turned toward the building she had to enter. There were several young men and women walking down the street, headed to the same place. *Oh well, here I go.*

One young man held the door open for her, and Kiki worked her way into the building. Inside the marked testing room, she slipped out of her rain jacket, lowered herself into a student chair, and stowed her crutches beneath the seat. Kiki glanced around and guessed she was sharing space with about seventy-five others, mostly high school juniors and seniors planning on future college enrollment, and a few older adults, some of whom looked uncomfortable—the same way she was feeling. She was glad to see the group was of mixed ethnic backgrounds, which meant others might struggle with some of the same language challenges she did.

A youthful male proctor with a three-day beard entered the room, barked instructions, and passed out the test booklets. Shortly the test was begun and, as Kiki expected, it proved very difficult. Every word required intense concentration, and each test section was timed. Sometimes, Kiki would feel that she had gotten the sense of a question, when a big word would throw her and leave her momentarily confused. Then she would get a grasp again and try to perceive the meaning of the whole instead of getting lost in one detail.

Thankfully, there were enough questions with clear answers that Kiki didn't feel at a total loss. The math was really hard, because she had never liked it in high school and had promptly forgotten every concept the minute the test on that material was completed. Admitting to herself that she would not score well in math, she put her major effort into English comprehension and grammar, where Nancy Raines had helped her focus.

When the proctor called the final "time," Kiki felt drained, exhausted and very hungry. She limped her way outside the building, waited, and within a few minutes, Nancy arrived to pick her up. Kiki flagged her down by waving a crutch and then worked her way into the car. Nancy watched her and also kept an eye on traffic—she was stopped in a yellow zone that was the only place she could find near the examination building.

"How was it?" Nancy asked after Kiki was seated and her seat belt fastened.

"Hard, but I did my best. I have to be satisfied, whatever happens."

"Well, I'll bet you're hungry," Nancy commented, as she carefully pulled out into a lane of traffic.

"Yes, I could hardly eat breakfast this morning, because I was so nervous, and now I'm famished."

"Well, I thought about taking you to a restaurant to celebrate, but then I decided, since you eat pizza and dining hall food all the time, that maybe a home cooked meal would be the best celebration? What do you say?"

Kiki smiled. "That would be great," she replied with enthusiasm.

"Good. I'm taking you to my home, which is near here in the Berkeley Hills. You'll enjoy the view and you can meet my life partner, Paula, who's a veterinarian. And our three cats."

Kiki was thrilled. *A good day was ahead, now that the test was behind her!* The thought of seeing a home in which two women lived together reminded her of Sal and Meg in Salt Lake City. She noticed that even the sky was clearing up—a good omen, she decided.

Before long, they reached the house, an older style two-story frame dwelling with a front porch, a fireplace in the living room, and lots of big windows. Compared to Kiki's tiny basement hideaway in the dorm, this house seemed like paradise. A calico cat sat on the front step, and inside she met a gray cat and a chocolate and white kitten. Kiki petted them and asked their names. "The calico is Muffins," Nancy explained. "We call the gray cat Phantom, and the kitten is Oreo."

Paula Franklin, tall and slender with hazel eyes and a light brown ponytail, came out of the kitchen. "Hello, Kiki," she greeted warmly. "Nancy has told me all about you. Welcome, please make yourself comfortable. I'll have lunch ready in a minute. I hope you'll enjoy a chicken casserole and a fresh salad."

"Sounds delicious!" Kiki exclaimed. She was instantly in heaven.

Nancy and Paula made over her, saw that she was comfortable at the table, fed her mountains of food, including a big bowl of ice cream for dessert, and asked her all about her adventures. Although Nancy knew most of the story, she enjoyed the retelling, and Paula was intrigued. Both of them agreed that Sal Turner must be somebody special and admitted that Kiki was very lucky to have met her at just the right time.

When Kiki finished her story, she suddenly realized that she was very tired.

Nancy noticed Kiki's heavy eyelids and suggested, "Kiki, you look like you need some rest."

Kiki nodded. "Yeah, I feel really exhausted." She yawned. "I guess I've been through a lot."

Nancy smiled. "Well, I can drive you back to school now or, if you like, you can have a nap in our guest bedroom, and I'll take you back a little later."

Kiki admitted, "I feel as if I could fall asleep right this minute, so if you don't mind, I'll just stay here."

Nancy showed her the room, pulled back a comforter for her, and left the door ajar. Kiki could hear the two of them talking in the other room, and she could sense their closeness and compassion toward her. Feeling supported by it, Kiki began to fall into a deep, contented sleep. As she slept, Muffins climbed up onto the bed, sniffed around, and curled up into a ball beside her, purring.

When Kiki awoke, it was dark. The house seemed very quiet. She climbed out of bed, found her crutches, and pushed the door open wider so she could enter the living room. Muffins followed.

Nancy was sitting quietly reading in the warm glow of a single lamp in the living room. She looked up and smiled at Kiki.

"You're awake! Did you have a good rest?"

"Oh, yes. I don't think I've slept that well in a long, long time. I hardly know how to adequately thank you for feeding me and letting me stay," Kiki said sincerely.

"Well, I'm glad it helped. We've had some dinner, and I saved a plate for you. Paula had an emergency call at the clinic. An Australian shepherd was hit by a car, and she went in to do surgery on its leg. I don't know how soon she'll be back."

Nancy found Kiki a comfortable chair in the living room and brought her a small plate of food. Then she relaxed in her own chair and watched Kiki for a few moments.

Finally, she spoke. "Kiki, a few days ago you asked me some questions about my sexuality, and I put you off at the time, because you needed to focus on the SAT. Now that the exam is over, I don't want to seem to be avoiding your issues, if that is still something you feel like discussing."

Kiki finished off the last of her meal.

"That tasted so good." She laughed and then looked at Nancy a bit shyly. "Well, yes, I am—well, uh, interested."

Nancy tried to make the subject easier. "Are you asking because of feelings inside yourself, or because you are curious to understand me, or—?"

"Mostly, I'm confused about me," Kiki admitted. "I've never been much into boys, except as pals. I'm not sure what I feel toward women or what I want or what I could handle. However, I seem to keep meeting, or being found by, lesbians, and I'm beginning to wonder if there is some reason this keeps happening. Is there something about me? I just don't know, and I want to understand why people are that way, and how do they know?" Kiki blushed. "I'm a bit shy about the topic, if you know what I mean."

Nancy nodded and gave Kiki a gentle smile. "Fair questions, and it sounds as if you have good reasons for asking them. Well, speaking from my own experience, I think people discover their sexual orientation at different times in their lives and for different reasons. Some girls just grow up knowing from the outset that they prefer women as friends, companions and, later, lovers. Other women start off being attracted to men, for any number of reasons, and later discover that they are more satisfied being with women. Still others push their sexuality down because of outside pressures from family, church, or society and then have to find a way to get in touch with themselves much later in life, if they ever do."

Kiki was thoughtful for a moment and then asked, "How did you know?"

"Well, I kind of always knew that I was different. At first I tried to elevate my feelings into some sort of spirituality, and then gradually, I realized that I couldn't use religion as a place to hide. Although religion provided me with a satisfying career, I needed to have a personal life as well. I explored the bar scene and social groups, and I was beginning to get a bit discouraged because I didn't seem to fit in. Then I was lucky enough to meet Paula, and we have been together ever since. We are a professional couple, and we are both private about our personal lives. We have a few close lesbian friends, but otherwise, we don't deal with our sexuality out in the world—and the world, for the most part, doesn't care."

With a warm smile, she continued, "Now, you're going to meet all kinds of lesbians, especially in a place like Montrose, where there is a special sensitivity over this issue. The school, as a women's college, is going to attract a lot of lesbians and women who are less dominated by an interest in men. Of course the institution doesn't want to be identified as a lesbian school, for rather obvious financial reasons, so the college will *acknowledge* sexual diversity yet not go out of its way to endorse it."

Nancy paused for a moment to let what she was saying sink in. "A few decades ago," she continued, "there was—throughout the country—active repression of homosexuality, and among older college faculty and staff, you will still find homophobic heterosexuals and closet lesbians who are terrified of being open about their lives. I feel sorry for both groups, because they are missing so much, but I especially feel sorry for the lesbians who have had to invent complex subterfuges to keep their personal lives secret out of fear of losing their jobs. In many places now, no one would punish them; however, many have lived this way for so long that it is hard for them to change."

Kiki nodded. "I guess it would be difficult after a lifetime of hiding."

"Among the younger adults and the students, you will find more acceptance, outspoken individuals, and even radical, political lesbians like Karen Fullerton, whom I understand is your friend."

Kiki laughed. "Yes, it's hard not to know where Karen is coming from. She's been helpful to me, but I have to be careful around her, or she'd be running my life."

Nancy grinned. "Well, at least you're aware of that fact. It is so important that you listen to your own inner cues and find your own truth, rather than borrow someone else's."

Kiki looked thoughtful. "That's hard to do, sometimes, since I've been hidden in the basement and lonely."

Nancy nodded. "Yes, I'm sure it is. Hopefully, all that will change soon. And whether you leave Montrose, or stay on as a student, you will encounter a variety of people, have difference experiences with your friends, and then find your niche. Just remember that your path to your own lifestyle and sexuality is solely *your* unique journey."

Sonia Yakimari, in her years as admissions head, had developed contacts in important places, one of them being among those responsible for scoring the SAT. She could, and sometimes did, obtain access to SAT scores more quickly than through normal routine channels. In this case, speed was of the utmost importance. Therefore, from the moment Kiki turned in her SAT answer sheet, it was marked for priority handling and went to the head of every list as it was forwarded, scored, recorded and distributed. Once it was scored, Sonia received a long distance call with a report on Kiki's performance. A hard-copy summary followed by FAX.

Sonia went over the report carefully and then called Melissa. The two administrators met for one of their hasty luncheon discussions.

"Well," demanded Melissa. "Don't keep me waiting. What are we dealing with?"

Sonia was direct. "Her math scores were disastrous. Of course, we predicted that. Her vocabulary is woefully lacking. So is that of most of our foreign students who are learning English as a second language. That's the down side. The up side is that her ability to reason—to understand the essence of the material presented and select among the options of matching ideas and concepts—is quite good. Not brilliant, but certainly acceptable. And considering that she has not had her senior year of high school English, even better. It's my opinion, on the basis on these results, that Kiki Rodriguez should be able to compete adequately at the freshman level in our classes and has the potential to grow as a student over time."

Melissa raised an eyebrow. "So, what are you recommending, as Director of Admissions?"

"Well, that's difficult, in this particular legal situation," Sonia said with a heavy sigh. Then she looked straight at Melissa and added, "But if we could remove that and just say that we have a young woman with a burning desire to study at Montrose College, I would probably recommend early admission on probation, with the probationary status to be lifted after successful completion of one semester."

Melissa allowed those words to settle while she took a good-size bite of her Cobb salad and chewed carefully. After a sip of iced tea, she commented, "That's a very interesting conclusion. What about money? This particular student with a 'burning desire to study at Montrose' hasn't a dime to her name, her parents—from what we can gather—haven't either, and tuition, room and board is, some $38,000 a year, more or less?"

Sonia nodded. "Closer to $40,000 at last count, and I've been thinking about that. Kiki found a job within twenty-four hours of her arrival in California. That's good. That's better than even she knows. It means, by late next summer, she'll be officially a California resident and she can apply for all kinds of scholarships, grants, loans, etc. And assuming her parents will cooperate, she should be eligible. That means we just have to find a way to get her through one year, and then she can have a chance to make it on her own merit."

"So," Melissa interrupted, "where do we get $40,000?"

"Well, first we have to win over Anita. When she returns on Monday, she's going to be hit with piles of paperwork and this scandal. I have no idea what kind of mood she's going to be in; however, the first challenge will be putting Anita into a positive state of mind over this issue. If she decides that it is not only in Kiki Rodriguez's best interest to be admitted, but also in the best interest of the college, she'll be a resource rather than a hindrance. She has more fundraising ability than any president we've ever had, and she is very influential with the board of trustees, many of whom are in turn very influential citizens in the Bay Area. I'm sure that someone, somewhere, can come up with the money, provided they understand it is important to do so."

Melissa nodded. "So, we wait until Anita gets back."

"No! Absolutely not!" roared through the hallway of the administrative offices. The secretarial and support staff, accustomed to Anita Collins Ryerson's moodiness, had heard her angry before. She was a redhead with all the temper reputedly afforded to redheads, and she had intense reactions to situations and events. Yet, once she calmed down, she was a brilliant problem-solver, and she was well loved as the current college president. Today, however, something had really set her off beyond all reason. "Right here, under our noses? No one knew anything?" she could be heard to yell.

Harold Seitzman and Dennis McNally sat across the desk from Anita in her well-appointed private office and were trying to calm her.

"I don't think this young woman had any malicious intent," McNally explained.

"She was dumped off at the front gate by some Berkeley students who gave her a ride from Salt Lake City," he continued as Anita stood up and paced around the room. "It was almost dark, she didn't know the city, and she saw what looked like a safe place to spend the night. When she woke up the next morning and realized what a beautiful place she had found, she tried to stay as long as she could. She got caught up in something bigger than she intended, and once it started, it was hard to stop. It would have been kinder if we had seen her early on, when it would have been easy to ask her to leave, politely but firmly. Once she had started sitting in classrooms and no one noticed her, she had made an investment, and she had made some friends. Now it is complicated."

Anita had stopped pacing and returned to her desk, where she listened impatiently and played with a paper clip. "Friends? What friends?"

Harold sighed. "Karen Fullerton, for one."

Anita threw up her hands in despair. "That dyke?"

McNally held up a hand. "Careful, Anita, no matter what you may personally feel, you'd better keep a lid on that stuff."

Anita forced a smile. "All right, *that* young woman?"

"Yes," Seitzman said with a nod, "that *particular* young woman."

"So," continued McNally, "it isn't very expedient for us to dump her out on the street. While you were gone, Melissa Johan and Sonia Yakimari did quite a bit of research, after Harold had checked out the girl's story. They've come up with a plan that can get the school off the hook, if you'll go along with it. And I think you should listen. If we try to strong-arm this girl, she may accept it. Fullerton won't. And you know that Karen has gotten the ear of the press several times during the past three years. All Fullerton has to do is make a couple of phone calls, and this young girl will become a sacrificial lamb. Once the media gets hold of the story, several other schools will be offering her scholarships, and we'll look like fools. So, please listen carefully and think seriously before you decide what you want to do."

"All right," Anita sighed with resignation. "I guess I'd better meet with Melissa and Sonia." She called her secretary over the intercom. A meeting later that afternoon was set up with the Dean of Students and the Director of Admissions.

By the time these two colleagues arrived, Anita had calmed down and was ready to be reasonable. Melissa asked politely about Anita's trip and then presented her case. Sonia followed with the SAT scores and a plan of action. Anita was not happy about any of it, especially about approaching the board of trustees for money, although she agreed to give the entire issue some serious thought before any action was taken.

"Well," she concluded, "I guess I had better meet this girl before I decide anything. Is she available?"

Melissa nodded. "Annibella Carrera, the RA in Olsen Hall, can round her up and bring her whenever you want to see her."

Annibella dropped Kiki off at the appointed time and went to park her car. As Kiki headed for the Administration Annex, Annibella called, "I'll see you inside. Just remember—be yourself."

Kiki was still hobbling with one crutch, although she expected to be rid of it in a couple of days. Her arm was also healing nicely. It had been just over three weeks since her accident, and so much had happened to her.

She sat down in the outer office, while the receptionist announced her arrival, and waited for President Ryerson. Kiki admitted to herself that she was horribly frightened.

Presently, the door opened and a tall, redheaded woman appeared. Attractive, she wore a very professional linen suit and heels and had tiny reading glasses perched on the end of her nose. Her green eyes peered over the glasses at Kiki appraisingly.

"Miss Rodriguez?" she queried, as if there were any question as to the identity of the lone visitor. She motioned Kiki to enter her office.

Kiki hobbled inside and sat where told and put her crutch on the floor. Anita Ryerson settled behind her big mahogany desk, looked down at some papers, and then looked again at Kiki, who squirmed a bit uncomfortably under her gaze.

"You seem to have caused quite a stir on our quiet little campus," Anita observed. Her voice had an edge that was difficult for Kiki to read.

"I didn't mean to, and I'm sorry for any problems that I've caused," Kiki apologized as sincerely as she could.

"You didn't understand when you came through our gates that you were trespassing?"

Kiki shook her head. "In the beginning, that wasn't my first thought. It was nearly dark when I was dropped off. I needed a safe place to stay for the night, and I didn't have much money. I was new in town, didn't know anyone, and was basically lost. I had been given a bedroll, and when I saw all the grass and tall trees, I thought it would be safe to sleep inside the fence. I saw the sign with the name of the college on it, but it didn't mean much to me in light of my situation. I'm from New York and I had never heard of the school. I wasn't thinking beyond that night when I first came in here. It was the next morning, when I started walking around and saw how beautiful it was, that I began wishing I could stay for a while. Nobody was around, and I wanted to explore. It was so beautiful that for me, it was something like being in Disneyland."

Anita had stood while Kiki was speaking and was now looking out her office windows at the tall Eucalyptus trees. "It is beautiful here, I'll admit," she observed. "That's one of our selling points." She looked back at Kiki. "I guess I can't blame you for being impressed when we spend a fortune making it almost seductively attractive so that students will want to come here and remain here."

Kiki nodded. "I grew up in tenements in the South Bronx. Except for a few visits to Central Park, I haven't spent a lot of time around open spaces with flowers and streams and tall trees. It was very exciting to me."

Anita forced herself to return to the subject at hand. "And you never really conspired to take advantage of the school, without proper admission?"

"I was curious, but I never really thought beyond day-to-day survival, and to stay here as long as I could. And," she added apologetically, "I tried not to use anything I didn't have to."

Kiki paused for a moment, and sighed, studying the college president's solemn expression. "I don't have a high school diploma," she continued, "so the thought of applying for admission was totally beyond me. I didn't know it was even possible. I just wanted to see what a college like this was like. After I managed to remain long enough for classes to start, I got caught up in the wonder of that, and I just wanted to sit and listen. I didn't expect anything, except just a chance to, well, absorb what I could."

Anita studied her. "So, how do you feel now, after having been here for, what, nearly two months?"

Kiki looked at the president directly. "I still love it. I think it's the most wonderful place I've ever seen, and I wish I could stay. I know that's not realistic, and I am prepared to let go and leave," she admitted, her voice shaking with tears that were just below the surface.

Anita looked away, studying the trees again for a long moment. "What if the college could find a way for you to continue here, officially, would you want to become a Montrose student?"

Kiki leaned forward in her chair, her heart pounding. "Oh, yes, I would do the very best I could. It seems beyond my wildest dreams, and I don't understand how it could be possible, but I would try my best."

Anita looked at her, this time her eyes a bit softer. "Well, I have a lot of thinking to do about this. Continue on as you have been, and very quietly, please, and either Dean Johan or I will be contacting you in a few days. Meanwhile, please don't talk about this until we have further word for you."

Kiki nodded. "Oh, yes, I understand." She stood up and adjusted her crutch under her arm. She tentatively stretched out her hand to the president. "Thank you for taking the time to talk with me. I know you are very busy, and I feel honored to have met you," she said, still in awe and with her voice trembling with fear.

After shaking hands with Kiki, Anita watched her leave the room and then looked down at her own hand, where she felt the remaining sensation of the young woman's grip. She again thoughtfully glanced out at the Eucalyptus trees. She wasn't sure what she was going to do. After a long moment, Anita touched a button on the intercom and said to her receptionist, "Jeanne, get me the Chairman of the Board, will you?"

12

Kiki

Several nerve-wracking days had passed. Kiki was seated in the administration conference room, facing yet again a panel made up of the dean, the college's attorney, the psychologist, the chaplain and this time Sonia Yakimari, Director of Admissions. Kiki was again accompanied by Annibella Carrera. The college president was not in attendance, and the security chief was also blissfully absent.

Melissa Yohan took charge, greeted Kiki, and began the meeting. "Well, Kiki, I am glad to see that you have largely recovered from your fall. Mrs. Trang reports that you have returned to your work in the dining hall. Do you feel well?"

Kiki nodded. "Yes, I'm fine, thank-you." She looked from one face to another around the room, wondering what to expect. To her, the assembled group looked rather like a firing squad, so she questioned if she would soon be packing her things and leaving the campus.

"That's good," Melissa said. The dean looked uncomfortable, as if not sure what to say next. "Well," she momentarily continued, "we have done a lot of research into your unique situation. I know you are well aware of that, since you studied with Chaplain Raines for the SAT and then took the test several days ago."

Kiki nodded. *Were they getting ready to tell her that she had failed the SAT?*

Melissa cleared her throat, took a sip of water, and then continued. "As I am sure you can guess, we have invested a lot of time and energy exploring the possibilities and consequences of your unexpected stay here. After consulting with President Ryerson, whom you have also met, and looking over your SAT scores, we have come to a conclusion. Perhaps Ms. Yakimari can explain better than I." She looked at the admissions director. "Sonia?"

Sonia glanced at her notes and smiled at Kiki. "Yes, Kiki, we have decided to offer you probationary admission to Montrose for the current semester. What this means is that you will be enrolled officially in the classes that you are now attending, and you will receive credit for the work you have done and will do for the remainder of the semester. If there are papers you have already written, you will be allowed to turn them in now, without their being counted as late. I'm sure this won't be easy, because you are starting behind in some ways. However, at the end of the semester, if your final grades are satisfactory, then probation will be lifted, and you will begin the second semester as a regular student. Do you understand what I am saying?"

Kiki nodded. She swallowed. She could feel her face turning red, and she was beginning to sweat. She couldn't believe what she was hearing. "It's wonderful, but how can I pay for it?" she dared to ask.

"Well, for the current year, that problem has been solved. President Ryerson contacted our board of trustees, and one of the members of the board was able to find an anonymous donor to insure the payment of your tuition for the remainder of this year."

Kiki was deeply touched. Tears welled in her eyes. "How can I thank all of you? It's wonderful!"

Sonia put up a hand to indicate that Kiki should wait. Then she resumed, "Now, assuming that you are successful in completing your freshman year, you should become eligible to apply for scholarships, grants-in-aid and loans to cover the remainder of your undergraduate education. This will be possible because you obtained employment and started paying taxes to the federal government and the State of California shortly after your arrival here. That was fortuitous. This money will not all be free, I must add, and by the time you graduate, you will have a debt of thousands of dollars to repay over a period of time. I'm not saying this will be easy—you picked a very expensive institution when you entered our gates. We will do our best to help you, although we cannot do it all."

Kiki nodded solemnly. "I understand and will do whatever I need to. I'm already working two jobs. I can work hard, I know that."

Dennis McNally coughed to get attention. "President Ryerson has set some conditions on your admission to the college," he explained, "and we need to be up front about these from the beginning. If you can't accept the conditions, then the offer of admission is null and void."

Kiki looked at him with apprehension. *What were they going to ask of her?*

"First," Dennis explained, "You are to promise that in no way will you take advantage of the college by seeking publicity or making money from any story regarding the way in which you obtained admission to this institution. The circumstances are most unusual and unorthodox, and the college would be embarrassed and compromised if the information were made public. If we help you to obtain the college education you seem so greatly to desire, then you must agree to protect the reputation of the school. This includes talking in detail with other students about your, well, adventure here."

Kiki frowned. "That's no problem, sir, except for the three students who already know and a friend of mine in Salt Lake City, oh, and my boss, Jim Williams, whom I haven't told exactly, yet he could probably put the pieces together if he wanted to."

Melissa spoke up. "I've already talked with Karen Fullerton, and she has been warned not to use this information. I think she understands that there would be consequences. I'm more concerned as to whether *you* feel comfortable about letting go of this past escapade and moving forward on a more stable footing here at Montrose."

Kiki nodded. "I can agree to that without any question. I wouldn't want to hurt the school, not after all the wonderful things that have happened since I came here."

Dennis resumed. "Now, Kiki, the second condition is that you contact your parents and let them know where you are and that you are safe. You had a right to leave home; however, as an institution that guides and educates young women, Montrose College cannot encourage the kind of situation in which you presently find yourself. Your parents have been worried about you. They have sought help from the police in New York to locate you."

Kiki's face fell and her eyes filled with tears. She had written a note when she left, but she hadn't really thought about the effect of her departure on the family. Now she felt deflated and ashamed. "I'll write them. I promise. I didn't mean to hurt them. I really only left for me."

Sonia inserted a thought. "We do not want to tell you that you have to be involved with your family if you don't wish it—just to let them know where you are and that you are safe. One thing you should remember, however, is that because you are under twenty-one, you will eventually need your parents to sign forms for you to obtain aid money from California. It may be in your best interest to patch things up, whatever your home problems are."

Kiki nodded. This was all so complicated. *Oh, she hadn't thought about Mama and Papa and how she must have hurt them.*

McNally continued. "Several of us have concerns that you be well guided during your stay here. We wish to make sure that you have some counseling available to you, both for selecting your course of study and for any personal problems you might encounter. Dr. Capehart, here, has volunteered to provide time for sessions for you, and we want to make sure that you understand this and will make use of her support whenever you need it."

Kiki looked at Dr. Capehart, who smiled at her warmly. Kiki hesitated because she didn't feel she could admit that she really wanted to talk with Nancy Raines, whom she already knew and trusted. She stole a glance at Nancy, who gave her a smile and a subtle wink. "Okay," Kiki nodded. "I can use all the help I can get, I know that."

Melissa took charge again. "Now, Kiki, although we can see that you are admitted to the school, we can't make it easy. There are no residence hall rooms available for this semester, so until January, you are going to have to make do with your little basement room."

Kiki swallowed and nodded.

"When the spring term begins, I feel sure that a room will open up in one of the halls, perhaps even Olsen, and we can move you into it. The arrangement for this semester is going to make it more difficult for you to integrate into the student body, but we just haven't found any other solution—besides moving you off campus, and that is fraught with all kinds of other difficulties. Looking at all sides of the question, we came to the conclusion that you've done well just as you are for the first part of this semester, and although it's not perfect, you could perhaps go on this way for another couple of months."

Kiki smiled. "It's fine. I can wait, if you just let me wait here and go to classes. That's what's important to me."

"Well," Melissa summarized, "it sounds as if we are in fundamental agreement. Ms. Yakimari will have admission papers for you to sign tomorrow morning in her office, and she will also have an agreement drawn up by our attorney, here, Mr. McNally, which she will have you sign and witness on behalf of the college."

Kiki sucked in a deep breath and gave a nod.

Sonia stood up. "Kiki, you picked a rather unique way to become a college student; however, now that you're here, welcome to Montrose." She reached out and shook Kiki's trembling hand.

Annibella ushered Kiki out of the conference room, as the college officials turned to talk with each other and seemed to move onto other issues.

When they were outside the building, Kiki could hardly contain herself. She laughed and cried at the same time and her body literally shook.

Annibella reached out and gave her a hug, and Kiki stood in the circle of her arms for a few moments, breathing deeply to calm down.

The RA smiled. "Everything is going to be okay, Kiki, believe me."

Kiki released her and a big grin gradually spread over her face. She walked toward Annibella's car, limping slightly. "I'm going to be a Montrose student!"

13

Mama

When Kiki returned to work at Big Jim's Pizza, she was still feeling both scared and thrilled. She also wanted to find some safe way to let Jim know about her college admission. Her enthusiasm suddenly dimmed when she found him sitting at a table over a pile of papers and looking very glum. He greeted her warmly yet looked unhappy.

"What's wrong?" Kiki asked, forgetting for a moment her own excitement.

"Well, I'm just not makin' it, Kiki," he admitted. "Gonna have to cut back somehow, jis' to make ends meet. I gotta keep a part-time delivery boy—ya can't drive, so I can't use ya for that. I'm jis' afraid I can't afford ya workin' for me, if business don't git better."

For a second, Kiki was crestfallen. Then her own positive spirit won out. "What can we do to get more business?" she asked.

"I don' know. I been sittin' here wrackin' my brain. This economic mess this country's in jis' throws me. They say it's 'most as bad as dat Great Depression my folks lived through." Jim sighed. "But no matter, I got a wife an' three girls to support, an' it's jis' not workin.'"

Kiki thought, trying to get a picture in her mind of what Jim could do. "Where do your customers come from?"

"The neighborhood, mostly. A few from the college, not a lot. Those girls got cars an' they takes off for nicer places. People aroun' here jis' don' have money right now. It's jis' a bad time." Jim was definitely in a funk.

"Well," Kiki observed with determination, "people still have to eat."

She thought for a few moments and then asked, "Could you cut prices a little, if it brought you more business?"

Jim thought and figured. "A little, if I did a lot more business."

"What about $1.50 off if someone bought two pizzas, two big ones?"

He calculated on a piece of paper. "I could manage dat."

"Okay," Kiki said, "I'm going to the library at Montrose and make up a flyer on the computer. I can get some colored paper in the bookstore and run it off on a copy machine. I'll put the flyers in all the dorms and on kiosks around the student union. It will be a special for Montrose students. Everybody likes special treatment, and everybody likes coupons, right?"

Jim nodded. "It sounds like a good idea. I never had much luck with those girls, but ya got my okay to try it."

Kiki rushed back to the Montrose library to whip off a flyer, after stopping at the campus bookstore for colored paper. She swallowed hard at the cost of this. However, if it made Jim some money and helped her keep her job, then it was worth the expense. Kiki made copies on the cheapest copier she could find and distributed the flyers everywhere on campus that she could hang them. She even slipped them on the windshields of cars parked in front of the residence halls.

This last move was almost her undoing. She was seen putting a flyer on a windshield by a security guard making his rounds. He approached her and asked, "You got a permit to do this?"

"No," Kiki admitted. "Do I have to get a permit?"

"This is littering. You have to go by the rules. There is a permit for distributing advertising on the campus, and you have to get approval of the student council."

"That'll take time, won't it?"

"I suspect so," the guard acknowledged.

So Kiki gave up that part of her project and walked back to the pizza parlor. She knew she had done a good job, yet it seemed she was always running afoul of rules and regulations. She showed Jim the flyer and told him of her experience. "It looks real nice," he said, admiring her work. "I don' know if it'll hep, but it shor' looks good."

That evening started off slowly, and Kiki picked at her nails, fearing that her job was about to be history. She hadn't even had a chance to tell Jim about her college admission, and this certainly didn't seem to be the right time.

Then, about 7:30 p.m., two cars pulled up in front of Jim's place, and several young women climbed out. They came through the door, laughing and talking, and one of them carried a copy of Kiki's flyer. "We want to order pizza," she announced.

"To go," added another.

Then a third spoke up, "No. This place is cute. I think I want to stay. I'll order a large Coke, to go with my pizza."

The others agreed to stay and settled at a table, where Kiki took their order in detail. She served them sodas and then brought their pizzas as soon as they came out of the oven.

One of the girls looked up at Kiki. "Don't I know you? Aren't you in my econ class?"

Kiki looked closer at her. "I think so, yes. I guess I am."

Another asked, "And you work here?"

"Yes," Kiki acknowledged, "on weekends." She was a bit embarrassed at the attention. She wasn't yet accustomed to her status as an official Montrose student. Returning to the counter, she told herself not to allow them to make her feel ashamed of working for Jim, especially after he had given her a chance in the first place.

As Kiki went about her work, one of the girls called her back to the table. "How do you like Dr. Ramirez?"

"I like her. I think she's a good teacher."

"Yeah, she is. But have you heard the rumor that she's a dyke?"

Kiki blanched. "No."

"Well, she has a cover story about some guy she was engaged to, who died in the Vietnam War. She supposedly never got over it, yet the story is she has a lover stashed away out near Stockton. What do you think of that?"

Kiki shrugged. "I don't know. How is it important? I mean, regardless of what she does in her personal life, she is still a good teacher."

"Yeah, it's just interesting, that's all." The girl winked at one of her friends then dropped the subject.

Kiki moved behind the counter to clean and help Jim. He had overheard the conversation, and his facial expression told her that what they had said didn't add to his appreciation of the Montrose student body. *"Bunch of spoiled brats, that's all they are."* Kiki could imagine what Jim was thinking.

However, when the girls left, they also left a big tip for Kiki and she had to be grateful even if she didn't agree with their gossip. And before the evening was over, they had sold twenty pizzas to Montrose students, all of them new visitors to the pizza parlor.

Jim was happy by the time they put out the closed sign. He dropped Kiki off at the front gate to the school and told her that she should keep coming up with good ideas. That way he could keep her working for him. Kiki promised she would, and by the time she reached Olsen, she had three more ideas of ways to create new business.

Early Sunday morning, Kiki sat down to write two letters, one to Sal that she really *wanted* to write and one to her parents that she *needed* to write.

Sal's was by far the easiest, because Kiki had a chance to tell her all about the meetings with the administrators, her admission to the college, and the agreements she had made to get in. She knew Sal was respectful of rules and would appreciate her situation. Kiki also realized that she had to have a confidante somewhere, and Sal was the best, and perhaps only, choice she had.

The second letter was to her parents, and this one was much more difficult to write. Although Kiki was excited about her new life and wanted to share it, she was aware that she had created real pain through her sudden departure. She hadn't been thinking of them at all when she left. Now she had to select her words carefully to acknowledge her family and all they had done for her, rather than to call attention to the realities that had driven her away from home.

Exhausted from the effort to express herself carefully and sensitively, Kiki mailed the two letters and then took a nap before reporting to work at Jim's.

A few days later, she was studying in her basement room when there was a knock on the door. Kiki stood and opened the door to find Annibella standing there.

"Kiki, there's a phone call for you upstairs."

Kiki was surprised. "There is? Who could be calling me?"

"I don't know. It sounds like long distance."

Kiki's heart pounded as she rushed up the back stairs to the main floor and went to the pay phone. She picked up the receiver. "Hello. This is Kiki Rodriguez."

"Kiki?" a delighted voice cried at the other end of the line. "This is Mama." Kiki was shocked. Her mama could ill afford a call to California.

"Mama, how are you paying for this?"

"Never you mind. I gotta know if my baby is okay."

"Mama, I'm fine. I wrote you all about my life here. It's okay, everything is okay." She felt her heart beating rapidly and her voice slipped into her natural South Bronx accent.

"We got your letter. It seems like everything is dream, so I had to call just to make sure. You are *really* okay? And you are student at this Montrose College?"

"Yes, Mama, I'm going to college. Isn't it wonderful?"

"But how you pay for it?"

"Read my letter again, Mama. It's all right there. This year is okay. If I can make good grades, then I can apply next year for scholarships. I may need you to sign some papers, but I can do everything else on my own."

"I didn't know what to believe, when Gusto he read your letter. Papa, he is very proud of you. Even though he don't say much, you can see it in his face. He is telling everybody he sees that his Kiki is in college in California."

Tears came to Kiki's eyes. "Please, Mama, you make me cry. Tell Papa I'll do good here." Then she added, "I'm sorry I left so suddenly. I didn't mean to hurt you. I just had to go."

"It's okay, now, Kiki. We forgive. Now we know you are okay, it's okay. You need anything? Can I send you something?"

Although Kiki could think of a million things she needed, she didn't want her parents to sacrifice when they had the boys at home to take care of. "No, Mama," she said. "I'm fine, I have everything I need."

"You maybe call sometime, and come home to visit?"

Kiki felt sad. Suddenly she very much missed home and the aromas of her mama's cooking. "I'll try," she promised. "Maybe I can come home next summer for a while. We'll see, okay?"

"I'm gonna write my sister in Sunnyvale. Maybe she come visit you."

Kiki felt another pang of sadness; she had never contacted her aunt. "That would be great, Mama."

In a moment, her mama had to hang up, and Kiki stood by the phone and cried. She loved every minute of her new life, but at times she felt very lonely and overwhelmed. Her family was nearly three thousand miles away, and right now hearing her mama's voice made her miss them all terribly.

Despite the difficulties, Kiki kept up with her studies and her two jobs. Jim's income took a turn for the better, and Kiki relaxed a bit. Her job was safe for the time being. The ads she dreamed up were within his budget and targeted the very people most likely to come to his store. And she was right; coupons were the answer. Jim thought that if he made good pizza, people would come. Kiki thought he need- ed to offer a bonus to get them inside the door. People always wanted to feel they were getting a little bit extra. Once they tasted his pizza, they would come back.

One weekend early in November, Kiki was serving tables and helping clean up, when she heard the unmistakable sound of a large truck screeching to a halt on the roadway outside the pizza parlor. Since it was a busy roadway, trucks were common, yet this one had a familiar sound. When it stopped, there was a single toot on its horn, and Kiki almost dropped the hot pizza pan she was carrying. Hastily serving a customer, she ran to the front door and almost bumped into Sal.

"Oh, Sal," Kiki cried with delight. "Where did you come from?"

Sal, while giving her a big hug and pointing to Aisha barking from the cab, just laughed. "Oh, I had a load bound for San Francisco. I don't get down here very often, and I've missed you, so I just mapped myself a little job that could get me to Montrose. I figured, because it's Saturday night, you'd be at work so I'd know where to find you."

Jim came to the door, having deduced the significance of Kiki's unusual behavior. He greeted Sal and invited her in for a cold drink and a pizza on the house. He had heard all about Sal from Kiki—as she relayed to him her cross-country journey—and he was glad to meet the woman trucker who had rescued her. While Kiki and Sal talked, he served up a giant "Jim's Special" pizza for Sal, who downed most of it with a glass of beer and saved a piece for Aisha. Sal grinned at Kiki. "Aisha loves to lick the sausage and cheese."

"I remember." Kiki chattered with Sal, and Jim left her alone, dashing about to take care of the tables by himself. He apparently felt Kiki deserved a few moments with her friend.

"How long ya here for?" Jim asked Sal, as he moved by with a loaded tray.

"Just over night. My load is being dumped right now, and I have to pick up a new one in the morning and head back to Salt Lake City." She looked at Kiki and said, "It's amazing to me that businesses can find people to load and unload trucks on a Saturday night. With the economy the way it is these days, people will work for anything at any time."

Kiki was smiling at Sal, yet her eyes held sadness. She was taking in the words that meant Sal would be gone again, just after arriving. Jim raised an eyebrow, obviously having noticed Kiki's reaction.

"That soon, huh?" he asked Sal, and she nodded.

"But yore gonna let this kid show ya her campus 'fore ya leave?" he added as he bustled by their table.

Sal looked at Kiki's stricken face. "I want to, but I've got to bed down for the night, and I know your campus security wouldn't look too fondly on the cab of an eighteen-wheeler coming through the front gate, especially after dark."

Kiki sighed. "Oh, you're probably right."

Jim came by again and stopped. "Look, I got a plan. Let me call my wife—we don' live too far away—and she can come down an' take ya home to sleep for the night. Ya can park yore truck right here in the driveway, by my place—dat drive is my property, an' nobody will bother ya here. We'll drop ya off at the Montrose front gate in the mornin'. Kiki can meet ya there and show ya 'round the campus an' then bring ya down here to git yore truck. How's dat for meetin' everbody's needs?"

Sal looked hesitant for a moment. "What about my dog—you have room for her, too?"

"If she don' mind us, we don' mind her. I got a big house—three daughters growin' up. If ya don' mind a little mess, yore more dan welcome. Any friend of Kiki's is a friend of ours."

Sal looked at Kiki's now hopeful face and caved in. "Sure, why not."

A few minutes later, Cora Williams arrived in the family Chevy. After introductions and hugs all around, she took Sal and Aisha back to their home. Kiki returned to work, feeling truly grateful to Jim for making it possible for her to spend more time with her friend.

Early Sunday morning, both suppressing yawns, Sal and Kiki met at the front gate of Montrose College. Marching by the security gate, Kiki gave the watchman a big wave. He had for some time been among Kiki's growing number of friends. No one seemed to be able to resist her constant smile, sparkling brown eyes, and unending enthusiasm.

Kiki was surprised that Sal didn't have Aisha with her. "Where's Aisha?" she asked.

"She's waiting in the truck at Jim's. It's not hot this morning, and she'll be fine. I didn't want to complicate anything while I visited you," Sal responded.

Kiki thought a minute. "Yeah, I hadn't thought about it. I don't see dogs around here, except for a couple of guard dogs belonging to the security patrol. Someone might challenge bringing her in here." Kiki was momentarily subdued.

"It's fine, Kiki," Sal said. "Now, show me your college!"

Sal was suitably impressed with Montrose's beautiful campus, its tall green trees, stream and walking bridges, campanile, Spanish and

Victorian architectural styles, and the amphitheater. Kiki walked her briskly around the entire school, pointing out buildings, showing her spots where she had hidden out the first few days—and how she had stowed away her belongings in garbage cans—and finally taking her to her room in the basement of Olsen Hall.

In the dormitory, Sal was visibly taken back by how small and dark the room was, and how few belongings Kiki had. Kiki quickly pointed out that she would be moving into a regular room in January, and that this was fine for the time being. Sal shrugged and nodded her acceptance.

Then they rushed up to the dining hall, where Kiki showed Sal the ropes about buying a meal ticket and piling her plate full of food that would last the entire day. Kiki even took Sal back into the kitchen to let her see where she washed dishes during the week. Sal sighed, and Kiki put a hand on her arm. "It's okay, Sal, it's really okay."

They sat at a table to eat the large meal they had selected. Sal admitted it was a lot of food for the money. They laughed and talked and Kiki asked about Meg.

"She's great, and she told me to say hello."

"Tell her hello back, okay?"

After a few moments, Sal patted her belly. "I'm full, and the food tastes good for institutional cooking."

Kiki beamed. "We have a family of Chinese cooks. Been here for maybe a hundred years. Since I work with them, I'm learning a few words in Chinese."

Sal shook her head with amusement. "You are absolutely amazing, Kiki. You are living in a dark basement, you are working two jobs—serving pizza and doing dishes—and you're happy because you are learning Chinese. I know you are going to be a success in life, because nothing gets you down!"

Kiki flushed. "Well, it isn't all easy for me. I am ready to give up once in a while. Then I look outside at how beautiful it is here, and remember all that I'm learning, and suddenly my sacrifices seem worthwhile."

All too soon it was time for Kiki to walk with Sal to her truck. Kiki was very thankful her friend had come to see her. Sal's visit made Kiki's life at Montrose feel more real—and it was special to share her world with a woman she greatly admired.

On the way back to the truck, Sal commented, "I'm really glad that things worked out this way, Kiki. Jim's family is quite nice, and they made me feel really welcome in their home. Aisha, too. You were truly lucky to find Jim the day after you arrived in California—it's almost uncanny."

Kiki laughed. "Just like I found you, huh?"

When they reached the pizza parlor, the two women gave each other goodbye hugs, and Aisha caught Kiki with a few sloppy licks. Kiki watched Sal drive away, as Aisha barked goodbye, and she then looked up into the blue sky. "Are you still there, Artemis? Will I see you tonight?"

14

Kiki

Kiki experienced considerable stress during that first semester. She worked and worried and worried and worked. She had precious little time for rest and kept going on sheer adrenalin. When final exams were over—allowing her finally to sleep around the clock for a couple of days—she woke up to the pleasant reality that she had survived her first semester at Montrose amazingly well. She had earned a B+ in psychology, an A- in economics, where the stock she had chosen very haphazardly was going through a phenomenal rise, a B in Spanish, also one in ESL, and a B+ in art history. She had received a pass in beginning tennis—Kiki liked the physical education class but had so little free time to go to the courts and hit balls that she felt lucky just to pass. She showed her grades to Nancy, who was very impressed.

"Kiki, I don't think you realize yet how bright you are," Nancy observed with a big smile.

"Don't you think the teachers were just nice to me?" Kiki asked, not believing her scores.

"No, I don't, Kiki," Nancy replied, shaking her head. "Remember, how you arrived here and the fact that you have not completed high school are not general knowledge. With the possible exception of Dr. Ramirez, no one knows anything about your story. Your instructors were given another reason for your late registration and graded your class work as it deserved. Given your two jobs, you are amazingly dedicated—and you learn quickly. I'm thinking that as you become more comfortable with your language skills, your grades will go even higher."

"Wow!" Kiki was stunned.

As the semester came to a close, just before the Christmas holidays, Kiki felt lonely. There had been such a whirlwind of activity around final exams that she was facing the winter break without having made any plans. For a college freshman without a dime to spare, closed residence halls and restricted hours at the dining commons meant a deserted campus and a deserted Kiki.

As the dorm emptied, she sat in the dark on her bedroll trying to figure out what in the world she was going to do. It would be Christmas, she was here alone, and she couldn't even stay in this room. Flying home to spend the holidays with her family was totally out of the question.

Unexpectedly, there was a knock at her door. Surprised and confused by someone coming to see her, Kiki got up to see who it was.

Jim was standing in the hallway, grinning widely.

Kiki was shocked. "How did you get in here?"

"Well, some lady upstairs, Anna somethin' or other, tol' me ya was down here in the basement." He looked doubtfully into the gloomy surroundings.

"Annibella," Kiki supplied. "She's the RA and runs the dorm."

Jim frowned. "Ya live in here?"

Kiki couldn't help but smile. She could read his mind all too well. "Well, this semester," she explained. "After the break, I'm going to get a regular room upstairs in the main part of the dorm. They didn't have any vacancies this fall."

Jim shook his head. "And now ya got Christmas vacation, and I bet ya don't have nowhere to go, right?"

"Well," Kiki nodded pathetically, "that's why I was sitting in the dark stewing. The dorm closes at noon, and that puts me out on the street for more than three weeks."

Jim shook his head. "No, it don't. Yore comin' home with me to stay wid the family."

"Really?" Kiki could hardly believe his words. "You'd let me stay in your house?"

"Kiki, ya practically keep my business goin.' Why wouldn't I want to hep ya if I could?"

Kiki felt a wave of excitement pulse through her body, because she knew that now she would spend the holidays surrounded with love and caring amidst a happy brood. Although she had been missing Mama and Papa and her brothers this morning, she knew instantly that time with the Williams family would be much less stressful and more loving. So, she packed her meager belongings and let her compassionate boss take care of her.

As they walked to his old pick-up, Kiki asked, "How did you find out I had to leave the dorm today?"

He chuckled. "Wouldn't ya like to know."

Kiki gave him a frown, and he put an arm around her shoulder. "Well, that lady friend of yore's, that trucker, Sal, she called yeste'day and said she was worried that ya might not have nowhere to go fer the holidays. She jis' figgered the school would shut down. I guess they all sorta do that."

Kiki looked up at the sky. *Artemis again! Looking out for her through Sal and Jim.* She'd have to thank her personal star tonight, provided it was clear outside and she could find her special blinking light.

The three Williams daughters were thrilled to have Kiki at the house. Karolina, a high school junior, had a room of her own, and Bettina and Sharrol, both in middle school, shared a bedroom. Karolina, tall like her dad with deep brown eyes and sporting dreadlocks, even had a double bed, so she made room for Kiki. Not having had a sister, Kiki was delighted.

Kiki spent hours hanging out with Karolina. Because the oldest Williams girl had tales of her own high school life to share, Karolina was interested and empathetic to Kiki's story about her family troubles in the South Bronx. Kiki overheard Karolina talking to her father before he went to work. "We have prejudices against us for bein' black, but Kiki has prejudice against her, too," Karolina said.

"Yeah," Jim told her. "Lots of folks git pushed around. Not jis' us black folks."

Clearly, the Williams family was not rich, yet their house was considerably nicer than the South Bronx apartments where Kiki had grown up. First of all it was a *house*. And pretty big. It was old, with faded wood siding, several big windows, a front porch, and three bedrooms. And for Christmas, there was a tall, decorated tree in the living room. Later in the day there was a holiday dinner with turkey on the table, all the trimmings, and a large peach pie for dessert. Kiki had never felt so full and happy. No pizza, she noticed.

After breakfast on Christmas morning, the family exchanged gifts. Karolina had helped Kiki find some little, inexpensive presents at a local thrift store that each person in the family would like. Kiki was excited about giving something to everyone else, because they all had been so nice to her. She didn't think much about getting presents herself. Being there with the family was present enough.

Yet, when the gifts were passed out, Kiki found she had several packages to open. Mostly, family members had given her clothing—tops and pants to help with her wardrobe. She was practically beside herself with glee, as she looked at the items around her on the sofa.

But that wasn't all.

Jim winked at her. "I got a call from Sal the other day, tellin' me dat a box was comin' from her an' Meg for ya to open on Christmas. It got here yeste'day. I don' know what's in it."

He pulled the box from behind his recliner and handed it to Kiki.

She was thrilled, wondering what Sal would have thought to send her. There was a card attached to the heavy parcel.

Sal had written: *"While I know there are many things that you need, I thought that this would help you most in college. Meg and I, and Aisha of course, send our love."*

When Kiki opened up the package, she found a laptop computer inside. "Oh, my God!" she exclaimed, her heart skipping beats. "I can't believe it!"

The Williams girls gathered around her, admiring the new computer. "We all have computers," Bettina said. "Daddy bought them for us, to make sure we'd do good in school. Karolina got hers first, then as soon as me and Sharrol got into middle school, he got us one, too. I'm glad you have one now. It can do *so* much to help you."

Kiki held the computer close, and tears filled her eyes. Karolina threw her arms around Kiki and gave her a warm hug.

"Dat Sal is a good woman. She knew what ya needed," Jim affirmed.

"Now I have to learn to use it," Kiki admitted happily, and with a sigh.

"Don't worry, I'll help you," Karolina offered. The two younger girls chimed in.

Later that evening, Jim and Cora watched the girls sharing with each other and having fun. Cora leaned close to Jim, whispering to him, "Now that she's been around here a few days, I understand why you think so much of Kiki."

Jim grinned at her and commented, "I thought ya would understand after ya met her!"

Much of the rest of Kiki's vacation time was spent playing cards and table games in the evenings with the girls, or ensconced in Karolina's bedroom learning about the computer. The family had

WiFi, so Karolina was able to show Kiki how to set up email and a Facebook page—using the computer's camera for pictures—and to generally get started navigating the Internet.

Kiki was amazed at what the laptop could do. "I have used the library computers," she told Karolina, "but I had them working like big typewriters to do my homework." *She had also typed up papers for Karen Fullerton and her friends—but that was over now.* Although the librarians had helped Kiki do a little research, she hadn't had free time to explore social media. This was all totally new to her.

When it came time to think about returning to school, Kiki got ready to depart from the Williams home feeling both happy and sad. Her stay with Jim's family had been everything she could have dreamed of and more. She wished her own family could have been warm and openly caring like this one. Although Kiki loved her parents and her brothers, their constant fighting had been very unnerving and scary. The Williams family members enjoyed each other, despite difficulties that they all faced in their lives.

In addition to Kiki's stay in Big Jim's home, the lengthy semester break brought additional excitement. Nancy Raines located Kiki via a visit to the pizza parlor and invited her to go skiing. Kiki had never touched a pair of skis, let alone stood on them, so she faced a day on the slopes of the Sierra Nevada Mountains with both great excitement and considerable trepidation. She reminded the women of her fall in the dining commons, and Nancy promised they would put a brace on her still vulnerable ankle.

Nancy and Paula picked Kiki up at the Williams' house early one morning, before daylight, and they spent almost six hours getting to the mountain ski slopes near the Olympic Village. "Wow!" was all Kiki could manage when she first saw a sloping wall of snow ahead of her. Once suited up and fully braced, and with help from her friends,

Kiki risked stepping out into the snow. Almost instantly, she knew she was going to love skiing.

Despite some initial fears and with only one lesson, Kiki did well, moving from the beginners' slope to the intermediate one before the day was over. She was tired yet exhilarated when they finally called it quits.

For dinner, Paula treated them to BBQ by a warm fireplace in a local eatery before they made the return trip to Jim's house in East Oakland. They arrived at nearly midnight, all three of them exhausted, satisfied, and thankfully uninjured.

"You are a natural skier," Nancy had assured Kiki during the drive home. "I think you would have real athletic skill if you had time to develop it. Although maybe it won't be possible in the near future, hang onto that information."

Kiki thought about that idea all the way back to Jim's house. "It was so much fun," she said in Jim's living room, as she handed the ski jacket and snow pants back to Nancy.

"Thank you for inviting me to go with you," she said to Nancy.

Nancy and Paula both gave Kiki a big hug and left the house. Kiki looked out the front window as the car pulled away from the curb. She sighed with satisfaction, because she had been very happy being with both women, sharing their laughter and fun.

The ever resourceful Karen Fullerton—who had completed her classes in December and now shared a San Francisco apartment with three other college students—also got in touch with Kiki at the Williams' house and invited her to come over to spend a day. This was a major event for Kiki. Having struggled all semester with classes and work, she had not had time for the luxury of crossing the Bay Bridge and seeing anything of "The City."

Following Karen's instructions, Kiki rode the BART into San

Francisco and met Karen at the Castro station on Market Street. First Karen showed Kiki her apartment in the colorful Castro District, which was home turf for the largest gay and lesbian population in the City. Next they walked to Union Square for a cable car ride to Fisherman's Wharf, where they had lunch. Although Karen's assertiveness and her desire to push her lesbian agenda on everyone around her were sometimes bothersome to Kiki, she realized that Karen was intelligent and had a good heart. The two spent a fun afternoon together. After a light supper, Karen asked, "Do you want to go back to Oakland right away, or would you be interested in visiting a lesbian bar?"

Kiki's curiosity overcame her hesitation, and she agreed to go.

They wandered through the crowded Castro, where "life" began after dark. Although Kiki thought she had seen just about every kind of personal expression in clothing and hairstyle at her high school, the Castro's profusion of leather, outlandish make-up and hair, chains, wigs, tattoos, and cross-dressing amazed her. She could not imagine wanting or needing to go to such extreme measures to decorate her own body. However, she had to admit that it certainly was colorful.

Karen pointed out sights Kiki might have missed, and eventually they ended up in a lesbian bar, where there was a minimal cover charge. Identification had to be shown at the door, so Kiki was thankful for her new ID card. Although she couldn't get served liquor at the bar, she *was* allowed in the door.

Karen seemed to know everyone, and she introduced Kiki to several of her friends. As the music blared at an ear-splitting level, Kiki nodded sometimes uncomprehendingly to this woman or that and soon found she had accepted an invitation to dance without realizing it.

A tall, dark and imposing woman led her onto the dance floor, as a KD Lang recording began—a slow, seductive, soulful number. Kiki's dance partner, whose name she never clearly heard, pulled her close and led her around the floor, amidst numerous very affectionate couples. Kiki's eyes grew wide, as everywhere she looked, one dancer or another was caught in an open-mouthed kiss while partners swayed to the sensuous music emerging from the sound system.

Kiki's partner pulled her ever closer and began nibbling on her ear and whispering intimacies to her. Then the woman pushed her leg between Kiki's thighs as they moved and put pressure against her crotch. Kiki's face grew red with both excitement and embarrassment. She also felt a touch of absolute fear. Shocked, Kiki pulled away and asked to end the dance.

Karen—who thankfully was keeping watch over her—realized that Kiki was in over her head and came to her rescue by stepping up and taking Kiki's hand. She smiled at the amorous dancer pleasantly and waltzed off with Kiki, holding her at a safe, non-provocative distance.

"Thank you," Kiki murmured.

"It's okay." Karen gave her a friendly smile. "Your eyes looked like a deer caught in the headlights. I knew you needed out of there."

Shortly afterward, they left the club. As they walked along the streets to the BART station, Kiki was very quiet and Karen seemed to feel a bit responsible. "I'm sorry that gal was so pushy. We all get carried away sometimes, but since that was your first experience, you weren't really ready for it."

Kiki, feeling overwhelmed and touchy, lashed out, "I don't know if that's the right thing for me, or if I'll ever be ready for it!"

Karen started to say something and then decided not. "Well," she apologized, "I'm sorry. I hope it didn't ruin the whole day for you."

Kiki sighed, took a deep breath, and forced herself to relax. "Oh, no, I had a great time. Thank-you, for inviting me. And I did agree to go to that place, so I can't totally blame you. I have to learn how to take care of myself. It's just all so new to me."

Karen waited with her until the BART train arrived and then

raised her arm in a cheerful farewell as Kiki looked through the window and waved back from the outbound train. Despite the uncomfortable dance partner, for Kiki it had been a marvelous day, indeed!

When the winter break ended, Kiki returned to a different world at Montrose. As promised, a room became available on the first floor of Olsen Hall, and Kiki moved in with the ongoing students. Having been so isolated in the dark and dank basement, she had been little noticed by hall residents. They now seemed to think of her as a new student and went out of their way to make her feel welcome.

Kiki was assigned to a suite of three rooms, each with windows looking out on the beautiful landscape of the college. She had two suitemates, Julie Anderson, from Seattle, and Jacinta Morales, from Mexico City. Julie was attractive and friendly; however, she had a boyfriend at Stanford University and was rarely around. Jacinta, on the other hand, was far away from her family and still dealing with culture shock, so she and Kiki found they had much more in common.

Jacinta, plump with dark brown eyes and short curly dark hair, spoke English fluently. Since Kiki had often spoken Spanish at home, the two sometimes slipped into Spanish for the fun of it. Jacinta fascinated Kiki, and they occasionally stayed up late into the night talking about their families, their classes, and life in general.

When Kiki told Jacinta about the South Bronx, her face clouded over, and she gave Kiki a big hug. "I wish I could take you home with me. There is so much love in our family," she explained. "My father is a doctor, and we have a really nice house. You would like it."

Kiki basked in the hug and gave Jacinta a broad smile. "I'm so glad we are rooming together," she admitted. "I didn't have anyone to talk with last semester. It was nothing except a long, hard grind of classes, study and work."

"Bueno, mi amiga." Jacinta gave her a big grin. "It will be fun times from now on."

Although Kiki knew deep inside that she faced another grueling semester, Jacinta's presence made it seem more possible to survive.

Having passed her courses with good grades, Kiki was relieved of her probationary status, and she sensed that the administration was pleased with her. Sonia Yakimari gave her more papers to sign and congratulated her for "hanging in there." Kiki also received the forms that her parents would have to sign for scholarships, grants, and loan applications for the following year. Kiki grasped these forms, which were her lifeline to continued education at Montrose, and wrote a carefully-worded letter to her mama and papa. She knew Mama would help and keep after Papa to round up the necessary tax forms and complete the applications. It would be humbling for him to admit that he had so few resources, but Mama would remind him how wonderful it was to have a daughter getting a good education. Kiki believed he would comply in the long run. She would just have to be *very* patient.

Her counseling sessions with Dr. Capehart were a mixed blessing. A valuable resource on the college's academic programs, Rita helped Kiki immeasurably in selecting classes and mapping out a course plan.

"It looks like you have a good start with your goal of earning a degree here at Montrose," Rita noted during the first week of the new semester. "But in planning your classes for next year, we need to look at what you want to do with your education after you graduate. That seems very far away right now, I know," the professor admitted. "However, it will come sooner than you think."

Kiki felt a frown crossing her forehead. "I certainly haven't thought that far," she admitted. "I have just been surviving day-to-day."

"I get that," Rita said, "but you will have to pick a major subject, and we will have to structure your classes to fulfill all of the degree requirements. It is not too early to be starting the process, for you to actually complete your bachelor's."

Kiki nodded. "I understand. My problem is that right now I love *all* my classes and I want to major in *everything*."

Rita smiled. "It's a good thing that you like so many subjects. Eventually, however, you do have to make choices. As you progress through your spring classes, it would be helpful for you to consider which ones appeal to you the most and how you would see yourself using what you are learning in them."

Kiki found that very confusing and admitted as much. "I don't know how to relate classwork material to a future job setting."

Rita smiled. "Good. That's bedrock information. We'll do some testing to help you see the connections."

During the next few weeks, Rita administered a variety of personality and aptitude tests that, with interpretation, helped Kiki better understand her abilities and interests and how those could lead to her college major and her life after Montrose.

Although the information was undoubtedly valuable, Kiki sometimes resented the weekly sessions with the psychologist because they took time she needed to do everything else on her crowded agenda. In addition, she sometimes felt that Dr. Capehart asked personal questions which went beyond what Kiki wanted to discuss. She asked about Kiki's social life—or lack of it—and Kiki felt her shoulders tense up defensively. She had so little free time to have fun with other people and also sensed that the psychologist had a preconceived notion of what Kiki's social life should look like. Kiki had never liked being defined by other people, and she didn't want pressure from the counselor any more than she wanted it from Karen Fullerton or an amorous dance partner.

After a session with Rita, Kiki sometimes sat on her bed for several minutes and stared out the window, attempting to focus on a world that was bigger than this campus she now inhabited. She tried to grasp what she was being asked to consider, especially about her personal and social life—not only now but as a post-college adult. It was hard to project out there into the future, but Rita seemed to be asking her to do just that.

Kiki tried to imagine being married to a Stanford or Berkeley graduate who could provide well for her and a family. While she definitely wanted something for herself that was happier and healthier than what she had known in the South Bronx, she wasn't sure that she wished to be saddled with a suburban house and a swimming pool, servants, a husband, and lots of baby diapers. She had seen plenty of those middle class families in the movies, if not in her own neighborhood. She wasn't sure yet what she *did* want. Yet the "good life" that traditional, middle-class people seemed to desire felt like a prison to her—undoubtedly attractive in a variety of ways, but a prison none the less.

When she listened to other students talking in the dorm, or the commons, or the pizza parlor, what most excited her were adventures—like traveling to foreign countries, perhaps backpacking through Europe, maybe even working in a foreign country. She always saw herself alone, with few belongings, going from one place to another and absorbing knowledge and atmosphere. *Like Artemis?* Perhaps she could even join the Peace Corps. At this moment in time, considering a life of ongoing routine seemed to Kiki dreadfully dull.

When Kiki remembered or had time to gaze up at the stars, she asked Artemis to show her the way. Artemis was the only guide she really wanted, and through her nighttime connection with her personal star, Kiki could really get in touch with herself and her own personal dreams.

15

Sal

Winter showed itself in the Bay Area through chilly, rainy days, and during this dark period that held only promise of the beautiful spring to follow, Kiki had her first opportunity to experience what Dr. Capehart would consider a "normal" social life. Darlene Henderson, a Montrose freshman who knew a lot of people around the Bay Area, invited Kiki to double date with her and two UC Berkeley upperclassmen.

The offer came early in the second semester, just as Kiki was finding herself on more solid ground as a student. The new computer made it possible to do class assignments in less time. Aside from that, everything seemed a bit easier now that the probationary status had been lifted, she had a regular room in the dorm, and she attended classes for the second time—beginning, legally, with everyone else on the first day. Kiki's ear for accents also was improving. She felt more comfortable in both her Spanish and English classes. There were many "aha" moments when she "got" it, and each time Kiki heaved a sigh of relief. She was still working long hours and found it hard to keep up but was beginning to believe she could actually *do* this college thing.

So, feeling generally good about her life, Kiki accepted the double date, although she admitted to Darlene that she didn't have a lot of fancy clothing. Darlene told her not to worry. An evening out provided a breather from her intense schedule—and was a special treat she could not have otherwise afforded. The four students planned to do dinner at a popular restaurant and then go to a movie. Other than feeling underdressed, Kiki loved everything about the evening—except that her assigned date, a pimply-faced computer geek, talked non-stop about comic books and computer multi-media. Kiki found him totally boring.

However, Darlene's date, Frank Symmons, kept watching Kiki, and a week later, the young man called her up at the dorm and asked her to go out with him. Inexperienced in such matters, Kiki decided to check with Darlene first. Darlene told her that she really didn't mind, because her relationship with Frank was casual. So Kiki finally agreed to the date and discovered that she was more excited about it than she had expected to be. She primped as best she could. She even raided the Goodwill box to see if she could come up with an appropriate dress for an evening out. Kiki wasn't quite sure what she wanted; whatever it was, she didn't find it. Later, she came to the conclusion that it was just as well, since dresses weren't really her thing and she would be creating an artificial facade. *Why do that, anyway?* She decided to wear a pair of new pants and a top that the Williams family had given her for Christmas, along with some flats that she did find in the Goodwill box. They almost fit and were not too worn out. Her leather jacket was the best she could do for the cold.

On an evening that thankfully did not rain, Frank—nice looking and not too tall for Kiki—picked her up in a sporty red car. He stepped out and opened the passenger door for her, and Kiki rather enjoyed the attention. He took her to a French restaurant and encouraged her to order anything she wanted. The complex menu entrees written in French presented her with a challenge, and she struggled, rather embarrassed.

"What kind of meat do you like best?" Frank asked, noting her discomfort.

"Fish, I guess, when it's fresh."

"Oh, it will be very fresh here. How about halibut?" He pointed out the entrée to her.

Kiki glanced at the page and smiled. "Perfect. Thanks."

Waiting for the food to be served, trying to fill the blank spaces of time and not knowing him too well, Kiki nervously began asking what she thought were normal getting-to-know-you questions, like "What are you majoring in?"

Frank smiled and warmed to her queries. He told her all about himself and his future plans, which were extensive. "After grad school, I plan to join my dad's firm in the City and then get married and live in Marin County. I think perhaps the country club would be nice, and two or three kids," he elaborated with a grin, and then added, "just kidding of course." Although he spoke lightly and looked a bit amused, she wondered if beneath his light touch this was a true picture of what he really wanted.

Just as Kiki started to tell him something about her own life, their dinners were served and they both became involved with eating. Kiki thought the fish was delicious, although she had had almost no comparative experiences with halibut. She and Frank chattered about food topics in general and about the foreign movie they were going to see. It was only later, when he dropped her off at Olsen Hall, that Kiki began to realize he had never asked her about her own goals and dreams.

Despite that fact, Frank apparently enjoyed her company. He called two or three times and asked her out. It wasn't easy, since she worked on the weekends and couldn't afford to take time off, yet Frank was persistent and Kiki did manage a couple of outings over the next few weeks. During the third date, Frank attempted to come on to her. Kiki quickly became disenchanted with him. *She was not ready for a lover, that she knew.* She clearly didn't know Frank very well and she was becoming aware that he didn't know her at all—other than perhaps as a fantasy that might fit into his Marin County dream life. She managed to extricate herself from his embrace after a few exploratory deep kisses and arrived back at the dorm largely unscathed. When he called again, she heaved a deep sigh and told him she couldn't go out anymore. Although Frank didn't seem happy, he moved on.

The only real positive outcome from this dating experience was that Kiki could report to Dr. Capehart that she had briefly dated an eligible young man. This brought a smile to the well-intentioned psychologist's face.

Kiki had found her own personal counselors on campus—Nancy Raines and Helena Ramirez. Nancy had become her personal confessor and one of the most important keystones to Kiki's being able to hang together under the stresses of her life at the college. Out of all her professors, Dr. Ramirez always held a special place in her heart. Her fondness for the economist started as gratitude for the way she had invited Kiki into her classroom and refused to turn her in as a campus interloper. As the months went by, Kiki realized that she respected Dr. Ramirez's teaching methods and really looked forward to her economics class.

Often Kiki would stay for a few moments afterward. She always had a legitimate question to ask, and Helena was patient with her. Then the professor would ask a question about how things were going, and Kiki confessed little details about her life on the campus. If Nancy Raines seemed like a big sister that she never had, Helena was like a favored older aunt.

One day Kiki stood around while a couple of other students consulted with Dr. Ramirez and then she asked her questions about keeping track of her stock for the ongoing class project. Helena smiled and explained what Kiki needed to do next.

Then Kiki suddenly remembered something personal she wanted to ask. "I heard that you live on a farm, right?"

Helena smiled, clearly amused by the question. "Yes, I do. Well, sort of. Although it used to be a real working farm, the suburbs have encroached so much that there is little left except the house and barn and a couple of acres. No room for horses anymore, yet it's fun."

"I've never known anyone who had a farm," Kiki admitted.

Helena smiled teasingly. "And I bet you'd like to see it sometime."

Kiki blushed. "Well, I would, but that doesn't seem realistic. I'll just imagine it. I'm good at imagining things."

"Yes, I suspect you are. You are a very creative young lady."

Kiki continued, "Do you have any animals?"

"A cow, some chickens, dogs and cats." Helena looked at her watch. "Well, my young friend," she sighed, "I have to get on to my next class. Maybe someday we'll just have to find a way for you to visit my farm. How's that?"

Kiki swallowed. "That would be wonderful!"

They exited the building together. Kiki waved goodbye to Helena and loped all the way back to the dorm, her ponytail swishing in the breeze.

When Sal arrived home from road trips, Meg was almost always waiting expectantly, and now there were email messages from Kiki to look forward to as well. Sal would open a beer—a luxury she could afford when she didn't face a grueling day of driving—and stretch out on the living room sofa with her iPad on her knees and read about Kiki's latest escapades. She would smile to herself and shake her head, then give Meg a big hug and share with her the details of Kiki's activities. They both got a laugh from her scrapes and her strong survival instincts.

Knowing that Kiki would always be short of cash, Sal considered sending her a small check or a gift card that she could use for whatever was needed. One time she actually did it.

Then, two weeks later, when Sal returned to Salt Lake from a long-distance haul, there was a note from Kiki waiting. In it, she said:

"Thanks for the money. I was very touched. I sat in my room and cried.

However, please don't do it again. My relationship to you means so much to me that I don't want to get money messed up in it. You've already given me a computer, so no more, please. I want to look for your messages and letters because of what you say—not because there might be money inside. I don't want to hurt your feelings but I hope you understand."

Sal shook her head when she read the letter. "I can't believe this kid," she confessed to Meg. "And yet this is just like her. She is so determined to make it on her own. Well, what can I do?"

Meg tousled Sal's hair. "You'll find other ways to show her that you care. I know you."

Sal thought and thought and then realized that she could contribute to Kiki's educational goals without sending her cash. Sal sensed that her extensive travels could benefit Kiki in another way. Sal could buy clothes, such as T-shirts, sweatshirts, pants, and hats for cold foggy days in the Bay Area. From then on, when she was on the road, she picked up a souvenir T-shirt, or sweatshirt and pants, and mailed the clothing to Kiki. The packages arrived at Montrose irregularly and therefore were always a surprise; through them Kiki acquired a useful wardrobe of casual clothes that helped keep her warm.

After the first package arrived in her post office box, Kiki wrote a thank-you note that made Sal feel really good:

"Thanks for the I Love NY *T-shirt you sent. I can forgive you this one. I've been away from home long enough now that at times I actually miss the place and wish I could see my family again. The shirt brings a little touch of NY, and I am strutting around on campus wearing it. In all honesty, I am beginning to be a bit proud that I made it here all the way from New York—with a lot of help, especially from you."*

As the spring semester drew to a close, Kiki acknowledged that she had indeed become a college student. Her grades were holding up, meaning the fall performance had not been a fluke. Although she felt exhausted from her very tight schedule, she was still enthusiastic and deeply satisfied. When finals began, she studied frantically to do her best but with a new nagging worry in the back of her mind—the coming summer and how to fill it.

During finals, she went to the post office and found in her mailbox a long letter from Sal. She rushed back to Olsen Hall and sat down to read Sal's humorous, detailed description of her latest experiences on the road. In the letter, Sal commented:

"I know you are getting out of school shortly, and I wondered what you are doing this summer. Work? Well, is there any chance that you could join me for a trip to the East Coast? If you want to visit your family, I might be able to get you there for a few days and bring you back. Let me know soon."

Kiki curled up on her bed and let the tears fall. It had been nearly a year since she had seen her mama, papa, and her brothers. Born in early May, she had just celebrated her nineteenth birthday alone and far from home. Somehow she really wanted to go back, not to stay, just to see everyone. And enjoy some of Mama's cooking.

Later that same afternoon, Kiki received an unexpected call from Sonia Yakimari in the admissions office.

"Kiki," Sonia greeted warmly, "I know you are always looking for work, and I wanted to let you know that we've just decided to hire a couple of extra clerks to work with admissions during the summer. The position could develop into a part-time job during the school year, and it would pay better than the dining hall. Are you interested?"

Of course she was! Kiki was nothing short of ecstatic. A full-time job for the entire summer and better work next fall! That was half of her immediate summertime problem solved, right there. She now just had to find a place to live when the residence halls closed. "Oh, yes, I'm interested. What do I need to do?"

Sonia instructed her to come "soon" to admissions to fill out the paperwork, and Kiki ran happily across the campus. Yet by the time she got to Sonia's office, she had remembered Sal's letter and her offer of a visit to New York, giving Kiki a conflict to face.

Kiki was mulling over these issues while Sonia finished a telephone call, and the administrator, ever observant, noticed that Kiki seemed troubled. "You were so excited over the phone, Kiki. What's happened?"

"Well, I want the job very much. I can't tell you how important it is to me. I just don't know where I'm going to live when the hall closes next week. I've been so busy just keeping up that I haven't had time to make plans. And I've just received a letter from an old friend offering to drive me back to the South Bronx to see my family. I haven't been home in a year, and I am really anxious for a chance to see everyone again." Suddenly overcome, Kiki put her hand over her mouth and dissolved into tears.

Sonia proved both sympathetic and resourceful. First Kleenex. And while Kiki sat beside her desk pulling herself together, Sonia called the campus housing office and learned that one apartment was available for summer rental in the hillside complex behind the music building. The apartment wasn't fancy, but it was furnished and the rent was reasonable in relation to Kiki's potential full-time employment. "You won't be able to save as much as you might wish toward your next year's expenses," Sonia told her. "However, you will be here on campus, which will reduce travel time and costs. So, all in all, you should come out okay if you take this apartment."

Kiki nodded. "Yes, yes, of course!" Her serendipity continued to amaze her, and yet the summer would be lonely without her friends in the dorm. Her mind was drifting off to that when Sonia continued, "Kiki, everybody needs a vacation. You've worked very hard this year, and I think that if you want a couple of weeks off to visit your family, I believe we can work around that. If you can commit to the rest of the summer and work part-time for us during the school year,

I believe we can survive your being gone for two weeks. Now how does that sound?"

Kiki teared up again; this time it was tears of gratitude. "Thank you, I don't know how I can ever thank you enough."

Sonia smiled. "Just hang in there and do your best. That's all you can ever do."

Kiki ran back to Olsen Hall to send a message to Sal that she had found a job, a place to stay, and could go to New York. *When do we leave?*

At the beginning of summer break, the entire administrative offices were being moved from the annex back into the completely renovated Montrose Hall. As a result, Kiki was extremely busy as she juggled learning about college admissions in the midst of a moving-box-and-van existence. Her work hours were anything other than dull and often very confusing.

After three weeks of struggling with all the admissions details, Kiki boarded a jet for a one-way flight to Salt Lake City. Never having flown before, she was alternately excited and then terrified. Jim drove her to Oakland International Airport for her late morning flight on Delta. He gave her a big hug and waved her off at the security checkpoint. "Ya have a good time now," he called before turning away.

Kiki kept her place in line but watched his kind, almost ageless face as she waved back to him and wondered if he had ever had a chance to have any adventures of his own, or whether he had been saddled with responsibilities as long as he could remember. The way he had taken to Sal, she suspected he was a dreamer at heart and probably would have wished he were doing something other than baking pizzas day after day to support his family.

Moments later, Kiki boarded her first jet. Delighted that she had a window seat, she watched their every move as the flight attendants completed the pre-flight procedures. She held on tight as the big plane rolled down the runway and lifted into a cloudless sky. Her stomach flipped a bit with nerves until the magnificent jet leveled off. Then Kiki began to enjoy herself.

A little more than an hour later, the plane touched down in Salt Lake City. As soon as Kiki passed through security, she ran to Sal, waiting by the gate.

"Hey, you made it." Sal greeted her with a big hug. "You have any luggage to collect?" she asked as she released Kiki and took a good look at her.

"Nope." Kiki looked down at her one small duffle bag. "Nothing else to pick up."

Sal led the way to the parking lot. "Meg wanted to come," she explained, "but she thought it would be nice to have a hot lunch ready when we get back. She's at the house cooking, and Aisha is waiting for you there, too."

As they walked to Meg's station wagon, Sal studied Kiki again. "You look really good. A year in college hasn't done you any harm. You've been getting some sun, I see, and your ponytail is growing really long."

Kiki laughed. "It really swishes, doesn't it? I should get it trimmed, but I just never seem to have the time. Oh, well."

Sal noticed with amusement that although Kiki was still wearing her backward pink ball cap, she was sporting fancy sunglasses. "Ray-Bans, huh? You're coming up in the world."

Kiki grinned delightedly. "Oh, these?" she asked, pulling off the glasses. "My friend Jacinta left them for me when she went home to Mexico City for the summer. Her father is an ophthalmologist—I hope I said that right—and they have tons of glasses all over the house. She told me she had these in every color they make, and since I didn't have any, she left a pair behind. She's really nice."

Sal smiled. "I like the blue lenses." It always made Sal feel good to hear that Kiki had made another friend and that her world was gradually becoming a little more positive and happy. The warm sense of satisfaction lasted all the way home.

As soon as Sal opened the front door of the house, Aisha was all over Kiki, sniffing, licking, and kissing as Kiki laughed with glee. It seemed to Kiki like forever since she had experienced Aisha's exuberant affection. And Meg was right behind with a welcoming hug.

After a delicious lunch, a long walk, a bit of sightseeing before dinner, and a good night's sleep, Sal, Kiki, and Aisha prepared to leave for the East Coast. On her way to work at the hospital, Meg dropped them off at a warehouse where the truck was being loaded. As soon as Sal signed for her cargo, she climbed into the cab. Kiki rubbed the pink passenger door affectionately and motioned Aisha to jump up. As soon they all were aboard and seat belts fastened, Sal pulled out of the lot.

Kiki had brought with her the tattered road map left from her journey west the summer before, and she and Sal laughed about their experiences then. Kiki felt that this trip would be a totally new adventure. On the first day out, rather than the last, she would pass through the Rockies, because they were starting in Salt Lake City instead of that little town in Kansas.

After initial awkward moments as they settled themselves and Aisha stretched out for a nap behind them, Sal began asking questions. "Okay, now that we have more time to talk than our occasional letters, tell me all about your year in school. Are you still happy there? Is it worth it?"

Kiki leaned back and thought for a moment. She warmed to the chance to put things in perspective. "Well, it was hard, *very hard*, in the beginning. When I was hiding out, it was all like a dream. I just went on from minute to minute, expecting to wake up back in the South Bronx. When I was caught, I had to start taking learning very seriously and I began to realize what an uproar I had caused. The people at Montrose were actually wonderful. I'm not sure that they were happy in the beginning with admitting me—"

"Well," Sal broke in with a warm laugh, "can you blame them? You did do a colossal bit of gate crashing!"

"Yes, I know," Kiki admitted as she flushed with a touch of regret. "I won't ever do anything like that again. It was pretty painful. Eventually, it turned out okay, and I think by the end of the year, I was able to prove to myself and the administration that they hadn't made a mistake in giving me a chance. But the burden, Sal. I felt so much weight from the heavy class load, trying to keep my grades up and working two jobs. I couldn't go to school just for me, I had to go for the college officials, too. Sometimes I got so tired, I wanted to give up, yet I couldn't let them down."

"Or yourself, perhaps?" Sal asked as she worked the rig around a slow-moving, heavily loaded van.

"Oh, yes, of course, or me."

"So, after a year, how do you feel?"

"Well, I still feel like I've died and gone to heaven, if you know what I mean. All the things I'm learning, all the things I'm exposed to, that I could never have experienced if I'd stayed at home—it's so amazing that it's almost unbelievable. I'm still awed by it. At times, I also get scared, lonely, and homesick and, when I'm tired, I just don't think I can keep it up for three more years."

"But you're going to try, aren't you?" Sal asked with a bit of apprehension.

"Oh, yes. I won't quit. I'm just fearful that one day there will be a challenge that's bigger than I am and I won't make it. That scares me a lot. However, as long as I can see a way through the problems, day by day, I won't give up."

"So far, when you've needed something, it's been there, hasn't it?"

Kiki nodded. "Money, jobs, housing. Everything. Not fancy, not easy, but enough. Each time I thought I was at the end of my rope, I got an idea or something opened up. It was really unexpected. People have been so good to me."

Sal smiled. "Perhaps they have been so good because you gave them reason to be."

Kiki shrugged. "I don't know."

Sal patted her on the shoulder. "Kiki, I'm trying to pay you a compliment. People can be nice or not nice, and quite often we give them the cues as to how they should behave. Deep inside, maybe where you don't even realize it, you have faith that people will come through for you, and because you believe that, they do. That's a wonderful quality, and I knew you were special when we met."

Kiki smiled. "Thanks, but it's hard for me to see that I'm causing good things to happen."

"Well, believe you me, you are, Kiki."

For a few quiet moments, Kiki watched the scenery out the window. "You know, Sal," she finally said, "when things get rough, I do sometimes wonder how important it is to have a college education. You don't have a lot of schooling, and you seem to be happy. Jim probably has a high school diploma, if that, and he owns his own business. Mrs. Trang manages the dining hall at Montrose, and I know she doesn't have a lot of formal schooling. Some of the most important people in my life are not educated. In the South Bronx I thought you had to have a degree to do anything. Do you really need one?"

Sal was thoughtful for a minute. "Well, in my case, I had a choice about schooling and if I wanted to, I could still return to college. Right now I'm happy because I'm doing what I like. I'm free to change my mind and do something different if I stop being satisfied. I don't know whether your Mrs. Trang ever had a choice about getting a degree, and having met Jim, I would suspect that in his generation and being African-American, he has risen above any expectations he ever had for himself. Yet if you were to ask him what he wants for his three daughters, what would he say?"

"That he'd want them to go to college," Kiki admitted. "And he doesn't make enough to put them through college, at least not a college like Montrose. He's helping me through, but I doubt that he's been able to save much for them." She thought for a moment. "You know, if I ever complete college and make some money, I'd like to help him, to pay him back, so his girls could have a chance for a good education."

"That's a lovely idea, Kiki." Sal smiled to herself and they both remained thoughtfully quiet for the next few miles.

A little while later, Sal again picked up the conversation. "So how's your summer, so far?" she asked.

"It's interesting. Working full-time in admissions is a real challenge. We spent the first week moving from one building to another, but now I'm into the real job. I don't think I like repetitive grunt work, like stuffing envelopes and making labels; however, I try hard to do a good job, because I am preparing packets for new students who are coming in the fall. It's so important that each packet be complete with all the information they need when they arrive on campus. It's a bit of a thorn in my side, because I am constantly reminded of how *I* got there. At the same time, perhaps I—as much as anyone— can appreciate how important it is to start off on the right foot. When school starts, the job will be part-time, and I think I can handle it. The pay is better than washing dishes and I like the work more than that, for sure. I have the chance to meet a lot of interesting people, too." Kiki bubbled over with enthusiasm.

While watching some traffic behind her in the rearview mirror, Sal grinned with amusement. "I notice that you've lost a lot of your

South Bronx accent."

Kiki laughed. "Thanks, I've been working on it all year, just by listening to how other people talk, but I bet when I get home, I'll drop right back into it."

"That's okay. You can lose it again when you leave," Sal observed. "Tell me about your apartment."

"It's a one-bedroom unit in the Hillview Apartment complex. Thankfully, it's furnished, because after I put my sheets on the bed, hung up my clothes in a corner of the closet, and put my underwear in one drawer of the chest, I already felt a bit stressed out with the move." She laughed and Sal joined her. "Actually, I was really lonely the first couple of nights. Then Jim loaned me a little TV that was not being used at his house, and that helped. Then I started to get to know some of the neighbors, and now it's fine. I don't think I'm ready to live alone for a long period of time, although I can handle it for three months, because I'm still on campus and can eat in the dining hall and be with people I know all day. Then I have my job at the pizza parlor on the weekends, and sometimes during the week, too. So, all in all, I don't have too much time to feel alone," Kiki summarized.

"Your friend Karen graduated, right?" Sal asked.

"Yeah, she finished in December but marched in the graduation ceremony in May. I watched the ceremony. It was really cool and emotional to see her receive her degree. Yet sad, too. She's spending a year in San Francisco and then may go to graduate school, perhaps out of the country. I probably won't see much of her. I liked her a lot, yet she was kind of pushy. I really had to stand my ground with her, and I'm not always sure how to do that. College is so different from the way we used to tease and push each other around in high school. You have to think and learn to use words very carefully. I'm not really good at it, yet I'm doing better."

Their conversation continued as they wound through the Rockies and then down the eastern slopes toward Denver. It was dark by the time they arrived, and Kiki was excited to see the lights spread out below her as they approached the city. She was recalling the previous summer as Sal pulled into a big truck stop.

While Sal set the brakes and prepared to climb out of the cab, Kiki looked around and her face lit up. "This is the same place we stopped going the other way last year, isn't it?"

"Yes," Sal nodded as she pulled down a lengthy diesel hose.

Laughing, Kiki climbed from the passenger seat and ran out into the middle of the gasoline island, where the giant trucks were lined up in a row. She pointed two directions. "Then this is where I decided whether to look for another ride going west, or go on to Salt Lake City with you and Aisha."

Sal nodded. Kiki twirled on the station island, with a big smile on her face.

16

Mama and Papa

As they neared her neighborhood, Kiki kept glancing nervously at Sal, trying to guess what she was thinking. When Kiki looked at the streets where she grew up, she felt nearly sickened by the graffiti, dirty barbed wire fences, aging buildings, and ragged looking kids playing on cracked concrete strewn with debris and the occasional dumped vehicle carcass. Sal made no comments, but Kiki pulled into herself. It had been a year since she had looked at this reality. *Better than it once had been, still worse than East Oakland, and not a nice place to live.*

Sal had dropped the trailer for unloading at a warehouse in Newark, and they had come on from there, slowed by rush-hour traffic and progressing in stops and starts through various recently-gentrified neighborhoods. Now they were in the thick of the South Bronx, and it wasn't very pretty. Somehow, to Kiki, it seemed worse than she remembered.

Fortunately, there was a place that Sal could park near Kiki's apartment building. The Rodriguez family knew they were coming, and Gusto was hanging out of a front window, watching for them to arrive. Now sixteen, he had shot up in height during the past year and was sporting a mustache like his papa. He called out to Kiki as she climbed down from the truck and she waved back. It was wonderful to see him again, she realized, but he had clearly grown a lot.

Before Sal could come around the front of the truck, the whole family had rushed down the front steps to greet them. Mama reached out to hug Kiki, and Papa offered a big hand to Sal.

"You hav' good trip?" he asked warmly.

Sal nodded with a gentle smile.

"Such a long way, all the way from California. Must be thousands miles? Si?"

"Yes," Sal nodded, "although Kiki flew part of the way to Salt Lake City. We started driving from there. Not quite so far."

Gusto examined the cab of the truck. "Yours?" he asked with wide eyes.

"Yes," Sal responded. "It's my living," she acknowledged, looking around warily, "and I hope it's okay to park it here."

"It's okay," Gusto said. "I got friends. We keep it safe for you. No worries. That your dog?"

Aisha was confused, alternately wagging her tail and barking as she waited in the cab.

"Yes, that's my personal guard dog," Sal explained, turning to calm Aisha. "I drive alone on the road, and she keeps me company. She's a good protector. Her name is Aisha, and she won't hurt you if I let her know that you're safe to be around."

"That's cool," Gusto said in awe. "It's hard ta keep a dog 'round here. They git shot, stole, hit in da street, or killed by a larger stray. An' it's too much money."

Sal agreed. "Dogs can be very expensive. I know I'm lucky to have Aisha."

Papa was admiring the semi cab. He walked around it, touching it very carefully and noting every detail. "Fine truck," he finally observed with a broad smile.

Mama became aware that they all were standing in the overbearing heat. "You come in? You want bring dog, too?"

"If it's okay," Sal queried.

"Sure, it's okay," Mama agreed. "She belong to you, so it's okay. Too hot out here, anyway."

Relieved, Sal let Aisha out of the truck, and Gusto whistled for some of his friends, who all gathered around the stoop to talk and make sure that the pink cab remained untouched. Meanwhile, everyone else followed in single file up the dark staircase to apartment 3A, where they could smell the pleasant aroma of beans, pork and Spanish rice cooking. Mama had gone all out for Kiki's homecoming.

While Mama bustled around putting the food on the table, Papa asked questions in his halting English. It was apparent that Kiki's standing in his eyes had changed since she had left home and was now a college student. He looked at her with obvious parental pride and love.

"You do okay in school?" he asked. "You get good grades?"

"Yes, Papa. I got mostly B's with a couple of A-'s. I really did well. I brought home my grades to show you. They are in my duffle bag and I can't wait for you to see them."

Papa shook his head with amazement. "Is hard to believe. Your friends, they just get out of high school, and here you come home from one year college. I don' understand this college with no high school diploma, but if they let you in, I guess it's okay."

Sal smiled at him. "It's a very good school, Mr. Rodriguez. Kiki has done extremely well, and you have every right to be proud of her."

Mama's meal smelled and tasted delicious, and they ate and talked well into the evening. Without air conditioning, however, the apartment became hot and sticky, so eventually Kiki took Sal up to see her rooftop hideaway. Pointing down to a spot on the roofing tiles, Kiki explained, "This is where I used to lie down and just watch the stars. That's how I found Artemis, and I used to talk to her every night, praying for things to get better."

"And did they?" Sal raised an eyebrow.

Kiki grinned. "You bet, and I thank her every time I can. See her blinking at us up there?"

Kiki pointed out her star, just visible in the hazy nighttime sky.

Sal watched for a moment and then looked at Kiki. "I don't want to change the subject, Kiki, but there's something we need to talk about. Tomorrow morning I have to pick up a new load in Jersey and leave for Salt Lake. You have another week of vacation left, and while I would love to have you ride back with me, I think it would be better if you spent that week here with your family. You haven't been home in a year, and who knows when you'll have a chance to come again. To spend one night and then leave hardly seems fair to you or them."

Kiki was surprised and perturbed. "That's great, except how will I return to school?"

Sal put her hand on Kiki's arm. "Look, I know you don't want to depend on anyone; however, I brought you along, and I promised to get you back to California. I didn't say how. I have a travel-agent friend who knows all the tricks with the airlines, and I've managed to find you this really cheap ticket back to San Francisco International a week from tomorrow. You can ride the BART back to Montrose from the airport. You might as well use the ticket, because it's one of those no refund, no change deals, so I can't return it, anyway. So please use and enjoy."

She pulled the ticket from her hip pocket and handed it to Kiki.

Kiki's eyes opened wide. She felt overwhelmed. She held the ticket tightly and stared at it, unreadable though it was in the darkness. "I don't know what to say. I thought it was wonderful just to be able to come along. I never expected this from you."

"I know you didn't expect it. That's what makes it easy to give it to you. I know we both would have enjoyed being together for the trip back, although I do drive to the Bay Area now and then, and we will have more opportunities to visit with one another during the year. Being here and sorting things out with your family—and all your old friends—is more important for you in the long run. And if I'm really your friend, I need to support the highest good for everyone."

Tears welled up in Kiki's eyes. "Oh, Sal," she said, leaning against

Sal's shoulder, "I've never known anyone like you. You are so special to me."

Sal gave Kiki a warm hug. "You're special to me, too. That's why I want you to stay here for a week."

Sal spent the night on the living room couch, with Aisha on the floor beside her, and Kiki lay awake in her old room. *A whole week ahead of her.* Not having prepared for it, her mind raced with thoughts of all the things she would want and need to do with the time. She had noticed that Javier had not been around at dinner or anytime during the evening. She didn't want to embarrass her parents with Sal there, but she had a feeling he was in trouble, or maybe worse. She would ask tomorrow, after Sal left.

Dawn came early, and Mama struggled out of bed to fix a good breakfast for Sal's departure. Mama clearly understood that Kiki's friend had a long day ahead of her. While Sal cleaned her plate of scrambled eggs and Mama's special potatoes, Mama watched her. "I want to thank you," she spoke carefully, "for making possible for Kiki to stay with us for a little while. I very grateful to you, and so is her papa."

"No problem, Mrs. Rodriguez," Sal replied. "It seems unfair to me to take Kiki away this morning when she has had so little time to visit."

"You, with dat big truck, you be very, uh, different. Yet I know you good person," Mama said. "You good to Kiki."

Sal looked at her deeply as she stood up and made ready to leave. "Kiki is a wonderful girl. You are very lucky to have her as your daughter. Any parent would be proud of her."

Mama nodded and her eyes became moist. Sal put her strong arms around Mama, and the two women held each other for a brief moment, connected emotionally by their mutual love for Kiki.

Gusto's friends showed up just as the family came down the steps to the street. Sal signaled Gusto over and handed him a few folded bills. "Share with your friends to thank them for protecting my truck," she commented.

Gusto seemed surprised and very happy. "Thanks," he said, his eyes glowing with appreciation.

Sal then hugged Kiki goodbye and climbed into the driver's seat of the semi, Aisha jumping in before her. Kiki's body trembled. Despite the fact that it was hard to say goodbye to Sal and Aisha, she knew that it was right for her to stay as long as possible.

Later in the day, Mama dug around in her secret hiding place and came up with a few dollars cash. "Let's go shopping for some clothes for you," she said, tousling Kiki's long hair. "I save a little bit, 'cause I wanna help with your college."

Kiki hesitated a moment. She knew from experience that her mama's fantasy would include Kiki in a beautiful dress—but hopefully by now she knew better than to insist on that.

When they arrived at Mama's favorite clothing store, Kiki pointed out items that she needed and would use, and her mama seemed willing to settle for a pretty blouse, a pair of good slacks, and sturdy shoes that were nice enough for Sunday best. Kiki was thinking about her new job in admissions, where staff members dressed a tad better than the usual student sweats, T's, and jeans.

After shopping, they stopped for a treat at an older independent drug store still equipped with a soda fountain. Having a chocolate milkshake was a major treat in Kiki's family, one savored only on special occasions. So Kiki sipped hers slowly, as she and Mama talked.

"What's happened to Javier?" Kiki finally asked.

Mama looked downcast and shrugged. "He got in trouble with the law, just like Raul. They arrest him two week ago. His bail, it was too high, so he's in jail waitin' for his trial. We pretty sure he not be home for long time."

Kiki put her hand on her mama's arm. "I'm sorry, Mama."

Mama nodded. "Me, too. I don' know what I do wrong. Two boys in jail. Very sad."

"Mama, you didn't do anything wrong. He was in a gang, so was Raul. They were influenced by the others, and before they knew it, they were in deep trouble. It's not your fault."

Mama sighed. "I wish I understood why."

Gusto had spread the word that Kiki was home, so before that evening was over, some of her old friends had come around to see her. After dinner, she took off with two girlfriends from high school so they could talk.

One of the girls was her best friend Manuela, always very outspoken, and the other was Rowena Manstead, who like Kiki, came from an ethnically mixed background. Rowena's skin was olive, her eyes brown, and her hair blonde, making her stand out among others in her class. Kiki had always figured that Rowena was a kindred spirit, in that she probably had to deal with bullying and prejudice at school and might have a tough home life.

Kiki watched and studied both of the girls affectionately. Their presence brought back memories from her childhood. Laughing and sharing stories as they walked, the trio drifted into a neighborhood café, sat at a table, and ordered cooling soft drinks.

Manuela did most of the talking and the asking. "The kids aroun' here couldn't believe it when they heard you left last summer," she began, not being able to wait to get all the news. "So what's it like being in college?"

Kiki didn't want to put her friends down in any way, so she just mentioned that she had been very lucky, college courses were hard, and she was hanging in there.

Manuela shrugged and let the subject drop. Her face then lit up, and Kiki could see that Manuela really wanted to share her own news. "Do you know only a little more than half our class graduated?"

Kiki was surprised, although immediately she knew that she shouldn't have been. "Why?"

"Well, between girls gettin' pregnant, and guys gettin' arrested, there was a lot missing at graduation. Carlotta dropped out after the first semester, then Rochelle, and then Cristina. They all got knocked up. Phillipe and Jose both went to jail. Carlos was killed in a drive-by shooting—they wounded his younger sister, too. It was awful. There was even two suicides, prob'ly because of drugs. You remember Antonio and Ruel? Antonio shot himself in the head with a pistol, and Ruel had one of those weird accidents in his car. He totaled it but there wasn't no other car involved."

"Wow," was all Kiki could say. The more Maneula talked, the more Kiki was glad she had left. "I'm happy that at least half made it through," she finally commented. "I hope some of them can go to college."

Manuela raised an eyebrow and then continued, "And they kicked Benita out because they caught her in the restroom doing something kinky with this girl from the junior class. Benita was always weird, but would you believe? She's been strutting around the 'hood wearing leather and chains. She is never coming back to school."

Kiki frowned. "I thought being gay wasn't so much of a problem anymore."

Manuela laughed. "Well, maybe out there in California and in college. But in high school, and when one of the girls is sixteen, it's illegal. All kinds of bad things could have been done to Benita, but when the junior admitted she wanted to do it, they let Benita off easy by just kicking her out of school. The younger girl was temporarily suspended and had to go to some kind of counseling—yuck!"

Kiki shook her head. She couldn't begin to tell them about the sexual complexities of her own inner world, so she just commiserated and let it pass.

Soon they left the café and strolled down the sidewalk, still hot from the afternoon sun. When teens out cruising in an old convertible started hooting at them, the three girls ducked into Rowena's tenement building. Kiki was in no mood to be hassled or have to fight— she just had to make it through a week, and she'd be gone.

Time passed very quickly. Papa got paid before Kiki's scheduled departure, and he, too, contributed a little of his earnings toward some clothing for her and a second duffle bag to take her new stash back to California on the plane. Gusto presented her with a little pin on a neck chain. Having little jewelry, she coveted the gift yet was afraid to accept it for fear that he had come by it illegally. Kiki started to challenge him, and he quickly protested, "Don't worry, it's not hot. I promise, cross my heart."

"Okay, then, thank you." Kiki gave him a long hug.

Everyone in the household made the trip to the airport to see her off. They could ill afford the cost in gasoline; however, it wasn't every day that a family in the South Bronx put a daughter on an airplane for the West Coast. This journey to take Kiki to her flight and watch planes take off would be their big entertainment for the summer. She could not deny them that, and besides, she didn't want to say goodbye until the last possible moment.

At the airport, Kiki tearfully embraced her mama and papa and pulled Gusto aside to beg him to please stay out of trouble. He promised to be good. Then she waved as she walked to the security gate. In two weeks she had flown twice. Kiki sighed happily—*she was now a seasoned air traveler.*

After Kiki returned to Oakland, she sat in her apartment, replaying over and over in her mind her visit home and feeling very alone without her family. Yet her full-time job at Montrose and her weekend job with Jim took up most of her time for the rest of the summer.

There were special moments—the evening Kiki had dinner with the Williams family, and the night when Jim and Cora took her with them to hear Chicago-style jazz at an African-American nightclub in the heart of Oakland. Having the only light-skinned face in a sea of ebony, Kiki at first felt a little out of place, yet as the evening wore on she felt honored to be included and began to really enjoy herself. Jazz wasn't *her* music, but it was good music nevertheless. And Jim and Cora were great company. She enjoyed watching their caring interactions on a rare night out together.

She received letters from Jacinta in Mexico City and post cards from Karen, who had taken off to trek around Europe for several weeks.

During the little free time that Kiki had, she rode buses and BART and explored Oakland and Berkeley and even ventured into San Francisco for the first time on her own. She had felt ignorant and curious about her new home, and as she learned to get around, Kiki became more confident and independent. Whenever she went exploring, she pretended that she was Artemis, wandering through the forest in search of adventures.

Almost too soon, the summer vacation was over, and the caravan of returning students rolled onto campus. Residence halls reopened, and Kiki moved back into Olsen Hall, relieved to see everyone and to know that classes were about to resume. When Jacinta arrived from Mexico City, Kiki gave her a welcoming hug, and they rushed to the teashop to sit and talk about the summer. They were still to be suitemates but Julie had moved into another living situation with a sophomore whose dating life paralleled hers. "Must be nice," Kiki sighed, and both she and Jacinta laughed.

Thanks in part to her job in admissions, Kiki was now a lot more aware of the complexities of campus life and the hurdles for new students settling in. Sensitive to those who were feeling homesick or lonely, she did her best to help them over the hump. Privately, Kiki thought about how lucky these freshmen were—she would never, *could never*, tell them her own story.

With her freshman year behind her, Kiki walked the Montrose campus with a new kind of pride. She even had a cocky stride, feeling taller than her five feet, two inches. No more nightmares about being discovered by security and thrown off the campus. No duffle bag in trash barrels. No dark basement room. No fears that she would fail all her classes. The new Kiki was legal, official, and funded. At the last possible moment, the paperwork had come through providing her tuition, room and board. It had been a private worry of hers during the summer months; however, Sonia had assured her that everything would work out, and finally, just a few days before classes were to begin, the confirmation arrived. She still had to earn enough from her jobs for books and supplies, personal needs and occasional entertainment. Books alone, she had discovered during her first year, would cost several hundred dollars.

When Kiki moved into her new room on the second floor of Olsen Hall, she put her things away and surveyed the room happily. *She was a sophomore!* This fall felt so different from the previous year. She was very pleased with her achievement, and at moments when the future—three more years of study, hard work, and probably very little time for fun—loomed ahead, she stopped a moment to think of her neighborhood in the South Bronx. Just a brief look backward helped her find gratefulness in her heart and hope for the future.

However, because of her job on campus, and her increasing academic load, she was forced to cut back at Jim's to one evening each weekend. He nodded sadly when she told him. "I'll miss ya, Kiki," he admitted. "Ya really helped my business, and I care about ya a lot. Ya know that."

Kiki reached up and pulled him into a hug. "I like you, too. You've been very good to me. I'll still be around, just not as often."

He nodded. "I know. I jis' don' know how I'll keep up." He sighed.

"I'll see if I can find you someone to help," she promised.

Kiki asked around the campus until she located another promising student whose financial situation was marginal and sent the freshman over to see Jim. Because this new girl had been referred by Kiki, he took a chance on another Montrose student.

Comparative religion emerged as Kiki's favorite class during the fall semester, because it was being taught by Nancy Raines and because on Sundays after chapel, several members of that class met for tea in Nancy's study, where they sat around for hours and discussed topics related to spirituality. The regulars included students from Asia, whose backgrounds in Islam, Hinduism, Buddhism, and Taoism brought a whole new flavor to any discussion. Kiki always felt that her brain was being expanded every time she attended this informal group. She admired the way Nancy was able to sift through the conflicts in different religious ideologies and see the underlying threads of commonality. After working on Saturday night at Jim's, Kiki sometimes couldn't pull herself out of bed in time for chapel, but she always managed to get to the tea sessions afterwards. *Yes,* Kiki told herself as she rushed across campus to make a meeting, *hard as it was, college was worth the effort.*

17

Dr. Capehart

There were two *big* items on Kiki's current agenda, after economic survival. The first was to settle down and officially select her college major, and the second was to consider what she was going to do with her education after graduation. These thoughts had not been particularly important last year, when she was struggling just to prove she belonged at Montrose. Now they loomed as major decisions. They both seemed so far down the road to Kiki that she wouldn't have thought of them at all, if Dr. Capehart hadn't given her all those tests and helped her to map out a class schedule for her sophomore year.

Kiki also had a private, *personal* agenda that she rarely admitted to anyone. This one focused on the question of her sexuality. Sometimes she felt that she was a lesbian, yet she wasn't really sure. Although she wasn't phobic about being a lesbian, she did think that whether she was or not could affect how she planned her future. Life would seem a lot easier, she felt, if she just didn't feel caught in the middle somewhere, without any true sexual identity. The many questions raised by this very complex issue were *not* something she wished to share with Dr. Capehart. Nancy Raines, yes. The psychology professor, no.

Meanwhile, Kiki's friends were also struggling with their own life decisions. Jacinta sat in Kiki's dorm room one evening and announced, "I've decided I'm going to teach school in Mexico City after I graduate. So I'm declaring a Spanish major and a minor in psychology."

"That makes sense for you," Kiki had observed. "I just wish I knew what I was going to do."

Jacinta smiled. "You'll figure it out, Kiki. You're very bright and resourceful. The answer will come to you."

Kiki nodded and kept mum about her *other* and most private issues.

Julie Anderson, who still kept contact with Kiki, ran into her in a dorm hallway and told Kiki she was going to major in art history. Since Julie seemed destined to marry well and came from an affluent family, Kiki realized that she could enjoy the luxury of an art major and perhaps advance to graduate school for further study. Kiki wasn't jealous. She liked Julie and wished her the best, although hearing these decisions underscored the fact that she hadn't a clue yet what she wanted to *do* or to *be*.

When she thought about *her* major, Kiki began to feel that she had to make a practical choice. She realized that being a Montrose student was a real luxury for her. Had she attended a junior college, maybe near Sunnyvale, she could have majored in business or computer science and been out of school with a usable trade in two years, and without a lot of debt. However, that fateful summer night Kiki had entered the gates of Montrose, where her mind and her whole world were expanding immeasurably. It was wonderful, except there was no clear career path. She now questioned whether a liberal arts education was really practical—especially for someone with such a limited background and future financial prospects.

After chapel the following Sunday, Kiki privately mentioned this concern to Nancy Raines, and Nancy had an interesting response. "I believe you were *meant* to be here, Kiki. Although I don't know all the reasons why, I don't think that such things happen by accident. You were dropped off at the front gate of Montrose for a reason."

Kiki sighed. "My friend Sal has suggested something similar. Sometimes I get it, and sometimes I don't. Right now it's hard to see."

Nancy nodded, "In the long run, I think you will find that a liberal arts education will pay you back many times over, yet I can understand that right now it's hard to visualize that. I can say, however, with some certainty that you are growing into a person that you could never have become if you had stayed in the South Bronx. That in itself is a very good thing."

Kiki sighed. "You may be right, yet I wish I could figure out where I'm headed. I need to have a major picked out—and soon."

Nancy smiled. "You will, Kiki, you will. Just be patient with yourself."

Kiki shrugged. "Okay. I'll try."

Not knowing just how to apply all these interesting and challenging subjects she was taking, Kiki decided she would have to think hard and ask lots of questions in order to decide on her major. She enjoyed every subject she took, and she did reasonably well in most of her classes. If money were not a problem she could pick any major she wanted. In her case, she had to find a good job not only to live but also to pay back the student debt she was accumulating.

Kiki finally accepted the inevitable and made an appointment with Dr. Capehart. In terms of selecting a major, the professor was very astute and helpful, when Kiki confessed to her the doubts she was feeling about being in a liberal arts college.

"I get it that you feel you need classes that have a practical application," Rita responded. "Let's look at that a bit. For your information, the college *is* moving in the direction of more business courses and even an MBA program. Although we don't currently, at the undergraduate level, have a business or computer major, we do have *courses* in these areas. We also have other classes that fit into a business-oriented program."

She sat down with Kiki and looked at her file, her test scores from the previous year, and her current list of classes. "This is what we could do that could meet both goals for you. If we select a major in communications, backed by courses in computer science, business practices, psychology, economics and Spanish, then—"

Looking at Rita thoughtfully, Kiki interrupted her. "Why Spanish?"

"Well, you have a bilingual background, right?"

Kiki nodded.

"If you decide to remain in California after graduation, then being able to communicate in Spanish will be very helpful in finding employment and advancing in the work force. I don't think it would hurt even if you go back to New York."

Kiki smiled. "I get it now. I think you are right about the Spanish."

Rita studied her for a moment. "I have seen your flyers for Big Jim's Pizza, and you are very creative. There is one other class I would suggest that you definitely include. That is graphic design, which is offered in the art department. It involves a combination of artistic and computer skills."

Kiki inhaled deeply and then smiled. "Wow, that makes me feel better. Like I have some kind of foundation to stand on." A little frown crossed her face. "I'm really hungry to have it all," she admitted. "Yet although I want more art history and some music and drama and English literature, I realize I have to make choices. I guess I just have to be grateful that this school will allow me to create my own special program."

Rita put a hand on her shoulder. "Once you have experienced the thrill of learning, you will go on learning for the rest of your life. It won't stop when you walk off the Montrose campus."

Once she had a clear study plan, Kiki threw herself into this second year at Montrose with all the enthusiasm and energy she could muster. Her job in admissions was at times tedious; every time she thought that, she reminded herself about the year washing dishes in the dining commons. She immediately stopped complaining.

As weeks flew by, Kiki began to realize that her sexual issues were much more complicated than choosing a college major. The questions of *who* she was, and *what* she was, kept pushing harder at her consciousness, and she needed safe places and people with whom to talk about her feelings.

Although she had guesses about a few students, they didn't wear signs announcing their sexual orientation, and Kiki personally knew no one on campus who was openly lesbian except Nancy Raines. So she sat in Nancy's religion class watching the petite instructor with admiration. Kiki really liked Nancy, and her class as well. Unfortunately, after meeting with Dr. Capehart, Kiki already knew that next semester she would have to focus on her core classes and give up the liberal "frills."

One day, after the tea gathering, Kiki hung around Nancy's study to talk with her privately. "I'm going to have to drop comparative religion next semester," Kiki admitted, "and I'm really going to miss it."

Nancy smiled. "That's too bad. Are you sure you'll miss the class, or the chance to stare at me? I sometimes think you have a little crush."

Kiki blushed. "Is it that obvious?"

Nancy put her arm around Kiki's shoulder and laughed good-naturedly. "Only if one is the subject of your long looks. I don't think the whole class knows, if that's what you mean. It's okay, I don't mind. Just so you know, you can still attend the teas on Sunday, even if you aren't enrolled in the class in spring semester."

Kiki felt a bit confused and uncomfortable. "I think I hang around you not only because I like you a lot but partly because you're the only lesbian I know, since Karen and her friends graduated. I'm not sure about myself, and I kind of look to people who know who they are, like maybe you know something that will help me figure myself out."

Nancy smiled kindly. "Look," she said, "I have somewhere to be in a few minutes. Let's make an appointment next week so we can talk about this, okay?" Kiki nodded and was relieved, because she so very much needed someone to talk with, other than Dr. Capehart.

The following Tuesday evening Kiki met with Nancy, and by that time, she had thought of several questions to ask. Nancy opened the discussion, moving right to the point. "We talked a little about this last year, right after you took the SAT. I can see you are still struggling. So, let's revisit the topic. What is it that confuses you about your sexuality?"

"Well," Kiki responded with a sigh. "I guess the fact that I don't really have one. The girls in my dorm mostly have boyfriends, and they talk about being out with them, and from the things they say, even casually, I know they are going to bed with them. In my high school, even, the girls were all dating by fifteen or sixteen, at least, and a lot of those girls are married, pregnant, or mothers by now. I somehow just never got around to it. I have three brothers, so I'm used to guys. I just don't seem to care."

Nancy raised a hand and then frowned a little. "But I remember from our few conversations that you lived in a stressful home environment, with fighting between your parents, financial problems, and your brothers getting into trouble. And you held a job at what, sixteen?"

Kiki nodded.

"So, in terms of your sexual development, we could label your childhood environment non-supportive and toxic?"

Kiki made a face and swallowed. "I guess that pretty well sums it up."

"So, it might have been hard for you to get in touch with your budding sexuality in a world where you were operating in survival mode."

Kiki shrugged. "Okay, so I'm here now, and it's not the same. I mean it's not toxic, and I know I'm growing, yet I'm so confused. One minute I feel jealous because others are talking about engagements, marriage plans, and children. The next minute I feel trapped because I don't want to fit into someone else's life plan. Guys seem to do that, at least the few I've met."

"So you have a rebellious streak, like your Artemis."

"I wouldn't be here without it, would I?"

Nancy laughed with amusement. "I suspect not."

Kiki frowned. "I also have to admit guys kind of bore me. When I spend time with them, I don't come away feeling—I don't know how to say it—well, I don't want to see them again because they want to kiss and more than that, if you know what I mean." She sighed. "When I spend time talking with another girl, later I feel good, happy, and I go around with a little song in my head. Then Karen Fullerton took me to a lesbian bar, and when this woman danced with me and became a bit provocative, I was frightened. So I came home confused, thinking maybe I'm not a lesbian either. Yet I'm lonely, and I wish I could be close to someone."

Nancy nodded and suggested quietly, "Look, Kiki, I can't assign you a sexual label. You will have to figure that out for yourself. Have you considered that perhaps you haven't met the right person and that sexual desire will blossom when you meet someone who feels really comfortable and whom you can trust? Just because it's not your nature to hop into bed easily doesn't mean you don't have normal sexual desires. Perhaps you need the safety and security of a trusting relationship before your feelings can emerge."

"But how will I know?" Kiki's tone was plaintive.

Nancy paused while Kiki bit her lip; she studied Kiki thoughtfully. "Lesbians have kind of a reputation for being quick to jump into bed with each other. My own experience is that lesbian women vary just as much as heterosexual women in their habits and natures.

"You have to be patient and follow your own instincts. If the men you've met bored you, you may not have met the right man. On the other hand, if you feel attracted to a woman, you may want to explore an intimate relationship. However, be sure you've had a chance to become friends first. Kiki, you may well be happier with a close relationship to a woman. Just don't rush into giving yourself a label."

"Present company excepted, I don't see any lesbians around to even talk to, let alone build a relationship with."

Nancy nodded understandingly. "Well, until recently women's colleges, including this one, were very repressive. Lesbians tend to feel at home in women's colleges, yet if a college becomes known as a lesbian hangout, then it becomes more difficult to attract students from the mainstream—something necessary for the school's fiscal survival. For many years, women's colleges were among the most restrictive of educational institutions. However, it's changing. At first there were just a few outspoken students, like Karen Fullerton, who openly admitted she was a lesbian. This open admission by Karen supports other lesbians to come out of the closet."

Nancy rose from her chair, signaling that her available time to talk had ended. She walked Kiki toward the door, where she offered a parting thought, "You may not have noticed that there is a very small lesbian and bisexual group on campus. They don't wave a rainbow flag, yet, but they're here. Sooner or later you'll find a notice of a meeting. Go to it, if you can fit it into your very busy schedule. You may be surprised to find that some of the girls who talk about boyfriends in the dorm do so only because it's a way to protect themselves. Yet their special friends are other women, not men."

Kiki's heart pounded. "Why do I find this idea so scary?"

Nancy smiled, "We live in a homophobic society. Many of us are taught that same-sex attraction is abnormal, perverted, even sinful. You probably went to Catholic Church when you were little. What did your priest say about homosexuality?"

"It was unnatural," Kiki recalled.

"So, as a little girl, what did you do with that information?"

"Remembered homosexuality as something to avoid," Kiki

admitted with a sigh.

"Well, that early teaching isn't overcome in a day. I know you've heard this before—just be patient. Your eyes will gradually open and you will see your own truth, believe me, if you can just allow it."

Kiki suddenly chuckled. "Meanwhile, I'm stuck with longing looks, watching the way a woman moves, and ogling the outline of her breasts under her blouse."

Nancy grinned. "Oh, Kiki, if that's what turns you on, just enjoy it."

The first half of Kiki's sophomore year thundered past like a passenger train at full speed. There was so much to do and so little time in which to do it. She was alternately exhilarated and enthused and then exhausted. Often, when she felt she couldn't go on, all she had to do was remember her life in the South Bronx, and she found courage to face another day.

Kiki worked so hard, especially as finals approached in December, that—just like the previous fall semester—she didn't think about Christmas or the holiday break. She ran from class to job to the dining commons to the library and to bed, sometimes as late as 1 a.m., then rose at 5:30 a.m. and started again. She barely had time to say hello to Jim when she worked her busy Saturday evenings at the pizza parlor.

After Kiki finished taking her last exam and was trudging exhaustedly back to Olsen Hall, she abruptly noticed that everyone was packing cars, and shuttles were arriving to take students to the airport. She stopped dead in her tracks. *She'd done it again. Now what was she going to do?*

When Kiki reached her room, Jacinta was closing her suitcase. She looked at Kiki happily and then, seeing the expression on her face, added kindly, "I wish I could take you home, Kiki, but Mexico City is so far away and so expensive though."

They hugged each other affectionately. "That's okay, Jacinta," Kiki sighed, "I'll figure something out."

The dorm was quiet that evening. Kiki paced the floor of her room for a while, then pulled on a sweatshirt, went outside and looked up at the sky. Although there had been rain earlier, now the clouds were broken and a few stars were visible. Kiki's Artemis appeared for a moment or two, and she focused on the pale blinking light. "Artemis, I need help. I don't know where to go or what to do. I can't go home, and I can't stay here. Please send me a sign." She stood looking up until her neck became stiff, and then she turned to go back inside the dorm.

Maybe, she thought, *if I just go to sleep tonight, when I wake up in the morning, an idea will occur to me.*

So she got ready for bed, climbed in, turned off the light, and tried to sleep.

Kiki awoke about 8:30 to sunlight peeping through her window. She sat up, startled, realizing a sound had penetrated her brain. A familiar sound. Not the chimes. The sound of an engine somewhere nearby. *Yes, it's the sound of a big truck!*

With her heart pounding in her throat, she pulled on her sweatshirt, jeans, and thongs and ran through the hallway, down the stairs, and into the lobby. Standing just outside the closed glass doors was Sal.

Kiki threw open the door and practically jumped into Sal's strong arms. "Oh, Sal," she cried out, "It's so good to see you. Where did you come from?"

Sal motioned toward the pink truck parked in front of the dorm. "Well, I had a load in the City, and I called Jim last evening at the pizza place. He said he hadn't talked to you and didn't know what you were doing for Christmas. So I decided, before I headed home, that I'd better stop by and see if you're okay."

Kiki trembled with emotion. "I was so busy taking exams, I didn't think about Christmas or anything else. Now the halls are closing. I don't have a thing planned and nowhere to go for the three-week break."

"Good thing I stopped." Sal gave her a warm smile. "Well, I guess I'd better hang around long enough for you to pack. You're coming to Salt Lake City to have Christmas with Meg, me, and Aisha. How's that for a plan?"

"That's wonderful!" Kiki said. "But are you sure? That's a lot to ask."

Sal nodded. "I spoke with Meg last night, and she told me to bring you home with me, if you wanted to come."

"Oh, wow!" Kiki was ecstatic.

She took Sal up to her room. "Don't look," she said, "it's a mess from exams. I haven't cleaned up yet."

Sal chuckled to herself as she looked at the papers and books littering the floor, the desk, and even Kiki's unmade bed. Clothes were thrown everywhere. "You know," she observed, "I was a college student once upon a time. This looks awfully familiar to me."

Sal pushed aside a few books and perched on the end of the bed while Kiki spent the next half hour locating and dropping into her duffle bags everything she would need for the trip.

As Kiki hurriedly packed, Sal thought about how sunny and how much nicer this room was—even if messy right now—than that cold, dark basement room Kiki had inhabited for one semester. She also noticed the bulletin board with pictures of Kiki's family, taken last summer, and pictures of Sal, Meg, Aisha and the pink truck, from the visit to Salt Lake City. It made Sal feel special that Kiki displayed them in her room.

When both Kiki's duffle bags were full, including her laptop, pink cap, and leather jacket, she locked the door to her room and followed Sal downstairs to the truck.

Aisha gave a big bark as they approached and covered Kiki's face with affectionate, sloppy kisses as soon as she climbed into the cab.

First they headed to Oakland's commercial district, where Sal pulled into a warehouse dock to pick up the trailer loaded for her next run. "I'm headed to Portland, Oregon," she explained, "and there I'll get another load for Boise, Idaho. We'll drop that load and then dead-head home to Salt Lake City."

"Cool," Kiki exclaimed. "I'm going to see the world with you!"

"I have to be honest with you," Sal admitted. "While you are at my house, I'll only be there part of the time, because I'll have one big run before Christmas. If I were headed to the East Coast I'd try to take you to see your family, but I'm not going that far. So you'll be seeing a lot of Meg, and you'll have some down time alone in the house to explore, rest, and think. I hope that's okay."

Kiki nodded. "Maybe I can read a book or two just for fun."

Delighted at Kiki's reaction, Sal grinned. "Good idea. We have lots of books in the study that you might enjoy. However, I assure you I'll be home for Christmas, and we'll have a special holiday, the three of us. And Aisha, of course."

Despite both of them having rumbling stomachs, Sal pushed the big rig along the I-980 headed eastward to catch the I-5. Once far from the Bay Area congestion, Sal decided to stop at a diner for break-fast. "Chow down seriously," she suggested, and Kiki ordered a big breakfast. In an hour, they were headed toward the I-5 northbound for Portland.

"So how's school?" Sal asked, as she worked her way through free-way traffic.

"Great! I'm learning so much! It's all wonderful and challenging—the classes and my job in the admissions office. There does seem to be no end to the studying. I'm moving forward and still playing catch up with my language skills, but I'm so much better at it than when I started that I feel really confident I'm going to come out okay in the end. I only have time for about five hours of sleep at night, so sometimes I'm terribly exhausted."

Sal smiled. "That's a common student complaint. Just be thankful that you're young and able to recover. When we arrive in Salt Lake, you can sleep all day, if you want."

"Ha! That would be a change—but I'd be afraid I'd miss something important."

"That's one of your strengths, Kiki. Your endless curiosity to know about life, learning, and maybe love," Sal observed with a smile.

"Well, there is so much I want to know and don't have answers for—" Her voice trailed off and she looked out the window.

Sal glanced at her with a raised eyebrow and let the subject drop.

They spent the night at a motel in Weed, California, deep in the Siskiyou Mountains. From the building they could look to the south and see Mount Shasta covered in snow. The next day, they crossed the rest of the range and continued down into agricultural valleys during a long day through Oregon, finally reaching the south side of Portland late in the day.

Sal knew a motel where she could park her rig, and they took to their beds after giving Aisha a much-needed walk and watching a little TV. After their complimentary breakfast the next morning, Sal drove the truck on to her next warehouse, left one load, and shortly picked up another.

Next Sal pointed her rig east on I-84 along the Columbia River Gorge. Kiki was beside herself with excitement over the beauty of the big river. "This sure is different from the East River or the Hudson," she observed with a big grin.

When they reached the turnout for Oregon's famed Multnomah Falls, Sal pulled off the freeway. Given the late fall, even with an unusually nice day, there weren't many tourists around. She could leave the truck in a big parking lot and walk with Aisha and Kiki up the path to the falls. Sal pulled out her cell phone and took photos of Kiki with Aisha beside her in front of the majestic falls that cascaded down several hundred feet. "I'll make a print of this and give it to you before you return to college," she promised. Kiki smiled gratefully.

Because of the midmorning start from Portland and the stop at the falls for a short hike and a sandwich, the drive to Boise made for a very long day. They not only had to negotiate the Columbia River Gorge but also climb onto the high plateau of eastern Oregon that was bathed in remnants of a recent snowfall. The up side of the lengthy trip was that I-84 would stay with them all the way to Salt Lake City.

Meg was at the front door when they pulled into the driveway the following evening. She rushed out to give Kiki a big hug. Then she kissed Sal hello and roughed up the fur on Aisha's head. Aisha jumped up and gave Meg a big lick on the cheek. Everyone was relieved and happy that Sal and Kiki made the trip home safely.

Kiki's room was ready for her, and she dropped her two bags on the carpet and stretched out on the bed. *Three weeks with Sal and Meg. This was going to be luxury.*

When they sat down to dinner that evening, Kiki made a little speech. "This is all very wonderful," she said, looking at both of them. "You're both so kind and generous to let me come and stay with you for the break. When Christmas comes, this is enough. I don't want some big fancy gift from you that I can't reciprocate. You understand?"

Sal and Meg both laughed and looked at each other.

"Okay, okay," Sal commented finally. "I get it. We are giving you room and board and transportation both ways, so that's all you'll accept. Is that the deal?"

Kiki nodded.

"Well, there might be one little present, nothing big like the computer last year. I promise," Sal said, crossing her heart with her hand. Meg just smiled, and they moved on to other things.

Later as they were having ice cream for dessert, Sal picked up the conversation again. "Now, I'm agreeing to your deal, but I want you to realize that you have to think of us as family. Meg and I are like your aunts. We're never going to have children, so we take great pride in watching you mature and fulfill your potential as a young woman. And now and then you are going to have to allow us a little latitude to give you something to help you along the way. Understood?"

Kiki mulled it over. "I kind of wanted you to be a big sister," she admitted, "since I've never had one. However, if you both want to be my aunts, that's okay too."

"Well, given the difference in our ages," Sal observed, "Meg and I thought that aunts would be more appropriate."

"But not a lot of presents. You do so much for me already."

Sal gave her a knowing look. "And you want to do it on your own, right?"

Kiki nodded. "As much as I can. If I'm ever in *real* trouble, I promise to let you know and we can talk about it."

Sal's face slipped into a questioning frown. "Speaking of aunts, did you ever contact that aunt of yours in Sunnyvale?"

Kiki sighed. "Yeah, I finally did. I haven't gone there to visit, but Aunt Fina and Uncle Roberto came up to see me once at Montrose. They had an old pickup truck that was missing some paint and had a few dents, and everybody stared at them when they parked in front of the dorm. I had them in my room, and I took them to the dining commons, and we talked about home and about their family and how they like California. I don't think they felt very comfortable, and as soon as they could see that I was okay at the school, they made signs that they wanted to leave. Their English was kind of limited, too. I haven't seen them since."

"That's tough," Meg observed.

"Well, with all due respect to your relatives, maybe it was best that Artemis led you to Montrose instead of Sunnyvale," Sal suggested with a raised eyebrow.

They all laughed, but Kiki put her hand on Sal's arm. "It's really more sad than funny, and I feel for them; however, you are probably right about where I ended up."

Meg nodded, and Sal agreed. "*You're* right, Kiki," Sal told her, "it isn't funny and we shouldn't make a joke about someone else's difficulties. Thank you for calling me on it—I'm proud to know such a sensitive and thoughtful young woman."

Kiki sighed. Looking at all of them around the table, she recognized her outstanding fortune to have met Sal and Meg, as well as Aisha, because the couple considered her family. Kiki felt a deep sense of belonging, a feeling she had never known before. *Thank you, Artemis, for leading me to Sal, Meg, and Aisha.*

18

Kiki

Alone in Sal and Meg's house, Kiki sat cross-legged on the floor in the spare bedroom that served as a work area and study. She was surrounded by a pile of lesbian romance novels. Sal and Aisha were gone on the road, and Meg was at the hospital working.

For the first couple of days, Kiki's time in Salt Lake City had passed pretty much as Sal had predicted. She slept a lot, watched a little TV, and thought about school, her future, and her sexuality. The latter topic had been coming up more and more often in her thoughts and dreams.

On the third day, left alone to explore, Kiki walked around the house and looked at pictures of Sal and Meg. She tried to project herself into their world, to feel what it must be like to be them. Kiki also made it into the study and noticed the lesbian romance novels. From then on, she spent every free moment pouring through the books. She found all of them intriguing, and they provided her with more questions to ask about being a lesbian.

Kiki noticed to her delight that explicit sexual scenes between women excited her. She had known physical sensations from the time she was about thirteen, as hormones first raged through her system, and she had talked with Manuela about it a few times, but boys didn't seem to bring out that physical electricity in her. In her high school years, she had had moments of thoughts and sensations, yet little time to focus on what was happening. As a consequence, nothing in particular had—until she encountered this group of erotic books—really aroused Kiki's strongest and deepest feelings.

Her imagination ran with the new information and images from the novels. During a couple of nights, when she couldn't sleep, she started exploring her body and masturbating. She realized that it felt good to touch herself, even though she did it very quietly. After some experimenting, she was able to bring herself to a climax and discovered that doing so relieved the tension she was feeling after reading explicit sexual scenes.

She wasn't sure she wanted to speak to Sal and Meg about this new life development, so Kiki put the books carefully back where she found them. She felt more comfortable with the thought that when she got back to Montrose she could talk with Nancy Raines.

That Christmas was perfect for Kiki. Sal and Meg put up a tall evergreen tree in their high-ceilinged living room and covered it with colorful lights and decorations that they had accumulated over the years. They shared a light dinner on Christmas Eve and then drank eggnog and played Christmas carols on the stereo. Later they all sat under the tree and exchanged presents. Aisha got a big bone to chew—this kept her busy while her humans opened their presents. Meg and Sal exchanged personal gifts and a couple of household items that were needed or wanted. Then there was one present for Kiki, as promised. When she opened the package, she found a pink sweatshirt that announced in beautiful script letters, "My Gal Sal, Long Distance Hauling, Salt Lake City," and a new pink ball cap with the words "My Gal Sal."

Kiki looked at Sal quizzically and Sal laughed. "I thought your pink hat was beginning to look a little grungy. You must wear it every day."

Kiki blushed. "Yeah," she admitted, "a lot, anyway."

Sal gave her a big hug. "That's quite a compliment to me, you silly girl."

Meg surprised her with another package, one even Sal didn't know about. "Before you get upset," she said to Kiki, "please understand where I'm coming from. Sal's present to you is personal, and I love it, and you'll love it. I can see you wearing the sweatshirt in the dorm on cool nights when you are studying—and feeling Sal's presence through the shirt. That's special. However, *I* want to give you something to show my, or *our* pride, in your achievement at Montrose."

Curious, Kiki opened the second package and inside found a Montrose sweatshirt in blue and gold. "Oh, my goodness!" she gasped. "I saw these in the bookstore, but there was no way I could afford one. Oh, thank you, Meg!"

Meg smiled. "It's from both of us. I found it online and ordered it for you."

Kiki wrapped herself around Meg and then Sal. "You are both so wonderful to me!"

The day after Christmas, Sal had to leave on a long-haul trip; she returned by New Year's Eve. After dinner that evening, they sat around and talked about what they hoped would happen during the next year, played card games, and waited for midnight to arrive. They toasted with a small bottle of champagne and allowed Kiki to have a glass. Then they offered hugs all around and tumbled into bed.

Kiki had one more week before she returned to Montrose. During her hours alone at the house, she continued to read. When Meg was around, Kiki watched her in the kitchen, because she liked Meg's cooking and wanted to learn. Meg allowed her to make several dishes, and Kiki did well. Everything she attempted was at least edible and sometimes pretty good. Meg gave her hints that helped her improve the less successful ventures.

When Sal was home, Kiki went on long walks with her and Aisha to different places in Salt Lake City. During one of these walks, Kiki tried to open up a little to Sal, because she could feel their time together was running out.

"I really think I am a lesbian," Kiki said abruptly, bringing Sal up short.

"What makes you say that?" Sal asked gently.

"Aside from some of the things I've told you in the past, I've gotten close to Nancy Raines at Montrose. She's the college chaplain and teaches religion classes. She's also a lesbian. I think she's really sweet, and I have long talks with her. She says I have a crush on her, kind of like my PE teacher in seventh grade, and maybe she's right." Sal chuckled as Kiki spoke. "If I do, I'm realistic enough to know it won't go anywhere. At the same time, she's my source of lesbian information on campus. It's hard for me to find lesbian friends this year—Karen Fullerton and her buddies graduated. I'm sure there are others around, but I don't know how to find them. Nancy says I must have blinders on and that I haven't developed 'gaydar' to recognize them."

Sal grinned. "For what it's worth, I suspect your friend Nancy is right. I would think on a women's college campus that twenty, maybe even thirty, percent are lesbians. However, a lot of them keep quiet about it. Students are vulnerable. It's only the very strong ones that dare call attention to themselves—while still under the thumb, so to speak, and subject to the opinions and prejudices of faculty, administration, and parents who often are paying the bill for their education. I suspect you will eventually find any number of lesbians to relate to, if that's where you feel most comfortable."

Kiki wrung her hands for a moment. "I hope so. Not that I have much time for a social life, but impulses toward it are growing and I'm beginning to feel a bit frustrated."

Sal laughed. "Oh, Kiki, you are so cute. I adore you—in an Aunt Sal sort of way. You are growing up and growing into yourself. Everything will come together one of these days. Just be patient with yourself and the world, if you can."

Kiki sighed. "Everybody says to be patient. I do try."

As Sal was preparing to drive Kiki back to Oakland, she received a phone call about a high priority load that needed to go east. The trucker who had originally signed on to take the load had encountered engine problems and could not have his rig repaired in time. The transfer company asked if Sal could pick up the load instead.

"Kiki," Sal called out.

Kiki came on the run from her bedroom. "What?"

"Would you be terribly upset if we flew you back to Oakland instead of going in the truck?"

Kiki swallowed. "No, I mean, I was looking forward to going with you, but if you have to work, I understand that comes first. It's just that I don't—"

"Shhh. Don't worry about the money."

Sal turned back to the dispatcher on the phone and told him that she felt sure she could shift her other load and could handle the emergency run. She took down the details on a pad and then hung up.

Kiki was still looking distressed. "I don't want you going out of your way and spending lots of money on me."

Sal laughed. "I'm your Aunt Sal, remember? And, as an aunt, I can do things for you, once in a while. Is that clear?"

Kiki sighed. "Okay, one airplane ticket."

Sal put up a hand. "And $20 for the BART to get you back to school."

Kiki turned away, feeling her lack of financial resources. "Thank you, Sal."

"You are some stubborn kid. But I win this one."

Meg took Kiki to Salt Lake City International Airport and waited with her until she had to go through the security gate. "Have a fabulous spring semester, Kiki. You're a sweetheart, and we both love you. Take care of yourself, and we'll see you again soon."

Meg hugged Kiki warmly, and Kiki's eyes filled with tears. "Say goodbye to Sal when she comes back, and give a hug to Aisha, please."

Meg smiled. "I will. Now you go and enjoy your college!"

In mid January, as students returned to campus for the spring semester, Kiki felt ready and excited to begin. Her rest over the holidays had given her the energy to tackle a new set of courses, both jobs, and the long hours of study in the library. Jim seemed happy to see her back at the pizza shop, Jacinta returned with stories about Mexico City and her family, and Kiki told her all about her time in Salt Lake City—well not quite *everything*—and her stay with Sal and Meg.

Classes had barely started when students began sneezing and coughing. A round of cold and flu—probably brought back by a returning student—passed around campus, affecting students and faculty alike. Rumors flew that the small campus infirmary, used for non-emergency illnesses, was overflowing with patients.

Having such a heavy schedule, Kiki worried that she might become sick. It would be so hard for her if she got behind and then had to catch up with all her classes. She tried staying away from anyone who seemed to be sniffling, carrying around Kleenex, or stifling a cough.

Kiki remained strong for more than a week, while student after student fell sick. And then one day, she felt very tired. She could hardly climb out of bed, and she struggled to eat, make it to her classes and function during her afternoon job. She drank lots of coffee and hoped the down feeling was temporary. The next day she began sneezing and coughing. By the weekend, she had to call Jim and tell him she was too sick to work. He told her he understood and to take care of herself. By Sunday morning, she had a hacking cough and her lungs hurt.

By Monday, she couldn't go on. Pulling a jacket over her pajamas, she struggled up the hill to the infirmary.

"You've got a bug all right," said Dr. Rose Arnold, the stocky physician who headed the staff of nurses and assistants in the small campus facility. "But worse than that, you've got walking pneumonia."

"Walking pneumonia?" Kiki asked between coughs.

"It's what we call it when you've got something that ought to put you in bed, yet you keep climbing out and trying to go on with your life," the physician explained. "You probably should have been in here two or three days ago."

The nursing staff put Kiki to bed, filled her with fluids and medications and ordered her to try to sleep.

Kiki was very troubled, because whenever she came to consciousness, she thought about all she had to do and felt the urge to climb out of bed. However, despite her sense of extreme urgency to return to her studies, classes, and work, her body would collapse and she'd fall backward onto the pillow to drop off to sleep again.

That evening a nurse leaned over Kiki's bed and shook her awake. "Kiki," she whispered. Her nametag read Penny Smiley.

Kiki forced herself to stay awake. "What, what is it?"

"I have a message for you. I think it's from your family. They've been trying to find you all day. Nobody could figure out where you were."

Kiki shook the sleepiness out of her eyes. "I don't have a cell phone." She coughed. "It's hard to find me, if I'm not in the dorm or at work." She began coughing seriously.

Penny handled Kiki a glass of water, watched her drink from it, and then waited for her cough to settle. "Look, I have a cell phone, and there is a number written down here. If you like, I'll call it for you, and when I've made contact, you can talk to whoever it is."

Kiki nodded. "Okay." Her words came out in a hoarse whisper.

Penny dialed the number. It rang a long time and no one picked up. Penny stopped the call. "There doesn't seem to be anyone home."

Kiki frowned. "It's late in New York. That's strange. Someone ought to be there." Through the fog in her brain, she wondered what could have happened. *Did someone die? Her mama, her papa, one of her brothers?*

Worried and exhausted, she fell back on the pillow.

"Look," Penny promised, "I'm on the night shift. I'll be here until seven in the morning. I'll try again a few times before I'm off duty. You get some sleep, and don't worry. We'll find out what's going on."

Penny straightened Kiki's clothes, pulled the covers up to her neck, made sure her pillow was just right, felt her forehead, and then said, "Now sleep, and I'll see you later."

The nurse's gentle touch was just what Kiki needed to drift back to sleep. She remained quiet for several hours.

Penny woke Kiki at seven, just before she was leaving the infirmary. "I'll try that number again," she said kindly and pulled out her cell.

This time the call was answered, and Penny handed the phone to Kiki, who could barely speak, "Yes?"

"Kiki, this is Mama. We try to reach you yesterday, all day. No one knew where you are. What happen?"

"I got sick. I'm in the infirmary."

"In hospital?"

"No, on the campus. I have pneumonia. They are giving me medications and I'm sleeping to get well." Kiki coughed several times.

Her mama sounded worried. "I am sorry to bring trouble when

you sick, but we call because Javier got shot."

"Where?" Kiki gasped. "In prison?"

"No, he was home. A few days. He was out with friends. Somebody drive by. Shoot him on street."

"Is he okay?" Kiki dreaded the answer.

"Now, maybe. Yesterday they thought he not make it. He had the fever and was weak and call for you. We try to find you for him. We thought he was dying. So much blood."

Kiki swallowed hard. "But he's better?"

"I'm not sure, but I think so. We hoped you come home."

Kiki sagged.

Penny, who was nearby and could hear the words, took back the phone. "Is this Kiki's mother?" she asked.

"Yes, si. Kiki's mama."

"Well," Penny said, "I gather you have a family emergency there, but your daughter is very sick. She will be fine in a few days. Now she needs to rest. I can ask the doctor, yet I doubt a cross-country flight would be approved until she's a lot stronger."

"Okay, I see. Just ask her to pray for Javier, okay?"

"Sure. We'll all send good thoughts for him."

"Okay. Goodbye, Kiki. You tell her?"

"Yes. Thank you."

Penny gave Kiki the message and then brought her morning medications and a drink of fresh juice. She helped her up to go to the bathroom and then saw that she was back in bed. While tucking her in, she repeated, "Don't worry, Kiki. Javier will do fine. I'm sure he's in good hands. Right now, you have to get yourself well. So try to go back to sleep." Penny patted Kiki's arm and then slipped out of the room.

Kiki closed her eyes and attempted to let go of consciousness, as she heard voices in the hallway. "Penny, weren't you supposed to be out of here half an hour ago?"

"Yes, Dr. Arnold. That girl in there, Kiki Rodriguez, she had a family emergency, and I had a cell phone. Not to worry. It's okay. I'm going home now."

Kiki remained in the infirmary for three days and then had orders for bed rest in the dorm for another four days. She talked with her family again from the dorm and found that the emergency was over. Javier would be all right.

After a week of recuperation, Kiki was allowed to return to her classes and her jobs. She felt terribly overwhelmed, yet she was stronger, the cough was almost gone, and she decided she was going to make it physically.

Once she was able, she called Sal and Meg and told them about her experience in the infirmary. "I hated being sick and not being able to go home to be with Javier, but I really hated the fact that my family couldn't find me. When Javier was calling for me, I wasn't available to talk to him. If he had died, I don't think I would ever have felt right about that."

Sal tried to reassure her. "Kiki, being sick and in the infirmary is nothing to be ashamed of. You had no control over that or over the fact that your brother got shot or that you couldn't get to him. I'm glad that he's going to survive and that you're back on your feet on this end."

"Well, the worst is over, I guess," Kiki sighed with resignation.

"I think you need to talk to Artemis," Sal observed.

"You're probably right. That always picks me up."

A week later, Kiki received a Priority Mail package at the campus post office. When she opened it, she found inside a new cell phone and a card from Sal.

Now don't complain, because this is necessary for OUR peace of mind. We don't want you to be out of touch anymore. We found a way to slide you into our family plan, so there will be no charges to you for using this phone until you graduate. Then it's up to you. With love from your 'Aunts,' Sal and Meg.

Kiki held the phone to her chest and tears rolled down her cheeks—tears of relief and happiness. *What a wonderful new family she had made in Sal and Meg.* Kiki was very grateful for all their kindnesses.

19

Helena

Kiki reclined on the couch with her legs outstretched and her cell phone in her hand. The TV, playing an old movie, was on mute. She had returned to the Hillview Apartments for a second summer, working days in the admissions office and most nights and weekends for Jim's pizza shop. When she had a moment to herself, she longed to go home to visit; however, there was neither time nor money to make the trip again. She felt sad that she had missed Manuela's wedding to Ramon, but it couldn't be helped.

Thankfully, her cell phone provided a saving grace, as Kiki had just hung up from a call to her family in New York. While fingering the phone, she sat thinking in gradually fading sunlight. Things were better at home, and she was relieved at that. Mama told Kiki that Javier was doing well. No details. Then Gusto took over the line, adding that his brother was getting court-ordered counseling and might be going to work or joining the military.

"And what about you?" Kiki asked.

"Me? Doin' good. Doin' what I promised. Staying in school. No gangs."

Kiki took a deep breath. "Oh, Gusto, you make me so proud. Please keep out of trouble. I know it's hard, but please, please stay in school."

"Hey, big sis, no worries. I'm fine." Gusto shifted the conversation away from himself. "Mama and Papa are gettin' along better," he told her quietly, so as not to be overheard, "and I think Papa's stayin' away from the booze. His new job has lasted several months."

After finishing the call, Kiki had hung up with a sigh of relief. The family, for once, seemed to be okay.

One Friday in mid July, Kiki's round-the-clock work schedule was interrupted by the unexpected arrival of Sal and Aisha. Kiki had been in her apartment for a lunch break and had just finished a carton of yogurt when she heard the unmistakable sound of a truck pulling to a stop outside her building. Her heart skipped several beats as she jumped up from her chair. *It had to be Sal.* Kiki rushed out the door to meet her very best friend.

Sal was already out of the cab, and she and Kiki embraced each other tightly. "I was hoping I could catch you." Sal gave her a big grin. "I'm on my way to Stockton with a load, and I have a couple of days free before I head back to Utah."

Kiki was thrilled. "Stockton, huh? Can you come inside for a minute? I've got an idea."

Sal followed her into the apartment and waited quietly as Kiki grabbed her cell phone and punched in some numbers.

"Hello," she said nervously when Helena Ramirez answered, "this is Kiki Rodriguez."

"Yes, Kiki," Helena responded warmly.

Kiki crossed her fingers. "You remember how we've talked about me coming to visit your farm sometime?"

"Yes," Helena replied. There was just a touch of hesitation in her voice.

"Well, I have a friend from Salt Lake City who's here in Oakland on her way to Stockton, and I think she could drop me off near your farm. If it's convenient for you, I'd really like to visit."

"Hmmm," Helena considered. "Well, there is nothing major going on here right now. I suspect I could manage to have you come see the place. In fact, now that you bring it up, that might really be nice."

Kiki wrote down instructions from the professor on the correct exit of the freeway and the closest location Sal could go with her heavily loaded truck. Kiki was to call on her cell when they reached that point, and Helena would come to pick her up.

When Kiki ended the call, she shared the plan with Sal, who nodded and smiled. "I see that phone we gave you comes in handy now and then," she quipped.

Kiki suddenly remembered Aisha. "Oh, I've got to go see her. And then we've got to leave. Oh, my job——" Her eyes grew wide as she tried to think.

Huffing and then calming herself, Kiki dialed the administrative offices. As Sal watched with amusement, Kiki told the human resources clerk that something had come up and she needed to use four hours of vacation time that afternoon. "I'm sorry it's such short notice," she added, "but I haven't taken off any time this summer." Once that job was settled, Kiki also gave Jim warning by phone, although she thought she would be on time for work the next day.

After throwing a few things into her duffle bag, Kiki closed and locked the front door to her apartment and followed Sal to the rig. She felt ecstatic to see Sal again. And Aisha, who stood up with her paws on the open window and her tail wagging ferociously. It seemed like forever to Kiki since their last time together at Christmas.

Kiki was also excited about visiting Dr. Ramirez. "This is really special," she tried to explain to Sal. "Dr. Ramirez has let very few—if any—students ever visit her farm. We've talked about it more than once; I just didn't think I'd ever have a way to go there."

As Sal smiled to herself with amusement, she climbed into the driver's seat. Kiki hopped into the passenger side, where she was greeted warmly by Aisha. The trio headed down Montrose Blvd. and onto the I-580 freeway.

Meanwhile, Helena Ramirez was hurriedly consulting with PJ out in the barn, where PJ was in the midst of a woodworking project.

Helena nervously paced. "I don't know what to do. Should we be open or make up some story? I've never had a student here. I don't know how to handle it."

PJ peered over her glasses at her partner and raised an eyebrow. "Helena. This is Kiki Rodriguez, the girl who hid out for nearly two months at Montrose. She adores you. I don't think she, of all people, is going to run around the campus and tell everyone she knows your dark secrets."

Helena frowned. "But I think she needs to look up to me. What if she is shocked or can't handle it?"

PJ laughed. "I think *you* have the problem, not Kiki. Are you afraid she'll hate you when she finds out you're in a relationship with, heaven forbid, *a woman*? Come on, Helena. Maybe this is a good thing that she's coming to visit. We'll get all this secret stuff out in the open."

Helena suddenly reached out and wrapped herself in PJ's arms. "Well, I'm scared, but she's coming, and I guess I'll just have to face it."

A little less than an hour later, Kiki climbed out of Sal's cab at a Livermore filling station, and Helena drove up beside the eighteen-wheeler rig in her aging Volvo. Kiki waved excitedly, as Helena pulled to a stop and climbed out of her wagon. She was clad in jeans and a T-shirt—a very different look from the professional attire she wore at Montrose.

Kiki introduced Sal to Helena and watched the two women sizing each other up. Both of them seemed to have expressions of amused surprise, yet no one said anything beyond "hello" and "glad to meet you."

Sal explained to Helena that she had to go on into Stockton with her load.

"Why don't you come to the farm when you're finished," Helena suggested.

"Okay," Sal nodded. "I don't know exactly when it'll be, but I'll find the place."

"It's pretty easy, from here." Helena gave her directions, and then Sal climbed back into the cab and, with a loud roar of the semi's engine, took off toward the freeway.

Kiki slid into the passenger seat of the Volvo to go home with Dr. Ramirez.

"I'm really excited," she confessed as she fastened her seat belt and glanced at the casual version of Helena out of the corner of her eye. The Volvo was old, Kiki noticed, probably a classic, and had a bit of a musty smell. Somehow all the people she met who owned cars seemed to express themselves by personalizing their vehicles. Kiki enjoyed looking at and smelling each of their cars.

"I hope you won't be disappointed." Helena was clearly a little nervous.

"I won't be." Kiki gave her a big grin.

Shortly thereafter, they arrived at the open front gate of the farm. Kiki was all eyes. "Oh, I love the house! Look at that swing! What a great porch! Nobody had a porch where I grew up—just high-rise apartment buildings. Look at all that lawn! Is that the barn?" She was a whirlwind of comments and questions.

"Whoa," Helena said with a warm laugh. "Slow down, Kiki. You'll be able to see it all. You'll have plenty of time to explore the whole farm."

The professor parked the car and showed Kiki to the front door.

Once inside the house, Kiki was speechless. She admired the beautiful wood used in the furniture, the grandfather clock against the wall, the colorful plants growing on the windowsills, and the warm and cozy living room.

Kiki asked to use the bathroom, and once inside she was amazed at the bathtub with lion's feet. She had seen old bathtubs before yet nothing as unique and attractive as this one. On her return to the living room, she peeped into Dr. Ramirez's office, surveying her desk and computer and her books lined up neatly on shelves. Kiki hoped to explore that room later.

"Would you like some lemonade?" asked Helena, a little unsure about how to begin this new relationship with her student.

"Sure," Kiki responded enthusiastically, "and can I see the barn?"

"Of course," Helena nodded "And you can take your lemonade with you." She cleared her throat. "There's someone in the barn I'd like you to meet."

"Oh, really, who?" Kiki inquired.

"A friend of mine. You'll see."

With a big glass of lemonade in her hand, Kiki hurried out to the barn, as excited as a small child. A bit unsteady in the wake of Kiki's exuberance, Helena followed her, trying to keep up.

Within the barn, just past an aging milk cow and several wandering chickens, Kiki encountered PJ's personal workspace, and then PJ, who was bent over a long piece of wood, smoothing it with a plane.

PJ stopped working and stood up, all five feet of her, and smiled. "Hi, I'm PJ and you must be Kiki," she greeted, wiping sweat from her forehead with a red-checkered handkerchief she had pulled from her hip pocket.

As Kiki looked around, she absorbed all the smells of freshly cut wood. "You make furniture? Did you make all the things in the house?"

PJ laughed. "Yes, I make furniture, and no, I didn't make all the things in the house. Some of them, not all."

"Do you live here?" Kiki asked. PJ's eyes twinkled.

"Yes, I do. Is that okay?"

Kiki blushed. "Sure. I'm sorry. I have a big mouth. I'm always asking things that I shouldn't."

PJ grinned at her. "Don't apologize. A healthy curiosity is a sign of intelligence. You just ask all the questions you want. If there's somethin' I don't wanna answer, I'll say so. Okay?"

"That's fair." Kiki laughed.

As PJ returned to her work, Helena showed Kiki the cow, named Matilda, and told her about milking, then introduced her to the chickens and explained how they laid eggs and how to collect them. Kiki was totally fascinated. "I guess I told you before that I've never been to a farm. I've only seen them in the movies," she admitted.

Shortly, they waved goodbye to PJ and returned to the house, where Helena had earlier begun to prepare dinner. The professor slipped a roast back into the oven and then showed Kiki her office and explained how she did her work at home. Kiki was intrigued by the way in which Helena could call up the stock market summaries for the day on her computer.

Kiki helped Helena prepare the rest of their dinner and set the table. "Save a spot for your friend," Helena instructed, "in case she makes it back in time to eat with us."

Having looked around the barn and having seen PJ, Kiki had lots of questions building up in her mind. "Have you known PJ long?" she finally asked, as they sat down in the living room to wait for the roast to finish cooking.

"Oh, yes," Helena admitted. "Nearly forty years."

"Is she from the South?"

Helena smiled. "Deep South. You picked up the accent, huh?"

Kiki blushed. "Well, kinda."

"You have an accent, too."

Kiki nodded. "Yep, South Bronx."

"But you've been working at losing it, haven't you?"

Kiki blushed again. "Well, yes. I've been trying."

"You have done a good job. It shows. Now, PJ, she's different. She was a real farm girl, and she's never had any desire to be anything else. I battled with her for years over the 'you all' stuff, but after that, I've long since given up trying to correct any more of her English or change the way she speaks."

Kiki risked another question. "How did you meet her?"

"In college, actually. Then she went off to the Navy, to be a nurse. And I went to graduate school. I lost track of her for a few years, but when she left the Navy and got a job nursing in a Bay Area hospital, she heard I was living out here on this farm and contacted me. PJ has been living here nearly thirty years now."

Kiki's mind raced ahead. "Is she——?"

"Kiki," Helena interrupted gently, "my personal life has always been very private. If I share any of it with you, I must feel very sure that the information will stay between us."

"Oh, yes," Kiki responded, blushing. "I would never talk about you behind your back."

Helena smiled, her anxiety beginning to ease a little. "I believe you, and I feel I can trust you. So, to answer what I think you are trying to ask, PJ is a very special friend. We share the farm, and everything else, only we're just very private about it. Do you understand?"

Kiki nodded. "Sal has a friend, too. Her name is Meg, and she works in a hospital in Salt Lake City. I've stayed with them. And Nancy Raines—everybody knows that she's a lesbian. It's really okay. I understand."

Helena blanched. "Kiki," she began, after taking a deep breath, "things have changed a lot over the years. When I was a young woman, no one talked about 'alternative life styles.' We didn't dare even think about such things. To do so was to feel deep personal shame and to humiliate our families. Most of us hid our feelings and our lives—what they now call 'being in the closet.' It's a real struggle for me to become accustomed to all this openness—T-shirts and parades and words like 'lesbian' and 'dyke' being bandied about freely."

"That's okay," Kiki said, not wanting to hurt Helena. "We don't have to talk about it. I just needed to understand who PJ is to you. It's really okay."

Before Helena could respond, Sal's horn sounded, and Kiki raced out the front door to let Sal know that indeed she was at the right place. Helena followed to show Sal where to park the cab and to welcome her to the farm.

Later, the four women sat around the table and shared a dinner of roast beef, rice and beans, a big salad, and tortillas on the side. Kiki felt like she was back home.

"Are you Hispanic?" Kiki asked as she passed a plate around.

Helena grinned at her. "You mean my name isn't a dead giveaway?"

Kiki sputtered. "Well, you don't talk like my roommate, who's from Mexico. I wasn't sure."

"Back there somewhere in my past there is Mexican history," Helena explained. "But I'm at least third generation in the United States, and nobody in my immediate family used Spanish very often. I know a few words here and there, certainly not enough to acquire an accent."

"The food is really tasty," Kiki said, as she tucked into her dinner. "It reminds me of home."

"Oh?" Helena asked.

"Well, my mama is part Polish, but she cooks mostly to please my papa, who is Filipino and Puerto Rican. We eat a lot of rice and beans."

Everyone at the table laughed, including Kiki.

Helena drew Sal out about her life on the road, and Kiki sat and watched two of her favorite women getting to know one another. PJ kidded a bit yet seemed to enjoy sitting back and watching the action. Kiki watched PJ's smiling eyes and thought that she must be a more contemplative person.

After they all played a few hands of Canasta, a game that Kiki had never known yet learned quickly, Sal's day on the road caught up with her, and she asked to be excused. Helena had prepared the guest room for her. Since there was only one spare bed, Kiki ended up on the living room sofa. She felt very content as she pulled the covers up around her shoulders and drifted off into a deep sleep.

Kiki was awakened early the next morning by PJ quietly slipping out the back door, clad in faded jeans, an old flannel shirt, and a pair of well-worn boots. Kiki vaguely had a sense that she had heard a rooster crowing, so she sat up, pulled on her jeans and a top, and followed PJ.

Kiki found Helena's partner in the barn, pail in hand, preparing to milk the cow.

"Good morning." Kiki's voice was still husky from sleep.

PJ gave her a good-natured smile. "Did I wake you?"

"I don't know. Did I hear a rooster?"

PJ laughed. "Yeah, probably. Ol' Toots gets me up every mornin.'" She looked in the direction of the rooster, who was parading through the barn with three hens following behind him.

"It's fine. He makes an amusing alarm clock," Kiki quipped. "How do you manage to milk the cow? It looks really difficult."

"It's easy. You wanna try?"

"Sure." Kiki wasn't *really* sure about milking the cow; however, she wanted to try anything that she was allowed to do. So, PJ sat her down on a little milking stool and showed her how to put her hands on Matilda's teats and just how to pull the nipples so that the milk could come out in a stream into the bucket. Although Kiki struggled at first, she was soon able to figure it out and was pleased with herself when milk began to fill the bottom of the pail.

PJ watched her approvingly. "This old gal doesn't have a lot of milk these days, but we go through the ritual every mornin', anyway. It's healthy for her to be cleaned out. I'm afraid she's gettin' old, just like us."

Kiki was curious about PJ. "I understand you served in the military."

PJ smiled. "Yeah. I loved it. Suited my personality. I liked the uniforms and all the rules—guess I kinda craved discipline. Except in one area. I was a bit of a stud, where the ladies were concerned. I was always chasin' tail, and the government, especially back then, didn't take to that very much. I was caught foolin' around with a nurse, and we both got the boot, real quick. Miss those days a lot." She looked wistfully off into space.

Kiki wanted more. "So you became a civilian nurse?"

PJ focused on Kiki. "You doin' a story for the school paper, or somethin?" she asked with a chuckle. "If you are, everythin' I'm sayin' is off the record. Get my drift?"

Kiki blushed. "Oh, I wouldn't tell anyone. I already assured Dr. Ramirez that I wouldn't talk about your life together on the farm. I just admire her so much, and you've been her—well, friend—for such a long time. I can't help being curious about you."

PJ put her hand on Kiki's shoulder affectionately. "That's all right, Kiki. I know you don't mean any harm. It's just that us old gals are so used to livin' double lives, the public ones for everybody else and the private ones for ourselves. I suspect deep inside, we're all dyin' to tell our stories to someone, yet we hafta be so careful—or we *think* we hafta be. Times are changin', but we haven't caught up with all the new freedom."

Kiki looked down at the ground and realized how difficult their relationship must have been in the past.

"Now, don't you get all worried. We've had a good life," PJ said reassuringly. "An' you know, I'm glad you asked to visit the farm. Helena has been talkin' about you for two years now, and I was beginnin' to wonder if I'd ever have a chance to meet you. You've given her a lot of pleasure, and your visit is puttin' the first crack in her wall of secrecy. Who knows, maybe before she retires she'll get a wild hair and invite the whole damn college out here. Wouldn't that be the day!"

PJ's body shook from her laughter, and Kiki joined in, her spirits lifted.

Later on, as Kiki and Sal drove back to Oakland in the truck, Kiki reflected on the visit. "I'm so amazed. I never thought about Dr. Ramirez having someone, I mean a lover. I guess I bought into that story about her pining away for some soldier killed in battle. I suppose I shouldn't really be surprised."

"I suspect you have several professors on campus who live rather quietly," Sal suggested thoughtfully, "and with cover stories, so that you don't guess what is really going on with them. Especially the older ones. They would have been fired—until even a few years ago—if even a whiff of rumor about their being attracted to women leaked out."

"Well, I'm not completely clear how I fit into all of this," Kiki commented, "but it's amazing to me that since I left home, almost every woman that I've met and become close to has turned out to be a lesbian. It's weird. And Dr. Ramirez? I've been in her classes for two years!"

Sal smiled at her. "And you don't know what it all means? Let me give you a hint. Very little in life is purely by accident."

With an amused frown across her forehead, Kiki studied Sal silently.

Starting her junior year at Montrose, Kiki became an upper class-man. She was thrilled! As a freshman she had feared she would never make it this far. Now that she had survived two years of college, she felt smarter and filled with a new understanding about many things.

While Kiki was growing and changing, Montrose was beginning to keep pace with evolving social values. Early in the fall semester, the faculty and staff voted to develop a festival day to celebrate the campus's "diversity." Although for many years, the student body as well as the administration, faculty, and staff had drawn from numerous ethnic groups—making the campus very clearly diverse—the college had not chosen to observe this fact publicly.

Planning for the event brought out all kinds of "diverse" ideas and opinions. During committee meetings, a group of current students asked that lesbian and bisexual students be recognized officially as part of campus diversity. And what about transsexuals? This request set off considerable controversy; ultimately the request was honored.

On the last Saturday in September—a date when sometimes vola-tile President Ryerson would just happen to be across the country on a speaking tour—the campus held its first Diversity Play Day, featuring a giant picnic on the lawn in front of old Montrose Hall. Ethnic foods were served and ethnic dances held on the lawn. The lesbians, who in their bars and clubs were fond of line dancing and the two-step, set up a huge conga line that moved and swayed around the campus to old Carmen Miranda music. Kiki got into the middle of the line and moved and swayed—until her cheeks grew flushed and she felt exhilarated but also so tired that she could hardly stand. She stopped, laughing to herself and the women before and after her. They closed up the line behind her and moved on with a wave. Kiki watched them go, as she collapsed on a wooden bench nearby, happy from the top of her sweaty head to the bottom of her aching feet and embracing her gratitude for all her good fortune.

After that day, which was considered by many a marvelous success,

Kiki noticed more T-shirts being worn that made reference to women-loving women. In the wake of the overall success, Montrose staffers officially affirmed that Diverse Play Day would become an annual event.

Attending and joining in the dancing had reminded Kiki of Karen Fullerton, whom she hadn't seen for more than a year, and the new T-shirts also made her aware that there were more students with whom she felt a personal kinship. Two of them were in Olsen Hall. Soon she began smiling at them and saying, "Hi," when they passed on the stairs. Eventually one of them handed her a flyer about a book reading the following Sunday afternoon at a women's bookstore in Berkeley. Kiki decided she'd try to go, and she began to feel excited about the event.

Jim supported her when she mentioned the possibility to him on Saturday. "Kiki, ya don' git out much. Ya oughta go to dis thing."

"But the buses don't run often on Sundays. I might be late to work."

Jim nodded. "I know, an' we'll make out 'til ya git here."

Kiki waited at the campus stop for the bus she needed, one headed into Oakland and then a second bus north to Berkeley. Although she was nervous about going into an area she didn't know well, just south of the UC Berkeley campus, she went anyway. It was a slow journey, with long waits for both the buses. Kiki felt relieved when she finally reached The Perky Poodle, an independent bookstore featuring both new and used books and with a deli attached. Kiki was glad to see the deli, because by the time she arrived at the bookstore, breakfast was a distant memory. The place was quiet, so Kiki settled at a small table with a sandwich and a Diet Coke and studied a printed flyer about the day's speaker.

Gradually, more women arrived, and Kiki watched them—trying not to be too obvious in her staring. An older woman approached her and asked if she could share the table. Kiki smiled and nodded. The woman sat down, also with a sandwich and a soda, and Kiki noted her short haircut, jeans and boots, and denim jacket with military-style trim. Her tanned face was lined from sun and aging, and she wore no makeup.

Kiki was curious, yet for a moment, neither of the two spoke. They focused on eating, although both glanced up as a few more women entered the bookstore, chatting with animation and gathering for the talk.

A small smile crossed the woman's face. "I never know if we'll have an audience," she commented, looking at Kiki.

Kiki's eyes widened. "Oh, are you the speaker?"

"Yes, I'm Ginny Forrester."

Kiki put her sandwich down. "I was just reading the flyer, but I didn't make the connection."

Ginny smiled. "Well, the picture on the flyer is of my mother. The book is about her. I'm on tour talking about the book and about her life. She lived at a time when it wasn't easy to be a lesbian."

Kiki swallowed. "Are you, uh—?"

"Not to worry. Yes, I'm a lesbian. Chip off the old block, I guess."

"But your mother was—"

"My mother was briefly married when she was young, and she had me. She had known she was a lesbian even when she was a child, but she was punished for it. She was jailed at one point, and later hospitalized—all efforts to cure her and make her 'normal.' She was basically forced to marry. It didn't last."

"And this is what you've written about in the book?"

Ginny nodded. "Yes, a chunk of it. Her life and what it was like for me growing up as a child of a single lesbian parent in that society."

Kiki picked up her sandwich again. "I can't wait to hear your talk."

"Hope I haven't given too much away already." Ginny grinned at Kiki.

"No. I'm just more intrigued."

Shortly Ginny excused herself and met briefly with a woman who was apparently the bookstore manager. Then in front of what Kiki guessed were about thirty women of various ages, she gave her talk and answered questions from the audience.

As Kiki's mind swirled over the personal lesbian history presented, as well as the questions asked, she used some of her precious money to buy the book and had it autographed. Hugging this treasure and shaking Ginny's hand with appreciation, she left the bookstore and hurried to catch her buses back to Oakland and her job at Jim's.

As she rode back to school, she thought to herself that if she was a lesbian, and she was really sensing that she was, she sure was lucky that she wasn't born back in the days before gay rights organizations began fighting for equality.

Kiki's developing sexual identity was impacted by another major campus event during the fall: the annual alumnae reunion. Every year in early October, the campus became a beehive of returning Montrose graduates. Classes were honored every five years, and among the participants were alumnae who had attended the college some fifty or even sixty years in the past.

As Kiki rushed from class to class, or to the admin building for her job, she noticed these women—trying not to bump into them as they walked around the campus, some with canes, talking with animation in casual groups and all wearing nametags. She marveled at the excited camaraderie and the dedication of these former Montrose students who came back to their alma mater from all over the world. The thought caught her by surprise that someday she might be among them.

During her first two years, Kiki had somehow totally missed the reunion weekend. Too overwhelmed, too preoccupied—she wasn't sure why she hadn't noticed. Now, filled with curiosity, she located a reunion program and learned that for the first time, there was to be a lesbian and bisexual reception on Saturday afternoon in one of the library conference rooms. The reception was open to current students, so Kiki decided to stop in before she left for work.

Not knowing what to expect, Kiki was a bit scared, but she pushed herself to go and quietly nibbled on snacks while moving around the periphery of the room, watching and listening as these women met and embraced and shared stories with each other. The noise level of chatter and laughter was almost deafening. Kiki felt that there was electricity in the air. By her own count, she saw at least a hundred women come and go during the reception, including perhaps twenty current students. Some were formally dressed and fashionably made up; others were clad simply or tailored; a few wore jeans and boots and no cosmetic touches. Some had long hairstyles, some wore their hair short and "butch."

Kiki was about to leave for work when she noticed a very attractive young woman standing rather quietly by herself in one corner. The woman was slender, a few inches taller than Kiki, and had blue eyes and curly, light brown hair. Kiki thought she was very pretty and wondered why she remained apart from the others. Did she want to be alone, or was she shy or uncomfortable?

Kiki's natural caring instinct led her to approach and introduce herself. The woman nodded, offering a soft, gentle smile.

"Hi, Kiki," she responded. "I'm Denise Walters, class of '05."

"Isn't this exciting," Kiki observed, "to see all these women talking with one another? There's one woman over there who's almost eighty. Imagine what she's seen in her lifetime."

Denise nodded. "Yes, it is exciting. There has never been an opportunity like this before at Montrose."

Kiki wanted to pursue a conversation with Denise, because she appeared to be a little older and out in the work world. Kiki always wondered how women made a living after they graduated from the college. "What have you been doing since graduation?" she managed, a bit awkwardly.

Denise smiled and warmed to the question. "I've been working for a publishing house in the City, doing advertising layout. I like it; I'm just more excited about a magazine I edit on the side, called *Belle Femme*. Have you heard of it?"

Kiki shook her head. "No, sorry, I haven't seen the magazine. Tell me about it."

"Well," Denise explained, "it's for women, lesbian women especially. But it's different from some of those sex magazines that I find everywhere. We try to include quality fiction, poetry, and good photography."

Kiki felt a light bulb go off in her head. "That sounds really special. I'd like to see a copy sometime."

Denise smiled. "Too bad, I didn't think to bring any with me, between all the reunion activities and everything. I should have brought some copies. Although it's carried in women's bookstores. You can pretty easily find it."

Kiki didn't want to admit that she had no car, little time, and that the one bookstore she knew of was two bus rides away. Instead, she just nodded. "Thanks. I'll look for it."

Her watch told her that it was time to leave for work, yet she felt unwilling to let this moment escape. "Do you," she blurted out, "need any help on your magazine? I mean, I don't have a lot of money, but I'm majoring in communications with an emphasis on computers and graphic design. There might be something I could contribute."

Denise's face lit up. "That would be great. We're always struggling to keep up with everything. I do have a card with me. Call me sometime, and we'll meet to discuss it." She reached into her purse to find a business card.

Kiki gave her a smile, accepted the card, and shook Denise's hand. After a quick goodbye, she rushed off to work. At the moment she couldn't put her finger on the importance of meeting Denise, but a little shiver ran up her spine as she dashed out the Montrose gate.

20

Denise

Following her Friday classes a week later, Kiki caught a bus and then transferred to BART for the ride into San Francisco. She couldn't decide if she was more nervous or excited about going to meet with Denise and seeing the workspace for her lesbian publication. Kiki's stomach was doing flip flops, and she tingled all over. In her pocket she had written directions for finding the small office building in the middle of a block just off Market Street and at the edge of the Castro District.

When Kiki left the subway and surfaced, as the sun disappeared behind tall city buildings, she felt very edgy about the neighborhood before her. Taking a deep breath, she swallowed her anxiety and followed the information she had been given. First she located the correct street, then found the right address, and finally saw the office number on the building directory in the lobby. She climbed two floors up a somewhat creaky wooden staircase. Then directly in front of her was a glass-paneled wooden door with the publication's name in red letters. She knocked.

A stocky, black-boots-and-leather dyke answered the door, and Kiki almost retreated.

"Hi, I'm Butch," the stubble-haired woman greeted. "Com'on in."

Hesitantly, Kiki crossed the threshold. Inside, she could see Denise working at a desk and talking on the phone, so she relaxed, relieved that she was in the right place.

Butch was friendly enough. "I'm the errand boy," she quipped with a wide grin and a touch of sarcasm. "I'm brute enough to keep myself out of trouble, so I go pick up things and bring in the food and all that good stuff—oh, and haul the magazines off to the post office when the issue is ready."

Kiki was surprised by Butch's masculinity and tattoos; however, she tried to return the welcoming banter. "Well, that sounds like a real asset, being strong and able to take care of yourself."

"Yeah, I think so," Butch quipped, as with a wave of one hand she was out the door.

Kiki looked around the office, at photographs on the walls of intriguing—if a bit different, by her own standards—women, design tables, file cabinets, and all the things necessary to produce a magazine.

In a moment, Denise put down her cell and came out of her little cubbyhole. "Hi, Kiki." Denise greeted her with a smile. "I'm glad you could make it. So what do you think of our little operation?"

"It's neat," Kiki affirmed. She immediately blushed, feeling awkward for not having anything more sophisticated to impart.

Denise did not seem to notice her discomfort and instead looked around the room at her own creation. "Well, it's not *Vogue*, and it has been pieced together with donations and other hand-me-downs. We operate on a shoestring budget, yet we're here, and I intend to make a success of it."

For the next hour, Denise showed Kiki the workings of the magazine, from copy submitted to layout and design, as well as printing. She explained which parts of the process they could do themselves and which had to be subcontracted out. "I wish we had the money to be self-contained; that's a goal for the future."

Beginning to sense the way things worked, Kiki felt truly excited. "I want to help. What do you think I can do?"

Denise thought for a moment. "Well, in time, I think you can learn to do a lot. For starters, I would appreciate it if you could help me catch up on that pile of mail over there. It's getting bigger and higher every day."

Walking to a table stacked with envelopes, packages, and sheets of paper, Denise sighed. "It needs to be sorted out. There are bills to be paid, there are people with subscription problems, there are authors trying to be published. Having a full-time job elsewhere, I come in here sometimes so overwhelmed with producing the magazine that I let the mail back up. I know I shouldn't, and that's why it would be so valuable if you would help me put it in order. Some things you'll be able to file right away, others I'll have to take care of myself, and some you can do with guidance from me. You'll learn a lot in the process, and as you watch me work, I can teach you to do other things."

Although the messy pile was a bit daunting, Kiki dug into it with determination. Within a few minutes, she was fully absorbed. She found each envelope and its contents very interesting. She went through short stories that had been submitted by writers from all over the country. While she couldn't stop to read them all, just knowing of their existence was fascinating. Then there were letters from subscribers—including publishable anecdotes and letters to the editor—along with orders for subscriptions and checks enclosed, a few complaints in one form or another, and a couple of unpaid bills. Kiki could see immediately how important it was to keep up with incoming mail.

Butch returned eventually, bringing a large pizza and some Cokes. Kiki smiled to herself, because her stomach had been growling. While they continued working, the three women shared the warm pizza slices. *Not as good as Jim's, but tasty anyway,* Kiki thought. Denise was in the midst of writing an editorial for the next issue, and Butch was heaving and shoving various boxes around. Kiki kept after the mail, disturbing Denise only when there was a problem she couldn't solve for herself.

By the end of the evening, the mail was in neat piles and the most urgent issues had been resolved. Denise, whose eyes looked tired, thanked Kiki gratefully for her help. Although worn out from the effort and concentration, Kiki felt very important.

When the office had been closed for the night, Butch walked Kiki to the BART station and saw that she got safely on the train. While Butch was not her type, Kiki decided she was really helpful, sweet, and protective of the other employees.

Nancy Raines was delighted when Kiki stopped by her office and told her about her volunteer job in San Francisco. "I'm so glad you have found a structured way to connect with the lesbian community, a way that suits your personality better than bar hopping," Nancy commented, "and I feel good that you are beginning to reach beyond the boundaries of Montrose College."

Kiki raised an eyebrow questioningly, and Nancy explained, "The college has been your haven, yet with senior year fast approaching, it's really time for you to start preparing to move on. Volunteer work across the Bay is a very good first step," Nancy told her honestly but very kindly.

Kiki nodded. "I get it now. Thanks for being up front about it."

Although Kiki kept Nancy informed about her work at *Belle Femme*, she didn't mention it to Dr. Capehart. She didn't see the psychologist very often, anyway; her school program had been decided, she was doing well in general, and she didn't want to open up her sexuality issues with the professor. Somehow, Kiki still didn't think she would truly understand. She figured that the volunteer job would be a positive for Rita—until she realized that the magazine was aimed at lesbians.

Even though it made juggling her life—especially her work schedule—even harder, Kiki took off on Fridays to help Denise with the publication, which had just gone from monthly distribution to every two weeks, doubling the work load for all the staff. After a couple of issues, Kiki's name went on the *Belle Femme* masthead as a contributor.

Denise smiled as she pointed out Kiki's name on a galley. "You've earned this," she told Kiki.

Kiki felt very proud as she looked at the magazine. She was happy to be making her mark at *Belle Femme*. And she was learning to do more than sort mail, although she took it upon herself to make sure that the incoming mail never got as badly behind as it had been the first evening she walked in the door. As the weeks passed, Kiki was able to use techniques she had learned in her computer classes and in graphic design to bring her own unique creativity to the look of the magazine. Denise showed enthusiasm over Kiki's efforts, and Kiki rode home on the BART each Friday evening feeling really good.

There was an additional plus to the new job. The more time Kiki spent in the magazine office, the more comfortable she felt with Denise as a person, and the more curious she became about her. At first Kiki had felt mostly awe and admiration toward this Montrose graduate making her way out in the world; however, continued hours of working closely with Denise allowed Kiki to view her as a real woman with strengths and weaknesses—not some kind of celebrity on a pedestal. As her comfort increased, so did her interest and her curiosity. Eventually, Kiki risked asking a personal question that had been on her mind. "I never see you come or go with anyone, or have any personal calls while you are here. Are you in a relationship? Is Butch your lover?"

Denise grinned broadly. "No, Kiki, Butch is *not* my lover." She stopped a moment and actually shook with laughter, rare for her. "And currently, I'm not in a relationship. I was, but I got hurt by an unfaithful partner," she admitted as a frown briefly crossed her face. "I've been nursing my wounds these past few months and just burying myself in work. One of these days, I'll come out of my shell."

"Oh, I see," said Kiki, now having more questions than she did before.

Denise looked at Kiki for a moment, seeming for once to notice her as a person and not just a young volunteer helper. "I'm sorry, I've been so into my own stuff that I haven't really thought about much else. Are *you* in a relationship?"

"No, I just have some lesbian friends."

Denise smiled. "You make that sound like that phrase 'some of my best friends are lesbian.' You know what I mean? Are you really comfortable with lesbians, or with being a lesbian, or are you still sorting that out?"

Kiki flushed and Denise looked at her seriously. "I'm sorry. I shouldn't have asked that."

Kiki shook her head. "You just hit the nail on the head, and I'm not used to my own stuff being out there."

Denise nodded. "I understand."

"But to answer your question," Kiki admitted, "I'm not sure. Nancy Raines, our chaplain—I don't think she was there when you were a student—is a lesbian, and I talk with her a lot. She thinks I may be the kind of person that needs to build a friendship first before I can have a lover. I think she's right, because although I really like women, I'm kind of private, deep inside."

Denise smiled gently. "Still waters run deep, huh?" She looked at Kiki, as if some bells had just gone off in her head, yet she didn't ask any more questions.

That evening a barrier had been dropped, and from then on Denise and Kiki began to talk, kid, and joke with each other more often. The business atmosphere lightened up, as a friendship began slowly and perceptibly to develop between them. Butch commented to Denise one day, "I don't know what that kid brought in here, but it's been good for you. You're in a lot better mood these days."

"Oh, really, I hadn't realized it."

"Maybe you got somethin' goin' on with Kiki that I don't know about," Butch suggested with a crooked smile and a raised eyebrow.

"Kiki?" Denise looked surprised. "Why she must be at least five years younger than I am and totally inexperienced. I haven't thought of her as anything other than one of the staff—but a valuable one, for sure."

Butch grinned at Denise. "Well, she's cute. It might be fun to teach her a thing or two. If you're not interested in her, maybe *I* could court her a bit. It would be a change from the bar gang."

"Oh, Butch, please leave her be. Go find one of your S&M friends and burn off some steam. I don't think Kiki's your type."

"Ah, you *have* thought about her," Butch noted, laughing to herself as she went out the door carrying several packages.

The next time Kiki came to the *Belle Femme* office, she quickly realized that something subtle had changed. She and Denise were watching each other now. Kiki noticed for the first time that she was particularly sensitive to Denise's perfume. She also admitted to herself that she liked Denise's femininity. Even though Kiki felt silly in a dress herself, she loved seeing women in beautiful, feminine clothes. Denise took care of her nails, had gorgeous hair and, although she wore little makeup, her features were strong enough that she didn't need anything extra. Sometimes she wore long skirts, yet even when she came to the office in slacks, she always had a feminine touch. She was definitely not what Kiki would have thought of as a "dyke." *In fact, far from it.*

Kiki also found that when she worked around Denise, she had funny feelings in her gut and a shiver would run up and down her spine. Kiki had noticed this for a few weeks, but she had shoved the awareness down and hadn't dared say anything about it to anyone. Each time she went to the office, the feelings got stronger, and Kiki began to wonder what to do. *Should she tell Denise? Should she leave? How should she handle this new development?*

One particular Friday evening, the two of them were working over the drafting table on a page layout, when Denise looked up to catch Kiki staring at her. Denise moved away as if the look made her uncomfortable. Finally, softening her words with a smile, she asked, "Kiki, are you staring at me?"

Kiki blushed. "I'm sorry. I think you're really pretty, and sometimes I forget that it's impolite to stare."

Denise gave her a gradually broadening smile. "Well, I appreciate the compliment, and I accept it. It's just that staring—well, I always wonder if there's an ink smear on the end of my nose and you just don't know how to tell me. It's much nicer to know that you enjoy the way I look."

"Oh," Kiki blurted out, "I do." Then she flushed with embarrassment and looked down at the floor. Her heart was pounding and she could hear her own breathing.

Denise gave her a long look and then moved closer and put a hand gently on her shoulder. "Kiki, do you have a crush on me?"

Kiki nodded. She was suddenly on the verge of tears.

"Do you want to talk about it?"

Kiki started to tremble and became speechless. "Yes, no," she managed. "I don't know." She looked up tearfully into Denise's eyes, scared how the truth would play out.

Denise took one long look at Kiki's expression and came to a conclusion. "Look, Kiki, I don't know what this will mean to either of us, but we can't go on working with you just sitting here in a pool of molten lava and hurting like hell. This is no place to discuss it with Butch in and out and the phone and other contributors stopping by. My apartment is just a few blocks away. Let's just put a sign on the door and go there and talk this through, whatever it means. I care about you and I'm a good listener and can keep secrets."

Kiki nodded her acceptance and silently followed Denise out the door and down the street. She was now so consumed with her feelings that she was beyond herself.

With great gentleness, Denise led Kiki into her apartment, seated her on the living room sofa and fixed her a cup of hot tea. Then she sat down beside her.

She put a hand on Kiki's arm. "I suspect you don't have any sexual experience with women, right?"

Kiki shook her head. She could not speak.

Denise paused a moment, clearly thinking. "Do you dream about being with a woman, do you have thoughts about a physical relationship with a woman?"

Kiki nodded. Although Denise had been on her mind and in her fantasies for weeks, she hadn't admitted it to anyone, even Nancy.

"When you have these thoughts, do you see yourself being active, or is your partner making love to you?"

"Me," Kiki stammered.

Denise paused and then asked gently, "Am I the person you think about?"

Kiki nodded again, flushing bright red.

Denise smiled and touched Kiki's cheek with her hand. "Kiki, I like you very much, and I wouldn't mind—in fact, I'd be honored—if you could tell me, or show me, what it is you think about doing."

Kiki's eyes grew wide in a combination of intense excitement and terror.

Denise looked at her and stroked her shoulder gently. "If it's too much, too soon, I can understand," she said very softly. "However, this *is* a threshold you are going to have to cross someday, and I'm a good person to do it with because I really *like* you and I won't *hurt* you."

Kiki could no longer contain herself. She turned toward Denise and kissed her, first gently and then long, hard and probing. Once

Kiki had begun to touch Denise with her lips, it was as if she had been waiting for this moment all her life.

Haltingly, yet directly and as if knowing exactly what to do, Kiki touched and kissed Denise everywhere she could—her face, her neck, her ears. She used her tongue to tickle and stroke, and her teeth to gently nip. Then she began unbuttoning Denise's blouse and loosened her bra so that she could find more skin to touch, caress, kiss and explore. She cupped her hand around a small, erect breast and touched the nipple with her tongue, sighing with her own excitement as she did so.

Denise allowed herself to relax in Kiki's embrace and let her do whatever she felt like doing. Although much more experienced in lesbian lovemaking, Denise had been alone for several months, and her body now thrilled to Kiki's touch. While remaining very gentle, she met Kiki's kisses and began kissing back and stroking in return and before long they were both completely aroused.

When they slipped from the sofa to the floor below, Denise stopped to take Kiki's hand, rose with her, and gently guided her into the bedroom, where Denise's large bed would be more comfortable than the hardwood floor. However, other than that one move, Denise surrendered totally to Kiki's lead. Somewhere along the way, they both lost the rest of their clothing.

The younger woman's intensity was so infectious that Denise climaxed easily and gratefully, and Kiki seemed both surprised and overwhelmed that she could create such a response in another woman. Denise lay still for a few moments with her arms wrapped around Kiki. Finally, she whispered, "That was so wonderful, Kiki. May I love you back?"

Kiki looked into Denise's face with unfocused eyes and nodded.

Denise released Kiki's long hair from the ponytail clip and allowed her shining and wavy dark hair to fall around her shoulders. "You are beautiful, Kiki," she said, as she began kissing Kiki's face and neck and shoulders. Then she moved downward, gently stroking Kiki's full breasts and putting her mouth around them, kissing her skin, and slipping a hand between Kiki's legs where Kiki was warm and moist. Kiki sighed and groaned with pleasure, and Denise continued stroking and loving her, teasing her body to the edge of a climax without forcing it. While Denise could not know whether Kiki would be able to climax the first time she made love, she did know that she had to help Kiki's passion become more intense than any fear or embarrassment that might prevent her response. Denise took her time and built the tension artfully until Kiki was squirming with desire. With fingers and tongue, she circled her breasts and sucked on them while stroking her skin, first on her chest and then gradually moving lower on her torso. Kiki was trembling and beginning to groan. Taking the cue, Denise slid her fingers slowly into Kiki's vagina and manipulated her clitoris with her thumb. Abruptly, Kiki arched her back and her body began to shake. She sweated profusely and cried out as she was swept into an intense climax.

An hour later, they lay locked in each other's arms. Kiki was exhausted, her dilated eyes proving that she had been to a heaven that her Artemis could never have foretold.

As Denise held Kiki gently, she thought to herself that if someone had to turn this inexperienced child into a passionate woman, she was glad *she* had been the guide.

Kiki's eyes closed, and for a few moments Denise was lost in reverie as she flashed back on her own coming out several years earlier. She, too, had been fortunate to have a sensitive and caring teacher. While Denise ruminated, Kiki slipped into exhausted sleep in her arms, and Denise gradually allowed herself to fall asleep as well.

When Kiki awoke, sun was pouring in through the bedroom windows. Denise was lying next to her, both of them covered by a sheet.

When Kiki shifted, Denise woke up.

"Are you okay?" Denise asked her softly.

Kiki nodded and smiled. "I feel great, wonderful. I could dance all over your apartment."

Denise laughed. "Well, you are a very passionate young lady."

Kiki leaned over and kissed her. "Can we do it again?"

Denise grinned warmly. "Yes, but this morning I've got to go to work, and I suspect you need to return to Montrose."

Kiki panicked. "What time is it? I have to go to work!"

Denise looked at the clock at the side of her bed. "It's 9 a.m. What time do you have to be there?"

"4 p.m."

Denise laughed. "I think you'll make it."

"Oh, Denise, you're wonderful. Thank-you, thank-you, thank-you." Kiki was beside herself.

Denise gave her a big grin. "You're pretty wonderful, too, my little one. Now hop into the shower and get dressed. I'll fix us breakfast and then walk you to the BART station."

On the way down to Market Street, Denise attempted to bring some closure. "We'll save some time next Friday to be together. Now that you know what lesbian sex is all about, you are going to be very hungry for it. I promise not to disappoint you."

Denise realized more than Kiki did that they had begun a sexual affair. Kiki was too intense and passionate for a one-night stand. Although Denise had not expected anything like this to happen, she was rather pleased. And while she had no idea where this encounter would lead, she knew that Kiki was sensitive and that she had to be gentle with her.

When Kiki arrived at the Montrose front gate, she waved at the guard and took off dancing down the sidewalk. At just that moment,

Nancy Raines was leaving the chapel. Kiki saw her, ran up, and gave her a big hug. "I got laid," she yelled, loud enough for the whole world to hear, and then ran onward toward the dorm.

Watching Kiki disappear down the street, Nancy chuckled to herself and looked skyward. *Now she knew for sure there was a God up there—and an Artemis, too!*

21

Denise and Kiki

While walking to the *Belle Femme* office from the BART station that morning, Denise felt a new spring in her step. And when she arrived, she noticed evidence of Kiki's participation everywhere she looked. The carefully organized mail, the layout design set out on the drawing board, the phone list typed neatly and hung exactly where Denise needed it to be. Denise now admitted to herself that she hadn't been fully appreciative of just how much Kiki had contributed to the publication. Somehow, at this moment, when her body still felt the sensation of Kiki's touch, Denise was acutely aware of her presence.

Butch came in an hour later and instantly recognized that something had changed—radically. "You went to bed with her!" she laughingly accused.

Denise flushed, and Butch's eyebrows shot up. She pestered Denise with sexual remarks until Denise protested, "Butch, Kiki is a very special young woman. Please don't cheapen it."

"Sorry," Butch apologized and walked off giggling.

Denise sat at her desk with a new energy for her work, discovering that this encounter had filled her with a positive glow. She hadn't realized just how down she had been these past several months until she caught herself imagining all sorts of little outings for herself and Kiki—the beach one day, dinner at the wharf, a harbor cruise. Having lived in the City for several years, Denise knew all the fun places, and she also knew that Kiki had neither time nor resources to check them out. What fun it would be to share all the sights with her!

Kiki meanwhile danced her way through her own day. She breezed through her studies and waltzed through her laundry duties with a smile on her face.

When she arrived at the pizza parlor, Jim apparently felt the difference immediately. He watched Kiki yet waited until a quiet moment before he questioned her about what was up. "Ya got a new boyfriend?" he asked lightly.

She gave him a lopsided smile.

Jim laughed and leaned toward Kiki. "I guess I didn't put dat right," he whispered. "Ya got yoreself some pussy."

"Jim!" Kiki was shocked.

Jim laughed so hard his belly shook. "Oh, Kiki, you ain't foolin' nobody. Ya got a way about ya dat's sweet but jis' a little bit tomboy. An' when yore truckin' gal friend came down, we all figgered out what kind of gal she was. But it's okay, Kiki, we all like ya, however ya is. Ya know, I live in a world of women, and I like 'em jis' fine. If I like 'em, I can unnerstand ya likin' 'em—jis' as long as ya keep away from *my* women!" He laughed again.

Kiki was both amused and embarrassed, yet as she set tables and served customers, she felt rather relieved that Jim understood her— maybe even before she had figured it out herself—and that he still cared about her. His relaxed attitude made it easier for her not to judge herself or feel ashamed.

When they closed up for the night, and he dropped her off at the Montrose front gate, she said to him, "Thanks, Jim, for accepting me the way I am, and my complicated life."

"Hey," he replied, gently, "I had a heap o' fear and prejudice dumped on me in my lifetime. I don' need to dump the same on ya, 'cause I knows what it feels like."

Kiki's week flew by, as her moods alternated between excitement and fear—excitement to see Denise again and fear that Denise would change her mind and that they would never be together again. The latter thought brought a stab of pain to her chest.

Midweek, Denise called to see if Kiki would be coming in as usual Friday afternoon.

"Absolutely!" Kiki assured her. When she had ended the call, Kiki suddenly realized that Denise could *also* be uncertain about *her* feelings after they had been sexually intimate.

When Kiki arrived at the office on Friday, Denise met her at the door. Butch was not around, and Denise took her hand. "I need a hug," she said, pulling Kiki into a warm and sustained embrace.

Then Denise led her to a chair and sat her down. "Look, Kiki, when a relationship is new, it is natural to think about it all the time and to want to make love all the time. I feel that way, and I imagine that you do, too. However, if we're going to work together, and deal with Butch and the others, we're going to have to be careful and to discipline ourselves."

Kiki nodded, not quite sure where Denise was leading.

"If you can promise to come over on Friday as usual, and we'll work hard on the magazine for three or four hours, then we can have a quiet dinner together and then, well, have some fun. If you want to spend the night, we can do something together Saturday morning, before you have to go back to work in Oakland. Then I'll catch up on the magazine later in the weekend."

At first Kiki didn't quite understand the need for all this structure. Yet she had been dreaming about being with Denise all week, and now that she was in the same room with her, Denise's presence was intoxicating. Kiki desperately wanted to start touching her, right here and right now, so maybe she did need to hear what Denise was saying.

Although it wasn't easy, they both managed to focus on their projects. Kiki organized the week's mail while Denise finished a writing project, and then they planned a layout together. At nearly 9 p.m., they finally reached a stopping place.

Denise picked up Chinese carryout, and they walked to her apartment. As soon as they opened the door, their discipline was forgotten, and the Chinese food sat in its containers growing cold while they kissed and touched and caressed each other on Denise's large bed. Their lovemaking was as passionate as the week before, perhaps more so because they felt certain about how to pleasure each other. A week of waiting and imagining brought them both to strong climaxes.

At midnight, Denise reheated the food in her tiny microwave oven, and they sat in bed munching on sweet and sour pork. Then laughing and teasing, they began making love all over again.

Somewhere about 3 a.m., Denise held Kiki in her arms. "It's so intense," Kiki admitted. "I never knew I had all this energy inside of me."

Denise stroked her long, wavy hair. "You and I are a good match for each other, Kiki. Lesbians can be very intense. That's the danger of it, because it is so easy to burn like a hot flame and then fade into ashes. I've had more than one sexual partner since college, and I can tell you that not all of them feel the same."

Kiki looked up at her in the dim light. "Did you always know you were a lesbian?"

"No," Denise said. "I dated a lot in high school, yet I never quite felt like I was getting what I wanted. So I ended one relationship even after I became engaged. When I started college, I turned inward for a long time. It wasn't until I moved over here to the City that I began to drift into circles where my attraction to women became clear. You know, even a decade ago, the environment at Montrose College was a lot more repressive. If there was any lesbian-bisexual student organization then, it was so secretive that I didn't know of it. Now, even the conservative alumnae association is waking up, but that's all very, very new. My college years were wonderful, and yet that time was very confusing sexually for me."

"Have you had a lot of partners?" Kiki asked.

"Just a few, but I'm careful. I don't bed hop, and I've been very sure about every woman I've been with, in terms of the partners she has had. You can't be too careful these days, with AIDS and all the other sexually transmitted diseases out there."

Kiki sighed, "It's a lot to think about, isn't it?"

"Yes," Denise agreed, giving her a squeeze. "However, we can have a lot of fun together, if we can just keep things in perspective."

"Okay, I trust you." Kiki yawned deeply and fell asleep once again in Denise's arms.

Dawn blossomed into a sunny warm day. Denise and Kiki rode the Geary bus to Ocean Beach and played and picnicked in the sand. Kiki felt deliriously happy. Denise kept her own commitment by seeing that Kiki got on the bus in time to catch the BART and to make her job at Jim's by 4 p.m. Although Kiki was sunburned and a bit rattled from tiredness, Jim was clearly so happy to see her having fun that he shrugged off the few mistakes she made at work that evening. "Kiki," he assured her, when she apologized for spilling a soda on the counter, "even when ya are runnin' on three cylinders, yore better dan lots o' folks would be on four."

As Kiki's new life with Denise began to unfold, some of her past relationships took a hit. When Jacinta, who had been Kiki's best friend since freshman year, figured out that Kiki had a meaningful relationship in San Francisco and that it was with a woman, she suddenly backed off. Coming from a very conservative Mexican family, Jacinta could neither understand nor accept homosexuality. She still liked Kiki and still spoke with her; however, there was now a wall between them.

Kiki talked with Nancy about Jacinta, and Nancy was honest. "Not everyone will be able to accept your lifestyle, Kiki. That's hard, but it's a fact. However, you will find that the people who truly love you and can accept who you really are will be even closer when you are open with them. Like your boss, Jim, for example. I expect he has a closeness with you now that wasn't there before, because this big question mark has been answered, and now neither one of you has to step carefully around forbidden topics."

Kiki reflected on her relationship with Jim, realizing that what Nancy said was true.

Kiki's life took on a new pattern. School, her part-time job, and study during the week, a trip to the City late on Friday afternoon and the night with Denise, some fun on Saturday morning, working at the pizza parlor Saturday and a quiet day on Sunday of rest and study. There was precious little time for anything extra, although she did manage a post card here and there to Sal and her family.

Sal called immediately when Kiki confessed in a brief note that she had found a woman to be with and was gloriously happy. "Hey, Kiki, what good news," Sal said with enthusiasm. "Meg and I are so glad for you. Details, maybe, for your aunts?"

Kiki laughed and told Sal how she met Denise on the campus, and about the magazine, and her trips over to the City, and how they gradually became close."

"That's wonderful," Sal exclaimed. "That's exactly the way I hoped it would be for you—that you'd find a smart and really good person with whom you have something in common. And you did it, good for you!"

"We have good chemistry, too!" Kiki admitted with a somewhat embarrassed laugh.

"That's great! Tonight Meg and I will drink a toast of champagne to you and Denise."

Kiki put off writing to her mama and papa for a long time. At first she was afraid her relationship with Denise would evaporate, and then there would be no need to tell them. Then, as Denise proved a faithful and dedicated friend and lover, Kiki began to feel uncomfortable. Perhaps she was waiting too long to write.

Finally, one Sunday, she made herself sit down and write a long letter about her life at the college, how things were going, and how she had felt confused for a long, long time about herself, but had met a wonderful woman and had fallen in love, and that she now felt sure about how she must live. She told them a little about Denise so that they would know she was well educated, had a good job and was a responsible person. Kiki enclosed a picture of the two of them that had been taken at Fisherman's Wharf.

Once Kiki mailed the letter, she lived in fear for the next few weeks. For a long time there was no answer, and she was afraid that she had alienated her family forever. She was about to call home, when a letter came to her, written by Gusto, who was now nearly eighteen:

I'm writing for Mama and Papa because, as you know, neither can write English good enough to compose a long letter. Mama says that she always knew you was different because you was always kind of a tomboy. She wants you to be happy and just says for you to be careful and not hang around people who might make you sick. I think she means AIDS, because it's on the TV sometimes. Papa was a little bit hurt at first, but he thought about it a lot, and then he remembered the nice woman you came here with, the woman with the truck, and he decided that if you had the good sense to find friends like that, that maybe this was how you were supposed to be and he could live with it. He is still very proud that you are staying in college. We all know how hard it is for you. We miss you a lot and wish you could come home, but we understand that it costs too much.

I need to tell you something from me, too. Your friend with the truck, she came through here last summer and she stopped to see us. She asked me if I had a job, which I didn't, 'cause you know there ain't no work around here. Then she talked with a man she knows at this warehouse in Jersey. He talked with a friend of his who has this warehouse on the edge of the Bronx, and this man offered me a job for the summer. It was too far to walk, so I had to ride two buses to get there. With the change, it took more than an hour to get to work, but I took the job, anyway. At first they had me loading trucks. I did good, and then they let me count inventory inside the warehouse and taught me to drive a forklift. When school started, I had to work part-time, so they found some work in the office that I could do late in the day and on Saturday. I'm still there, and the money is good. The neat part is that I was so bored on the buses that I started reading comic books and then I used the time to do homework for school. My grades went up, even though I was working, and now the school counselor is encouraging me to go to junior college when I graduate in May. My boss, he says that if I will study business at college, after two years, he can make me a manager trainee.

And here's the really good news. Javier is well again and has stayed out of jail, and my boss offered him a job if he would promise to avoid trouble. So he's working at the warehouse, too, and between the two of us, we're bringing home enough money so that Mama and Papa may be able to move to a better apartment in a nicer part of town.

Kiki, I don't have no friends in gangs no more, and I know that will make you happy. I wanted you to know that I am proud of me, and I am proud of you. 'Cause if you hadn't left and showed us all we can change things, I'd probably be out of school and in jail now too, and Mama and Papa would be real sad. We don't hold much hope for Raul, but I think Javier might make it. I know I will.

We love you, Kiki. Gusto.

If Gusto's life and schoolwork were improving, so were Kiki's. Even though she had less time to study, her grades kept getting better. She was amazed, yet Nancy assured her that she had been using a lot of energy suppressing her sexuality, and now that she had a healthy outlet for that energy, it was natural for her to be able to do the same amount of work in less time and with a lot more inspiration.

At the end of the fall semester of her junior year, Kiki made the Dean's List for the first time. Word rippled through the administrative wing that Melissa, Sonia, Rita and even President Ryerson had openly admitted how proud they were of Kiki. Furthermore, they were now very pleased with their decision, albeit a big risk, of admitting her to Montrose.

Rita Capehart rather missed her sessions with Kiki because Kiki was positive, creative, and responded to encouragement—something always rewarding to a counselor. She used the Dean's List announcement as an excuse to reach out to Kiki and to encourage her to apply for an internship during the summer between her junior and senior years. "It could really help you prepare for the workplace after your graduation," she suggested.

Kiki was both stunned and grateful to Rita for this information. She would never have thought of an internship herself, but she explored the possibility and applied to a public relations firm in San Francisco. Secretly, Kiki also thought the internship might give her a chance to see more of Denise; however, she didn't mention that to Rita.

Although Kiki's life was going marvelously well, she was still living a hand-to-mouth existence financially. She had twenty hours of work a week at the college, plus Jim's pizza place on Saturday evenings. Twenty-seven hours a week only provided a limited amount of money, which kept her in books, supplies, and clean laundry, gave her a few treats each week, and was enough for her fare to the City.

It didn't buy clothes, cover vacations, or do anything to prevent the student loans from piling up. When she graduated, she would owe a lot of money. Kiki knew she would have to work hard to pay off those loans.

In the short run, Kiki was covered as long as the college was in session, but every Christmas and summer, she still faced the issue of housing. As a junior, she sublet an apartment on the hill for the winter break and was taking care of a hamster named Puffball, or Puffy for short. As Kiki sat in the living room reading a novel and watching Puffy roll around the floor in a plastic ball, she mused to herself about her situation. Arranging the sublet this holiday break felt lonelier compared to being with Jim's family or with Sal and Meg—although Puffy's antics helped—but also more grown up as she faced a holiday period on her own for the first time. She spent Christmas Eve and Christmas Day with Denise yet didn't hang around afterward because Denise had to work and Kiki definitely didn't want to strain their relationship. Besides, there was Puffy to consider.

Kiki hung out in the apartment when she wasn't working for Jim. She played with the hamster, read novels for pleasure, and watched some lesbian films on television. Nancy had loaned her several lesbian romance DVDs when she heard that the apartment had a large-screen TV.

"Don't get carried away," Nancy teased when she handed her the movies.

Kiki just blushed.

While Kiki could admit to herself that she adored Denise and was deeply involved with her, she also recognized that Denise was older and had lots of commitments of her own, like *Belle Femme*, that took much of her extra time and resources. Having the magazine meant a great deal to Denise, and Kiki felt that if she leaned on her too much,

Denise would eventually resent it and a wall could grow between them.

So Kiki focused on being thankful for every week that their love-making and fun together continued. Beyond that, she was a bit afraid to think of their romance as permanent. From what she had gleaned from friends and books, many lesbian relationships were hot and heavy but didn't last long. However, Helena and PJ had been partners for many years. So had Nancy and Paula and Sal and Meg. She didn't think that each of them had started as a first partner, though she didn't know for sure, and Denise *was* Kiki's first. Although she *hoped* it would last, it would appear too much to ask that Denise would be her "one and only" forever. Kiki didn't mention her fears to Denise, because she was afraid that her feelings might dampen the fun they were having now. She knew *that* discussion would be a risk. Kiki was emotionally immature in some ways, yet she was smart enough to realize that fact on her own. So she gave herself—and Denise—room to grow.

In the middle of the spring semester, Kiki found a letter in her post office box from JJ Jackson & Co., San Francisco. The firm promised her an internship for the summer. The pay was rather low, and the letter admitted that fact; it also stated that if she did well, she might be hired after graduation for a permanent position at a very healthy salary.

Struggling with the information and the decision she must make, Kiki went to Nancy Raines, because she felt the chaplain was the one person in her college life whom she could count on to be objective. "I don't know what to do," Kiki admitted to Nancy. "I want to take the internship, because it's probably in my best interest, and it would allow me to see Denise and learn more about the City and the business world. But it means giving up a good and comfortable job in admissions this summer and a guaranteed place to live that I can afford."

"Could you stay with Denise?" Nancy asked.

"I don't want to put that kind of pressure on our relationship. I mean, the idea of it sounds wonderful, yet it would make me very dependent on her and push into her space, and I don't think that would be right." Kiki's shoulders rippled with tension.

"So you're not going to talk to her about it?" Nancy pursued.

Kiki sighed. "Okay, maybe it isn't right for *me* yet. Maybe *I'm* not ready for that much closeness all the time. Once a week is great. However, I have a lot on my mind and that's completing my degree."

Nancy smiled. "I'm relieved that you're admitting that it's *you* who feels uncomfortable. Denise might love having you live with her, but if it's too soon or not right for you, then don't set yourself up."

Kiki's shoulders relaxed. "Thanks for understanding. I was kind of afraid that you would say I should ask her."

Nancy gently suggested, "Well, personally, I think you should at least discuss it with her. For such an arrangement to work out, it has to be right for both people, and it sounds like you're saying that it wouldn't be right for you, at least not yet. If you are clear about that, then I don't want me or anyone else, including Denise, to push you into something that's not good for you."

Kiki gave her a lopsided grin. "Thanks. I still don't know what I'm going to do for the summer."

Nancy thought. "Well, I have one suggestion, but I certainly won't push that on you either. Paula and I are going to Europe to do some backpacking during the summer. We have been planning to hire a sitter to take care of our house and the cats while we're gone. I hadn't thought of you because you usually stay on campus and don't drive a car. And now you'll have to go into the City to work, which will consume a lot of extra time. You might want to think about it. There would be no rent to pay. However, in order to survive, you would have to learn to drive a car and pass the driver's exam between now and the end of May. Whether you can accomplish that, I don't know.

Or whether you'd want to."

"Can I have a little time to decide?"

Nancy chuckled. "Of course, you can."

Kiki thought and thought and asked everyone she knew. Jim laughed and said it was a great idea. Denise seemed almost envious yet remained very supportive. When Kiki mentioned that she was afraid she couldn't learn to drive in time, Denise just grinned. "I know you can do it, honey."

So Kiki went back to Nancy and told her that if the offer were still open, she would like to try to make the deadline. Also, was the car a stick or an automatic?

The remainder of the spring semester morphed into a "teach Kiki to drive" marathon. Jim volunteered to help her on Sundays for an hour or so before he opened his pizza parlor. He brought his old green and white Chevy to the campus and demonstrated to Kiki how to start it, go forward, back up, and move in and out of a parking place. Then he traded seats, had her buckle up and let her drive slowly around the campus—which was very quiet early Sunday mornings. A security guard assisted them by putting out cones at just the right spots Kiki needed for the parallel parking test, and Jim good-naturedly helped her try again and again until she had learned to move the big car into the tiny space. He kidded her when she finally succeeded. "If ya can do it with dis' big ol' Chevy, ya can do it with dem tiny foreign t'ings ever'body drives these days."

Meanwhile, Kiki had ridden the bus to the driver's license bureau, picked up a manual, studied it and successfully completed the test for her learner's permit. She was proud of having passed a milestone that allowed her to go out on city streets as long as Jim was with her.

As Kiki's confidence began to grow, Jim went with her around the neighborhood and then onto the freeway for the first time. Kiki felt very nervous; however, they both came back in one piece. Thankfully, Sunday morning traffic was light on the I-580.

A few days after Kiki's first freeway challenge, Nancy invited her to come to dinner at her home in the Berkeley Hills, with the proviso that she had to drive. Nancy came to Montrose to pick Kiki up, but then she put Kiki behind the wheel and had her drive all the way to Berkeley and back, a journey that required headlights and night driving before the evening was over. Kiki felt particularly anxious, because Nancy had a nice car and it was a lot different from Jim's spacious and clunky Chevy. Although she was terribly afraid of making a mistake, they returned safely. Nancy smiled and patted her on the shoulder, and Kiki ran into the dorm, climbed the stairs, and collapsed on her bed, emotionally exhausted from the ordeal.

Just before the end of the spring term, Kiki took the driver's test and passed—just as everyone else knew she would. As fate would have it, she became eligible to drink and to drive in the same month. Kiki would always remember her twenty-first birthday!

At the end of May Kiki moved into Nancy and Paula's home in the Berkeley Hills and even gave them a lift to the San Francisco airport to catch their flight to Europe.

Having a real house, fully decorated, was an incredible experience for Kiki. She felt Nancy and Paula's nurturing presence in each carefully selected detail throughout their home. At the same time, she was beginning to feel very grown up, living on her own, taking care of the cats each day, and driving the car, careful not to let the tiniest dent mar its shining surface. She remembered being in that house once before, the day she took the SAT exam just before being admitted to Montrose, and it amazed her to consider how far she had come since then.

Thinking of that particular Saturday sent Kiki to the backyard that evening, where she sat in a rocking loveseat, holding Muffins in her arms, and gazed up at the stars. She studied Artemis, still blinking, and asked, "Can this really be happening to me?"

The summer internship at JJ Jackson & Co. offered a real challenge for Kiki. At first she felt terrified; gradually she realized that her work at the college and with Denise on the magazine had prepared her for this experience. The tasks Kiki was asked to do were just a step beyond what she had already done, and before the summer was over, she felt very comfortable working there. She watched what other employees did, and she saw several jobs that she thought she would enjoy.

Each Friday evening, Kiki stayed for a while to help Denise with *Belle Femme*, yet she had to get home to take care of the cats, and she still worked for Jim on Saturday evenings. She would have liked to take the summer off, but she needed the extra money. Kiki and Denise were able to have lunch together during the week occasionally, but their real private time together came on Sundays. Denise rode the BART to Berkeley, and Kiki picked her up at the station and drove her up to the house. First they had lunch together, a meal that Kiki often prepared because while staying at the house she was working on improving her cooking skills.

By the time Kiki and Denise had eaten and shared their week's events with each other, they had overcome any initial nervousness and were ready to make love—and then lie around listening to music or watching a DVD. Kiki was totally enthralled. She did miss the Friday overnights they had enjoyed together, and she wished for more time with Denise. Kiki felt that Denise wanted more time as well, but Sundays were all they could do this summer—at least all that Kiki could manage. Kiki wondered at times if their relationship would grow, or whether they would have trouble connecting during the very busy senior year ahead at Montrose. Once she was out of college, Kiki hoped to have only one good job to worry about and more time for a personal life.

That summer was also punctuated by the arrival of Sal, who wanted to see Kiki and managed to arrange a load to the Bay Area. She stayed with Kiki for a couple of nights during a weekend and commented on how grown up Kiki appeared in stature and maturity. "I'm still only five feet, two inches tall," Kiki quipped.

Because Sal's timing was just right, she managed to meet Denise, and before Sal climbed into the cab for her trip back to Salt Lake, she commented to Kiki, "I really like Denise, and I hope the two of you will do well together. She is exactly the kind of intelligent, sensitive, and dedicated person that I would have picked for you." She laughed, "You know as your adopted aunt, I am very protective. I want you to fall in with the right people. I'm sure your Artemis does too." She gave Kiki a hug and then—with Aisha panting out the passenger-side window—shoved off in the big truck.

Waving at Sal going down the street, Kiki remembered something else that Sal had said kiddingly that morning, "Now that you have your driver's license, you'll have to come on the road with me sometime. Wouldn't that be a kick?"

Kiki was initially enthralled with Sal's idea; she later realized that those easy days on the highway in the pink truck seemed very far away. So did her fantasies about world travel and joining the Peace Corps. Now she had college to complete, a significant relationship, a full-time off-campus job, and a growing debt of student loans. She would always be an adventurer, but maybe the scale or the nature of her adventures was changing—at least as far down the road as she could see.

22

The Family

Kiki literally bumped into Nancy Raines in the college bookstore one sunny fall morning. "Oops!" she gasped, suppressing a giggle.

"Hi, Kiki," Nancy smiled. "No damage done. How are you anyway? I haven't seen much of you this semester."

Kiki's senior year at Montrose had started out at high speed. Everything seemed to be pushing her toward an ultimate day in her young life—graduation from Montrose College for Women.

"I just run as fast as I can go," Kiki admitted to Nancy. "I'm keeping up with everything, just barely. Life is good. Denise is really special. I can't believe she's best friend, my lover, and the woman having my back, all rolled into one. It's fantastic for me! Jim and his family are good. One of his daughters was accepted at Berkeley with a scholarship, and he's very excited for her. Word from back home is positive, for once. Sal gets down here now and then," Kiki gushed. "Oh, how are the kitties? And Paula?"

Nancy smiled. "We're all fine." She looked around the shop. "I don't want to hold you up, but it is really good to see you. Stop by sometime. You can always bring Denise, too."

"Okay," Kiki blushed. "I'll do that."

She and Nancy parted, and Kiki thought a bit how strange it was to have lived in someone's house all summer and now have barely enough time to say hello.

As Kiki carried on with her day, that thought about Nancy led her to consider where she was in her life. Before she was eighteen, everything in her world had pushed and molded her in such a way that led her to take to the road looking for something better. Now everything during her twenty-second year pushed and molded her to move on from her college cocoon out into a wider world. Just like not seeing Nancy very often anymore, her senior world was constantly changing—leaving some things behind and adding new ones.

As the school year began, everything appeared to be a good fit. All Kiki had to do was put one foot in front of the other day after day, and she'd arrive at her destination. *Hard at times and exhausting at times, but basically as simple as that*, she thought.

Kiki was thrilled when they drew numbers for room assignment to senior sleeping porches. She picked a high number and was able to select the porch where she had slept a few nights when she was hiding out at Montrose. Somehow, it seemed appropriate to return full circle to the scene of her early adventure on the campus.

Shortly after classes began, the Human Resource office at JJ Jackson & Co., notified Kiki that the firm was satisfied with her summer work as an intern and that she was officially invited to apply for a full-time position the following year. The work there would involve many of the things she had studied in college, and she pinched herself every time she thought of it. The letter sounded so positive that she found herself making the assumption that the job was hers, and she immediately posted her application.

On the academic front, her grades remained high, and Kiki was well on her way to making the Dean's List for the second time.

Her ability to drive a car opened up new dreams and wishes for the future. She could see herself exploring the country and visiting friends, especially Sal and Meg. She could apply for jobs anywhere that she could reach in a car. Although she thought she wanted to work in San Francisco, being able to drive meant she didn't *have* to work there if something better came along.

In the meantime, having a license also increased Kiki's options for fun and romance with Denise. There was always someone willing to loan her a car on a Sunday afternoon, and she explored the world as much as time would permit. She was ecstatic when she took Denise on their first trip together across the Golden Gate Bridge. Kiki sang "California Here I Come" at the top of her lungs all the way across the fabled red span. Denise joined her in singing and then laughed with amusement.

During the fall, Kiki marched in the first Gay Pride celebration ever held at Montrose, including a parade through the main street of the campus and onto the greens before the campanile. Many students, staff, and faculty attended the event, including Rita Capehart who watched the parade at a respectful distance and focused with a stern look at Kiki, who carried a large sign proclaiming "Love Is Love."

Nancy Raines, who coincidentally was standing next to Rita, leaned over and commented, "Don't take it so hard. Kiki was born this way, and there is nothing you could have done to change it."

Rita glanced at Nancy with a look of surprise and, in an unguarded moment, asked, "Have I been that obvious?"

Nancy laughed and then quipped, "Not too bad, maybe a little." Rita looked a bit taken aback, but she managed to smile good-naturedly.

Kiki also attended the reception for alumnae during Montrose's reunion weekend in early October. Denise came, partly to visit with good friends who had made the trek from out of town because their class year was being honored. Denise introduced her friends to Kiki, and then the two lovers sat together quietly holding hands beneath the table during the alumnae dinner.

Throughout Kiki's senior year, Denise and Kiki continued their relationship, which appeared to blossom. Any initial reservations Denise might have had seemed to lessen as Kiki continued growing in maturity and self-confidence.

After working together on the magazine one Friday evening, and while the two walked back to her apartment, Denise held Kiki's hand and shared something that had been on her mind for a while. "Shortly after we met," she said gently, "you expressed the concern that we could not last as a couple because I am older than you are and more experienced. Do you remember?"

Kiki swallowed and then nodded. "Yes, I remember."

"Well, at the time I understood where you were coming from, and I didn't know *what* my role in your life would be—beyond introducing you to lesbian sex," Denise continued. "But the longer I know you, and the more you grow, the less I feel those five years between us. I think by the time you graduate and spend a few months working, you won't feel I'm too far beyond your reach any more."

Kiki looked at her questioningly. "You think not?"

Denise shook her head. "I've developed a great respect for your tenacity, your creativity, and your ability to turn difficult situations around until they work for you."

Kiki looked at her with amusement. "I do that sometimes, don't I? Maybe that's the Artemis influence."

Denise squeezed her hand. "I also feel very lucky to have met you first, because you are becoming a very special young woman."

"Really?" Kiki—caught up in the rush of senior life and events— didn't quite see herself from the outside. She still looked up to Denise with adoration because her intelligence, wit and capabilities were much more firmly in place. And Kiki could not believe how beautiful Denise was and the fact that she was in a relationship with her. At times Kiki actually felt overwhelmed with the love she felt toward Denise.

Denise did not say anything more and made no open projections about their future together. Kiki was quiet, too, thinking as they walked on together.

Kiki was feeling so good about everything by the end of the fall semester that during the winter break she risked staying with Denise. "I think I can handle being in your space a lot better now," she confessed, and Denise just beamed. They made every moment of the three-week holiday count as they celebrated their second Christmas together. Denise even took a few days off from her job so that they could have quality time with each other enjoying the City's holiday cultural events—as well as quality time together in the bedroom.

They toasted with champagne on New Year's Eve, and Kiki confessed, "I don't think my life could be any better than it is right now."

After the winter break, Kiki returned to Olsen Hall with one semester to complete. She was happy and hopeful, skipping along as she was and feeling that the world was now on her wavelength. *She had come so far from her life in the South Bronx, and there was no going back.* Ahead of her, just four more courses to complete, her thesis project, graduation, and then a job in San Francisco and time to spend building her relationship with Denise.

Very suddenly, Kiki's bubble burst. In February, she received an upsetting letter from JJ Jackson & Co. There had been several applicants for the full-time position for which she had applied, and apparently one of them, a young woman from Stanford University, had been so outstanding that the firm had awarded her the position. The letter concluded:

You were our alternate choice and will remain on our list of desired candidates should another similar position open up in the near future.

Kiki was devastated. She went to see Nancy Raines and literally cried on Nancy's shoulder. "What's going to happen to me now?" she wailed. "I'll graduate with nowhere to go and owe all this money for student loans."

Nancy soothed her as best she could. "Something will turn up.

You know that. It always has. Maybe there is a better job waiting for you out there, one you just can't see right now."

Kiki dried her eyes. "Maybe you're right. But I feel like I'm on the edge of a cliff and about to fall off."

"I understand," Nancy told her gently. "This makes everything harder, and there's no way around it," she admitted. "You'll have to do all the things you already do and still make time for job hunting—doing job research, writing resumes, and placing applications. It's going to be hard, I don't deny that. However, you'll do it, I'm sure, because you know you must."

Nancy reminded Kiki that the college's placement office might have some listings and that she should start there. Caught so off balance, Kiki had forgotten that there was one resource right at Montrose that could help her. After all, they had assisted her with the internship at JJ Jackson.

As the semester progressed, Kiki's emotional life shifted several notches upward on the stress scale. She spent precious hours scouting job possibilities, exploring the Internet and local newspapers, even looking for positions out of the area. She felt compelled to do that for her own survival, although she admitted to a concerned Denise that she certainly didn't *want* to leave the Bay Area.

There were several consequences of this flutter and flurry. Kiki nearly lost her job with Jim, because she had so much homework to do that she was very late to work one Saturday and totally missed another Saturday's time slot. Jim acknowledged that he understood her situation, but he also gave Kiki a stern lecture. He needed to be able to count on her, especially on Saturday evenings, and if he couldn't, he'd have to find someone else for the one shift she was currently working.

Kiki failed to make the trip to San Francisco on more than one Friday afternoon, and Denise, although she understood, also became tense. She admitted that she was disappointed because she needed Kiki to show up for work. And personally, she acknowledged that she missed Kiki and worried that maybe their relationship wasn't as solid as she had hoped. Kiki told her that it was just a few weeks to graduation, and things would get better. "But what if you find a job elsewhere and move away?" Denise countered. "That would be the end of our relationship." Kiki gulped and tried to reassure Denise, yet in reality, she knew that if she couldn't find work here, Denise was probably right.

Kiki's senior project for her major in communications was to be a fifty-page thesis with photos and video about African-American musicians who played in the bars and clubs of old downtown Oakland. Jim had introduced her to that culture, and he was also supportive in rounding up some of those musicians that she needed to interview and videotape for her report. While the idea had excited Kiki in the beginning, after she received the JJ Jackson & Co. letter, she was so busy with job-hunting that she didn't have sufficient time to make the trips on a regular basis into the nightlife scene of Oakland to do the research. She was late finishing and assembling the report. The deadline approached and passed, and Kiki had not turned in her project.

Stressed to the max, Kiki was putting the finishing touches on the written part of the thesis that accompanied the video, when she got a phone call from Denise, who hadn't seen her for three weeks. Kiki was beside herself. "I can't talk," she practically screamed into the phone. "I'm late on my senior project, and if I don't get this done, I won't graduate. I can't talk to you now." And she hung up.

Kiki began crying, tossed her papers around the room, and collapsed onto her bed. She curled up into a ball and rocked herself. *Was this the end of her dream?*

Shortly afterward, Rita Capehart called Kiki into her office for a conference. Kiki looked grim, and her distress was obvious from her mismatched attire and her straggly uncombed hair.

Rita met her face-to-face at the door. "I'm concerned, Kiki, by a call from your communications advisor, that your senior thesis has not been turned in. Is something going on that we need to know about?"

Kiki exploded. "I just can't do it all! I have to find a job and a place to live, and I don't know what's going to happen to me." Tears poured down her cheeks.

Rita looked pained. "I gather you are totally overwhelmed," she observed gently, guiding Kiki to a nearby loveseat. "You must be very scared, after you've worked so hard to get to this point."

Kiki hunched over and nodded. "I can't eat, and I can't sleep. I've never felt so messed up like this. I feel like I owe everything to everybody, and I just can't keep going."

"Okay, I understand," Rita said kindly. "Let's try to sort this out."

Kiki sighed, and her shoulders sagged as she wiped her eyes with a Kleenex.

Rita sat down beside Kiki and put an arm around the troubled senior. "You have maybe ten things before you," she noted, "all of which you are trying to juggle, and you are dropping some of the balls, right?"

"Yes," Kiki acknowledged. That much was clear.

"Of all the balls you have to keep in the air, which one is the most important right at this moment?"

Kiki wanted to scream "ALL OF THEM," but she held her tongue and tried to think rationally. "Well, I can't graduate without completing my senior project, so I guess that is number one. The other things are dependent on that."

"Okay," Rita affirmed. "You're right. You need to go back to the dorm and settle down and finish the project and turn it in to your advisor. Focus on that, and while you are working on that one thing, do try to eat something, drink lots of water, and get some sleep. And take lots of deep breaths."

Kiki nodded and started to stand up.

Rita put a hand out. "Wait a minute. When you turn in the project, I want you to come back here again, and we'll look at what comes next. You need to focus on all these things, yet only one at a time."

Although Kiki's nerves were still frayed, she walked back to the dorm, drank water, forced herself to eat a snack, and inhaled deeply several times. *Just finish this one thing*, she said to herself repeatedly like a mantra, while she gathered up all the papers she had scattered earlier and sat down in front of her computer.

Before the day was over, Kiki had completed the paper and proofed it. She created a package to hold the written copy, the photos and the video, with a cover that featured the best photo that she had taken of the musicians. Kiki felt pretty confident that the report was a good one, and she hurried across the campus to print it out at the library and turn it in to her advisor.

The next morning, Kiki went back to see Dr. Capehart. With one less ball to juggle, she already felt a little better. She had even eaten breakfast and combed her hair.

Rita gave her a pat on the shoulder. "Good job! One down. And did you sleep last night?"

"Not a lot but much better than I have been."

Rita nodded. "Okay, that's good. Now, what comes next?"

"I'm behind in my homework for all my classes. Nothing serious; I know I need to catch up so that I will be able to do well on my finals."

"How many hours of work do you have to catch up?"

Kiki sighed. "If I spent a whole weekend, and did nothing else, I think I could be caught up by Monday morning."

"What is keeping you from doing that?" Rita asked.

"Feeling that I'll lose my job if I don't go to work on Saturday evening, and the guilt I feel toward my partner in San Francisco for screaming at her on the phone and not going there to see her."

Rita thought for a moment. "If your boss at work knew ahead that you couldn't come in, and it was just for this one Saturday, would he fire you?"

Kiki sighed. "He's not happy with me now, yet maybe if I called ahead, so he knew, he would accept it, as long as it's this one Saturday only."

"Okay. What about your partner? Would it give you some peace of mind to call her and apologize and tell her that you need one more weekend to catch up, and you'll be able to see her after that?"

Kiki shrugged. "I don't know if she'll even speak to me, but I could try."

Dr. Capehart advised Kiki to make the two necessary phone calls and then focus the entire weekend on her homework.

Although Jim didn't sound very happy when Kiki called, since she gave him warning so he could find another worker to take her place, he did not threaten to fire her. He just told her that he'd see her the following Saturday. Kiki was very relieved by his reaction, thanked him, and hung up the phone.

Contacting Denise was harder. Kiki nervously paced the floor a few times before making the call. Denise's number rang and rang and there was no answer. Then the call went to her answering machine. Kiki frowned, put her cell phone down, and returned to her studies. She had piles of books on her desk and scattered all over the floor. There was so much to do!

Later in the evening, as she buried herself in one of her textbooks, the phone rang. Kiki jumped up, nearly in panic.

"Hello?" she said hesitantly into the cell.

"Kiki? This is Denise. What's up?" Denise sounded cool; at least she had called back.

The color rose in Kiki's face. "I want to apologize for my outburst," she began, almost choking on her words. "I was so overwhelmed and so late on everything here at school, and I don't have a job yet, and I just wasn't handling anything. It wasn't fair to take my stress out on you, and I'm very sorry."

She could hear Denise take a deep breath. "Well, thank you for calling me and letting me know. It certainly was upsetting, and I didn't know what to think."

"I can understand that. You've been wonderful to me, and you didn't deserve that from me. I went to see Dr. Capehart, and she helped me figure out what I had to do first and get it done, and then second, and now I'm seeing more clearly how to keep going. I have to spend this weekend on my homework, because I am way behind," Kiki explained, tears forming in her eyes.

Denise sounded cool again. "Well, your homework does come first. And you are about to graduate. You wouldn't want to screw up now."

Kiki squeezed the phone and paced around the room. "Denise, I really miss you. I know I've made some mistakes. I just hope you won't write me off."

Denise was silent for a moment. "No, I won't write you off," she finally promised. "I'll try to be patient. The last semester is always hard, and I've been there, too—only I think my load wasn't as heavy as yours. And I miss you, too."

Kiki promised to let her know as soon as she could come over to San Francisco, and they said goodbye. Kiki leaned against the wall for a moment and felt as if she would faint. After taking a few deep breaths, she sensed her heart rate slowing down. Her head cleared, and she was able to sit down at her desk and return to work.

The following week, Kiki attended her classes, and her homework was current. She also put in her hours in the admissions office.

By Friday, she began to feel more hopeful that she would be able to graduate.

Kiki rode the BART into San Francisco and struggled to walk to the *Belle Femme* office. When she arrived, Denise was working alone. Kiki dropped into a chair across from her desk and stared at her. The ravages of the past few weeks were obvious on her face.

When Denise looked up, it took only a glance for her to see just how hard a battle Kiki had been fighting. She came around her desk and took Kiki in her arms, and they both cried together. "I'm so sorry," Kiki wailed, and Denise soothed her gently.

Very little work was completed that evening; they shared a meal and made love. Their jangled nerves settled and their relationship began to heal.

The following week, Kiki received a note from her communications professor:

Your senior project is excellent. It deserves an A grade, and had it been turned in on time, it would have received an A. Because it was late, I have to give you a B+. I'm sorry to have to do so, because your work is worthy of an award, but I have to treat everyone by the same rules.

Kiki cried over the message. Yet most of her tears were ones of relief, because a passing grade on the project meant that she could graduate.

From that moment on, Kiki was better able to keep her priorities straight. She wrote a thank-you note to Rita Capehart, and she made sure to get all of her other papers in on time and to prepare carefully for her finals.

Kiki still had a difficult time keeping the clouds away, because she didn't know what would happen to her after graduation day. She was only able to keep on going because she looked back at all the good things that had come to her and the way people had helped her. Late one evening, she sat on the end of her bed and looked up from the sleeping porch tarp, studying the stars and searching for Artemis. "Everyone has been so good to me, from that first day on the bus when I met that little lady Grace, and she saw that I had dinner and then a place to spend the night. Then there was Sal, and Jim, and—" Kiki sighed. *So much goodness, it made her want to cry.*

Kiki needed very much to hang onto her hope that something good would come again. Somehow this whole crisis would surely turn out for the best, even if she could not see how at this moment. She promised herself that she would go outside, breathe in the May night air, look up to Artemis, and offer a prayer of thanksgiving. *Being thankful would be a lot better than complaining.*

One week before graduation, Kiki's ship of life righted itself on the stormy sea of that final semester. An unexpected letter appeared in her mail box from JJ Jackson & Co. The letter read:

Our original candidate for the full-time assistant position has received a prestigious scholarship to attend graduate school in Europe this fall and therefore will not be assuming our proffered position.

In that you were our alternate candidate, we are now proffering you this position, effective June 1, if you are still available and wish to work for this firm.

We regret that this offer comes so late; however, please advise us of your availability.

Kiki screamed and danced and ran around the post office and down the street to Olsen Hall. She waved the letter in her hand high over her head and whooped. Everyone she passed gave her a questioning glance, as if she had lost her mind.

Within an hour, she had notified Denise, Nancy, Rita, and Jim. She had called Sal in Salt Lake City and her mama in the South Bronx. She had also called JJ Jackson & Co., and told the firm she would be delighted to accept their position. Whether she was number one or two or ten didn't make any difference. What she needed was the job!

Almost before Kiki could blink, it was Graduation Day. On a beautiful sunny May morning, she stood on the lawn before the campanile, with more than two hundred other Montrose students clad in black caps and gowns, all waiting for the magic moment when President Ryerson would present them with their diplomas.

The night before the ceremony, Kiki had received a phone call announcing that Mama, Papa, Javier, and Gusto had arrived at the Oakland airport to see her graduate. They were staying in a motel downtown. Taken totally by surprise, she marveled that her family could have put together the money to make this long journey. She realized it had to be the result of Javier and Gusto both working and living at home. For that she owed Sal a huge debt of gratitude.

Sal had sent a congratulatory note along with a graduation present, and Kiki secretly wished she could have been here too. Sal had once made her promise, she remembered, to invite her to her graduation. Although Kiki understood the difficulties of planning with Sal's trucking responsibilities, she still felt an empty space in her heart.

Late that evening, Kiki had gone outside the dorm and spent a long time sitting on the grass looking up at the stars. It had been clear, and she could see her beloved Artemis blinking at her. "There is so much I should say," Kiki said aloud to her star, "and there is no way I'm going to find the right words. But thank you. I've come a long way since the South Bronx, and you've been there with me all the way. I can imagine you, Artemis, in your flowing robes and with your bow and arrow, wandering freely through the universe accompanied by your trustworthy dog. You have inspired me, and I will always be grateful to you!"

Kiki's family arrived on campus by cab early graduation morning, and Kiki delightedly walked them up and down every street and into every courtyard and building to show them the world in which she had lived for the past four years. Papa and Mama were impressed, and Mama kept hugging Kiki. Javier and Gusto were quiet, respectful, and clearly in awe, and she could see the wheels turning in Gusto's mind. At one point she saw a smile cross his face and realized that her younger brother truly wanted more out of life just as she did. Kiki hoped he would find a way to get an education himself because his thirst for knowledge had now been awakened by her accomplishment. Her mama had told her on the phone, a few days before, that Javier was thinking of joining the Army, and Kiki wanted to tell him that she was proud of him and that the Army might be a good way for him to get ahead and eventually go to school himself, if he decided to do that.

Kiki led them all up to the dining commons, where they shared a big breakfast together. Mama kept saying, "So much food. They give you so much food! And this is where you work in kitchen for a year?"

"Yes, Mama." Kiki remembered that first, most difficult year at Montrose.

The ceremony was scheduled for 11 o'clock, and shortly after breakfast and a bit of walking and talking with her family, Kiki returned to the dorm to dress in her cap and gown. It felt so strange to slip into this garment, which symbolized her passage from Montrose student to college graduate. She studied herself in the door mirror, giving smiles and assuming all kinds of glamorous positions. "You did it, kid," she said out loud with a grin.

Once dressed, Kiki waltzed down the central stairs to meet her family in the dorm living room. Everyone smiled and laughed as Kiki twirled with delight in her black robe and cap, and Gusto took pictures with his cell phone. Then she walked with them to the central grass oval where the ceremony would be held.

They were looking for seats when Denise arrived, and Kiki introduced her to the family. Everyone gave Denise a welcoming hug, and Mama especially reached out for her with open arms. Kiki shed a secret tear or two as the two women embraced. *Her cup was indeed running over.*

The graduating seniors were called to form a line, and Kiki started to join her peers. Just then she saw Jim, his wife, and three daughters cross the lawn. They looked a little lost, and Kiki ran to welcome them. She quickly introduced them to her family, and both groups found space to sit down together. As the students began arranging themselves in alphabetical order and organ music sounded, Jim laughed heartily. He leaned over to Mama and whispered, "That is some daughter ya got!"

Mama smiled and replied, "Si, I know."

Kiki started to run to find her place in line. Then she remembered something else. She turned back, went to Denise and slipped a piece of paper into Denise's hand. Questioningly, Denise opened the paper and read the brief note:

I'm ready to live with you, if you still want me. Kiki

Denise's face broke into a broad grin, and Kiki blew her a kiss as she ran to catch up with the other seniors.

Kiki finally found her spot in the line, after giving hugs to Julie Anderson and Jacinta Morales as she passed them. Both excited and nervous, she looked around her and thought to herself—*I can't believe I'm graduating from Montrose!* Then she glanced back toward her family and noticed Sal and Meg on the fringe of the crowd. She waved to them, and Sal waved back. Kiki pointed out where her family was sitting, and Sal nodded. Kiki's heart pounded double time. *Her entire extended family had made it to her graduation!*

As the faculty marched by to the traditional "Pomp and Circumstance" by Sir Edward Elgar, Kiki looked for Nancy in the group and then Helena in her colorful regalia. She located Helena first, and then Nancy, who smiled and winked at her. She also saw Rita and Sonia Yakimari and the faces of Dean Johan, and President Ryerson, who would personally hand out the diplomas.

The class valedictorian gave her speech on the importance of women as leaders and role models in the emerging global community. A shiver ran up and down Kiki's spine; she felt thrilled as well as scared to be on her way out into that complex world.

Soon, award winners were announced, and Kiki's name came up as being among those students on the Dean's List for the spring semester. Her cheering section clapped and hooted. She tried not to feel disheartened that she had failed to receive an award for her senior project—that misstep had cost her, but thankfully she had survived and was here to become a real Montrose graduate.

She squeezed herself and risked a glance heavenward. *Thank you, Artemis, for always being there.*

The organ music began in earnest, and the graduates filed across the small stage area, as their diplomas were handed to them one by one. There were a few who were cited as graduating with honors, and Kiki admired their achievement.

Finally, she heard her own name over the sound system. "Patricia Loretta Cristina Rodriguez, Early Admissions student graduating with Honors in her major field, Communications." She could hardly believe the words, as with trembling hands and rubbery legs, she crossed the platform and accepted her diploma from President Ryerson. The president looked at her warmly and added, "We are all proud of your achievement, Kiki." They shook hands, and Kiki, blinded by tears, walked on as her rooting section cheered.

After the ceremonies, everyone circled around Kiki and hugged, talked, and laughed together. Grasping Denise's hand tightly, Kiki beamed as she passed her diploma around. She was especially excited to see Sal. "I didn't think you could make it," she admitted.

"Well, it wasn't easy," Sal explained to them all. "It took some last minute juggling and taking someone else's load, but I had to come, and Meg wanted to come as well, so here we are. Security is tight at the entrance gate. The guards ran their bomb-sniffing dogs around the truck and then took pity on two women from Salt Lake City and allowed the cab to come inside. Speaking of dogs, Aisha's out there in the truck, because I didn't think it would be appropriate to bring her up here."

"Oh, I want to see her!" Kiki cried, and her surprised entourage of family and friends trailed after the flying cap and gown as Kiki ran across the field to find her favorite traveling companion.

On the main street of the Montrose campus, foreign sports cars, family sedans, SUVs, and limousines lined up bumper to bumper. Right in the middle stood the imposing and outrageous pink cab of Sal's truck. And inside, a tail-wagging Aisha panted with anticipation as she sat looking and waiting for her pal.

Acknowledgments

The Artemis Adventure was written over a three-week period in 1994 and left as a first draft. It was intended as a story about a teen-age girl growing into womanhood and perhaps should be considered a young adult novel. However, because of still controversial themes and supporting characters of various ages, I have decided that the "young adult" label might be too limiting, and hopefully, I've made the right choice.

This novel would have remained a rough draft forever, except for the loving encouragement of my late partner, Vera Foster, and my current partner, Connie Jenkins, both of whom told me the initial version of this book was too good to leave tucked away inside a box. So this past year, I began seriously revising and updating the novel for publication.

My thanks go to all my friends and Facebook pals who read a "beta" draft—including Ruth Messing, Lisa Salazar, Kyra Humphrey, Mary Ellen Bartholomew, and Deanne Lachner—and helped me mold the manuscript into better shape. A special thank you goes to Myrna Oliver for her wisdom and "reality checks" and to Teri Louise Johnson for her enthusiasm, insights, and extensive editing.

About the Author

Dorothy Rice Bennett grew up in the Midwest. She began filling spiral notebooks when she was ten years old with fanciful stories that she shared with her classmates in school. Her heroines were women of action—they flew Navy jets, competed in hydroplane boat races, drove Indy cars, and raced horses as jockeys. In short, Dorothy was way ahead of her time, but little could she dream as a child that women would someday do these very things.

Dorothy earned a bachelor's degree from Mills College, a master's degree from the University of California, Davis, and a Ph.D. from Tulane University, all in the field of theatre. She also holds a master's degree in counseling from Arizona State University.

As an adult, Dorothy still loved writing, yet her busy careers in mental health and in journalism, as well as parenting an adopted daughter, commanded her time and energy. Eventually, in retirement she pushed other tasks aside and began to put words on paper. *NORTH COAST: A Contemporary Love Story* was her first published novel in 2015, and *GIRLS ON THE RUN* followed in 2016.

Dorothy lives on the Olympic Peninsula of Washington State with her partner and two toy poodles.

Dorothy Rice Bennett may be found on Facebook and Twitter and reached via email at <u>dorothyricebennett@yahoo.com</u> or at <u>www.dorothyricebennett.com</u>